THE
PERSIAN
GLORIES

By

Susan Wakeford Angard

Tudor House

Editorial and production management by Flying Pig Media with typesetting and cover design by Circecorp Design.

A CIP record for this book is available from the Library of Congress Cataloging-in-Publication Data.

ISBN: 978-1-7338984-4-7

For my Grandfather Joseph who sang opera

For my Father Joseph who played Jazz

For my Husband Joseph the love of my life...

PROLOGUE

NIAVARAN PALACE, IRAN
September 1942

I t was a night of great celebration, the "Night of a Thousand Stars," an annual ball given by the crown prince of Iran, Mohamed Reza Pahlavi, the future Shah. High on the gentle northern slopes of Tehran, Niaviran Palace, solid and resplendent, stretched toward a deepening indigo sky, its immense curved marble brow softening the vivid purple horizon.

Inside, the brilliantly lit palace glowed with festivity, smothering any hint of discord felt by a people shaken by invasion and domination by their supposed allies, the British and the Russians. More than half the world was wrenched apart by war, and all the powers involved continued to vie for Iran's black gold: oil. But tonight on the road leading to the palace, as the stars came out and the moon rose into a golden orb over Tehran, a procession of limousines and foreign state cars snaked up the royal thoroughfare through the palace gate. The war was far away from Rena Ajani's mind. She took Valik's hand and climbed out of the black 1939 Rolls Royce Phantom III, then tossed back her head and looked up at the sky over Niavaran Palace. She took a moment to breathe in the wonder of the night, letting herself be filled with the royal ambience.

Bursts of fireworks exploded overhead in cascades of starry radiance, like a cosmos newly born to the heavens to announce her. At eighteen, she was a bride of four months, and this was her first palace ball, a night she had craved throughout a seeming eternity of dullness.

Many nights she had seen her family—her father, mother, and older sister Ilyia—seeking favor from their monarch, the Shah. Many nights she had jealously watched them sweep off to the palace, dressed in their finest silks, brocades, and tails, while she, three years younger, had been forbidden to leave the house.

She had hated the sense of imprisonment she'd felt being left alone—and most of all she hated that it was always Ilyia first. Ilyia, delicate, lissome, and beautiful as a spring willow, whose graceful shape sharply contrasted Rena's own voluptuous curves, exotic face, and more energetic nature.

Rena knew she was beautiful because of her sensuality.

Ilyia, she admitted, was simply beautiful.

Rena was too young, her father had insisted, to go to parties, dances, or with friends, though not too young to be married off. But then, Valik's proposal had surprised even her father. She didn't mind. Being wed to a powerful man had opened the world to her at last.

"You are ravishing, Rena, my love." Her husband's lips caressed her fingertips, and she brought her gaze back to the man at her side. "This is your night to shine," he said.

Valik Ajani was only twenty years her senior and the prime minister of Iran, she thought proudly. With a shiver of excitement she watched courtiers and dignitaries approach and greet him with deference.

Valik was tall and lean, with a keen intelligence reflected in his intense, dark features. He commanded respect from everyone as they crossed the palace courtyard, and the feel of this veneration brought a new kind of thrill to her, a thrill that assuaged a hunger for acclaim long starved.

And now I will share his power, his wealth, and his place in the sun. I will have all that I desire, this man will see to it, I am certain, because of my fervor in the marriage bed.

When they made love on their honeymoon in Egypt, it had been an entirely new and wondrous adventure for her, and for Valik, he seemed overcome with ecstasy. Instinctively her hand moved to her throat, where she touched with pride his finest gift, an astonishing Burmese ruby necklace.

Yes, the honeymoon trip had been a good beginning. Tonight she would greet her family from a new vantage point—that of power. She smiled inwardly, relishing the glow of triumph she felt. And for once not even Ilyia could ruin the moment.

"Shall we go in, my love?" her husband asked. Then in a sexy voice, he whispered, "I have a surprise for you."

Confidently, she smoothed her red Coco Chanel ball gown and gave him a coy glance. "What surprise?"

Valik smiled. "The prince has arranged for the Persian Glories to be removed from the vaults of the Bank of Iran and put on display tonight in the reception hall. I know you'll want to be the first to see."

"The Persian Glories! Yes!" Since she was a girl of seven, she had been captivated by the romantic story surrounding these famous jewels, as were so many Persian girls.

Years ago, a lovestruck Russian prince, overcome by his passion for a young Persian beauty—a girl he was forbidden to marry—commissioned Carl Fabergé, the great Russian artisan, to select flawless diamonds from anywhere in the world to design an astounding gift for the beloved he would be denied. Fabergé fashioned perfect stones into a glorious collection finer than any in the czar's own coffers: yellow diamonds rivaling the brilliance of the sun, pure white diamonds like glinting stars.

It was said the Persian Glories possessed a great legacy and when unselfishly given to one you cared for, brought great love. Great love indeed! Those jewels were priceless—they could bring fortune and power! Rena felt the cool stones of her own magnificent necklace against her skin. Could the famous Persian Glories possibly be as beautiful as her rubies?

"Sir?" A barrel-chested man in an elaborate tux interrupted her reverie, touching her husband's arm.

"Go in and see the jewels, my dear. Take your time."

Palace guards in dress whites guided Rena along a marble hall flanked by niches filled with precious European art. Her excitement was great; she could barely acknowledge all the greetings and nods of respect from elite Persian guests.

Rena stepped inside a lavish salon lined with satiny walls of exquisite wood paneling and carved Louis Quinze gilt furniture. A massive chunk crystal chandelier dangled from the towering ceiling like a colossal bauble.

A figure came forward from the shadows; a lieutenant in formal attire melted toward her. Lieutenant Omar Houdin. She had not seen him in months. Shocked, she tamped down the last of her attraction to him.

"Rena. I've longed to see you. I missed you."

"Omar! What are you doing here?"

"I'm now part of the prince's guard. I waited to catch a glimpse of you."

"You must stay away from me, Omar. I'm a married woman. I can never see you again."

He reached for her.

Quickly she pulled away. "It was not meant to be, you and me. Stay away." He was young, handsome, virile. But she should not even remember the small dalliance she'd had with him in her father's garden before she had any idea Valik was interested in her.

She had teased Omar, led him on out of a young girl's boredom. That was all! "Please go now."

His smile, almost lethal, stunned her.

Fists clenched, Omar said, "For now, Rena, for now."

He bowed and faded away.

Rena shook off the meeting, gathering her wits.

Then she saw them.

She stood transfixed before the glass-enclosed display housing the astonishing Persian Glories. The tiara, bracelet, necklace, brooch, earrings, and ring all glinted up at her with a power to light the sun. Never had she seen anything like these. Something extraordinary emanated from these diamonds. A force she felt to her bones took hold, filling her with energy, potent and erotic. Entranced, she wanted to touch them—she wanted to own them. Her fingers lightly gliding over the case, she quelled her hunger and compelled her hands away.

All at once she was conscious of being observed. Valik had come quietly into the salon and moved to her side, his gaze probing, as if he perceived her arousal by the diamonds.

"Enthralled, my love?" He gathered her hands and pressed her fingers to his knowing smile. "Oh, I feel your craving, Rena." His words were eager; his breath felt hot on her skin. "How I would love to cover your naked body with the Persian Glories if they were but mine."

Her body tingled from the encounter with the gems. She breathed deeply, barely able to let Valik guide her to the ballroom. Within seconds friends and courtiers surrounded them, welcoming them back from their trip.

"How wonderful you look, Rena," she heard.

"Such an extravagant ruby necklace! Valik knows how to spoil his bride."

Taking the arm of her husband, her chin tilted, she pushed the Persian Glories for the moment from her mind and basked in the praise.

Then she heard a familiar voice of welcome. "Good evening, Madame Ajani." She looked up into the radiant face of Prince Mohamed Reza Pahlavi, only twenty-two and imbued with the regal self-assurance of a future monarch.

The prince was resplendent in his official dark jacket and trousers trimmed in gold braid and epaulets. He took her hand, his large dark eyes flashing. "You look lovely this evening, Rena." His smile she remembered well from the brief time she had visited the court before he had married Princess Fawzia of Egypt. The Shah's wife was not with him but in Egypt, visiting her brother, King Farouk.

"Your Majesty," she said.

"You've chosen an incomparable beauty, Prime Minister," the prince said, glancing at her husband and then at her. "I would like the first dance with her."

"But of course, Your Highness." Valik beamed his agreement.

Prince Mohamed guided Rena onto the dance floor. With natural grace he waltzed her around the ballroom for all eyes to see, and her spirit soared above the heavens. With this honor she had outshone every woman there. Her status was secure.She felt as if she were spinning through stars when the waltz ended. Then, from the edge of her vision, she noticed a group of guests whose entrance was causing a flurry of interest.

The prince's warm gaze left hers and traveled across the room. "Ahhhh...the guests of honor."

Guests of honor? What guests of honor? Rena strained to see.

Before she knew what was happening, the prince had escorted her back to her husband. "A pleasure, Rena," he said and promptly turned away.

Rena searched the entrance. She took Valik's arm, and they moved to get a better look.

A party of couples entered, led by a tall, blond infidel—blindingly handsome with emerald eyes and an enticingly warm smile—dressed in British military dress uniform. He and the prince embraced affectionately.

Rena was stunned. His majesty embracing an infidel!

"Reza, *insha allah*," she heard the infidel say to her prince.

"Evans, you devil, you've snatched the prima flower in our Persian garden."

Evans chuckled at the prince's remark.

The room buzzed with speculation. From behind the infidel stepped a vision in white chiffon, more beautiful than anyone had a right to be. Rena staggered, gulping down a fierce need to shriek out in rage, every part of her quivering with hate. It was Ilyia.

Rena grabbed her husband's arm. "The infidel, who is he?" she asked. Her voice sounded harsher than she intended.

"British. Lord Richard Evans, the next Earl of Edyton. He is the prince's close friend from Le Rosey School in

Switzerland. But don't you know this, Rena? It is your sister to whom he is betrothed."

The infidel close to the future Shah?

"How could I know any of this? We've been away for four months."

"But there was a cable from your family telling us the news, don't you remember?"

"Cable? What cable?" But she did remember. There had been one in Egypt announcing Ilyia's engagement to some Englishman. Ha! *English*, a mere infidel! Skimming the telegram, she had tossed it aside, not wanting anything from home to spoil the best time of her life. A slow, bitter grimace sliced across her mouth. She had been right to not dwell on the cable, because the news turned out to be devastating. Her sister was going to marry into English aristocracy and be close to the highest-ranking member of Iranian society, in the inner circle.

Rena blanched, holding down irritation.

"Richard Evans," the prince continued, "will protect our peace and keep Iran's wealth in our country."

The prince then turned to a steward and lifted a black cloth from a velvet-lined tray. Instantly, the room was bathed in beams of refracted light emanating from the Persian Glories.

"The legend of the Persian Glories speaks of selfless giving and the flourishing of love. I bestow these jewels upon you, Lord Richard Evans, with love and friendship, cementing our countries' bond for our lifetime."

Rena gasped and took in the reactions of the crowd.

Those closest to the prince registered surprise. From the back of the room she heard excited muttering.

The prince gazed at Ilyia, and Rena thought she saw longing in the look. "It is as it should be."

Lord Evans nodded to the monarch and said, "For my bride, a symbol of Persian grace, who will stand beside me and our future children to protect Iran."

Rena watched in horror as the brilliant necklace was lifted from the tray and placed lovingly around Ilyia's slender neck. Then the bracelet was circled about Ilyia's delicate wrist, the earrings put in her ears, the tiara put in her gleaming hair, and the perfect twenty-carat ring handed to her betrothed. The infidel's gaze, fixed on Ilyia, burned as powerfully as the extravagant ring he slipped on her finger.

No! Rena shrieked silently, her mind swirling with hatred. *The Persian Glories should be mine! I saw the prince first—he loved* me *first!* But the Persian Glories now belonged to her sister.

Everyone watched in silent awe as the prince raised his glass in a toast to the glorious couple. The room cheered. Ilyia stood there in her splendor, as radiant as the sun. Rena's sister had outshone her once again, for their entire world to see.

At that precise moment, something snapped inside Rena, and the world changed color, washed in a grotesque dead gray like the skin of a decaying rat. She stood apart, shaking with envy, cursing her sister, wanting to rip everything away from her: her betrothed, their future heirs, and especially the Persian Glories. Then, as if Ilyia could read her mind, she looked over at Rena with a smile of compassion and extended her hand. Ilyia was urging Rena to share the spotlight.

Rena shot her sister a withering look. *Don't you dare pity me, you slut!* she screamed inside. Involuntarily she backed away. Excited guests quickly filled in the space, edging her back, back, until she was forced into the shadows at the far end of the ballroom. There she stood, shuddering in disbelief, consumed with rage.

This would be the last time, the very last time, that bitch would ever shine.

CHAPTER ONE
Teheran, October 1978

At dawn, startled from an uneasy sleep by General Houdin's call, Mirdad Ajani opened his eyes, so hung-over he felt like a blunt slab of cement rammed his head, slicing his optic nerves. He vomited over the side of the bed. "Ugh."

"My God, man! What's wrong?" the general shouted. "You're sotted again! The ministry will fire your dumb ass. By God, stepson or no I'll—"

"I'm too handsome to fire." Mirdad wiped his lips on the sheet and mouthed a reply. "And how is my dear mother."

"The package was moved from the palace," Houdin said.

Iran's Crown Jewels, moved. Mirdad's attention ramped up.

"The Glories too. Our informant doesn't know how, but they're gone. It's Evans, your cousin!"

Mirdad lifted up, leaning on his elbow.

"Rena is enraged. She wants those Glories. Find them! You hear!" Houdin growled. "And terminate this Evans."

Irritation made Mirdad's voice terse. "I told her I would."

Dizzy, Mirdad staggered to the shower. He dressed with care, forcing himself to wait before alerting Houdin's favorite thug, Captain Aran. He wanted no one but Aran to handle this special assignment, but with absolutely certainty that Kathryn was safely away from Anthony before he acted. Taking the chance of having her fall into the hands of a beast like Aran was unthinkable.

Shortly after 5:00 a.m., Mirdad, in his immaculate gray suit paced the Tehran Imperial Hilton lobby, smoking Turkish cigarettes, suppressing his anxiety and a hangover.

It had been an hour.

He viewed the various lobby seating arrangements grouped around an immense Persian carpet and slouched onto a stiff leather sofa. Sounds from a vacuum cleaner in the bar grated on his nerves.

It was now 6:05 a.m. He waited to escort Kathryn and her crew to the airport. Annoyed, but driven to see Kathryn once before she left, he had arrived too early.

His anguish over Kathryn had become torture so extreme he almost enjoyed it. He had donned it like a coat of nettles and had worn it since the first moment he'd looked at her. She had touched him in some forgotten part of himself where dreams and goals had once lived. His delight in film and history, poetry and conversation had awakened with his need for inner truth. He could love and laugh with a friend, a beautiful blond friend, and have fun like he hadn't since his youth. She made him come alive.

There had been no denying Kathryn left the palace with Anthony last night. He would have put his spies on Kathryn.

But why send others to find out what he already knew?

Finally, the hotel elevator doors opened, but Buzz and Peter emerged without her.

"Hey, Mirdad," Peter greeted him.

They said nothing about where Kathryn was, but he could guess. He'd watched Anthony chase after her last night from the palace. Anguish seized Mirdad's gut. Anthony, that son-of-a-bitch, was a dead man.

Kathryn Whitney awoke at first light, grasping where she lay—Anthony's bed, the man she loved, the man she would marry. Warmth from Anthony's body sheltered her, his scent surrounded her, enticing as always. The pull between them was powerful; they were drawn to one another more intimately than either expected. She'd not tell anyone he'd proposed in a bathtub.

She smiled, though wretchedly aware it was time to go.

Scattered light and shadow played over Anthony's tosseled dark hair, his ridiculously handsome face a blend of his Persian and British heritage. Her senses screamed to run her hands over his body shaped by endless polo matches and riding break-neck across desert plains with Kash'kai tribesmen. But no.

They'd meet in London in two weeks—a promise.

She'd watched this celebrated photographer risk everything to save his Iranian countrymen. His passion pulled her in. Seeing a mother swaddling an infant, her pleading eyes saying, 'help us,' emboldened her. A small boy, patting his little sister's head, as if she were a puppy he didn't want to lose. Who could resist? Naturally, she focused her fearless flying ability on joining his covert missions, filming by day, flying death-listed families safely into Iraq or Kuwait by night.

It was amazing they were both still alive. Few knew of his bravery; he was their hero. None knew of her escapades. She'd keep it that way.

She had to leave.

Her exit from Iran was inevitable, her failed film shoot; her saving lives of death-listed families. Her secret flights had put her in danger. But Anthony's danger was worse— his name now topped the ruthless Black Glove terrorists' death list.

Anthony's dark eyelashes fluttered when she kissed his forehead and slid from the bed. There was no way she'd wake him, or departure would be impossible. She was terrified of goodbyes. They always meant the end.

Time to go.

I'll never leave you, Kathryn. We'll be together in two weeks.
Move.

She lifted her crumpled white Dior gown from the Jules Leleu headboard, slipped on the dress and grabbed her shoes, drive pushing her to make today's only flight to London.

Trouble had found her on her Persepolis Boeing set. Revolutionary Guard artillery fire shot down her Jet Ranger helicopter. The chopper was totaled, her crew brutalized but alive. But she had a small window tomorrow to get final pick-up shots at the British Museum where twenty-five-hundred-year Persian Artifacts packed the lower floor. If she failed, her directing career was over.

There was someone who would delight in her ruin.

Her crystal evening bag she tucked into an old canvas camera-case with documents and her betrothal gift, a legacy from Anthony's mother, the famous Persian Glories. She carried to the kitchen the flawless Faberge canary diamonds, hidden in a twelve-by twelve inch jeweled box wrapped in a tribal scarf, placed inside the scruffy canvas bag. Sliding into her shoes, she dialed Anthony's driver's downstairs apartment.

She heard a dazed male voice say, "This better be good, Anthony."

"Ali, it's Kathryn. I need to get to the Hilton now. My crew and I leave Iran this morning. Can you take me?"

"At once." His voice perked up. "I do whatever you ask. I'll never forget you saved me from those scum desert soldiers. Meet me in the garage. We'll take the Rolls."

"On my way." She hung up, penned a note for Anthony, placed it next to him and took one last look, wishing to feel his intense green gaze on her once more. But no, better not.

She slipped out of the apartment.

It was somber this morning in Tehran, but not even the choking cloud cover hanging gloomily over the city could dampen Kathryn's ebullient spirit of hope for the future.

Ali drove Kathryn past the wreckage of the previous night: overturned buses and flaming cars, burned-out storefronts, smoldering in the haze. She came to Iran full of hope determined to resurrect her damaged film career unaware that cities in Iran exploded with revolution.

But today she couldn't fully register the destruction. Not when joy bubbled inside for her future. Anthony Evans.

She had left her dark knight sleeping and longed for the heat of his body, the closeness they shared.

Groggy and floating on clouds, they arrived at the Hilton. She counted on it being too early for anyone to see her in her evening gown, creeping into the lobby.

Ali pulled up to the hotel entrance and opened her door. All looked quiet.

From the seat, she grabbed the castaway camera-bag she'd found in the corner of Anthony's studio to carry the treasure and customs documents he had given her and draped the strap over her shoulder. The Glories she would deliver to his grandfather's vault in England.

Ali jumped out of the car and opened the passenger door for her.

She climbed from the car.

"Take care of yourself, Ali, my friend."

"Of course." His smile warmed her.

"Thanks for being there when I needed you. You're courageous. And take care of Anthony for me, will you?"

"As always, when he is not taking care of me."

She squeezed his hand and he blushed, shifting feet, uncomfortable, she guessed, with any public show of affection, as were most Iranian men. She stepped away and waved.

Rushing into the Hilton at 6:15 a.m., Kathryn ignored a glance from the doorman, surprised that Iranian Police Guards flanked the glass double doors. It felt good having protection after viewing the extensive damage in the city.

She hurried past them, thinking what a fright she must look. She'd done nothing to her appearance since last night's bath, her luscious white gown was crumpled like a Goodwill rag, and she wore no makeup. She giggled, adjusting the crude, olive-drab bag drooping over her shoulder. Oh, what the hell! At this hour nobody was up but the chickens.

She marched past an empty front desk and crossed to the elevators.

From behind her, she heard a cat whistle and stopped in her tracks.

"Way to go, Kat!" came familiar voices, followed by clamoring applause.

"Chalk one up for Kat!"

"She scored!"

Mortified, Kathryn whirled around and faced them. There sat her crew, rocking with laughter, enjoying themselves completely at her expense. Buzz, her uncle and account exec for Boeing, groomed to the nines, from his salt and pepper grey hair, his Turnbull and Asser striped shirt to his polished dress shoes.

"Hey! You look great, Kat," Buzz said. "Never better."

SUSAN WAKEFORD ANGARD | 19

"That one of your designer originals?" said Peter, her tall, lanky A.D. and best friend since UCLA film-school, applauding. No sign of his usual Grateful dead shirt or faded jeans. He dressed for business and London.

"The Grunge look, huh?" Peter said.

"Would you guys stop that!" she whispered.

They laughed harder.

She covered her face with her hand, wishing she could disappear, edging toward the elevators.

But Buzz grabbed her hand. "Damn!" said Buzz. "Catch that rock!"

"What'd you have to do to get that?"

"Whoa, look at the size of it! Is it real?"

"Behave yourselves. Shhh!" And then she saw Mirdad, Anthony's cousin, sitting on the adjacent sofa, looking grim, staring at the fifteen-carat diamond on her finger. He must have seen it before, since it had belonged to Anthony's mother his own aunt Ilyia...*He's jealous,* she thought.

"Good morning," she said.

Mirdad cleared his throat. "Good morning. Are congratulations in order?"

"Yes." She beamed with unbelievable joy. "I guess you could say that."

"And where is the lucky man this morning?" said Mirdad.

"I left him at his apartment, asleep." She smiled.

Buzz jumped up and embraced her. "Congratulations, sweetie. You and Anthony together could light up Times Square. See, Peter, she's not a fallen woman. It's legit, she's engaged."

"Damn!" Peter said.

"You better get changed," said Buzz. "We've got a plane to catch. From what Mirdad says it could take a while to get there."

The expression on Mirdad's face never changed. It was as though he'd been sculpted in stone. The deadness in his eyes, which traveled from her face to her hand and back, made her uncomfortable. She put her hand at her side and stepped toward him. "Please be happy for us Mirdad." She gave a tentative smiled. "We'll all be family soon."

He raised an eyebrow, with a smirk.

She turned away, allowing him to think on it. "I'll be right down. I didn't even unpack."

When Kathryn finally entered the hotel lobby this morning, looking like a fallen angel in her crumpled white gown, Mirdad had only wanted her more, regardless of what Anthony had done with her. He wanted to take her and bathe her slowly, cradle next to her and be held. Aware this was his only chance to redeem himself for the film location fiasco in Persepolis, Mirdad continued to sit passively with the others, while the thorns of his torture gouged him.

He gazed across at the man who had become his friend. Buzz had gotten drunk with him last night and had made Mirdad laugh harder than he'd ever laughed before. Americans had a way of making fun of themselves that made him feel better, until this morning, until now. Seeing what he'd lost, what Anthony had stolen, the way he grabbed everything good in Mirdad's life, only deepened his hatred for Anthony to a fathomless hell.

Excusing himself from their group, he crossed to the bank of telephones and dialed General Houdin's sadistic thug, Captain Aran.

Mirdad and Buzz, Kathryn's producer, exited the elevator on the hotel's eighth floor to get Teddy, Kathryn's cameraman. The door was open, the radio blared, and Teddy looked like Mirdad felt, like hell.

Buzz shook his fox-grey head. "Move it, man. Our plane, remember?"

"Didn't sleep," Teddy struggled. As he stuffed his bag, his red-rimmed, fear-filled eyes darted a look at Mirdad.

"Buzz and I saw you drinking in the Euro Lounge last night." Mirdad watched Teddy pack like he was still drunk.

Teddy looked Mirdad over. "You there, huh?"

"Sure was." Mirdad ignored the urge to sit and hold his throbbing head. His hangover savaged his skull. "Let me do it." He yanked Teddy's bag and zipped it. "Your plane won't wait." He hoped they still had seats on their flight. Reservations meant nothing these days.

"Damn," Teddy said, "I hate flying."

"You were fine in the chopper." Buzz grabbed the bag.

"Before those bozos shot me down."

Mirdad caught snatches of news from the Tehran British radio station through the static. A baritone voice calmly stated,

"...pro Khomeini supporters block entrances to highways..."

Teddy whirled, staring at the blaring radio. ". . . rebel troops near the Mehrabad International Airport..."

"Shit! Not those insane zealots." His face turned redder.

"Time to go." Mirdad threw Teddy's jacket at him, his exasperation rising.

"What the hell!" Shaking, Teddy gripped his hat and spun toward the radio, as if he could see into it. "Crap." He wiped sweat from his face.

"Move!" Mirdad shouted. "Let's get out of here." He tugged Teddy out of the room, rushed them past the slow elevator, blowing down eight flights of stairs, visions of the fucking militia, gnawing at him. They emerged into the hotel lobby panting, but cool-headed. There, sat Peter, reading *Newsweek*. But where was Kathryn?

Mirdad spoke to the desk clerk in Farsi. "Turn on the TV! Iranian news." Boisterous truckloads of militia on the screen, moved past a mosque where demonstrators shouted. He needed to see what routes were open.

His concern for the Americans' safety mounted.

Peter. Cool as pool of water, picked up the camera in his lap. "Buzz wants his shots." Peter quickly organized the group. "Mirdad, get in the picture."

Crazy Americans, always taking photographs. Mirdad bunched in with them, not wanting to set off alarm bells about their exit, an iffy situation at best. No matter, they must go.

"Teddy, get over here." Peter grimaced. "On second thought, you look like you need a nurse. What's wrong?"

"Are you crazy, Peter?" Teddy grabbed his arm. "Didn't you even hear the news? Look at the TV!"

Buzz nudged Teddy. "I wanna shot of the hung-over cameraman."

"I'm serious, man," Teddy shrugged him off. "Those Green Band bastards are all over the airport. Mirdad, tell 'em what's up."

"Nothing serious." Mirdad had to keep them calm. If trouble found them on the roa they'd need their wits. "Nonetheless, you have two minutes—then we go."

Buzz nodded, looking around. "Where's Kat?"

"Screw the pictures." Teddy pulled away.

"Here I am." A fresh-faced Kathryn joined them. "Face it." She nudged Teddy and looked over at Mirdad.

She was radiant in a navy-blue pantsuit, her blond hair billowing around her shoulders. Mirdad wanted to grab her and run out of there.

"Buzz won't leave a location without photos," she smiled.

"Shit!" Teddy shuffled into the group for three quick shots.

"Let's go, Buzz," Mirdad insisted, motioning for Kathryn's luggage to be gathered up. "We have to deal with customs. Teddy, sit up front with the driver. It'll be fine."

"Hell, don't care where I sit, just get me on that plane."

Mirdad called out to the driver in Farsi. "Don't stop for anything."

Eisenhower Avenue was clear to the junction with Tehran-Karaj Road where they turned off for the airport and raced ahead.

Mirdad sat back between Buzz and Kathryn, with Peter in the jump seat across from them. Their conversation was the lively banter of familiar friends, and he found himself included, unlike the pain he suffered years ago. He'd been a lonely political outcast after his father, Iran's prime minister, was falsely imprisoned for murder. He swiped away memories of his brilliant father's untimely death in prison.

"Yeah," Peter said, "we're on this cruise ship through the Panama Canal. The captain, who looked like some Danish movie star, was taken with Kat, who, at the time, was our lowly production coordinator."

"Peter, must you tell this?" she said.

"Mirdad wants to hear it."

"I do." He wanted to absorb every nuance of her, every moment of her life into his.

"So, at night," Peter continued, "we dine at the captain's table, very formal, Kat, the beauty queen, putting everyone else to shame. I mean, she looked good at night."

"That's your best shot, Peter?" she said.

"And every morning," Buzz added. "Captain Busik looks for Kat, casual like. Well, she was with the film crew."

"Right," Peter leaned forward, "in cutoff jeans, sweatshirt, hair scrunched under a baseball cap, and high-top tennis shoes, doing her thing, having passengers act natural when we shot them. Captain Busik comes up, looks right at her and asks, 'Where's the lovely Miss Whitney.' She says, 'I have no idea!'" Peter slapped his knee laughing.

"Why you delight in these stories about me, Peter, I'll never know!"

"Yeah? Well, I'll bet Mirdad'll never forget when he first laid eyes on you. I can still see your face, Mirdad, when you realized she was *the* Miss Whitney you were looking for."

Mirdad smiled in spite of himself. "Yes, I nearly choked asking you to dinner at the Paradise Club. I kept thinking who could I get to replace me."

They all laughed

Kathryn crossed her arms, "I can beat any poker hand you've got," she said, peering straight ahead. She was unlike any woman Mirdad knew, funny and natural. Beautiful, yet she was easy being one of the guys. No charade.

Buzz mussed her hair and patted her head. "And you're such a good sport too, Kat." That made her smile.

"I'm not giving up my high-tops. That's final!"

They approached the airport, and the driver signaled to Mirdad.

Mirdad looked out the back window. A small army of military trucks and jeeps filled with troops followed them.

"Looks like we're part of a parade." Buzz scowled. Instantly, they were aware of a battalion of tanks and artillery closing in on them.

Mirdad cringed.

Next to him, Kathryn stiffened with a harsh intake of breath.

The driver slowed down.

Back in his Tehran apartment, through a haze of sleepy bliss, Anthony Evans felt morning light creep across his bedroom. His mind filled with images of Kathryn, smooth and warm next to him, and he wanted her. He reached for his woman.

She was gone.

He sat up, looked around, listening for her in another room. The apartment was silent. Beside him was a note.

Couldn't bear to disturb such peaceful slumber, you, so content ...as I am. Missing you already, hope two weeks passes quickly! I'll put the jewels in your grandfather's vault as you requested. Love you, Kathryn. P.S. I'll be at the Savoy on the off chance you can call.

Gone. She'd just left. No goodbye.

She hated goodbyes.

In an instant, Anthony was alarmingly awake. The jewels! Naked, he bounded into the studio, her note still clutched in his hand. The Persian Glories were gone; the chest, gone. My God, he'd forgotten to tell her not to take them, that it was dangerous. She had no idea what else was hidden in that gold cache. Some of

Iran's most written about gems. And the papers were still in his desk.

She couldn't leave without the papers. She carried a global fortune in jewels and no way to get through Customs. Not only the Persian Glories, but the treasure entrusted to him by the Empress of Iran. Christ! Got to catch her. He glanced at the clock. 8:00 a.m.

He picked up the house phone and dialed Ali.

"Yes, sir..."

"Ali, what have you done with my lady?"

"I took her to her hotel."

"Did she say what time her flight leaves?"

"No, but a limo from the ministry was there when I pulled up. Must be the nine o'clock to Heathrow."

"Warm up the Ferrari. I'm leaving for the airport."

"There's trouble in the city," Ali said. "I'm going with you."

Racing through Tehran streets, Anthony searched for a shortcut, turning down a side street, only to come upon a group of frenzied Green Band rioters, yelling and beating a car with clubs and boards. The occupants, ripped from their vehicle, shoved up against a wall at the mercy of the mob. Soldiers shot them. Their car overturned, was set ablaze. Horror everywhere he turned.

"Damn!" Smoke blurred their way. "Look for a way out," Anthony coughed and punched the Ferrari into reverse.

Ali wiped at his eyes and reached for the concealed .38 under the driver's seat. He slid it under his belt and pointed to a narrow space between two buildings. "There, turn! We can make it. Go!"

Anthony turned sharply, skidding into a dark alley littered with stinking refuse, hearing shrieks of panic and suffering that echoed through the corridor. He drove toward the light at the end of the alley. Reaching the end, Anthony downshifted and roared out onto a wider street, relieved to leave the violence behind, the thought, goading him to greater speed.

"Hold on, Ali. I'm driving like an Iranian."

"Do it!"

Forty minutes, Anthony calculated. He'd have to make it in twenty to catch her before customs. God, he hoped the flight was delayed!

He thundered through the city and finally turned onto Eisenhower Avenue, his foot to the floor, his thoughts accelerating in concert with his driving. In his coat pocket were documents Kathryn needed for clear sailing through customs once she reached England. Without them she'd be accused of smuggling or theft, and if he didn't reach her in time? Jesus! If Iranian customs searched her bags... He shuddered. Any number of horrible pictures flipped through his brain, things that could happen to her before she got out of Iran. *Who is this woman I chose?* The love of my life has a penchant for heading into disaster. Why hadn't he stowed the chest in the safe last night? And why hadn't he placed the papers she'd need with the jewels? And then he recalled how she'd sprawled on his bed wearing nothing but the Persian Glories.

He'd shot all those rolls of film, and then his cock had taken over for his brain. God, one hot night and the roof caved in.

Mirdad reacted quickly. "Kathryn, you must cover your hair."

She rummaged in her carry-on and dug out a large black silk square banded in color and tied it under her chin.

Mirdad tucked the Shiraz tribal scarf in around her face. "Be certain to keep your eyes down. Don't look at anyone."

"Right." Eyes downcast, she clutched her hands in her lap.

Mirdad's limo halted on Eisenhower Avenue, only minutes from Mehrabad Airport. "Sir," The driver sounded near hysteria. "Trouble. Trucks, soldiers." He jammed on the emergency brake.

Screaming, jostling, Green Band militia surrounded them. Mirdad swallowed his fear. The vehicle was rocked back and forth, jostled by surrounding troops. Mirdad tamped down his panic searching for a way out other than death.

"Sir, what should I do?" the driver yelled.

"Close the window!" Mirdad ordered, knowing the bulletproof glass would be insignificant with this mob attacking. His survival instincts roared on alert.

"Everyone. Keep your head." He'd need every bit of cunning he possessed to save Kathryn from being raped and killed. "Kathryn, fix your scarf."

A mass of angry, riotous Green Bands, clamoring anti-Shah slogans and exalting the Ayatollah Khomeini, circled them, crushing in on the car, pounding on it, tilting it. He clamped down his nerves.

Everyone inside grabbed on to seats, straps—anything to keep them from injury, swearing, their expressions near panic. The driver blasted the horn, and the car settled. Mirdad dug deep for the courage he'd not drawn on since years ago in a refuge-strewn ally, facing bullies like these Green Bands outside.

Kathryn and my friends will be dead within minutes if I don't act quickly.

Kathryn shoved her canvas camera bag to her side, hiding it, obviously very frightened.

Mirdad squeezed her hand, dug something out of his pocket, and forced his way out of the car. He adjusted his dark glasses, emerging with a brusque, dignified manner.

"Who's in charge? I demand to know."

An officer in his early twenties came forward, bearing his M-16 like a trophy in Mirdad's face. "What imperialist pig is here?" he roared. His eyes blazed with hatred. "You have five seconds!" He spit.

Enraged, Mirdad grabbed the man by his throat. "You loathsome dog!" he yelled. "You dare speak to me with such disrespect!"

The crowd moved in on Mirdad. Suddenly, all assault rifles aimed at his head.

"Shoot him!" came the rabble's roar, hungry to kill. "Death to Imperialist pigs! You die!"

Reluctantly, Mirdad eased his grip on the young soldier. He swept his face of feelings. He needed to take control, but inside fear twisted, threatening paralysis. Desperate for a next move, a sudden jolt of recognition hit him when he studied the soldier's crooked nose, all of his facial features. They had a chance if he played this well.

Mirdad said to the soldier, "I know your face...and you know mine!" He released his grip on the soldier. "You served under Captain Nubriand in Shiraz, did you not?"

Mirdad kept his gaze on the young man who ruled his fate, ignoring the arsenal pointed at him. "You know who I am." His voice was firm but low. "Don't you, Lieutenant? It seems you've been promoted since I saw you last at Persepolis. You were a mere sergeant there."

A sharp intake of breath came from the soldier.

Satisfied, Mirdad removed his dark glasses with regained composure. "Don't you realize who I am? Colonel Ajani," he said loudly, making sure they could all hear as he looked into their faces. "How many of you know what became of the legendary Captain Nubriand when he disobeyed my orders? How many?"

With authority he displayed the Green Band Revolutionary Guard identity card he had palmed, holding it high. "Captain Nubriand disgraced himself," Mirdad paused. "Disobeying his general and me. Nubriand was a blight on our goal. Now he's dead."

The lieutenant took Mirdad's lead. "This is true," he boasted to his men. "I recognize his Excellency. He is a brother in our cause. Let him pass!" With that, he raised his rifle in the air, taking up the chant exclaiming, "Praise to Allah! Most high is God! God is Great!"

Mirdad too shouted, "God is Great!" He exhaled a mountain of stress, and with great relief re-entered the car and the driver sped away.

Crowds jammed the doorways at Mehrabad International Airport. Noise and mass confusion assaulted them. Reports had reached Mirdad of clogged airports and people desperate to leave Iran, but this was far beyond his expectation. The stricken faces of his American friends heightened Mirdad's need to get Kathryn safely on the plane, away from this powder keg.

He paid a porter to follow him with their luggage and led them through crushing crowds, boisterous and rowdy, where problems threatened at every turn: violence, pickpockets, kidnappers. He was ready to pay more *pishkesh*, the usual bribe and he knew a few shortcuts. Still he would need a small miracle to get them on the flight.

"Don't worry," he said. "I'll get you through. Don't let customs officials catch your eye."

"Whatever you say," Buzz said.

"Can we make the flight?" Peter asked.

"Shit!" said Teddy. "I knew it. I knew it!"

"Quiet, Teddy." Kathryn nudged him. "It'll be all right."

"Okay, okay," Teddy muttered, "but I don't like it."

"Here, Kat," Peter said, thrusting the 16 millimeter Bolex at her. "Use it."

She checked the film gauge, popped off the lens cap

and cranked, looking up for a second at Mirdad. He nodded, reminded of their time filming at the souk in Shiraz, catching a glimpse of her as she lost herself filming. "I'll get you passed this mob," he said.

They all grouped close to Mirdad, skirting the terminal perimeter. He moved Kathryn in front for a better vantage of the wave of people trying to leave Iran, and led them behind a counter, through airport officials' doors, down a long gray corridor lined with offices, some empty, some with closed doors, shouting heard behind them.

Kathryn hesitated, lowering the camera. "I don't like it, either." She sounded nervous and tightened her scarf. "This is too familiar to me."

Mirdad smiled. "You don't have to worry with me. I'd never let these corrupt officials harass you again." He realized he meant it, that he'd always mean it. No one ever made him feel as good about himself as Kathryn did. She inspired him. They laughed together, teased and shared passionate interests for film, literature, philosophy. No pretense. She was everything he admired in a woman.

"This way," he said. They barreled ahead and came to the airport director's office at the end of the jammed corridor. Here pandemonium reigned. Fists full of money waved in the air on the smell of sweat and fear. Shouting people frantically made deals to get on any flight out of Iran. Mirdad collected passports, visas and held Kathryn's hand. "Stay together." He broke through the crowd. "Out of my way!" His booming voice cleared a path to the director, Devi Saed's desk.

"Our guests from the Ministry of Culture are leaving on this morning's flight to London," Mirdad intoned. "Kindly stamp their papers. I'll personally see them to the plane."

Devi Saed looked up, incredulous. "Surely you know the flight is overbooked, Deputy Minister. There's no way." The flesh on his face shook, as if affirming his own answer. Airport security guards were staggering as they held people away from his desk.

Mirdad leaned over the desk close to Saed and slapped down a stack of rials, holding his hand on top of them. "Stamp the papers at once." He lifted his hand slowly, revealing his SAVAK card, another gift from Houdin, "or you'll live longer than you're able to bear."

The man jolted up, surprise sweeping his features.

"You must understand the situation," said Devi Saed. "Others are ahead of your guests. I'd love to fill your wishes but..."

Mirdad smiled with cold understanding. The swine raked in money from people fighting to get on the flight and had probably sold it four times over.

"Stamp them now!"

"It will cost you..."

"It'll cost your life if you defy me longer, or I'll call Pavriz Sabeti from this office."

Saed's eyes grew large. The name of the head of the SAVAK carried its own power. Saed's mouth opened then closed with a snap. He stamped the documents. Mirdad snatched them from the desk and turned to his charges.

"Come quickly." Mirdad rushed Kathryn and the others back through the crammed corridor, through metal gates, out onto the scorching tarmac. They looked toward the glistening 707 aircraft with Air India on the tail fin.

"Oh God, the plane!" Teddy hesitated.

Kathryn nudged his arm, handing him the Bolex. "Move it. We're getting out of here."

Mirdad stayed close as she made Teddy shoot footage of everything around them; people, aircraft, officials arguing, while they hurried to the plane.

Hot winds gusted, crackling dry and angry like everyone on the tarmac. Panicked people shouted while other passengers overran officials who tried to check boarding passes.

Mirdad remained with them as they waited their turn at the ramp.

Peter shook hands with him. "Thanks, man," he said over the din. "See you in the States, right?"

Teddy hugged him with one arm. "You did it, Mirdad. You're okay." Mirdad smiled.

The roar of jet engines, the smell of fuel, airport carts and baggage trams, the explosive hysterical energy pulsed around them.

Mirdad was about to see Kathryn fly out of his life, the one person who knew the best side of him.

"See you, Mirdad," Buzz said. "You're quite a guy. You ever want to join an ad agency you've got a deal. Think about it." They hugged.

"Safe journey, Buzz."

Mirdad turned to Kathryn, taking her hands in his.

"Kathryn..." He tried to disguise the longing he felt, but with her, it no longer worked. She had unmasked him.

Gazing at him, she said. "I have no words to say how grateful I am, my dear friend. Please don't let this revolution suck you under, Mirdad. Live your dream, go to Paris, study film noir." She gave him a tight hug. "I'll never forget you." Quickly, she started up the ramp. "Come see me!"

"Kathryn!" Mirdad called to her.

Halfway up, she stopped and looked back. "I'll send you my film," she said. "You'll be in it. Wait till you watch it! Ooh la la!"

He smiled through his pain. "If you need me, I'm there, Kathryn."

A look of gratitude brightened her face. "Yes, friends!" she yelled back, blew him a kiss and disappeared into the plane.

But we'll be more than friends with Anthony gone. I'll win your love. Soon.

Kathryn boarded the plane and took her seat next to Buzz, relief seeping into her every pore, calming her racing nerves with their narrow escape. She was leaving Iran, her goal on the horizon with her career once again on the line, but surprise, surprise she'd found a love she hadn't dreamed existed for her. Two weeks and then...

Together in London, she would meet Anthony's adored grandfather, Lord Charles. She thought of her own family, Uncle Buzz, her equestrian mother. She giggled, recalling her mother's last taunt to her. "When you go into the Garden of Love, Kathryn, must you always pick a lemon?" Not this time mother. Not this time.

Could this bliss truly last? Of course it could. She leaned back and gripped the arms of her seat surrounded by the sound of soaring jet engines.

Anthony's silver car skidded onto the airport turnoff, roaring up the road for fifty feet, then screeched to a halt in his desperate attempt to reach Kathryn before her plane departed for London. He had to give her the documents she would need to enter the U.K. with the Persian Glories in her possession, not to mention Iran's crown jewels.

"Damn! What the hell...?" Ahead lay a massive array of military vehicles in mayhem. Shadows of a passing storm swooped overhead, disappearing over the Elburz Mountains.

"Hold on, Ali." Zooming backward almost to the corner, Anthony swerved onto a narrow service road.

"If I hold any tighter, I will crush this door into pulp!" Ali shouted over the whine of the Ferrari engine and the roar of Pirelli tires eating gravel. They sped toward a barbed-wire-topped iron gate.

Anthony yanked his ministry I.D. card from his coat pocket, waving it for the armed guards to see.

They jumped to open the gate. The generous *pishkesh* Anthony had paid in the past secured a speedy entrance to airport tarmac. He shouted a greeting to a young guard in Farsi, then asked if the morning plane to London had departed.

"Just now, Excellency." The guard pointed northwest. "She's in the air."

"Damn!" He couldn't see anything in the steel-hued sky, but the roar of aircraft was deafening. Anthony waved and continued toward the main terminal.

"What can you do now?" asked Ali.

"Saed's phone. If the phones still work I can get through to London. Either that or I've created an international incident."

Ali's booming laughter grabbed his attention.

"What the hell are you laughing at?"

"You," Ali cackled. "I can't wait until a woman makes my heart jiggle like a pudding, too."

"Yeah, we'll just see what kind of fool love makes of you, my jolly friend." Anthony roared up beside the Airport Director's private entrance.

"Wait for me." Anthony jumped out of the car.

"Don't worry." Ali maneuvered into the driver's seat.

Riddled with panic for Kathryn if customs had detained her, Anthony dashed into the crowded terminal, and headed for the director's private offices. Devi Saed was a man whose friendship it had taken five years to cultivate, for the man hated most everyone. But he and Anthony shared a mutual interest, polo horses, and they'd formed an informal camaraderie.

Anthony skirted a noisy throng, shoved his way along the corridor, nodded to an unfamiliar guard who looked like SAVAK outside Saed's office. The man frowned.

Anthony heard a voice from behind the door and pushed inside.

He stopped short, his mind reeling. The bleak olive-green walls, the scarred metal desk, picture frames over-turned, filing cabinets jammed to overflowing with bent manila folders, chairs forced against a wall, and Saed, disheveled, cowered in the corner. Mirdad, breathing hard, hair mussed, sat behind the desk on Saed's phone, halted in mid-sentence.

Anthony processed appalling implications of Mirdad, alone in this office. Alarm blared. Only SAVAK had the clout to take over Saed's office. "Mirdad?"

"Just a minute," Mirdad said into the phone and looked over at Saed. "Get out!"

Saed scrambled to the door with a dejected look at Anthony, as if he would say something. He just shook his head and got out.

"Anthony."

For once, innocence had vanished from Mirdad's face. Hardness replaced it, jolting Anthony's nerves.

"You're too late," Mirdad ran a hand through his untidy hair. "She's gone. But you know that, don't you?"

"What's going on, Mirdad?"

"Permit me to conclude my call, cousin," Mirdad said.

"Finish it later." Anthony strode toward the desk.

Mirdad shot his arm out to halt him and went back to his call. "Captain? Try Shiraz. They must be there. And carry out my orders. Whatever it takes." Mirdad flushed, replacing the receiver. "You were saying, cousin?"

It wasn't Mirdad's usual bright smile, like sun, bursting through clouds, lighting his face, but one dark and tortured, meant to mask feeling.

With great sorrow Anthony finally understood the things others had told him, that he had explained away. Though he had watched and listened, hoping to glean insight into Mirdad, now all at once, it was there. Mirdad giving orders, dismissing Saed, his hookup with Houdin, flight plans copied from Anthony's office safe, the escalating kill-list he now topped. A sickening stab of clarity pierced Anthony's gut and a lifetime of filial trust crumbled until only a thick film of suspicion was left.

He reached across the desk, and grabbed Mirdad by his shirt. "What have you done?"

Mirdad sputtered, then roared with laughter. But there was no laughter in his dark eyes.

"Tell me!"

Mirdad shoved him off. "What typical arrogance! Can't you tell when you're despised?"

Anthony shoved him back. "You're a bitter man, Mirdad. Let go of regrets before they kill you."

"What would you know of regret? YOU LEFT ME— ALONE!" Mirdad threw a punch. The blow clipped Anthony's jaw.

He staggered and groaned. "You idiot! I never abandoned you. I did everything I could from a distance."

"Alone—tossed into the street, beaten..." Mirdad's arms waved wildly.

"I'd have given anything to protect you," Anthony said, moving closer.

Mirdad backed away. "While you went off with your rich family. An English lord..."

"I was fourteen. My parents had been murdered."

"Never reaching out to me—not a word!" Mirdad retreated behind the desk, leaning on it head down, panting.

"I sent letters," Anthony said, "money. I called from school—you were never there." *Damn!*

Mirdad shook, not listening.

Anthony turned to leave but couldn't. Since he had returned to live in Iran eight years ago, Mirdad would not speak of the past. It just hung heavy in the air around them. Mirdad misconstrued everything.

With his head bowed, Anthony whispered what he'd never uttered. "Don't you know I suffered, too? Stripped from my home, all I'd grown up with." He felt like he would explode.

Noise from the hall intruded, boots thundering down the corridor, shouts in Farsi, Arabic, Russian. Women crying. It was all getting away from him: Kathryn, his family, his home, his country—all falling apart. He couldn't hold back the destructive tide rising to crush what mattered. He turned back, searching Mirdad's now inscrutable face for a glimmer of feeling. None.

"I waited for so long. Hoping." Mirdad's voice sounded dead. "To think I cared."

"In my mind, we were brothers," Anthony said.

Mirdad's veneer cracked. "You lie!"

"...in my heart you were my little brother, *baradar koochooloo*."

"Liar!"

Anthony gripped his feelings, steadying himself. "I was gone, but I always loved you—my family."

"NO! I will not hear these words! Never! My mother warned me...We're finished!" Mirdad vaulted over the desk shouting, "I hate you, hate you!" He lunged at Anthony, knocking him to the floor, landing on top of him, fists flying. He punched Anthony's face.

"Damn you!" Enraged, Anthony punched back. CRACK. His fist split Mirdad's lip. Blood spurted. Anthony shoved him over, pinning Mirdad to the floor.

"Get away from me!"

"I'm sorry, Mirdad, for all you went through. But let it go."

Mirdad looked up with such pain, his eyes wet with tears. Suddenly, Mirdad grabbed Anthony's head, pulling his mouth down in a bruising kiss. Mirdad clung to him, deepening the kiss, hanging on, clutching him.

Anthony struggled, his pulse slammed in his temples, his mind whirled. He pushed off, too stunned for words.

Eyes wild, Mirdad leapt up, straightened his clothes, and stormed from the room.

Anthony swept his hair from his face and wiped away the taste of Mirdad's smeared blood from his mouth. His knuckles ached. Shock and disgust paralyzed him. *My cousin, my brother.* And despair at the wrath his cousin could pull down on them engulfed him—Mirdad was SAVAK. Then he thought of Aunt Rena, Mirdad, and Houdin last night at the Embassy ball huddled together—conspirators, married. The Black Glove surrounded him.

Mirdad stormed past the Mehrabad Airport crowds toward the exit and flew through the open terminal door. His thoughts and emotions a jumble until he spotted the limo. *Thank God!* Escape. Lungs heaving, he jumped in.

"Go!" he shouted. The car sped away.

I'm suffocating! He tore his tie loose. Sweat and blood dripped down his face. He fumbled in his pocket for a handkerchief, dabbing his face and neck. His head pounded like raging surf dashed on cliffs of despair. *I never stopped loving you. Liar!*

Mirdad shuddered. His hidden fury and lust smoldering warm and safe for so long, burst into flames of hate. But he had kissed Anthony, tasted him, felt his warm breath on him, his blood smeared onto that full mouth. He'd had an erection. Then he'd run from the room. Desire and humiliation warred in that moment—loathing won over them both.

Why? Anthony had asked. *Why indeed!* How he had longed to tell Anthony. *I loved you above all others. You were my sun, my hero, all I ever wanted and you left me.* Mirdad's heart cried out.

"The apartment was empty, Excellency," Captain Aran had said on the phone, even as Anthony stood across the desk from Mirdad. *"The paintings, gone from the walls, the silver, the statues, everything personal, gone."* Then Mirdad had heard words that would bring Anthony's death: *"He will be taken care of, sir, have no fear."*

Baradar koochooloo, beloved little one.

Craggy mountains loomed in the distance, bathed in a copper glow. Clouds, steely grey, crowded the sun, smothering the light with scorn. Mirdad tried relaxing, his breathing heavy. Soon they would be over the first winding mountain pass, then Shiraz and his refuge, the Paradise Club.

He would stay there in a plush apartment until it was over, until the jewels and Anthony's head were delivered to him. Then he could indulge himself in anything he wanted, go anywhere. But none of this made him feel better. He sank deeper into the seat and stared out the window at nothing, craving the warmth of Anthony's body over his.

Anthony's head reeled. Mirdad's total freak out, the fight, and the bizarre kiss shocked him to the core. Mention of his home and Kathryn in flight, a red flag. *Danger, danger!* his mind screamed. Quickly, he shut the airport director's office door and grabbed the telephone. His gut churned like a poison worm slithered inside, into his thoughts. He dialed London; he must get through. Telephones in

Tehran had grown more unpredictable with Khomeini's escalating revolution. Green Band power censored every aspect of daily life. Finally, he heard a ringing on the other end. Be there he prayed—please!

"Philippe? My God, I was afraid you were out!"

"Anthony! You sound unhinged."

"Listen. I've botched things up. I need you to pay attention. Kathryn is on the morning plane to London." Anthony sucked in a breath. He was going to sound like an idiot. "She's carrying something that belonged to my mother."

Silence.

"Philippe? Did you hear me?"

"I see."

"No, you don't," he said through annoying static. "The documents for entry have been forgotten. And that's not all," he said. "She's bringing in the gift I told you about from my client in the same package. However, she's unaware of that, doesn't know anything about it."

"How the hell...?"

"Forget that now. You must secure a waiver for entry. Use every contact with Heathrow customs."

"Calm down. I know what to do. I'll have the plane hijacked."

Anthony groaned in exasperation. "Can you handle this?"

"Not to worry. I'll arrange something. I thrive on pressure. How did you manage this *faux pas*?"

"Things got out of hand since you left."

"You besotted bastard! You're in love!"

Anthony held the receiver away from Philippe's laughter.

"You haven't heard anything yet, Philippe. We're going to be married. Now you can go into shock."

"Shock! More like cardiac arrest."

"I want you to stand up with me. That is if my bride doesn't end up in London Tower."

Philippe's voice lowered. "Don't worry. I'll take care of it, but you might find us handcuffed together at Scotland Yard."

Anthony didn't laugh. "Philippe, its serious. Now I've gotta go..."

"Something else is wrong. Is it the shipment?"

"The shipment is fine, exactly as planned. But...I've got a bad feeling about Mirdad. He's embroiled with the Black Glove—Houdin."

"I warned you, you know."

"I've been blind. But not anymore." Anthony exhaled tension. "Philippe, I'm counting on you. Mirdad mentioned Shiraz to someone on the phone. I have to get there— Raymond, Tali. Phone lines to Shiraz are down." Saying Raymond's name made him uneasy. "Tell Kathryn I love her. I'll explain later." Anthony hung up with thoughts of Kathryn. He made one more call to London.

CHAPTER TWO

Anthony's Ferrari roared through the mountain pass. He raced to his home in Shiraz. Two more frustrating hours left to drive.

His mind replayed Mirdad's airport outburst, over and over, the telephone call to some nameless captain on the other end: *"Then try Shiraz. They must be there. And carry out my final orders."* All Anthony's reluctance had been blasted away. Mirdad, the Black Glove son-of-bitch, was after something. There was only one thing he coveted: the Persian Glories. Unless somehow he had learned of the crown jewels.

No, only he and the empress knew about those, no link to Kathryn there. She was on the plane. But SAVAK had long arms. Surely his MI-6 link would protect her if Philippe made contact. No choices were left. He must get across the mountains before the Black Glove arrived at his Shiraz home. Ali, desperate to warn his father, had gone to the guard-gate office phone. The lines were dead. Obviously, he'd been lucky earlier to get his calls through to London.

Anthony refused to endanger Ali further, convincing him to get a ride to his secretary, Nina's apartment and keep trying to reach anyone in Shiraz. Tell them to get Ali's father, Raymond and everyone away from the house immediately.

He accelerated past a truck full of squawking poultry, convincing himself Ali's warnings would be heeded. Raymond would take his household members to family outside Shiraz. Later, Anthony would meet his pilot, Hans at a nearby airstrip, but Hans would know to wait.

Images of Kathryn crowded his thoughts: flying in the Cessna next to his, late at night zig-zagging across Abadan oil fields, rapid fire pelting their planes from machine gun turrets below. The look on her face when they'd entered a hidden airplane hangar near Shiraz, with a sitar player she admired sheltering his wife and child, waiting with sixteen other frightened men women and children to be flown out of Iran.

"You're missing a pilot," she said, circling the two Cessna.

"He was just picked up by Black Glove for questioning."

"All these people won't fit into one Cessna," she said. "I'll fly the second plane."

They'd argued. She won. People were saved that night. Getting back alive, tired and shaky had taken some daring with fuel gages on empty, engine sputtering, Kathryn just didn't back down.

The first class Air India cabin bound for London was filled to capacity. It would be a long flight, Kathryn thought, carefully placing the drab camera case under the seat in front of her, protecting the jewels, her Vuitton carry-on next to it. Leg room was non-existent on this flight. Passengers escaping the revolution carried everything possible: photos, appliances, bedding, the family silver, china, artifacts, lots of shoes—as much as their arms could bear.

People were crowding the aisle, refusing to sit down and talking loudly over the heads of nearby passengers to friends and relatives in other rows.

Pressured flight attendants strove to accommodate those in the crowded cabin, working through the raucous noise and hysteria filling the aircraft.

A desperate voice said, "What if the airplane isn't cleared to leave?"

"Green Bands can interfere," said another.

The din in the cabin rose to a cacophony of paranoia.

Suddenly there was a crackling in the public announcement system as the captain began to speak. "This is the captain. Listen up, please." His voice boomed over the P.A. as the crowd toned it down a notch. "Until everyone cooperates we'll remain on the ground. Do you all understand? Find your seats, sit down, and stop talking. You have three minutes to settle down." His voice boomed.

People calmed to a quiet, nervous murmur. The plane taxied forward.

"We're damn lucky to be on this plane," Buzz whispered.

The jet liner roared forward on the tarmac, lifting through the haze and streaking up into a brilliant blue sky, in and out of tremendous, cumulus clouds.

Buzz said, "If it weren't for Mirdad....Gutsy move."

"You guys wouldn't listen to me," Teddy hissed from the seat across the aisle, his fists clenching and unclenching. "If those soldiers had gotten us, we'd be rotting in a pile of cow dung."

Kathryn reached across the aisle, patting Teddy's hand. "We're safe now. Relax," she said. "When we're out of Iranian airspace, I'll buy you a Remy."

"Deal." Teddy exhaled, taking his anxiety down a notch.

Uneasiness circled through her gut. She tried to let it go. The Boeing shoot teetered on the edge. Could she pull it out of the fire? She wasn't sure. Wally, her Boeing client, would be in London, Brett her ex-husband and producer, too. He'd try to take her down. One should never underestimate Brett Whitney.

She breathed in and out steadily, ignoring the chatter around her. Unconsciously she twisted her engagement ring around to see the dazzling blue-white diamonds and sank back into her seat nervous, excited, and so in love. Engaged. Wonderful, but hard to believe it had happened so quickly.

Beside her, Buzz nudged her arm. "I'm happy for you, kiddo." He leaned in. "I know you're crazy about the guy, and is he crazy about you! When you walked out of the palace party, he breezed past that brunette like she was a gnat."

Smiling, Kathryn pulled the light wool blanket around her, wishing she were still nestled beside Anthony's warmth.

There were obstacles, obligations, logistics, but they would make it all work.

Kathryn was startled awake on Air India's final descent from a clear afternoon sky into an airport blanketed by English fog. The flight crew had worked through raucous cabin noise, now calmed to snores and chattering.

A harried stewardess turned to her and said, "Don't forget your customs form, miss," then smiled. "They're serious about checking everyone coming in from Iran these days."

Groggy, Kathryn looked out at the mist. "How much longer is our flight?" she asked the attendant.

"About forty-five minutes. May I get you something?"

"Black coffee, please."

Kathryn glanced down at the form in her lap, too drowsy to think clearly. She reached into her camera case for the manila envelope addressed to Lord Charles Evans, her documents for the Persian Glories. She'd look it over privately and made her way to the bathroom and splashed her face with tepid water hoping to clear her mind. She dried it, the paper towel rough against her skin. It didn't do much. She was about to apply fresh lipstick when all at once it hit her. She got a queasy feeling and opened the manila envelope, pulled out the papers and stared at the heading she hadn't checked earlier.

Inventory and bill of lading for Shiraz household shipment. Inventory!

Customs! The wrong documents, She didn't have it, *the Persian Glories provenance.*

No problem. Other than her bazaar purchases of the ivory miniatures costing five hundred dollars, she had bought amber beads, lots of silver bracelets, tribal purses made of different brocades edged in crusty gold trim, and a few silk scarves. The total valued could be no more than six hundred dollars. That was it, except for an eighteen-carat gold box twelve by twelve inches, studded in small ruby and emerald chips housing a famous parure of flawless canary diamonds, valued around—priceless.

No problem. Piece of cake.

She leaned into the mirror, glaring at her reflection. What have I done? He showed me the papers last night. *"You must carry these stamped documents from the Royal office to pass through customs."*

How could she not have checked the papers she'd grabbed, pulled them out of the envelope to be sure she had the right ones? But she hadn't been focused on papers this morning, lost in dreams, hurrying to get back to the hotel. And now she was stuck. How could she bring rare jewels into England without provenance? Jewels she didn't have when she entered Iran. She was going to land in hell, be arrested for stealing, or treason for smuggling a national Persian treasure. There would be no career to worry about serving time in a British prison—or worse, extradition to a Tehran prison. Prisoners there were raped, urinated on and forced to stand naked for hours according to the *New York Times*.

She had to save herself!

Calm down. Anthony.

He couldn't help her now. *"I won't be in touch for a few days."* And this morning, he hadn't said a word.

Well, he'd been asleep. She'd taken a heart-melting look at him and left without a word. Goodbyes were her nemesis. *Her husband, Brett, her father.* Goodbyes meant the end. Old fears still ruled, she guessed.

But she should've settled this last night! No, last night wasn't about papers. God! I left before getting my head straight. It's my fault. I'm toast if I don't do something.

The plane angled downward. She grabbed the sink, hyperventilating, then ripped the bathroom door open, seeking air. Two chatting stewardesses stared, one cracking her chewing gum.

"When do we land?" Kathryn asked, her smile awkward.

"Just thirty minutes left, and you need to go back to your seat," the gum-chewer said. "Your customs form ready? They're really on us." She cocked her head. "They can be nasty."

"I'll do it now," Kathryn said. *But how am I going to do it?* In her seat, she tried to print legibly. With Buzz next to her she wondered about telling him. No. He was better off not knowing. Peter? He'd handled so many customs problems for crews all over the world. But this was personal. God, she couldn't involve them. She was running out of time.

Kathryn tapped her pen on the customs form in front of her as if she could knock it into giving her an idea. She looked across the aisle from Teddy to Peter, and back to Buzz, searching for a plan. Film crew. She was part of an American film crew coming into London. How could she use this?

Peter was leaning back, legs stretched out, his hair flowing about his shoulders, over a blue dress shirt and grey slacks.

Teddy wore jeans, a cowboy shirt, boots and jacket. "Teddy, where's your sacred hat?"

"In my pocket, where it always is if it's not on my head."

"I want to borrow it for an hour or two. Okay?"

"Well, I don't know."

"And your jeans jacket."

"My jacket?"

She held her hand out. "Do you mind?"

"Geez! Well, no, but...Ah, what the hell." He took it off and tossed it in her lap. He swallowed his Remy Martin and stood up. "I'm outta here before you strip me naked."

If it would help, she'd do just that. It would be a distraction. She gulped the last of her coffee, grabbed Teddy's things, her purse, and the camera case, and headed back up the aisle to the bathroom.

Cautiously, Anthony slowed the Ferrari and turned onto his narrow street in Shiraz. Blocking the gates to his own house were three cars: SAVAK cars. One stood out like a tarantula on an anthill: Captain Aran's bulletproof Mercedes 600. Anthony's gut tightened as if screws were being inserted.

If the phone lines were down, Raymond and his staff would still be inside. Images of atrocities he'd witnessed over the last eight months jumbled his mind: the Ozamis, the Devis, so many others. He shook the horror away, making a U-turn on his street, and pulling down the alley at the east end of his property by the citrus orchard. He stopped adjacent to the eight-foot stucco wall. He didn't think he'd been spotted. How many were there: three cars; ten, possibly twelve men at the outside?

He reached under the driver's seat for his .38. Gone! Ali must have kept it. He fumbled further and found his knife. He tried the trunk and grabbed heavy gloves, a wrench, and the canvas tarp he used when taking pictures. He skirted up the path to a portion of the south wall, trying to control his fury. His little Mecca, purposely hidden from the outside world, had been violated by the lowest demons.

The top of the eight-foot wall surrounding the property was encrusted with wicked shards of glass and a bulging spiral of barbed wire. He backed up the Ferrari and climbed onto the hood. He slipped on the gloves, listening to leaves rustle, insects buzzing, but hearing no human sounds. Not wanting to dull his knife blade yet, he aimed the heavy wrench three feet up the wall, smashing the rigid surface. Again, he listened. Still no noise. His blow had taken a chunk out of the wall's thick plaster surface. The canvas tarp hoisted over the wire, he looked up at the wall and singled out one piece of glass to aim for with his free hand. He dug his shoe tip into the crevice, grunted, and thrust his body upwards with all the agility he could summon.

He missed. His foot slipped, banging his knee and scraping his leg down the wall. He ignored the pain and tried again. This time he counted to set a rhythm for the leap. One, his foot wedged into the hole, two, he grabbed the glass, three, and he hurled his body up over the wire, hitting the ground in a roll to offset the fall and landed with a thud against something that felt like a sandbag. Anthony turned over and almost gagged. He was wedged against the body of his gardener, face down in the flowerbed; his aged, gnarled fingers had clawed into the earth with death. A senseless murder. A pool of blood spread from a bullet wound to the head. Bile rose in Anthony's throat. Not five feet away lay the gardener's young helper.

There was no doubt; Ali had not gotten through by phone.

Bullet holes riddled the boy's spine and neck. *The butchers!* This boy must have been harder to kill than the old man. He had to get to Raymond and Tali, her girls, the Iranian family of his heart. Hearing faint voices, he held his emotions in check and scurried across the open area toward a snarl of shrubbery. He disappeared beneath tangled boughs.

Two men in camouflage fatigues with automatic rifles slung over their shoulders came toward him, dragging a struggling young housemaid between them. She was Tali's youngest daughter, Lila, not more than fifteen. Her hands were tied, her mouth gagged. The soldiers laughed as they ripped her clothes away and shoved her nearer the shrubs.

A sour, sweaty smell announced their proximity. Anthony edged closer, swallowing his rage as he watched one of the soldiers hold the girl down with a .45 automatic pressed to her head. One shot and she'd be dead. The other fell to his knees, pushing open her legs, ripping at her panties.

Anthony only had his knife, damn it. If he moved too quickly, he and the girl would both be dead. He steeled himself, seething inside, barely able to hold back before he unleashed his fury on these bastards.

Laughing, the man pulled down his pants, pumping his cock in his hand, then rammed himself into her.

Her muffled cries were covered by his grunts.

He shooed the other soldier away to give him more room. Silently, Anthony lifted himself off the ground the instant the second man backed closer. He was obviously enjoying the sight of his friend humping away on the young girl struggling beneath him, her black eyes wild with pain and terror.

In one quick movement, Anthony's right hand grabbed the soldier's mouth and his left sliced the blade deep into the man's larynx and across his throat, almost severing his head. He let the body fall, and in one step, was behind the rutting pig who had seen nothing through his lust. He saw the child's pleading eyes just before he wrenched the man off of her and slit his throat. Then, before the vile man's dying eyes, Anthony cut through the base of the man's engorged penis with one slice of the blade. *An eye for an eye*, he thought, momentarily sickened by his own rage. He lifted the weeping girl and moved her away from the bodies.

Anthony released her bruised wrists and covered her with his jacket. "So sorry, *koochooloo*. Shhh, it's all right now."

Removing her gag he placed his hand over her mouth until he was sure she would not cry out. He lifted her, cradling her against his chest. "Is Raymond inside?" he whispered, still hoping that somehow Raymond had gotten away.

"Yes...and so is my mother."

His jaw clenched, holding back a shriek of rage. It just got worse. Christ, his timing was off.

Anthony heard a movement in the bushes, then the girl's name whispered. Before he could move, he saw another girl, Tali's older daughter, Mira, creeping toward them.

"I saw," she muttered, moving to her sister. "I was hiding and I saw what you did." Tears streaked her pretty face. "I will take care of my sister," she said.

He nodded. "How many men are there?"

"Many...eight or ten, but more in front of the house." She pulled a letter from her pocket. "Raymond said I must give this to you."

"Thank you. He stuffed the letter in his shirt.

The younger girl, Lila, gripped his hand, "Please help my mother!"

"I will." He touched the older sister's arm. "Can you find a way out of here, Mira?"

"I know a way."

"Good. Go to your uncle's house and stay there."

Anthony kissed each girl on her forehead and clasped them to him before quietly sending them on their way.

Grabbing one of the soldier's AK-47s, Anthony glanced around and headed toward the house. In the distance, across the expansive lawn and through French doors into the house, he could vaguely make out Raymond, drooping between two soldiers, and Tali, precious Tali, in her kitchen apron, sobbing. Then Captain Aran, Houdin's most cold-blooded henchman, walked into his view, and Anthony broke into a run, heedless of being spotted and knowing the rifle would be useless at this range. He might hit Raymond or Tali.

As he got closer, Anthony saw Raymond slump against his captor's bulky frame, facing the windows. Anthony caught a look of recognition on his agonized face.

He wanted to scream, *I'm coming*! He ran harder to reach them, watching Raymond labor to raise his head and defiantly spit in Aran's face. Aran raised his luger to Raymond's chest Anthony's heart broke as the Arab fired once then turned to Tali and fired again, then he turned and marched out of the room.

No! No! Anthony howled silently, tears springing to his eyes as he stumbled, racing to the house. "No-o-o!"

Anthony stopped and clung to the terrace balustrade, out of sight, weeping. He forced himself to wait till the men were gone. Then he smelled smoke. He couldn't wait any longer; he dashed in through the French doors—no signs of SAVAK. Knowing the futility, he checked Raymond for a pulse, then Tali. *Nothing, no life.*

He moved quickly through decimated rooms, his studio, searching through the shambles of his home for survivors. Furniture, bedding, all torn apart, burned. Covering his face, he staggered through smoky haze. In a back room, Anthony found the body of a young houseboy. In the servants' quarters, he found Ali's cousin Hassan—dead. Anthony thought Hassan was safe with family in Tehran. It was a massacre. Everyone was dead, except Mira and Lila.

He ran back to Raymond and Tali flooded with regret. And for a moment, smoke seeping into the room, he kneeled cradling Raymond's body, blaming himself for arriving too late. Raymond clearly had used his last gesture to distract those vermin, sacrificing himself. He wiped the congealing blood from Raymond's face with his shirtsleeve, rocking his beloved friend's body, tears blurring all around him.

Potent images of the years under Raymond's care, wisdom, and unspoken love came to him. It was like his father dying all over again. *Father, Father, I've lost you forever and now Raymond, too.*

He should have respected his grandfather's advice and sent his servants to safety with their families weeks ago, and Raymond to Qom to stay with Hassan's father. Too late, it was all too late.

Fire leaped up the walls around him, devouring his drapes and tapestries, blistering walls billowed with flames.

Coughing through smoke and scorching heat, Anthony lifted his lifelong servant's body, the man who was as close as his own blood, unable to bear leaving him to be consumed by the flames, and ran with him out of the house to the garage.

"I'm taking you home, my friend," he said and laid Raymond's body in the Range Rover, leaving the Ferrari.

He thought of all whom the Black Glove had crushed. And then he remembered how many he'd saved, his spirit lifting. Now it was him they sought to bury. He wasn't far from the airport. All he could do was run for it.

For months it was as if he'd skied before an avalanche, one wrong turn and he would be under it. This onslaught had increased momentum, interring people he cared about. He crouched as low in the car as possible. Everything he'd done in the past few weeks had been off, the close calls, ignoring warnings about Mirdad, everything, except for meeting Kathryn. Even that, he had almost blown, had almost lost her.

As Anthony swung his Range Rover away, a black SAVAK car raced back toward the Shiraz house.

They'd spotted him.

He swerved in a U-turn. Thirty seconds sooner, and they would have missed him. He downshifted, taking off across the city toward the airport. Their car might be faster, but he knew every short cut. The gray cloud cover had brought gusting desert winds, hot and dry off the plain. The sky cleared, a giant cap of cerulean hinted of paradise or the Caspian Sea. The image hurt, so distant from his reality.

Once on the highway, he thought he'd lost them. Adjusting the mirror, he caught a glimmer of black, gaining on him. *Shit!*

His timing was definitely off.

The car continued to gain on him.

A man leaned out the rear, aiming an automatic rifle. CRACK!

He swerved the Range Rover across the road then back, making their target difficult. Bullets flew by his vehicle. Five more miles.

He fought to stay on the road, avoid bullets, and search for a way out—a path off road—anything!

A bullet grazed the Range Rover, more ricocheted off its metal. With a jolt, a bullet pierced his shoulder, then another. He swerved but hung on. Then he heard it. *Shit! The gas tank!* They had struck their mark. *Get out!* His mind screamed, before—

Within seconds the tank exploded in flames, sending metal and debris flying. Red-hot pain shot through him. Smoke and fire surrounded him. As a black void overtook him, Anthony's last thought was of Kathryn.

CHAPTER THREE

Kathryn ignored the pounding on the bathroom door and stayed put, planning to be locked in the 707 lavatory bound for Heathrow until the last possible moment before landing. She studied the props assembled for a risky transformation and assessed herself in the mirror. Making a spectacle of herself could backfire. But on the other hand, being busted for smuggling was a terrible option. Her hands shook; her resolve was just as shaky. But she was out of time and had to get a grip. *Just follow the plan.*

Her navy linen jacket discarded, she rolled up the sleeves of her white shirt and opened several buttons, displaying an ample amount of cleavage above edges of her white lace bra.

Removing the Persian Glories, one piece at a time, she dusted each with a fine coat of face powder, dulling it and cringed at her irreverent act. An image of her being stoned as an infidel, the daughter of Satan, sprang to mind. She trounced it and fastened the diamond necklace, topping it with amber beads. She adorned the earrings, brooch, ring, and the tiara around the crown of Teddy's Hemmingway legacy hat. An added tribute, she tied a tribal scarf to the hat and slouched one around her hips.

Fumbling, she pulled out her comb, teased her hair into a "working girl" 'do then opened her make-up case, extracted a kohl eyeliner pencil, and got to work. *She could do this.* She caked on mascara.

Ten minutes later, red lights flashed under the lavatory mirror, a sign to return to the seats. She gazed at the result of her makeover, appalled and scared. Get into a tough role, she coached. Rizzo, *Grease. No fear.* Right.

She felt the angled descent, gathered her things, and beat it back to her seat.

The stewardess did a double take.

Peter was absorbed in the window view. Teddy was too busy white-knuckling it to notice her. But Buzz leaned away from her as if she'd contracted an infectious disease. *He'd never hire her again.*

"What are you up to, Kathryn?"

"Full moon, no other way to explain it," she whispered, cheeks hot. "Let me in."

He moved his long legs, and she eased into her seat and buckled her seat belt.

"I won't ask!" Buzz said. "Just get over it before Lord Samuelson's party tonight." Buzz shuddered. "We're going to thank him, and that get-up will say something different to his ritzy crowd."

Kathryn glanced down at herself. She counted on a good relationship with Samuelson Film Service to finish her shoot. "Uh, I'll change after Customs."

"Then I'll see you there."

"Right." If she wasn't apprehended at customs. "Got any gum?"

Mirdad bolted from the limo he had taken from Mehrabad Airport, and charged into the Paradise Club in Shiraz, to Houdin's private office. He slammed through the office door and leaned his hands on the intricate Boule desk, panting, nerves ragged from his encounter with Anthony. *Was it done? Was Anthony dead? Had this thing ended?* He wanted to get out of here and go have Siri, his little whore, hold him.

At the sound of footsteps, Mirdad whirled around. Captain Aran opened the door and strutted into the office carrying a burlap bag. Harsh afternoon light spread across the room, filling the hollows of Captain Aran's face. Standing erect, Captain Aran was dressed in a black suit, the SAVAK emblem stretched over his bicep. Aran's appearance was impeccable, as if he'd just stepped out of a dinner party instead of a slaughterhouse. The bag he was holding held an odd shaped object.

"The servants were resistant," Aran reported.

"You disposed of them?" A twinge of discomfort assailed Mirdad. "All of them?"

"Yes, all of them. And the house, burned to the ground as per your instructions."

Mirdad turned away, concealing the triumph he felt at those words. *You deserved to die, Raymond, for betraying my father with your accusing lies. Father, I avenge you for a murder you never committed!* Composing himself, Mirdad faced Aran. "And Evans?"

Aran raised an eyebrow above cold black eyes, a smile twitched at his mouth. "Anthony Evans is dead."

"Dead?" Mirdad repeated, a moment of regret surfacing for his lost childhood and love.

Captain Aran brought forward a burlap bag in one of his black-gloved hands. He opened the bag and extracted a reeking object, the stench horrible.

He held the offending object over the beautiful boule desk as if to drop it there.

Mirdad froze, searching his pocket for a handkerchief and clutched it to his nose.

"No! Over there." Mirdad gestured to the black marble coffee table in front of a brocade sofa, drapes rustling behind it.

Aran plunked the thing down with a thud on the marble table.

"Yes. Evans arrived at the house after we'd left. If we hadn't gone back to look for two of our men, we would have missed him."

Mirdad couldn't focus on the words. He saw only the object—a scorched human arm, black, purple, mottled with brownish red dried blood. The attached hand wore a ring Mirdad recognized. He turned away, crouched over, fighting the need to gag.

Regaining composure, he stood up in front of the gloating captain.

Aran took hold of the ring finger of the burnt hand and snapped it off, like breaking a chicken bone. He handed Mirdad the finger.

Mirdad cringed, his body flushing heat, but he took it, examined it, noting the blackened Evans family crest. "Ah," he said, anger and sadness warring with his sense of victory.

He handed the body part back to Aran.

Captain Aran worked the ring off the digit, wiping it with a corner of burlap and gave the ring to Mirdad. "Then you recognize the seal, Mirdad? He was related to you, after all."

Mirdad's gut churned, his emotions careening from heavenly revenge to the depth of hell. "You got him," he stated lamely, shoving the ring in his pants pocket.

Aran swaggered to the window, pulling aside the brocade drape. A shaft of light struck the table red, illuminating the scorched limb, a gory entity raised from death in sun shards stabbing the room. Mirdad shrank from the sight.

"Evans, the arrogant bastard, tried to escape," said Aran, "on the road to the airport in his Range Rover. We chased him. Our best marksman found the gas tank. The explosion left a million pieces of metal and human remains. Of course little was retrievable, but this," he gestured to the limb defiling the marble table. "This, I trust you'll agree, was a significant find."

Mirdad shoved Aran's gruesome details from his thoughts. *Anthony dead!* They'd fought at the airport in Teheran but a few hours ago. Passion had roared through Mirdad, shocking Anthony and himself with the provocative kiss. Lust or punishment, Mirdad was uncertain. Probably both, if he were honest. Anthony, blubbering about affection for him, got more than he had bargained for.

"I brought you the papers from his safe in Shiraz." Aran handed him a packet. "There was nothing in his Teheran apartment."

Mirdad stared at the large envelope, wildly exhilarated. There before him was a glimpse into Anthony's private world. His fingers itched to rip it open and expose Anthony's secrets. He looked up into Aran's smug face. "And the jewels. Where are the jewels?"

"They were nowhere to be found..."

"The general's orders were clear, were they not?" Mirdad kept his tone crisp. He wouldn't want Aran to forget he outranked him in the general's Black Glove coterie. "But you will find the jewels, am I correct?"

"Yes, Colonel, I'll not fail my orders."

Mirdad didn't give a fart about the jewels. He had what he wanted: Anthony dead, burned alive! How good, how delicious was revenge.

"You've done well, Captain. And when you complete your task and get the jewels, our general will reward you. I'll see to it personally." Mirdad clasped his comrade's shoulder, refusing to touch his hand.

Mirdad walked away from the sofa, gesturing nonchalantly toward the gory remains. "And take that with you. I've no need of it." Mirdad moved to the chair behind the boule desk.

"But—" Aran gestured.

"You may go now, Captain, and finish your mission. The jewels."

Aran stared at Mirdad, his steely eyes unreadable.

"As you wish," he placed the arm back in the burlap bag.

Mirdad turned away when Aran departed. With a tremor of excitement, he sat behind General Houdin's desk. He picked up the phone and placed a call to his mother's new Caspian villa. She must know. In Shiraz, at least, the telephones still worked. As he waited for the call to go through, he tore open the envelope and spread the papers before him.

"Yes, what is it?" came the sharp sound of his mother's voice on the other end. He swiveled the chair around to face the windows across the room. He gazed out at the Paradise Club's gardens, verdant and lush. A brilliant peacock strolled languidly across the lawn. Orchids fluttered on the breeze.

"Mother, how are you?"

"Mirdad? Do you have news?"

"Yes, Mother."

"The Glories?"

"I'm afraid not, but Anthony, Raymond, the rest at the Shiraz house..."

"Dead? Tell me they're dead."

"Yes, Mother. The Shiraz house is no more, and our enemies have all departed for paradise."

"There is no paradise where they go!" Her voice was venomous. "Where are my Glories, Mirdad?"

"We're tracing them. I'll let you know as..."

"TRACING?"

He held the receiver away from his ear.

"WHERE ARE MY JEWELS?" she screamed.

"Please calm yourself. It's not good for your health."

"You imbecile! You killed them before they told you where they were, didn't you? You let my diamonds slip through your fingers!"

"Mother, please..."

"Understand me, Mirdad. I'll be patient for now. But find them for me, my son, because if I don't have what I want, there will be trouble you cannot imagine."

He heard a sharp click, then the dial tone. He shivered against the sensation the dark tone his mother's voice brought to his spine. Even he, the orchestrator of his own cousin's death, thought it evil.

Mirdad swiveled the chair around and replaced the receiver, gladly turning his attention to the papers spread before him. There were letters from Anthony's dead mother and father, deeds to property in Iran, and Anthony's will. Mirdad read, "*I, Anthony Evans...*" He skimmed down the page to where it said, "*...leave my estate in Shiraz and all the property in it to my cousin Mirdad Ajani, along with...*"

"No!" Mirdad shouted, jumping out of the chair. In his mind he saw the beautiful house, and felt the flames leaping out of it, smoke engulfing it. His pulse pounded in his ears and he snatched the papers from the desk and read on.

"*...along with the house in which he and his mother now reside, and all my funds in the Bank of Teheran...*"

Mirdad searched through the other deeds on the desk,

unable to fathom the words before him. What did Anthony mean? The house I reside in with my mother? *My mother owns that house. She paid for it.* He found the deed to the house in Shiraz, now burned to the ground. He tossed it aside. There was a deed to a ranch in the northern part of the country, resort property on the Caspian Sea, a ski lodge in the Elburz Mountains—all of it was left to him, *baradar koochooloo.*

The last paper he picked up was the deed to his mother's house in Teheran. The date of purchase was 1964, fourteen years ago. Anthony would have been twenty-one. *No!*

Digesting the scope of his mother's lies, Mirdad shot out his hand, swiping the desk clean. Paperweights, the clock, inkwells tumbled to the floor. He shook. His eyes squeezed shut, but behind his eyes the hatred, everything he had ever believed, dissolved, melted, disintegrated with images of his lying mother—lying to him for years. Raymond, who had always been kind to him, helped him. And Anthony at the airport. *"I've always loved you."*

He covered his ears, trying to block out Anthony's voice, low, choked with emotion.

"...you were my brother...I never abandoned you...did what I could from a distance...I never stopped caring...I loved you, baradar koochooloo." Tears drenched Mirdad's face. "Anthony, Anthony. You, you..." he whispered, choking on saliva, "You were such a fool! I hated you. But loved you, loved you so."

Clutching the papers, he spun toward the door and lurched out to his limo, his stomach burning. He would have to forget this, forget everything he'd seen in that office today. He would wipe it all from his mind as if it never happened, the anguish, guilt, sorrow. *The rage.* No matter what that took. No matter what.

LONDON

Crowds flooded into the Heathrow terminal with Customs lines jammed. Kathryn, her nerves tight, and her crew crowded in along with droves of anxious travelers fleeing Iran, some tourists and business people, arriving on this gray day, but none looked as anxious as she. They shuffled through passport control. Kathryn peered out from under Teddy's jewel laden hat and stepped into the centerline behind Buzz, putting on her poker face. *She could do this.*

Harried customs officials, working in pairs, wore frowns.

Others behind her in the lines seemed as tense as she was. *What did they have to hide?* She overheard snippets of conversations in front of her.

"Take it all out, sir, or we'll do it for you." Disgruntled officials dug through an enormous duffle bag in front of them.

She looked away.

"Next."

She looked up. Buzz was gone. It was her turn. Inner panic hit her like there was a rock in her gut.

She stamped down fear, chomped her Dentyne, and moved in front of a heavy-set customs guy and his lanky partner, heads close, whispering. "Have a look at this onslaught of Middle Easterners, mate," Lanky Guy said.

"Pouring in every day, clattering incoherent languages." She heard him groan in complaint.

Customs Guy pointed at her then Teddy and Peter.

"Film persons," Lanky Guy muttered. "Yanks."

"They're no better. Degenerates, the lot."

"They're not gettin' their hashish and cocaine by me." Customs Guy guffawed and hiked his stomach over his belt. He glared at Kathryn.

She moved her things along the counter, hiding behind her sunglasses as if glasses could disguise the jewels.

"Anything to declare?" he asked.

This was it.

She forced a smile, chewed her gum, and handed him her declaration form.

He took it and stared at her until she removed her glasses, then he scanned her appearance. From Teddy's ratty felt hat over teased hair adorned with a tribal scarf and glittering brooch, to her kohl rimmed eyes, her over-extended bright pink lipstick, her jaw clacking. Teddy's filthy denim jacket had seen better days. It hung open showing a flagrant amount of bosom.

Customs Guy stared at the dusted yellow stones around her neck, amber beads piled on top and a crumpled scarf over that. He muttered something that sounded like,"Trashy."

"Nice outfit, dearie." He shook his head, and leaned closer. "Take off your hat, miss."

"What?" she asked.

"What's that up there? You rob some Pasha?"

"Isn't it something? I find great stuff."

"Let me see it," he held out his hand.

Carefully she removed the hat, handing it over without shaking.

He examined it. "You wanna tell me where you filched this lot?"

"Hollywood Boulevard," she said. "Looks real, doesn't it? Like maybe Marlene Dietrich would wear it, don't you think?"

He scrutinized the jewel-adorned hat and her. "Yeah, 'bout as real as the rest of the stuff you have on. Bet it cost all your inheritance, huh, princess?"

"Almost." Her poker face held.

"Marlene Dietrich," he mumbled, shoving the hat to her. "Take it. Now open your bags. All of them." Arms folded across his chest, he watched.

She steadied herself and opened bag after bag. He searched through cosmetics, hair products. He dug his fingers deep into her bath powder, smelled his fingers and grimaced. He proceeded to open every small container, including her toothpaste.

"Okay, love, put it all back." He wiped his fingers on a paper towel, chuckling, as if he was a nice guy. "Unzip the big one there."

Kathryn struggled with the oversized case. *Stay cool. These guys were probably all on double shifts, cranky as hell.*

He flipped back the suitcase top, pulling things out from all sides, seeming to enjoy his work. He grabbed two evening dresses that had been previously rolled on top and shook them out.

"What have we here?" He scanned the labels in mock surprise, looking she guessed, for tags. "Valentino? Christian Dior?" He looked her up and down. "Really?"

"Beverly Hills Thrift Shop," she said.

"Figures," he smirked. "Okay, close it up."

She was still struggling with her mangled make-up case when Peter came forward.

"Step back." Lanky Guy frowned at Peter with his long hair and sparse Manchu mustache. "The lady can manage on her own."

"If I help it'll speed things up for you, sir."

"You in a rush?" Customs Guy took over.

"Our people from Samuelson's are waiting." Peter smiled. "They're on the clock."

"Really?"

"It's okay, Peter," Kathryn stuffed everything back in her Samsonite. She had to keep her friends away from her until she was away from here. "I can manage. You guys take the car from Samuelsons. I'll get my own cab."

Peter looked her up and down. "Get it together, Kat."

But the customs official wasn't through yet. He picked up her canvas camera case and dumped the contents on the counter. Film, lenses, and her Nikon toppled out. As well as a twelve-by-twelve inch gem-studded box entrusted to her tender care, tumbled from her battered camera bag onto the metal counter.

Her breath caught. She thought she might faint. Give her a mission under gunfire any day.

"I suppose you have papers for this camera?"

"Right here." Peter handed them over.

The official examined every item of film and equipment and picked up the gold box and shook it.

Kathryn bowed her head. *Oh God, this was it. We're finished.*

"Open it."

Kathryn felt helpless. Her anxiety rose a notch.

"Open it," Customs Guy demanded.

Cringing, with shaking hands she lifted the lid of the box, revealing a jumble of silver souk jewelry. "It's all on the list." The ring to the Persian Glories she stuffed in with the junk jewelry. She held her breath.

"Seven rials, twenty rials, five rials. Big spender." He dropped the box. "Next!"

She flinched, wondering if he'd broken the latch.

The customs official caught her pause.

"You want this thing?" They both reached for the box, grabbing on. Her pulse surged.

They eyed each other, both gripping hard. She could yank it away and run like hell. "Thank you, sir," she said instead.

His eyes narrowed, grip tightening.

People behind Kathryn called out. "Come on!"

"Let's move it."

"Hurry up!"

He raised an eyebrow at the riled up passengers but eased off. "Go on, you're done."

Peter shoved a metal cart up to her.

Kathryn loaded her heavy bag and the rest onto the cart. The gold box she clutched under her arm like a football. The room's clamor crowded in on her. The cavernous area felt cold. Her body was stiff with fear, alternating chills then hot flushes. She exited Customs, the heavy double doors sliding shut behind her. Relief nearly felled her. She fought the need to look back for Peter and Buzz, afraid to attract attention. Who was she kidding? Dressed like a tasteless tart, she caught the tight-lipped glimpses sent her way and plunged into the flow toward the fluorescent terminal exit sign, a taxi symbol underneath.

She wouldn't feel safe until her butt was in the cab pulling away from Heathrow.

A river of travelers gushed in opposing currents through Heathrow. Noise blared from a P.A. system, arrivals, departures and messages for passengers—all a cacophony against her pounding temples and frayed nerves.

There were no smells of Shiraz; coriander and jasmine, just damp wool and tired bodies. But her mind, caught in jetlag, held visions of Iran, where a piece of her heart dwelled. The contrast from Heathrow to Teheran's air terminal shimmied into her mind, her memories of Shiraz bursting with exotic sounds, the blazing heat, Farsi and Arabic tumbling through outdoor markets, stalls draped in magenta, turquoise, ochre, and above all that, her love for Anthony. God, she missed him. *Two weeks.*

Heathrow's high-ceilinged glass and metal structure shifted back into focus. Travelers wore crisp, conservative, dark or neutral outerwear; hats, scarves, gloves worn against the cold.

Kathryn's relief melted and fear from carrying the Persian Glories without provenance surfaced along with fear for Anthony's safety, the people she had helped and those left behind. And looming ahead stood her towering fear of career failure. She shoved it down. She would get the jewels to Anthony's grandfather and focus on salvaging her shoot.

She trudged forward; gaze downward, picturing a steamy shower and warm bed.

Dark wing-tipped shoes entered her peripheral vision.

"Hold it right there, miss."

Sweating she stopped and looked up.

Men with badges and dark expressions surrounded her. "You'll come with us. Now," a square-jawed man in a black suit said.

Panic surged. "Who're you?"

"MI-6."

"What do you want with me, I finished with customs? I'm leaving." Kathryn shoved ahead of him.

"Sorry." The black suit moved in her way. "You're not leaving yet," he said.

"I protest! What's going on here? Let me see those badges. I'm a U.S. citizen. I have rights."

He nodded, showing her his badge, but explained nothing. An officer seized her luggage cart and headed away from the exit sign, down a dark corridor, the creaking wheels echoing. "You can make this easy or hard, miss," he said, taking back his badge. "I don't much care which."

Out maneuvered, she reluctantly followed.

"This woman is not involved here," she heard from across the hall. She swiveled toward the deep, cultured and familiar voice.

Philippe Kahlil, Anthony's best friend, strained against the grip of two policemen, his look pleading. "Kathryn," he mouthed. Then a silent, "Anthony."

Had Anthony called Philippe to meet her?

But why had he brought police? *Involved in what?*

An officer shoved Philippe back, down the dark aisle, shoes scuffling across speckled linoleum.

"No, No stop!" Philippe shouted. "You've got this wrong!"

A prickly sense of déja-vu engulfed Kathryn: another hallway, dark and foreign, flooded her consciousness, danger, threats in Farsi. With the memory, anxiety heightened. Airports were clearly not her lucky charm.

She was ushered to the end of the hall.

A mahogany paneled door flew open. Harsh light splashed her face. Kathryn squinted and was pushed into an office, Philippe behind her.

Before her stood a tall distinguished elderly gentleman dressed in a Vicuna coat, a dark suit underneath. The knot of his silk tie rested against his shirt collar. Silver hair and pinched eyebrows set off his obdurate glare. Behind him a row of radiators hissed steam, fogging the windows above them. Yellowing shades bumped against the sills in uneven rhythm.

Philippe shoved himself forward. "Charles," he said, "leave her out of this."

Philippe knew this man. How?

The gentleman grunted. "As if I would listen to you."

"It's not what you think, sir," Philippe said.

"What I think is you're a disgrace, Philippe! Enormous gambling debts to the worst people in London." The gentleman shook his head. "You should've come to me!"

"Sir…"

"My own godson. Take him away!" The gentleman waved him off.

Philippe struggled, dragged away, shouting, "She's in danger."

Kathryn sucked in a deep breath. *What danger? The Glories?*

The elegant silver-haired man stood before her, an aging aristocrat, she guessed. He looked her up and down. She straightened.

"So," he said, snatching Teddy's felt hat adorned with diamonds from her head, his jaw set like hardened steel. He unfastened the dazzling brooch, collected the necklace, wiped the dusty surfaces, slid them into his coat-pocket, tossing the hat into a wastebasket.

She gasped appalled at her lack of autonomy and horrified she would let Anthony down. "Sir, Anthony entrusted those to me."

"Just how are you acquainted with Anthony Evans? I'd like to know."

"Just who wants to know, and why?" Kathryn said. Her hair, teased and sprayed, fell forward. She shoved it back off her forehead, holding on to her bravado. Oily make-up smeared over her skin: mascara and kohl stung her eyes. She swiped at it; smudges of black came off on her fingers. Any credibility she might have called on had melted with her make-up.

She looked down at Peter's jean jacket gaping, tawdry, exposing her cleavage. Embarrassment shook her. She took a deep breath, summoning courage to deal with her new disaster. "I'm in the dark, sir. Please tell me what's going on here."

"Answer my question."

Anthony. Here goes. "Anthony Evans photographed the Boeing commercial I directed in Iran. We...fell in love." She held out her left hand and swiveled around the fifteen-carat diamond ring on her finger. "We're engaged."

"My God, woman! Have you no shame?"

"It's true," she muttered. "Call him."

"Anthony's gone missing. His home in Shiraz burnt to cinders, servants dead, his studio in Teheran ransacked."

Chills coiled around her heart. Anthony. The staff he loved, Tali and those wonderful girls, his home. He'd warned her of the danger. But this couldn't be. "It can't be true."

"You're wearing a fortune in jewels belonging to him." He took a steadying breath. "You had better tell me what you know."

"I was with him last night, at his studio," she said. "He was fine then, and you need to acknowledge Anthony is fine now. Tell me you made this up to scare me." Her insides clutched, she felt dizzy but too hurt and angry to back down.

The gentleman no longer looked at her. He'd noticed the gold box gripped beneath her arm. He seized the glimmering object, examining the edges, his gaze intense. "Clever," he said, fumbling then pressing an oval cabochon stone on the side. A tray popped out from the jeweled box, then another, revealing the most enormous stones Kathryn had ever seen.

"What on earth?" she choked out.

"The Dari-a-Noor. The second largest diamond in the world, also in your possession." His fingers skimmed cherry-red stones. "The priceless Maharani Rubies, and," he held up another stone, examining it, "an emerald the size of a Reed avocado." He glared. "You have a lot to answer for, having crown jewels of Iran in your possession."

Kathryn shook, her emotions imploding. "Where is Anthony? He'll explain everything."

"Book her."

"No! I need to call my producer, Buzz Anderson, at the Savoy. "

The gentleman stormed away.

"Somebody, please listen to me!" she cried.

CHAPTER FOUR

SHIRAZ

Through a hash and alcoholic haze, Mirdad grew melancholy. His hand shaky, he dribbled champagne over blond Siri's lovely breasts, hearing her squeal, watching her nipples grow taut, and holding his traitorous thoughts of regret over Anthony's death and his mother's infinite lies at bay. He had to bury this hideous pain before it took him down. Sweat soaked his back.

A naked brunette perched on his other knee lunged. Her lips parted to taste the cool wine from Siri's fair nipple, the spot she'd been gazing at hungrily. Amusement colored Mirdad's mind and arousal tightened his loins. Suddenly he grabbed a handful of dark curls, yanking the brunette's head back from the pink jiggling breast.

His mouth opened, ready to order her to bed, when he stopped, his own eyes widening. There was something about her. She reminded him of...of...?

He jumped up, spilling Siri from his knee, toppling the brunette, her face a younger version of his mother's face.

An uncontrollable need to punish her seized him. Yowling, he swung at her. The girl recoiled, missing the full impact. She fell backward, his fist grazing her cheek. With one hand he reached down and threw her across the room, and he seized Siri with the other. His breathing heavy, he turned Siri's pretty, pale-eyed face, blinking in terror, to his.

"Did I startle you, little blond princess?"

Siri trembled.

"Don't be afraid, I'll make you so happy now."

He had her sprawled before him on the dark satin bedcover, her limbs writhing. He stared at her creamy flesh and leaned back on his heels unsteadily, squinting, his heart racing. In his mind, she was Kathryn, at last where he wanted her, on her back with her legs apart.

The brunette crawled back to him, unafraid, and wound herself around his ankles, whimpering, easing her way up to his hard cock, her tongue slithering like a wet snake over his balls.

He closed his eyes for a moment, smiling, moving to his own rhythm, then pulled the brunette off him, turning her on her hands and knees toward the waiting blond, who, at his command, spread herself with her fingers. The brunette came closer and licked Siri's fair pussy.

Mirdad crouched behind the darker girl, stroking her round firm ass, marveling at her slim waist.

"Such a lovely derrière," he whispered, plunging himself inside, groaning.

Images of Kathryn's face and mouth, the curve of her full breasts sprang before his eyes. He'd longed to strip her naked and fuck every inch of her. He pumped himself deeper, deeper into the girl.

An explosive orgasm crested and his head flew back in a howl. An image of Kathryn in a gold lamé gown swam before him: she smiled at him, pushing her breasts together, taunting him, so beautiful. But another face crowded into view. It was Anthony, stripping off her clothes.

"No-o-o-o!" he cried.

Kathryn shivered against a cold draft locked in a six by nine Heathrow holding cell and her own dank prison of disbelief. She had to find out about Anthony. Why wouldn't they tell her where he was? Why didn't anybody try to reach him?

She sat on the metal jail cot, wrinkled shirttails of her re-buttoned blouse bunched around her hips. She might have been delivered from the Iranian revolution, but she'd landed in hell—as a jewel smuggler. Her matted hair hung about her shoulders like the childhood doll she had tucked next to her at night when her father had been in the Middle East. The men she'd loved were gone. Fists clenched at her sides and hyperventilating, she held back sobs, because if she let go she might never stop. She needed to move, to run, and mostly to get out of this stinking nightmare or be swept away on river of misery.

Where was Buzz? He should've been here by now.

Scared, all she could do was wait and think of those frightened families in Iran. She knew she just couldn't give up. Night after night those people had huddled in freezing sheds, fearing execution, clinging to a thread of hope to reach safety with nothing but dirty clothes to start new lives. Adversity could push you under or it could give you a shove forward.

She had to figure this out. What else had Anthony told her about the jewels? What had she missed?

"I won't be in touch for a few days,..." He must be on a mission...or with Tabriz and the horsemen.

He'd said, *"I'll arrange everything tomorrow."* What had kept him from the arrangements? Surely he was okay.

He'd said, *"You can rely on Philippe."*

Not really. Philippe wasn't the reliable gent she'd thought in Iran, but a gambling reprobate in cahoots with a jewel thief. Anthony was not a jewel thief, so who was in cahoots with Philippe? Why were those enormous stones in her case? What were her options to get out of here? Buzz was out. She'd have to call her mother.

Lord, help her because somehow these MI-6 guys had all missed the truth.

Nothing made sense.

Her head bowed, Kathryn massaged her temples, remembering. Just days ago Raymond was proud, hearing her praise his son, Ali. Tali had prepared a feast with her teenage daughters peeking around the door, giggling and watching Anthony serve each course. Sneakers, memories of sneakers loaned to her from Tali's younger daughter with big feet like hers, the smile of pride for the loan. Kathryn had left her red stilettos—a trade. It had all felt so solid, so real.

The fond recollection faded through iron bars in front of her as footsteps from down the hall came closer, voices arguing grew louder.

Kathryn leapt up, over to the bars, straining. *Let it be Buzz.*

But it was the older autocrat, with two beautiful well-dressed women. Philippe followed, with Buzz. Her heart sang music of hope. The younger of the two women, a lovely young redhead, rushed forward, holding a camel hair car coat over one arm.

"Hullo, I'm Emmaline, Anthony's friend and neighbor in Buckinghamshire and this is my mother, Samantha."

"What a terrible mix-up," said Samantha, a beautifully coiffed blond, "and a rotten welcome. Sorry."

Emmaline turned to a uniformed official. "Sir, can you please hurry?"

The grumbling official unlocked the cell door and swung it open. Kathryn stepped out.

Emmaline, stepped up first and thrust the car coat at Kathryn. "It's all I had with me, but it's warm."

Kathryn slid into the coat, and Emmaline's mother stepped forward, unwrapping a cashmere Burberry scarf from her own neck and placing it around Kathryn's. "This should help against the cold outside."

Buzz pulled Kathryn away from the cell, hugging her. "Another fine mess, huh?" he said.

"Oh, Buzz..."

"Well, you missed Lord Samuelson's party."

Emmaline gestured. "Oh, my parents give tons of parties. You'll come to the next one."

Emmaline's smile warmed her.

The older autocrat took over. "Harrumph. We haven't been properly introduced. I'm Lord Charles Evans, Anthony's grandfather."

Stunned at this disclosure, "Hello," was all she could squeeze out.

"Come, my dear, let's get you out of here where I can apologize profusely."

"As long as I'm away from here, you can try," Kathryn said.

It was almost midnight when Lord Charles' Silver Cloud Rolls Royce drew up in front of London's Hotel Savoy, and Kathryn stepped out into the cold night. It was late, she was anguished, exhausted. She needed sleep and was too angry to let him keep the jewels. She huddled deeper into Emmaline's coat, her canvas camera case with the returned Persian Glories inside. The distinguished gentleman who'd had her thrown in jail, Lord Charles Evans, 11th Earl of Edyton and tyrant, was also Anthony's grandfather. He stepped out beside her. "Again, my dear, I apologize for my mistake, believing you to be a gold-digging jewel thief...and jezebel."

"I hope we're past all that, Lord Charles."

"Just, Charles, please," he said.

"Okay." She was too tired to care and too relieved to be gone from the grimy cell. She wanted to get to her room, get cleaned up, and get in touch with Anthony, but how? Arms crossed over her chest, she moved toward the hotel entrance.

"Kathryn, wait." Lord Charles cleared his throat. "Please, let me escort you inside."

She looked up at his pleading expression, which must have cost his pride for the offer and just couldn't refuse his olive branch. "Thank you." She took his arm.

They passed through the etched glass door held open by a Savoy doorman and entered into pandemonium.

Detectives, police officers, and hotel patrons swarmed near the front desk. In the elegant lobby, chandeliers sparkled overhead, shimmering cocktail candles adorned round marble tables. Jittery and unhappy looking clients occupied the surrounding chairs.

"Oh, dear," said Lord Charles. "What now?" He moved to the desk. "Wait here, my dear."

Kathryn barely registered the chaos. Then she felt her elbows nudged.

House detectives edged her to a marble pillar by a wrought iron railing overlooking the famous Savoy Lounge. In her getup, they must think her a trollop.

"Stop that," she said, pulling away, tired of being corralled by cops. "What do you want?"

Lord Charles appeared next to her. "I'm afraid, Kathryn, there's been a robbery. The hotel safe. And several suites, including one you're booked into."

"My luggage?"

"Gone. I'll have things sent round for you tomorrow. Can you manage till then?"

"I guess I'll have to." *What was one more speed bump?* She shifted in her grimy clothes. Whatever was in her carry-on would do. "Am I in danger?"

"I'll make certain you'll be in a suite on a locked floor," Charles said.

While he spoke to the detectives, Kathryn scanned the lobby and caught the eye of a hall porter.

"The ladies?" she asked, unwilling to have more questions thrown at her while dressed like a tart.

His posture erect, in the deep red uniform, hands behind his back, cap square over tight brown curls, he said, "Just over there, miss," and nodded to his right.

"Do you, by any chance have a rubber band?" She noticed his nameplate. "Robert?"

"Rubber band, you say?" He hunted in his right hand pocket. "Thin or wide, miss?" He held out two.

"The wide, please." She took it with reverence as if he'd handed her a diamond. She was over diamonds. "Thank you so much."

"Think nothing of it, miss."

"Kathryn," she said.

"Miss Kathryn." He staunched a smile over crooked front teeth, but his brown eyes sparkled.

Kathryn excused herself and rushed into the marble and glass ladies room hoping to make herself look less tawdry. She finger-combed her hair and scrunched the mess back into a ponytail with Robert's rubber band.

She used hand soap on her face, neck and wrists, scrubbing and rinsing again and again, drying with rough paper towels. Then she noticed the monogrammed linen hand towel on a carved mahogany chest and used that, too. She still had owl eyes from smudged mascara and eyeliner above chaffed cheeks, but she felt better. Unraveling the tribal scarf from around her hips, she retied it around her neck as if it were from Hermes.

With this hotel robbery she was bound to face more questions with no answers. She had to be finished with all this before 5:00 a.m. the next morning. Just a few hours in the British Museum was all she needed to complete her shoot, her goal. Her career would rise from ashes.

Footsteps alerted Kathryn, and a woman in a business suit, smelling of Tweed cologne, rushed toward her. "Miss Whitney, I'm sorry but they're waiting for you. You must come now."

"They?" Kathryn asked.

She followed the woman into a small foyer and faced several fierce looking men in black suits, including the Iranian counsel, and the general Kathryn had met at the palace ball, General Omar Houdin, waiting for her, eyeing her with a penetrating Omar Sharif expression. Wasn't the general married to Mirdad's mother?

Lord Charles stepped forward; his stern look softened when he looked her over. He must have noted her more reputable appearance.

His gaze met hers briefly. A gentler emotion flashed in those eyes before his tyrant persona took over.

"Miss Whitney has been through British customs, sir, and had nothing to declare," Lord Charles said.

The general smiled, but his eyes were deep pools of venom. "Perhaps we can see the customs list of her items, if you would be so kind?"

"So sorry, gentlemen," said Lord Charles, now her ally. "Miss Whitney is exhausted from her trip and cannot possibly speak to you at this late hour." He supplied them with customs documents of her six-hundred-dollar entry, no mention of the MI-6 event.

"We will return tomorrow," said General Houdin, his smile brittle.

"Sorry, I'll be working tomorrow. Goodnight," Kathryn said. She took Charles' arm and walked away.

Twenty minutes later, Kathryn entered her upgraded hotel suite, courtesy of Lord Charles. She fumbled tipping the bellboy and clutched her camera case to her chest, waiting for him to set down her lonely Louis Vuitton carry-on and leave.

She closed the door and turned the extra bolt, sinking back against the door, her nerves raw and her heart heavy. She shoved away revulsion of the last several hours and the extraordinary discovery; the angry aristocrat was Anthony's beloved grandfather. She would explode without a moment to sort out her predicament before trying to sleep. She had a 4:00 a.m. wake-up call.

She savored the privacy, as if decades had passed since

she had any. She made sure her suite's doors and windows were locked securely and drifted through her soft sea green sitting room, into the ivory and green bedroom, and flipped on the radio from which gratefully she heard soothing music and her shoulders relaxed.

The bed beckoned, a vision of plump pillows and billowing down comforter clothed in a soft jade Patesi duvet cover. She longed to crawl in and drift away for just a wink of time from a world grown frighteningly confusing and exhausting. Fleeting images teased her mind, her last magical night at the Palace Ball, Anthony's lovemaking, and his proposal. All now seemed a deflated fantasy. She would find a way to reach him. He must be crazed with grief. She knew he wouldn't stop until Raymond and Tali's killers were captured. Before succumbing to fatigue, she coerced herself away and in that moment Kathryn spotted the flowers.

An exquisite Steuben bowl, placed on a table near the window, overflowed with creamy gardenias. The aroma filled the room with memories. She jumped for the card, hands trembling.

Until we're together in another garden, my heart has wings to find you, my love, my future.

Till then, as always, Anthony.

P.S. Forgive the unthinkable situation I placed you in, but darling, you're to blame. I've become a besotted idiot.

As her gaze lingered on the fragrant blooms, her lethargy lifted. Dear God, he was okay!

"Get moving." She ordered. "Undress, take a shower."

With monumental effort, she continued into a sizeable bath and dressing room of wall-to-wall mirrors and stopped, almost slipping on smooth marble floors. She was struck from all sides with images of an owl-eyed stranger. For the first time since leaving Iran she saw her head-to-toe reflection and laughed.

What an entrance I must have made! Even British stoicism must have been taxed.

Poor Lord Charles. He had escorted her through the Savoy lobby without a flicker of embarrassment. She almost gagged at the thought while carefully removing the Persian Glories from her camera case, returned to her, for now, from Anthony's grandfather. She set the jewels on the marble counter, rinsed off the powder, dried them and unfastened the remarkable brooch, which caught a million points of refracted light, glinting back at her. She set it gently on the counter and undressed, carefully hanging up the same clothes she'd have to wear tomorrow with her luggage stolen, everything except the Persian Glories.

Whisking her hair up in a tight regency coil, she fastened the brooch in front of it and crossed her arms over her bare breasts, standing tall, showing off the necklace, bracelet, ring, and earrings, never taking her eyes off her image in the mirrors.

Golden light splashed over her and she murmured, "There you are, Kathryn, just as you were last night when

Anthony photographed you, when he stole your heart so completely."

Kathryn moved across the room remembering and watching herself, as Anthony had just last night....

"I am going to photograph you like this. Foolish to miss an intoxicating opportunity."

When he picked up his camera, he was transformed into something she'd as yet never seen. Wild music had filled the room from his stereo. Anthony's voice was deep and commanding, his body had vibrated control, his energy savage.

In his black silk robe, he stalked her, crouching, moving around, ordering her to move with his commands. His eyes, like green steel, his mouth, a sly half grin, he laughed deep in his throat and pressed the shutter button. He changed positions, his directions changed with his desires, firm and cold, exuding something infinitely dangerous. In a flash, he became coaxing and caressing, like a coat of silk charmeuse. At first, she was startled and confused, but quickly shifted her mode, reacting to her director.

"You're a queen, Kathryn, a goddess. Move like one," he commanded, "and don't stop until I ask you to. Move for me."

She moved, as he demanded, into the role.

"Nice, very nice."

She barely breathed as he kept shooting her. It was like a dance, consuming them.

She reached up and unpinned her hair shaking it out.

"Stand with your back to me, baby, feet wide. Good. Now when I tell you, turn your upper body and look at me, hard. NOW. See me! How I want you? Oh yes, you do." He stopped

shooting for a moment. "You don't know if you want to run away or come to me, do you?"

Her lips tilted up. She stalked him, gliding in cat-like stealth.

With a most dangerous look about him, he grabbed her and put his camera down. "You got too close," he said.

His hot mouth covered hers.

CHAPTER FIVE

LONDON

B arely visible, the enormous carved frieze over the British Museum's Great Russell Street entrance was steeped in dense morning fog that wound through the museum's towering ionic columns. It wasn't yet 5:00 A.M.

A familiar twinge of pre-shoot excitement stirred Kathryn—excitement and vigilance. From behind a column, she stared at the maze of trucks, scaffolding, lights, cranes and baffles, parked in the museum courtyard.

Hands crammed into Emmaline's coat's deep pockets, she exhaled into the mist, showed her I.D. to a guard with a clipboard, and entered to an astonishing sight.

Unbelievable. Her crew, cameras, lights—everything was already set up. The call wasn't until 5:00 a.m. They must have been there for an hour at least. Camera assistants loaded film, sorted lenses, and Teddy Wright, perched atop a forty-foot camera crane, directed the lighting crew over an enormous, stone statue of a half-bearded man, half winged beast, the same artifact depicted on SAVAK emblems.

Peter, off to the side, was engrossed in a conversation with the British crew and Brett. *They're working with Brett.* She fingered Teddy's sacred hat retrieved from the waste-bin at the jail.

Buzz walked up to her.

"The crew call was for five," she said. "My call."

"I warned you." Buzz looked at his topsiders. "That's not all, Kat. Prepare yourself."

"What?" She turned, hearing rubber-soled Italian boots squeak against the cold floor.

"You dare show yourself on this set, Kathryn? Are you nuts?" Brett pushed up in her face.

A crew of thirty stopped setting up, grips, sound, camera crew, everyone. Some looked away, others gaped at her.

"Why wouldn't I be here? It's my shoot, Brett."

"So she's here." Boeing's Wally Brandt sauntered up next to her. "Got your wings clipped, missy." He crossed his arms over a plaid flannel shirtfront, his gaze harsh.

"Nice to see you too, Wally." She had almost smiled seeing Wally. She liked him.

"Well, it's lousy seeing you!" Wally said. "Screwed up the works."

"Excuse me?"

"Cut the crap, Kathryn," Brett chimed in. "You're two-hundred-and-fifty-grand over budget, late and—"

"One day, which I'll finish here."

"You'll finish nothing!" Brett growled. "You're history. You crashed a fucking Jet Ranger, for God's sake. The pilot was injured. Men were killed."

"Rebel militia fired on us," she said.

"Right. You should've gotten the hell outta Iran after two days. It was enough!"

Wally stepped in close, his expression neutral. "Spectacular footage from the first few days, Kathryn." His expression hardened. "But you took chances with peoples' lives. Inexcusable."

"How could you get it so wrong?" Brett said. "You were in charge." His eyes sizzled rage.

Kathryn's body vibrated fury, fury at Brett, who she knew only too well.

A standoff.

She couldn't tell them what really happened. That she had flown secret missions getting families out of Iran before they were murdered, that the soldiers who'd died chasing her over the pass were scum-sucking lowlifes. Not until she knew Anthony was no longer at risk. She took a deeper look at Brett and saw through him.

He didn't care about the Jet Ranger, the pilot, or the soldiers.

He had won.

Winning was all he had ever cared about. She could blame her own stupidity for letting her guard down in Iran. She had asked herself so many times, "What does he still want from me?" *To win, dummy—win it all.*

"You're a conniving bastard, Brett Whitney."

"Get off my set. Now!" he snarled.

Wally's hard stare fixed on her. "I took a chance on you, girl. Damn." He walked away, shaking his head.

Hefty guards marched up and took hold of her elbows. "You have to leave, madam."

She sucked in her rage, cold, hurt, humiliated.

"Kathryn!" Over her shoulder she saw Emmaline Samuelson, her new production assistant, charging after her. Brett shook his head, a warning at Emmaline. She stopped.

The guards hauled Kathryn to the exit, opened the door, and nudged her out onto the wide front steps. The heavy door clanged shut, and wind whipped her chafed cheeks.

She spun around, her palms pressed on cold glass. She peered in, the light so dim she could barely make out shapes. No words had been spoken to her crew, no goodbyes or...anything.

It didn't matter. *She'd screwed up. Failed.* As if she'd never been the director or even part of the production. As if she'd never counted.

Raindrops slid from her forehead to her nose.

She flipped up the hood on Emmaline's car coat, wiped her face on her sleeve, and turned toward the street.

A black chauffeur-driven Daimler idled at the curb. A tall figure stood next to it.

If only it were Anthony. She longed for him.

Philippe nodded, gloved hands clasped in front of him, watching her. Rain-flattened hair dripped over his forehead.

Was she supposed to trust him? Anthony's "best friend" who was mired in gaming debts and London mobsters?

His sad eyes beckoned.

She stepped to the curb. He looked like hell, dark circles under his eyes, disheveled attire, like he'd dressed in the dark. *He can hardly look at me*. She didn't mind. Her mood was dark with failure and resentment.

"Please," he said, opening the rear door.

She climbed in the back without a word, Philippe edged in next to her, and the driver drove the quiet car away from her career, the last she'd see of it.

"I didn't have a chance to tell you at the airport with our mutual arrests." Philippe smiled wanly. "You're a clever woman." He studied her. A glint of amusement lit his azure eyes. "Such an unusual display of priceless jewels. I've never seen the like." He shook his head as if dispelling the whole episode. "What you did was brave. Ingenious, really."

"I felt like a thief." She scanned his face, wanting answers. He took out his handkerchief, handing it to her. She dabbed at her cheeks and handed it back.

Philippe blotted his own, exhaling a ragged breath.

Why was he here? "It's a little early for a museum visit, Philippe. Did you know I would have trouble this morning, too?"

"There are many things you don't know...things I'm loathe to tell you."

"You've heard from Anthony. For God's sake, Philippe, tell me!"

Philippe sunk low in his seat, quiet.

Kathryn leaned back and looked out the window, waiting for him to speak, scenery passing in a blur. It had stopped raining.

The driver pulled up next to Hyde Park, glistening in half-sun, rain clouds still threatening. Philippe asked him to wait. "Let's step outside."

It was barely 6:00 a.m. and chilly. *Oh, what the hell.* She got out. They walked side by side on the grass, avoiding the muddy path. Well into the park, Philippe stopped, breathed deeply and said, "The Black Glove has made good on their threat."

Wind blasted against her, a new storm brewing, she thought, avoiding her fear of what Philippe would say next.

"It's about Anthony."

Her muscles clenched.

Philippe cleared his throat, and Kathryn noticed red-rimmed eyes behind his glasses.

"There's been an accident in Shiraz. Anthony's house was burnt to the ground. Many were killed. Tali, Raymond, and other staff members were shot."

"It's true then," she mumbled, clenching back tears.

"Anthony escaped the house, carrying Raymond's body to the Range Rover. Black Glove militia chased him." Philippe shook his head. "His car went off the road."

Her mouth opened partly, but terror halted her words. Her eyes searched his.

"It's worse, much worse. Anthony was killed."

"No. No, you're wrong. Anthony's not dead." Kathryn felt herself breaking apart. She stepped back, away from the nightmare.

"I'd give anything, anything for it not to be true," he said. "Kathryn, I am so, so sorry." Philippe reached for her.

She snapped away, suffocating. "I don't believe you." She sucked in a breath.

"Kathryn..."

Why was he doing this to her? She had to get away. Backing up, she whirled around, her head spinning with disbelief, and took off running across Hyde Park, running against the wind, against his words.

No. He didn't die. He couldn't die. Her legs pumped, gaining speed, across the soaked green.

"I'll never leave you," he'd told her.

In a whirlwind, her mind chanted, *It's not true, you didn't die.* She ran, finding her rhythm. *You're not dead. You're not!*

At a steady gait she moved toward something, something that had to be out there, proof that he lived. Her feet barely skimmed wet ground. *Oh God. You can't be gone. You wouldn't, I know you wouldn't leave me.*

Lightning splintered the sky.

Panting and sobbing Kathryn passed a herd of horses being led to stable. Images popped into her head of Tabriz and his horsemen thundering across the plains, Tabriz at the head with Anthony....

Don't go, Anthony! Her mind screamed and she dashed among a stand of rain-soaked trees. *I'll find you.*

Her feet flew across sodden lawn, over a bridge, past a splattering pond, heading for the stables. *You promised we'd be together. Oh God, where are you?*

Thunder cracked through the clouds. The sky darkened, releasing a torrent of rain.

Blinded by tears and pain, she yelled, "I won't let you go!" and picked up speed, sprinting. Another bolt flashed, the terrain lit up, illuminating an oak tree directly in her path. She couldn't stop. Angry thunder resounded in the dark, and she crashed into the hulking tree trunk.

Kathryn crumpled to the ground.

Dazed but conscious, the wind knocked out of her, she reached toward the sharp pain in her head. Her forehead was sticky. Blood. She tried to stand, clawing her way up the bark, wet and whimpering. "Take me with you, Anthony....I don't want to stay without you. Please!"

Then everything went dark.

CHAPTER SIX

SHIRAZ, IRAN

The sun still blazed in the Persian sky when a furious Rena Ajani, Mirdad's mother, accompanied by Black Glove Colonel, Dimitrius Nassiri, and four other uniformed SAVAK officers burst into Mirdad's private Paradise Club lair.

"Seize them!" she yelled, pointing to three naked women draped over her son's like-wise naked body. She was repelled.

"Yes, at once, Madame Houdin," said Nassiri.

Mirdad grabbed a black satin sheet and bolted up, wrapping the stained fabric around his body. "What is the meaning of this, madame? My private quarters, really?"

She waved her hand about. "A brothel, Mirdad? This is our goal for a better life?" She marched over and slapped his face hard. "Get dressed!"

He winced, agitated, rage surfacing and struck his mother back, full on her rose-tinted cheek. CRACK!

"Uhhhh!" She pulled back, sucking in air, her surprise evident.

Mirdad's face contorted in frustrated rage until his expression became stoic. "I've done all that you asked, Mother. The traitors have been dealt with. And all you've done is lie to me."

She touched her face, lightly. "The Glories, Mirdad. Where are my Glories?" *Would he never learn?*

Mirdad straightened up to his full height, his indifferent facade shattered. "Everyone in the Evans' house is dead, Anthony, Raymond." His raspy voice broke. Tears streamed from his bleak eyes.

"And you, Mirdad, are alive." She looked him over. "For now."

"You would threaten me, madame?" Mirdad snarled.

Rena turned to Colonel Nassiri. "Get him out of here. And see that he is never allowed to return. Ever!" She whirled to face the other officers. "And if a word of this incident is breathed, I'll have you all shot."

She stormed from the brothel. Omar would deal with his son.

St George's Hospital

Antiseptic white surrounded Kathryn. She raised an arm, shielding her eyes, a harsh awakening. Clanging metal, medicinal odors, and heavy footsteps clomping down hallways assaulted her senses. *Hospital.* She was in a hospital bed. Her head pounded under a bandage; stitches pulled at her forehead. Disconnected voices in her room and over the P.A. were driving her nuts.

Concussion...Give it a few days...She'll be fine. She didn't recognize the voices but wanted them to go away.

It was day two in the hospital, and she refused medication. The pain distracted her from reality. But on the third day, feeling almost normal, she sat up and drank tepid soup.

Buzz, Philippe, Peter, Teddy, and her new friend Emmaline Samuelson visited, rallying around her with news of an editing bay assigned to her any day at Samuelson's Film Services.

"We can put together *Faces of Iran,*" Peter said. "We have all the film we need."

She had not forgotten their moonlighted documentary.

"With Emmaline's help we've secured the footage in Samuelson's film vault," Buzz said. "It's just waiting for you."

Emmaline took her hand. "I'll act as your P.A. I know this town."

"We can do this. Come on, Kat, give us the go," Peter said.

"Thanks guys, you're great. But I need time." Feeling weak and disoriented, she wasn't up to editing or anything else. And she still rankled over her crew working with Brett. But hey, she was grateful the Boeing commercial was still slated for Super Bowl airtime. And she needed to face reality and get back to work for her own sanity. *But not yet.*

She pulled back the covers. "Where are my clothes?"

"No." Buzz stepped forward. "You've got to rest today. Seven o'clock tomorrow morning, I'll come for you."

Peter swung a duffle bag up on the end of her bed. "Clothes, your project notes, list of setups."

She looked inside the duffle bag and smiled. "My high tops." They all high fived. She watched them file out. Her crew was back, depending on her. She leaned back in the bed, pulling the covers up around her, knowing she couldn't fool herself. She was not someone they should count on. Despair smothered her, worse than the accident, than any of it. She couldn't shake it. People she adored, good people, were raped, killed left to burn. *And, God, Anthony.* How could she ever get over Anthony...? *Never. Never.* She would love him forever.

Lord Charles, Anthony's grandfather, visited that afternoon. He sat on the chair beside her, his head bowed.

Conversation was difficult between them, but when their anguished gazes met, he took her cool hand in his, warm and strong, and it was enough, sharing grief quietly.

They both shed tears and most likely would never speak of it after today. To her it was remarkable how he moved through his day, having lost his only grandson, his heir and last hope for renewed family.

The next morning she left the hospital and walked behind Sloan Street and tried to enjoy the cheery houses off Cadogan Place. She headed for a real estate office to let a London flat. Why not? What was there for her to return to in L.A.? Buzz came with her.

The real-estate agent promised to call when something suitable came up.

Maybe it was time to hook up with her crew and go back to work. *Faces of Iran*, her documentary, had to be edited, a daunting job, but she needed a challenge. From her hotel she called Peter, just the slightest hesitation in her voice. "Let's get to work on *Faces*. You in?"

"Seen enough bridges and suits of armor for a lifetime. Let's do it."

She let out a nervous laugh.

Peter chuckled. "You're back. We'll celebrate tonight, right?"

They both knew there'd be no dinners out once their reel threaded into the Moviola, not until *Faces* was complete.

"San Lorenzo's at seven, an early dinner for us, dude."

"Got it. I'll bring Teddy up to speed."

"Maybe he has a movie to shoot back in the States or some other gig?" She heard Peter laugh.

"Hey, we've both just been waiting on you, Kat."

"Whew! I was worried."

"Teddy and I have a score to settle with those fuckin' Islamic terrorists," Peter said. "And film is our battlefield."

"And with all the footage we shot, *Faces* can be a seriously good film."

He laughed. "Goes without saying. It'll be great. Four months of solid editing."

"Did I mention we can only have the editing bay for six weeks?"

"We have to do a full-length documentary in six weeks?"

"Guess so."

"Is anything ever easy with you, Kathryn?" Exasperation oozed from Peter's tone. "Just keep hot coffee and pizza coming, and we'll get it done."

"Better get used to fish 'n chips and strong tea."

For the next five weeks, Kathryn and Teddy worked in Samuelson's editing room, selecting shots, splicing footage, editing music, sound, and voiceovers until they had a rough hundred-and-twenty-minute documentary cut together. A close-up of Iran as Khomeini's revolution swelled and exploded, dissolving a lavish Persian culture into dust. Teheran, the Paris of the Middle East, sank into anarchy, where lovely women had once dressed in the latest fashions and had strolled busy streets, dining in chic cafés. Shots of the carpet museum, the crowded Paradise Club dance floor, strolling peacocks, children in classrooms, boys and girls playing outside together. A rich Persian theme, dramatic and haunting played over the footage. The dramatic and haunting theme was a gift, composed by their rescued Sitar player.

Overlays of the revolution emerged: shattered faces lost in the struggle, children alone in the streets, soldiers whisking them away. An emergence of a different Iran crowded the screen. Groups of veiled women huddled in rooms, reading condemned western books at their peril. All women now veiled from head to toe in black, scurrying through the streets. Trucks loaded with chanting soldiers, "Kho-mein-I, Kho-mein-I." Militia with assault rifles threatening citizens in their homes, offices, college campuses—everywhere. Burnt out cars and boarded up storefronts announced a brutal cultural throwback to a dark, repressive age.

"Whoa," Peter said. "We're almost there. Few more weeks."

"Make that one," Kathryn said.

"No way," Teddy muttered. "Got our special effects to load in."

Carrying a stack of papers, Emmaline Samuelson rushed in. "Sorry to be the bearer of bad news but..." She handed Peter the papers. "Production bills, music charges as well, and of course invoices for voiceovers—shall I continue?" she asked, her voice shaky, her face pinched with concern.

"Hell, my Amex is maxed out," Teddy said.

"Mastercard, Visa, tapped out," Peter said. "Even held on to Brett's production Amex." His grin was brazen. He shrugged. "We'll face that one later."

"I'm broke, too." Kathryn shrugged, sheepish. "My mom paid the rent, so we have a place to crash."

Teddy grimaced. "I can't face more greasy fish 'n chips. No way." He clutched his stomach.

Emmaline said, "Philippe will cook Beef Wellington tonight. Dinner will be served at nine-thirty sharp, so be there or starve."

Embarrassed, Peter clutched his gurgling stomach. "Guess I'm hungry."

Emmaline handed over a pastry box full of scones. "Something to tide you over."

"Gee, thanks, Emmaline." Teddy dove in, handing one to Peter.

Kathryn absently grabbed a scone, preoccupied with finances. "Somehow we're going to finish. We're almost there. Have to find a way." She glanced around.

"We're all in," her crew of three chimed in.

But how?

A week later Kathryn sat alone in a small Brompton Road bistro on a green vinyl seat, sipping terrible coffee, feeling anonymous in a city far from home. No one bothered her. No one knew that if she moved too fast her heart would crumble.

Her gaze fell to the uneven brown and pink floor tiles. It was the first time she'd gone out by herself since Anthony's death. Convincing Buzz and Peter she'd be all right hadn't been easy.

She had walked through mist, rising and sinking around her, diffusing the day. She wanted to focus on what was next, but images of Brett swam before her, his protruding veins, his booming voice yelling at her, echoing off the cavernous museum's marble hall of antiquities and yanking her off the last day of the Boeing shoot.

A day late and mega-money over budget.

She'd made a half-hearted attempt to make things right. But Wally wouldn't take her calls.

Things would never be right.

Her career mangled, she was *persona non grata*—again.

She needed direction. The pain of missing Anthony cloaked her, squeezing tightly.

Days working on her film passed in a haze of denial, giving way to nights of despair envisioning Anthony's face. She heard the low husky sound of his voice and a flood of memories—vivid, sensual—left her drained, wishing for oblivion.

Around her friends, she allowed only the quiet appearance of grief. But her mind raged, never leaving her alone. A voice inside urged her to let go, to fall into an endless abyss. She pulled her thoughts away from that direction, gazing outside the café window. The incessant fog still draped the neighborhood.

A gum-cracking waitress appeared in a pink uniform, carrying a pot of coffee. Kathryn stared at her empty cup.

"You won't find what you've lost in the bottom of a cup, dearie." The waitress poured more coffee.

Kathryn nodded politely, stirring the refill, absorbed in melancholy and growing increasingly sick of herself, sick of everything around her. She hated London, its gloomy weather, but felt somehow she must stay. She despised the food, the traffic, the homes filled with families. She pictured blazing the tarmac at dusk along San Vicente in her old Porsche, wind whipping through the open car, a drive on Sunset Boulevard to the beach, where sand crunched between her toes as she ran along the shore. Tennis at the Mulholland Club, streaming sweat, the ball popping off the racket. Even lunch... yes, lunch with her mother. Imagine—she even missed her mother.

She took a tasteless bite of a sandwich and forced it down with a gulp of lukewarm coffee. Home. She nudged that thought aside. Home meant where the heart dwelled and her heart futilely craved Anthony. She had no home.

What am I doing here? She clunked the cup down, drawing attention. She blushed, wanting to be invisible. *Get out of here.* She paid the bill, stepped out into the vaporous day, and moved along the Chelsea streets.

She was running on empty, aimless as the fog. If she didn't face herself soon, she'd have real trouble coping with her life. Enough!

I've made mistakes, many mistakes, but had successes, too.

She thought of the trophies she'd won for her AFI film work, the Clios—all cavalierly tossed into boxes and dumped at her mother's house. Could she only accept screw-ups and not all her high moments? Why?

Everyone she loved left her. She wasn't good enough, really.

Her father, constantly leaving home, died in a foreign country. Her mother, who couldn't stand to look at her, had sent her off to boarding school. Brett cheated on her—a humiliating form of abandonment. And Anthony. Anthony loved her, but he had lives to save. She couldn't fault his bravery and concern for others. But she'd never been quite enough to be truly loved. Had never put herself at the head of the pack, had she? Would she ever be enough??

Maybe she just didn't feel good and was letting her failures bury her under.

Well, perhaps not this time. She could do something, for Anthony, for herself, something more than fight for her career. Prove her personal worth. Thinking back on the suffering in Iran, of terrorists like the Black Glove, that odious General Houdin, she knew she could do it. She had to. She walked faster, an idea forming.

Who said *they* got to win?

Twenty minutes later, Kathryn arrived at Philippe's Mayfair gallery, excitement propelling her. Together they would set the stage to catch Anthony's murderers.

Whoever they were. Her hunch was the killers hungered for another opportunity to grab the Persian Glories. With Philippe's help, she would provide their second chance. She stepped inside the gallery and stopped.

Philippe, red faced, glared at a man across his desk holding a sheaf of papers. Kathryn stayed back at the entrance.

"Sir," the man said to Philippe, "you are mistaken. That inventory was destined for Morocco and was off-loaded in Casablanca port."

"Impossible," Philippe said. "You've made a mistake! The shipment was bound for England! Can't you read?"

"There's no need to shout. I have shipping papers for all the art in front of me now. They're clearly marked Casablanca, Morocco, not England."

Philippe shook with rage.

Kathryn stood against the door, not wanting to interrupt.

Philippe jabbed his pen at the man and said, "Somebody has to straighten out this colossal mistake! Unless..." Philippe sank into his chair. "The shipment meant for Iranian families has been stolen." He looked away. "Oh, Anthony...Mirdad."

What did he mean, Mirdad? Kathryn had to get to the bottom of this. Lord Charles. He would help her. In her pocket she dug for a business card. J. E. HARTMANN, MI-6. Quietly she left Philippe's gallery, her plan revised.

At Riverhouse, MI-6 headquarters in London, Kathryn met with Lord Charles and the agent who'd detained her at Heathrow, Jess Hartmann. He had apologized then and handed her his card, hoping for more information on the terrorists butchering Khomeini opposition in Iran. Therefore Mr. Hartmann listened to her plan to lure the killers out of hiding just as Lord Charles entered his office.

"Jess," Lord Charles said.

They shook hands.

Charles leaned in and gave her a peck on the cheek. "My dear, good to see you. How is your film coming?"

She couldn't tell him the film was on the brink of financial disaster. He had enough to worry about. "We're doing well. Almost finished." Well, that part was true.

"Good, good. But Kathryn, I can't say I'm in favor of

your potentially dangerous plan," Charles said.

"I can't imagine living a life of regret, doing nothing. Can you, sir? If we don't act to capture Anthony's killers, who will? Anthony fought the terror brought down on innocents in Iran. We should fight for him."

"It's a bold plan, Kathryn," Hartmann said. "But I agree with Charles. Dangerous."

"I possess something the killers seem to be obsessed with, however."

"The Persian Glories," Charles said. "Hmm , , , ,"

Kathryn had to get back to Samuelsons; she'd been gone for hours. Emmaline had finagled another week of editing time, but there was still no way to pay production bills to finish the film, and more upcoming post-production costs.

When she arrived at Samuelsons, Emmaline met her at the door with a cable from the States. *What now?* She took a deep breath and opened the cable slowly:

> *So Missy,*
> *Heard from an Iranian ex-pat. You did some flying over there under Iranian gunfire—saved his life—on my dime, yet! Hell, if I'd known you were a war hero, I might not have fired you. So, I plan to fund your documentary,* Faces of Iran—*also shot on my dime! Next time lunch is on you.*
>
> *Wally*

TEHERAN

Mirdad slumped between two of General Houdin's men who supported his drunken body under his armpits. They were in Houdin's office at the Paradise Club.

Houdin stood before him shrouded in shadow, backlit against light shot through the windows like arrows into Mirdad's squinting eyes. He winced.

Captain Aran swaggered up next to the general, his usual sneer in place. "We traced him to Madame Shala's in Teheran."

Mirdad squirmed against the men holding him; their grip tightened and Mirdad caught a whiff of himself. He stank like bad meat. He looked down at his attire. Mother of God! He wore a filmy red negligee, soiled feathers trimming the neck and wrists.

"Evidently he hadn't bathed or shaved since he arrived at the brothel. The lout had been there for days."

"You're a disgrace!" Houdin bellowed. "Throw him in a bath, groom him, dress him, and for the love of Allah, sober him up and bring the bastard to me in two hours." Houdin turned away. "It's time for him to grow up."

As Houdin's men dressed him, Mirdad shook violently. They'd thrown him into a scalding bath and lathered him with some wretched-smelling soap. He gagged and threw up over the side of the tub. One of the men became furious and punched him in the stomach. By Allah, he felt worse than death. He'd behaved like undignified vermin. Ashamed, he hated himself.

The two men shoved him back down the hall to the general's office like a criminal. And this after the general had lifted him out of oblivion and delivered on promises of wealth and favors in return for hard work. They stopped at the guarded door and knocked.

Mirdad fought to hold his throbbing head high, his bloodshot eyes focused straight ahead, uneasy.

"Come in," he heard. The doors swung open.

Mirdad's stomach lurched. He battled to keep its contents. His pulse racing in a miasma of fear and dread, he stared at the man behind the desk, who faced away from him reading a document.

"You men may go."

When they were alone, the general swiveled around in his desk chair to glare at him. "Sit down, Mirdad. It's time I dealt with you."

Mirdad sat, looking solemnly into Houdin's dark, angry face.

CHAPTER SEVEN

SOMEWHERE IN IRAN

Noise...unspeakable pain, scorching flesh...dread. *Dear Lord! It was his body burning!* A tormented cry ripped from searing lungs. "God...help...me." Clawing his way from a deep and dark underworld into consciousness, Anthony urged movement from his body. His world was grim, filled with flames, clawing limbs, and distorted faces melting like shadowed candle wax. Was this hell? *Was he alive or dead?* He didn't know.

He concentrated on his right leg. *Christ! It wouldn't move.* He tried the other. Pain engulfed him, something, at least, other than dead weight. His arms. *No! Too much.* His head fell. He struggled for breath and felt the ripping rise and fall of his chest. He coughed, gasping.

There could be little left of him. He doubted he was whole. Surely he'd be better off dead.

Sound. Concentrate on sound. Was it horses' hooves, thundering around him, voices shouting? His head pounded...he was so disoriented. Flames leapt behind closed eyes with the smell of burning flesh. Was it his? He called out a garbled yell. He couldn't find his voice. Was he falling? Falling in a vortex of noise, torment...too much.

He shifted, but was restrained, strapped on something huge. Wings! Great wings. A roar, and he knew then what it was. The lion. Wind whirled, and he was borne away on wings of a lion...whatever was left of him.

The lion roared, lifting him.

He saw her in the distance, calling him—the spirit. She wore white. Golden hair floated over fair shoulders, and she reached for him, arms beckoning. He must get to her.

Kathryn! He fought to cry out.

She turned away.

Wait! No! Wait...

CHAPTER EIGHT

A Villa on the Casablanca Coast

Rena leaned into a supple chaise; her sun-drenched skin caressed by cool Egyptian cotton, a thread count of over a thousand, the color of toasted almonds. She enjoyed each day spent away from Iran in Omar's luxurious villa overlooking the ocean. She kicked off Dior sandals, curling her legs on the cushion, her pomegranate toenails gleaming under the Moroccan noonday sun. She gazed out through a Moorish sandstone balcony with turned columns and pointed arched windows reaching for the sweltering sky, waiting for news, vaguely aware of Omar across the terrace patio on a black square mat.

She loathed the idea of returning to Teheran. The revolution had destroyed any chance of her regaining a lost life in the top one thousand Iranian families. They would either flee Iran or be slaughtered. Militant Shiite Fundamentalists would rule; women would be treated like dogs, their rights and education a thing of the past. Back to the middle ages. Once again religion was used for a reign of terror. No. Her dreams for Iran were shattered.

But Paris. Paris and London offered a venue for fabulous living. And with her esteemed man, finally their wonderful son could have the life dreams were made of.

No. She would never go back to Teheran.

Any minute they expected a messenger would bring fulfillment of her dreams—the Persian Glories.

With detached interest she watched Omar, immersed in some martial arts ritual. He stared at his opponent, Major Demetrius Nassiri, his adjutant, who assumed the stance of an Aikido warrior. Omar's mind would be clear behind a steel door of concentration. He had moved into the void of still awareness, the presence of survival instinct. He had explained all this to her each day as she watched.

Omar never missed a day of discipline or a morning's meditation. He had learned early how to elevate himself above those around him, he'd said. He removed his thoughts from another's scrutiny, to hold his energy where it could constantly be refueled, thereby making his knowledge of others—even that which they wanted withheld—available to him, he claimed, from their most vulnerable secrets.

She had been attentive since she'd been there, fascinated by the nature of discipline. She'd never had discipline; a torrent of emotion always had ruled her. *Patience, Mother, one must be patient.* She recalled her son's words and watched a man with power operate: her man. It was an acquired skill, learning when to remain still and when to pounce.

He looked inscrutable, but she had caught the mood shift. Without warning Omar struck his opponent with a blow to the chest. Supposedly it was meant only to stun not paralyze. But Omar, it seemed, had allowed his dark rage to surface, flattening Demetrius Nassiri or Demi as Omar called him, who sprawled on the mat then curled into a ball. For some reason, this amused Rena. Omar had bested three soldiers before his bout with Demi. She hoped that was enough for one day.

Omar helped Major Nassiri off the mat. Demi's touch rested for a moment too long, Rena observed. They turned to one another and bowed. Omar shifted his glance to her, as if sensing her sexual energy. Omar bowed to her as well and waved Demi on. He came to her, and Demetrius' eyes narrowed before he filed out the door.

"Your life-force burns a path into my consciousness, Rena." He smiled darkly. "And I feel I must do something to resist you, but truth is, there's been only one woman who truly affects me, and that is you." He breathed deeply his gaze warm. He reached for her and the sound of approaching feet interrupted.

A knock, then his chief henchman, Captain Aran, entered. What they needed to discuss, she knew, had to be done face to face. Secure lines no longer existed in the Middle East.

"Have you found the shipment?" Omar gestured for Aran to come in.

"Sir, a hundred and fifty-two containers rest in the hold

of the *S.S. Amsterdam*," Aran said. "I have intercepted these riches intended for the sniveling creatures who escaped Iran. The ship bound for London is now coming to us in Casablanca."

Houdin laughed. He turned to Rena.

She said, "Evans spared you the trouble of killing those fools, no doubt?"

"Yes, my dear, and now their wealth, neatly packed, will be delivered to me, for sale to Arab trade."

Rena controlled her agitation.

"The problem," he said, "is still the jewels, the crown jewels and, of course, your Glories." He paced. "We questioned the arrogant Brit grandfather." A breeze off the balcony caught his sweat-glistening hair. "The rude bastard, indignant that *his* family's Glories had gone missing under Iran's watch, *his* family assets!"

Omar turned back to Aran. "Where the devil have all these jewels gone, Captain?"

"The jewels are another matter. We have no trace."

Patience withered. Rena screamed. "What is wrong with all of you? Can't you manage one small case of jewels?"

Houdin gathered her close, but she threw him off.

Her rage unfurled at Aran, "Finish, you imbecile, so I can be done with you."

Captain Aran's eyes widened at her tone. Women never spoke to Iranian men so. He raised his hand to strike.

Houdin growled, and stepped in front of him with a murderous look. "Is there anything you do know?" he said, his voice frigid.

Aran stepped away, backing down, regaining his military stance.

Rena smirked.

"We know," Aran continued, "that the jewels could have been taken out of the country by the art dealer, Kahlil."

"Philippe Kahlil?" Rena said.

Aran nodded.

Houdin paced, his agitation mounting. "Kahlil left before the treasure was moved from the palace. Now Evans is dead, his safes are empty, his servants terminated," Houdin recounted.

Get on with it. Rena clenched her jaw, blinded by fury.

"Yes, dead," Aran said, solemn.

Rena watched Aran, his iron legs firmly planted, his hands folded behind his back, his eyes coldly unreadable. She sensed his ambitious mind working to remain in Houdin's good graces.

"That is," Aran glanced at his general, fire jumping to his irises, "all but the chauffeur. Ali, was not with Evans, nor was he found in either household."

"Raymond's son, Ali?" Rena said.

"Very good, Captain. You have struck upon our answer." Houdin's smile was ice. "Find him at once!"

Captain Aran snapped to attention. "Sir, I obey you."

"And then a promotion, perhaps," Houdin said.

Aran's mouth twitched. Disappointment, she thought. No promotion for him today. He turned to leave. She tossed her hair. *Men were such idiots.*

The door clicked shut, and Rena's mind was elsewhere.

She pictured the crowd at the Iranian Embassy Ball a week ago: and Mirdad's date, the one wearing the diamond gardenia with an insanely large pearl. Ilyia's brooch. Yes, Anthony's eyes had smoldered, wanting the American blonde. Jealousy, hot as burning coals. Who was she? She searched her memory. Where was she? Rena paced more. Of course, her wonderful son Mirdad would know. Another woman, she grinned; who else could be a more formidable enemy? Fists clenched Rena swept from the room. She wanted to take care of this matter herself.

CHAPTER NINE

ABADAN, IRAN

He clung to life, drifting in and out of consciousness, pain and heat searing his body. Where was he now? Was he whole? Damaged? He smelled pipe tobacco, tumeric, horses, and sounds of prayer. *Tabriz.* His friend watched over him. He drifted off.

Covered in ice, freezing cold, he tossed his head, wanting escape.

"You're safe, man."

The voice? *Ah—Hans.*

"We've got you in a remote hospital along the Irez River, remember?"

Irez...burn specialists, yes. He faded.

"His surgery went well," Anthony heard later.

"Don't fret. We've smuggled SAVAK victims in from Teheran before," Hans said.

"But safety," Tabriz argued.

"No one outside of us few know he lives."

They spoke as if he were not there. And in truth he wasn't. He'd not spoken since he had been there, hadn't wanted to, didn't know if he could. But he was more aware of his dim surroundings, of his loss. Time passed. Awake, he listened, hearing it was no longer safe for him in the hospital. Covered in burn blankets, they shot him with morphine, loaded him aboard Hans' Jet Ranger from the hospital's roof, and flew him to Tabriz's mountain compound.

"It's been three weeks," he heard.

Anthony kept reaching for life. He gathered four more weeks had passed as he grabbed life with a vengeance and finally awoke. A different torment was then unleashed on him—recovery.

Tabriz watched over him. Anthony suppressed un-speakable agony with Tabriz's style of physical therapy. But determination to get well set his path.

He was forced to move his body, to stand, to walk—but always he needed help, always he had to stay out of the sun so his scorched skin would not leave him with a lifelong purple discoloration. He'd been slathered in bacteria-killing Sulfamylon cream.

Then one day he walked on his own.

"He heals well." Tabriz frowned. "At least, his body heals." Tabriz shook his head. "I'm not certain about his spirit."

Hans just shrugged. "I'm not one to speak of a man's inner life."

"This makes me ache within," Tabriz said. "He is like a son, as Anthony's father was like a brother."

Anthony had known this most of his life. "I'm here, you old goat. And I hear every word you say."

"I guess it's time to wean him off of drugs, then," Hans said. He and Tabriz laughed hard.

Anthony wished they'd shut up. He knew this weaning would not be funny.

But without Tabriz and Hans forcing him to refocus, to rebuild his body, he would be a weak mass of bitterness. Their loyalty was difficult to ignore. The hard discipline they inflicted was another matter. This he could resent, later.

Eventually Ali found them in the mountains through Tabriz's scouts.

He cried like a ninny when he'd learned Anthony lived.

Ali's father, Raymond, had burned in the wreckage. Except for the arm the bastards had sent to Mirdad as Anthony's. The identifying factor was the Evans' crested ring he'd worn—the last gesture of love Anthony had given Raymond before carrying him from the burning house. And yet he'd burned anyway.

Anthony's friends, Tabriz, Hans, and Ali, he knew had agreed to be tough as yak hide with him. "It's the only way he will heal and become strong."

Anthony heard this over and over.

They insisted upon turning a blind eye and deaf ear to his struggle, forcing him to fight.

Hans and Ali trained his body. Though his burned right side still healed, his right leg was in a cast, and his left shoulder with two bullet wounds hurt like hell, they made him work. Each took a different shift, always after the sun had gone down, slathering him with malodorous Thermazen and collagenase ointments, yak butter mixed with vitamins, making him walk and stretch the scarring skin and muscle, insisting he eat and sleep. Sleep was mostly impossible. Nightmares came often.

Still no one outside of Tabriz's small band knew Anthony lived.

"When our recovery goal is met and you are out of Iran, then the old grandfather can know. Not before," Tabriz said. "I know a fire inside fills you, gives you the will to do what you must. Let it."

After the hospital the first training weeks at camp were rough. Anthony, barely able to walk, had lost weight—a pale Englishman, thin and white.

"This is not my friend," Tabriz would shout when Anthony faltered. "This is the devil Houdin's work. Anthony hides inside this walking corpse."

For five painful weeks, they worked, rode, lifted weights, sparred with weapons and martial arts.

Anthony was aware of being watched—always. "Move it! Hoist that log and get your ass up the mountain," Hans would yell.

"Chop more firewood."

"Fill those buckets from the stream and bring them inside."

He moved his skinny ass slowly at first, then, as the pain meds, antibiotics and muscle relaxers, tranquilizers and whatever other drugs they'd fed him worked their way out of his system, his appetite increased and so did his temper. Until one night he lost it with Hans.

"I'm sick to death of you bullying me, dammit!"

"Shit." Hans threw up his hands and stomped off.

What was he becoming? These men were in this mountain camp late in the fall for one reason: to save him, heal him, put him back together, body and soul. And then they would help him take down his enemies—their enemies—the Black Glove, Houdin, Mirdad, Aran, Nassiri—all the crooked cutthroats.

One day at dusk Tabriz, Kash Kai Tribal Leader, mentor, friend and savior said as he had when Anthony was a boy, "Hold this knife. Look at the blackened twig on that tree."

Anthony saw the tree thirty feet away.

"Wait!" shouted Tabriz, "is that a tree or is it Houdin?"

"No," Anthony said, "it's Mirdad!" The knife whizzed past Tabriz's head, splitting the twig.

The day came when Anthony leaped on a horse and rode hell-bent, his body pale, leaner, but his strength greater than before, defined. The martial arts he practiced daily were far more deadly. He felt ready to do battle.

Tabriz seemed pleased at first. But then...

"Anthony, you have changed." Tabriz leaned against a tree. "I don't like the icy hardness I see in your green eyes, the hard set of your jaw, nor for the driving hatred I see settle on your heart."

Anthony slicked his long hair back with grease, gazed out over the mountaintop, and said, "Ice cools the burns I still feel. And hatred drives me to seek my goal." He tied his hair with a leather cord. "Vengeance."

Snow fell in the rugged Elburz mountains. It had been two months since Anthony had been brought to Tabriz's lodge. Thickly coated Ibex goats foraged on juniper berries in the day, moving further away from their summer homes with winter approaching.

Anthony sat on an old log watching a white kid determinedly attempting to keep up with its mother, who foraged for berries in a continual descent, searching for cleaner pastures. Birds swooped downhill, seeking protection from icy winds. Anthony had seen a brown bear early this morning not far from the lodge. He wondered how many bears were out there.

He stared at the valley blanketed in clouds. It was early and gray, and for a moment he indulged in memories of Kathryn, his brave beauty—his no more.

Mangled in mind and body, not an ounce of gentleman left in him, the last thing he'd do would be to inflict his degenerated self on her. But protect her he would, if he could get to her in time. The Black Glove had spies enough to realize who had the jewels they coveted. He shook off useless thoughts, turning his attention back to the mountain.

Today he'd hike to the top before Tabriz arrived to goad him with his torture called physical therapy. He was strong again, but not agile. Making his stiff leg perform took constant force of will. For this, he used yoga and Tai

Chi and meditation skills, expanding his consciousness outside himself, releasing the notion of pain or pleasure. There was only one goal: getting to the mountaintop.

Over steep, jagged rocks coated with ice, slippery and perilous, he climbed. The temperature had dropped. He clutched with his fingertips, pulling himself up, gripping the mountain with his knees and his will, eleven thousand feet above sea level. At this altitude, freezing air tore at his lungs.

Through the rigors of the past months, Anthony wasn't certain if he'd been blessed or damned having Tabriz and Hans discover him thrown from the twisted wreckage of his Range Rover, dying. Now, he knew; it was a blessing. He could climb and ride when he hadn't thought he would ever walk. Still, he was impaired with a noticeable limp and scarred along his right shoulder and hip. He chuckled, ironically grateful to be left-handed.

Anthony searched upward for the summit, but that too was cloaked in mist, as yet a mystery to his eyes.

Sweat dripped from Anthony's back through a protective layer of clothing. The chill wind whipped at corners of the tarp covering icy ground where a steel bench press held the canvas firmly in place. He watched angry storm clouds move closer to the mountain behind Tabriz's lodge. He raised and lowered the bar over his chest, his concentration focused, muscles burning.

His thoughts turned to Kathryn. Was she alone or had some guy waltzed in to ease her distress over him? *Mirdad. Please no!* He recalled Mirdad as he'd last seen him at Mehrabad Airport in Teheran, screaming, *"I hate you, I hate you!"* Yes, hate me, bastard, because I'm coming for you. Dark feelings drove Anthony forward, drowning out screaming shoulder pain from healing bullet wounds, leaving only an obsession for strength enough to face adversity.

From the day's stillness he heard the alarm, a wolf cry. Someone was coming up the mountain. Anthony replaced the two-hundred-fifty-pound weight, grabbed the towel next to him, and headed toward the stone lodge. A second signal, the sound of a great owl told him to come quickly. He sprinted up wooden stairs and leaned into the porch railing searching to see if friend or foe approached.

Bursting from the trees, Tabriz and Ali carried a ragged old man into the clearing. The man's head fell forward, his maroon tribal turban drooping, his breathing labored as Anthony lifted him and brought him inside, laying him on a cot by the door. He looked from Tabriz to Ali. "Who is this man?"

Ali's eyes blazed hatred at the man, something Anthony had not seen in Alies=0-890999.

"Houdin's men came close today. They were after me," Ali said. "Thanks be to Allah, not you, because they believe you're a dead man."

"You're certain?"

"They did not get that close, my friend," Tabriz said. "We killed all but three."

"Those we made speak," Ali said.

Tabriz turned away and went to the hearth, unsheathing his curved knife, grinding the blade against a sharpening stone, his movements exact, as if preparing for battle.

"One soldier bought himself a quick and painless death," Tabriz said, "with his knowledge. He told us his orders were to bring Ali back to his commander alive. He knew of Ali's connection to you and Mirdad." Tabriz moved back to the cot. "He also told us of this decrepit creature."

Anthony glared at the wretch; beard tangled, fingers gnarled, skinny as a rat in rags, his rheumy eyes pleading, but for what?

"We found him hiding in his village and brought him," said Ali, "so you hear for yourself what he says." Ali stood rigid, teeth clenched. "This man will tell you the secrets haunting you for years." He prodded the man. "Speak, old one!"

Anthony looked at the crumpled wreck on the cot. He knelt beside him, bringing water to his lips. "Drink this," he said in Farsi.

"You needn't be kind, Anthony," Ali said behind him.

The old man looked up into Anthony's face searchingly, his eyes wide and with some recognition Anthony didn't understand. He'd never seen the man before, he was certain. "We'll not harm you, old one. I swear."

"It wasn't me, Excellency! It was not." Words difficult to understand rumbled out. "The woman, the young wife of the general, she paid." The old man sputtered.

Anthony gave him more water.

"My brother needed money—hungry—poor. Child sick."

Ali spit on the floor. "Coward! Worm!"

"Quiet, Ali," Anthony ordered. "You were saying, old one? Wife of what general?"

"Has haunted me—years. My brother—dead, killed him. I, afraid." He sobbed, frail shoulders heaving, then looked up again. "I cannot go to Allah with this guilt—must tell."

A grinding wedged in Anthony's stomach. He'd rather be on the mountain, wind whirling through the trees, chilling him to the bone. Because he had a premonition that what this man was about to divulge would change him forever.

"The airplane—the murdered people. The explosion—a bomb, hidden aboard the plane, killed those people. The Englishman with eyes like yours, and his wife, twenty years ago. Prime minister's young wife," his voice, barely audible, he choked out, "she paid my brother to do it."

Anthony's mind whirled, a spiraling vortex, and fought to reject what he'd heard.

"You're certain?" demanded Tabriz. "You know this for certain?"

"Yes."

Hidden truth spread like an oil slick around Anthony, slimy, ugly. "Who else have you told?" Anthony said.

"The general's men."

"Houdin?"

The man nodded. "This woman is now his wife."

Fury surged through Anthony's veins, searing more deeply than flames had scorched his flesh. "Houdin's men were in your village?"

"Late this summer," the old man sputtered. "They came raping our women, killing many." He swallowed, sagging against the blanket. "A major, mixed-blood Greek, Nassiri, his name." He coughed. "With this truth I bargained for my life. Even then, he beat me and left me to die. Allah. Now I am free of this guilt."

Anthony had heard enough.

He stormed from the lodge and ran to his horse, grabbing the reins, leaping on, almost grateful for the pain shooting through his damaged leg, deflecting the frenzy inside. Part of him had felt a glimmer, had known somehow, that Rena had played a part in his parents' death. So it was never Mirdad's father. It was his mother, Rena.

He galloped along the ridge to the river. Tomorrow he would leave the compound, the hunter, laying traps for his prey, sparing no mercy.

If the weather held, Hans would arrive at dawn. They would fly a circuitous route into Iraq, refueling at arranged sites, avoiding Iranian aircraft and radar, rebel artillery. They had no clearance with the insurgency strangling Iran and would fly at great risk. And somehow he would find Kathryn. But that was tomorrow.

Anthony slowed, listening to the calls of black-headed thrushes. Tilting his head back he viewed a massive vulture on alert for remains probably left by last night's growling leopard. Winter would be severe, he knew. *So many predators.*

CHAPTER TEN

PARIS

"*Bonjour, bonjour*, Monsieur Ajani," came a welcoming voice from the owner of the French cafe, Mirdad's favorite bistro on the Rue Madeleine not far from where he stayed in Paris. Sent here by Houdin, who with a generous offer, demanded Mirdad redeem himself by studying finance with a successful banking investment adviser, Jean Paul Natef, and learn to handle his family's assets.

Mirdad had jumped at the chance. Though Houdin did mention what would happen if Mirdad failed to achieve the banker Natef's respect. Banishment, and his funds would be cut off.

But today in Paris, Mirdad was blissfully anonymous: He knew no one and no one knew him. He had no history, no shame, no memories. In Paris, he was a new, free man, free to fulfill his ardent dream of a new life. He would never look back at his foul deeds thanks to the opportunity Houdin had presented.

He glanced up as the small rosy-cheeked café owner bustled up to greet him, one of her favorite patrons, she insisted. "Where have you been for *zeez* last tree days, uh? I save *la table pour vous tout le matin,* and you don't come."

"Et vous, Madame Tourneau, comment ça va aujourd hui?"

"Bien, bien, monsieur." Mirdad kissed her on both cheeks before she guided him to his favorite outside table where he enjoyed watching the enchanting Parisians pass by. Although it was winter, the outdoor area had heaters and wind breaks.

"I've been in the country sightseeing," he said. "My first visit to Versailles and its magnificent gardens."

"Oui? And you enjoyed?"

"You know, I would be there still, if it hadn't been for the aroma of freshly baked *brioche* beckoning me all the way from La Petite Trianon!"

"Ooo la la, monsieur," she chortled. "You *'ave bonne chance."* She leaned closer to him, and he caught the smell of freshly baked bread, blended with her own body odor carrying a trace of lilac cologne. "Not only has Henri baked *brioche,* but today 'e prepared a *gateau St. Honore."* She stood up to her full height of five feet, her hazel eyes twinkling.

"Has he?"

She nodded. "

"Could it be that today is a special day?"

"Well..." she said.

"Then that must be why I have this." Reaching inside his coat he brought out a small box wrapped in gold foil. *"Bonne Anniversaire,* Happy Birthday, madame."

"*Monsieur!*" A look of pure amazement swept her blushing face.

"Please, open it."

"But, monsieur, why 'ave you done zis?"

"Could I forget my first friend in Paris on her birthday? Please accept my little gift."

"*Avec plaisir*, monsieur," she said almost shyly, "*et merci.*" Her chubby fingers moved quickly as the paper fell away. "*Mon Dieu! Magnifique! Merci bien, Monsieur* Mirdad."

For a moment she studied a pair of finely crafted tortoise combs, inlaid with gold and ivory before rushing to a pub mirror near the front door of the bistro. In a preening gesture, she smoothed the errant wisps of gray hair around her face and inserted the combs, all smiles before rushing off to the kitchen shouting, "*Henri, Henri, maintenant, le petit dejeuner pour nos ami Mirdad, et n'oublies pas le gateau.*"

Mirdad had surprised even himself by this gesture. But then the last few months had been nothing less than astonishing. He remembered staying drunk for days before Houdin had found him at Madame Shala's and sent him to Paris. Drunk and disorderly, screwing every young piece he could get his hands on, male and female. He'd had an insatiable need, until he was jolted awake by the general's men and ripped out of bed.

Wiping the past away like chalk on a blackboard, he was determined to forget everything. Get a new life. Money was no longer a problem with a substantial amount tucked away safely, waiting for him. His mother was out of Iran, and there was nothing to take Mirdad back to Persian life, nothing.

Paris offered an electrifying change of scene, streets bursting with galleries, boutiques, people bustling about in the crisp winter air, sharing their easy humor. He'd become acquainted with a charming café culture, free of censorship, the streets free of militia. He felt young for the first time in years.

Each month a tidy sum was sent to his orphanage and clinic. Tashi sent back reports to him and photos of the boys in front of improvements made with his money. But he'd never go back to Iran.

At first, he soaked up the sights, like a conventional tourist, getting a feel for France and the French people. The gaiety and style of those in the *chic* areas fascinated him.

On Rue Faubourg St. Honore, he often passed the finest men's couture shops: Cerruti, St. Laurent, and Dior. But it was weeks before he felt compelled to go in and be fitted.

When finally he did, it was at the request of his new friend and boss, the investment banker, Jean Paul Natef. Tall, his full black hair slicked back away from his handsome face, and a cocky smile, as if he owned the streets, Jean Paul slapped Mirdad on the back and said, "You're not a bad looking man, Mirdad." Jean Paul looked him over. "Pfff, the ladies, they might say you're good looking, but your wardrobe! Are you crazy looking like that, like you're fifty? Come now. We're going to my tailor at Cerruti. He'll fix you up." Jean Paul snapped his fingers, and they were off.

Once Mirdad walked through Cerruti's door, he was ready. He ordered clothes he had only dreamed of having, suits, shirts and ties of course, but mainly casual clothes, leather pants, and raw silk Raphael shirts, expensive bomber jackets, finely crafted shoes, and two dinner jackets, things he had seen in western magazines and had always desired. Not a lot, just enough to get by. No hurry.

He'd changed his hairstyle and his walk, both now easier, relaxed, truly enjoying himself for the first time since he was a boy. He immersed himself in finance, stocks, international markets, and the language of money. Working through his stilted French accent, slowly he developed an ear for French meter and cadence. He now spoke fluent French, as well as four other languages, as he'd assuaged his thirst to learn at Shiraz University. This helped him immensely with the bank's various clients.

During his first week in Paris, Mirdad had stayed at the George Cinq, but soon tired of the frivolous life in a luxurious hotel. And after searching for only a day, he had ensconced himself on the top floor of a discreet but charming pension. There he had behaved with reasonable decorum, getting to know the people he came in contact with daily, like Madame Tourneau.

When Jean Paul took him to pick up his newly tailored clothes from Cerruti's, Mirdad put on a new suit.

"*Voilà!*" Jean Paul pinched his fingers together in front of Mirdad's face, gesturing. "What did I tell you? Not bad." He laughed, pleased with himself. "Now we are going to lunch at Laserre. The bank's clients are in from Spain."

Mirdad's new knowledge saw him through the lunch conversation, and from there he went to dinners, meetings, and for cocktails on the bank's behalf, in a whirlwind of business. He had found a productive niche in which he excelled and which he enjoyed. Maybe he would find a chic townhouse one day, but for now, life was perfect.

Until the night when he received a message from his mother.

"Return to me, my son, at once. I'm in Casablanca." In that moment, the joy burgeoning inside him started to shrivel, his old stomach pain resurging. He tore up the message and tossed it away and immediately felt better.

CHAPTER ELEVEN

In Omar's Casablanca villa, Rena stood in the bedroom at her dresser mirror shaking with terror.

"Rena, where are you, *joon-am*, my life?" Omar called from the other room.

Omar, oh Omar, he would help her, if she could speak. She felt helpless as a small child, a feeling unfamiliar and unwanted. In a tenuous voice she pleaded, "Help me."

"What is it? What's wrong?" Omar's deep voice crooned to her from the doorway, but she couldn't look at him. She stood quite still, her eyes squeezed shut, frightened of what she would see on his face.

"Omar, look at me...really look at me. Tell me, what do you see?"

"What games are you playing? I thought something was wrong. You were supposed to be resting before lunch."

"Please, Omar, tell me!"

"I see you, Rena, standing before me naked. Your hair is wet, drops of water trickling over your bare breasts. Open your beautiful eyes, *joon-am*."

"What?" Her eyes flew open.

"Let me see a smile on your exquisite face."

Did she dare ask him? Yes, she must. "Am I beautiful, Omar?" She searched his face for the truth. "Tell me, please."

"Turn around and look. See for yourself, *joon-am.*" His voice was low and soft, not mocking.

With tremendous effort, she forced herself to turn around and face her reflection in the glass. A woman she barely recognized gazed back at her. She raised a trembling hand to touch the skin. *Could this be her?*

She was beautiful, really beautiful. More now than she had ever been in her youth, more than she had ever dreamed of being. The face was slightly different, but the eyes—the same. She stared and magnificent dark eyes with lighter smoky motes sparkling looked back at her. How could she have forgotten? The dream—always the terrible dream haunting her. Ilyia, her dead sister, laughed at her ugliness; Aziz, the blackmailer, chased her with a blade.

But every inch of the woman Rena saw before her was breathtaking. Reworked from her now straight toes to the tip of her gently upturned nose, until a younger and infinitely more alluring woman had emerged from her unsightly form.

She smiled at the woman, who smiled back with luscious lips and straight white teeth.

It had been worth it, worth all her discomfort. She was something glorious.

"Rena, speak to me," Omar said.

Slowly her hand moved down her smooth neck: her fingers tingled at the touch of her warm flesh as they slid over her high full breasts that she couldn't resist caressing. Her other hand glided down over her tight flat stomach, a product of endless hours of careful working out since the surgery.

In the mirror, her eyes caught the outline of Omar standing in the open terrace doorway, peering at her, backlit against the vivid sun, as her hand reached lower into the nest of curls between her legs where she was hot and wet.

He smiled, moving across the room, his brooding Persian face, the deep-set almond eyes, smoldering as the space between them narrowed. "Are you all right now, *delbar-am*, the one who has my heart?" The muscles of his bare torso rippled as he discarded his swimming trunks. He was so handsome for a man in his fifties.

"Omar." Her voice was husky with desire.

"Don't move, *joon-am*. I will find you." His silky voice caressed.

He moved in behind her. Strong arms reached around her waist and pulled her against his warm, hard body. His large hands slid up to her breasts.

She strained toward his touch, while he rolled his thumbs over her tightening nipples. His breath was hot on her throat.

He licked circles up to her ear, whispering, "Don't stop touching yourself, *joon-am*. Show me how hot you get, *atashe del-am,* fire of my heart. I want to taste your heat."

His thickly lashed, dark eyes watched her as one hand drifted between her legs. He slipped two fingers inside of her, then pulled his fingers into his mouth, tasting her wetness. She moaned her desire.

"You're so wet, Rena."

"She wants you, Omar. She cannot live without you." Rena pushed her buttocks against his arousal, breathing rapidly.

"Then she'll have me." Omar spun her around to face him, taking his wet fingers, rubbing them lightly around the outline of her lips, his face intense. He brought his mouth down to hers, plunging his tongue inside. He breathed in the perfumed smell of her. He lifted her to sit on the dresser and spread open her thighs. "This is mine, Rena."

"Fuck me, Omar, please fuck me now."

And he did.

He arched over her and plunged his cock into her hot center, roaring his pleasure, pumping until—"Come for me, Rena, come for me now," he demanded in a hoarse voice.

"Oh, Omar," she moaned, wanting it, needing it. He moved inside her to a growing rhythm, as she met his every thrust.

"Take it, take it," he ordered. And she did until he erupted into her, calling her name, over and over.

"Renaaaaaaaaa."

Together they collapsed, half on, half off the bed, wound around each other like serpents on a desert rock. If he only knew how much she craved it, she thought, knowing she would never tell him. He lifted his head and looked into her eyes as if he knew what she was thinking.

She smiled, knowing he would take her again.

Satisfied an hour later, Rena leaned over, kissed her sleeping lover, and headed for the shower. As the hot water streamed over her sensitive flesh, she thought of him.

The first time just months ago she had caught the light of desire in his glance and had doubted it, still thinking of herself as an old hag. But what she saw reflected in his eyes was something else. Something wonderful. She felt ageless and desirable with him, something she thought never to feel again. And if she were to fulfill her plans, she needed Omar.

Before her new marriage to Omar, it had been over twenty years since she had been with a man. The only pleasure she had known had been alone, in the privacy of her darkened bedroom.

She had fantasized again and again, but always for her first love, this man, the man who should have been her first husband. But fate, she thought, looking back at what had happened, always played a hand. And if she were to keep him now, she would have to know exactly what she was doing, for there was no one, she was sure, anywhere, with more sexual prowess than Omar Houdin, the man she craved. The man who would help her fulfill her need for the Persian Glories.

While Omar slept, Rena padded barefoot from the bedroom in her bikini onto the wide tile terrace of their rented Moroccan villa and stood gazing down at the Casablanca Yacht Harbor in the golden sunlight. She smiled hearing Omar's occasional snoring and marveled at the recent life-changing events that had finally occurred for her.

All those years of having no idea, no plan of how to extricate herself from the agony of moral captivity, impoverished, a woman alone in Iran, was the foulest prison she could imagine.

She shuddered as she recalled the isolation and futility, the yearning for more. Would there ever be enough for her? But she must never forget the torment she lived, or one day she could find herself there again, only older, and without hope of ever being free—free to have love, pleasure, and her greatest desire, her Glories.

She gauged from the sun that she had about an hour before Omar awoke from his nap. An hour to lounge. She settled herself comfortably in her favorite chaise, drenched herself in sunscreen lotion, arranged a stack of new magazines on the small table next to her, and glanced back at the bedroom and the recumbent form on the bed before reaching for a box of Belgian chocolates concealed among her periodicals. She lifted the lid, selecting her two favorites, eagerly popping them onto her salivating tongue, savoring the taste.

"Rena! Don't you dare," came an accusing voice from behind her.

"Merde!" she grumbled under her breath.

Omar held his hand out in front of her, his eyebrow raised. She looked up; her lips curled in a smile, while behind her dark glasses, her eyes gleamed murder. If it had been anyone else, she would gladly have slit their wrists.

She squashed the melting chocolates into his palm.

"Where's the rest?" His voice cooed.

She had asked him to help her stay fit, but she'd never dreamed he'd be so damned vigilant! Grudgingly, she handed over the horde, watching him take them away then return to her, offering instead a tall cool glass of mineral water.

"Here, this will refresh you, cara."

"How thoughtful of you, my love." She ungraciously snatched it out of his hand.

Omar laughed. "You're such a good sport."

Good sport, my ass, she fumed, watching his ass move as he sauntered to the balustrade still naked. He stood confidently, hands on hips, staring at the sea.

The sex had made her ravenous. Damn! She was sick of salad, fish, and vegetables, but she sipped again. She curled her lip and spit water across the burnished tile floor, causing a starling that was busy pecking at an errant piece of breakfast roll to flutter off chirping irefully.

"Rena, the water is good for you. Your body needs hydration in this sun."

But Rena wasn't listening. She stared at the cover of *Harpers Queens*. Her mind fought to grasp what she saw. She couldn't believe her eyes!

Her jewels! *Her necklace around another woman's throat.* Her earrings, bracelet, ring, brooch all of it. On the cover of *Harpers Queens*!

They're mine, mine! Her mind screeched at the image. She tossed the glass over the edge of the terrace into the bushes and frantically searched through the pages for the story, her hands shaking so violently she could barely hold the magazine.

"Rena, did you hear me?" Omar said, unused to being ignored.

He threw his hands up. "I'm going in to shower."

"Wait, my love. You must hear this." Finding the story, she read:

"The famed Persian Glories, a spectacular and legendary parure of flawless canary diamonds, worn by Miss Kathryn Whitney, will be on display at London's Kahlil Gallery in Mayfair for the opening of the long overdue exhibition of photographs by Sir Anthony Evans, the brilliant young photographer who recently disappeared while in Iran."

Rena looked up at Omar, catching her breath. "Is this the blonde from the embassy ball?" She watched him pondering.

Omar wrapped a towel around his waist and pulled up a chair. "Go on, Rena." He sat.

"The unusual artistic quality to Evans' work won him acclaim from his first sitting with Princess Grace of Monaco in 1970 for *Life* magazine. From there he continued his work for many royal families around the globe. In 1971, he became the official court photographer to the Shah of Iran and his family, a first for the royalty of Iran, blah, blah, blah....A charity gala will follow.

"Evans and Miss Kathryn Whitney had planned to announce their engagement at the opening of his exhibit, says Lord Charles Evans, grandfather to Anthony. The Persian Glories were a betrothal gift to Miss Whitney from Sir Anthony. They are currently valued, Sotheby's tells us, at somewhere in excess of two hundred million pounds."

They exchanged glances, and she read on.

"The gems are completely unique, each canary diamond is of the highest grade for yellow diamonds, fancy intense, and the immense white diamonds..."

"Enough!" She hurled the magazine across the terrace. "How could this be? From under our noses, this slut steals my jewels. How dare she!"

"They said two hundred million?" Omar grunted. "Great Allah, I never knew they could be worth that much."

She sprang from the chaise, a frenzied feline set to pounce on her prey, dizzy now, hyperventilating. *Mirdad. How could he have let this happen? What has he done?* She rushed to the edge of the terrace, struggling to catch her breath.

Her thoughts whirled, whipping her mind with every recollection about Mirdad and this woman. From the ministry calling Mirdad to Persepolis, a liaison to the American film crew's director, the Whitney woman. He'd taken his dress clothes and had searched his library for some book on film to bring her. He'd been happy. And at the embassy ball celebrating her marriage to Omar, her first foray into society in twenty years and her son had caused a ruckus, fighting with Anthony over this woman, almost coming to blows. She gasped, clutching the terrace railing. Mirdad loved this American. Mirdad. This was the first time she had thought of her son in months, but he wasn't here when she needed him.

No, he was lying around in Paris, saying, "Be patient, Mother, the Persian Glories can't be found." *Ha! I found them.* Idiots, all of them. Or was Mirdad protecting this Kathryn Whitney? Had he known she had the Glories? Had he betrayed his own mother?

Wait, calm. Be calm. She pondered.

Who knows? Perhaps this is a benefit to me. At least now I know for sure where the diamonds are. I no longer have to concern myself with getting them out of Iran. She paced back and forth the length of the wide terrace.

In actuality, now I can make certain there will be no way to implicate me when they are stolen and the blonde bitch is sliced to shreds! I'll be nowhere in sight.

She swept across the terrace retrieving the magazine and shoved the *Harper's Queens* into his hand. "Omar, did Mirdad know of this? Has he been shielding this woman—lying to us?"

He flicked his fingers, thumping the magazine cover. "You will know soon enough. My pilot readies my jet. You'll leave for Paris in three hours."

Brushing his shoulder with her fingertips, she breezed past him into the library and picked up the phone, dialing a number she hadn't called in years but knew by heart. She waited while the connection was made. Rena tapped her lustrous fingernails against a glass tabletop, keeping a rhythm that soothed her until she heard his voice.

"Charles," she said.

There was a pause then, she heard, "How kind of you to call, Rena," Lord Charles said. "How long has it been?"

As she stared at the telephone Rena envisioned Lord Charles Evans sitting in his palatial estate surrounded by luxuries and servants.

"Too long, Charles, I know. But Mirdad and I are both devastated to hear about Anthony. Horrified. Perhaps we can see Anthony's exhibit when we're in London."

"Then come to the charity ball afterward as my guests."

"How kind of you, Charles. We're only too happy to come."

"Then I'd consider it my pleasure for you and Mirdad to join us." Lord Charles cleared his throat. "If Anthony were here, he'd insist you attend. Your invitations will be with the concierge at the Hotel Savoy."

Rena hung up the phone laughing. She was going to the ball, the ball commemorating the late Anthony Evans. Lord Charles, the old fool, had played into her hands.

The day after receiving the message from Casablanca, a message he'd tossed away, Mirdad strolled out of his lunch meeting at the George Cinq after having eaten lunch with colleagues, and celebrating the success of his three month training program. Dressed in a new suit and enjoying a feeling of well-being, he caught a glimpse of his reflection in a lobby shop window. He stopped, surprised by the smiling well-dressed young man he saw there. Could it be? Yes! He was happy! Through the glass he noticed two lovely girls smiling back at him. *They thought I was looking at them. Well, why not?* He checked his watch, assuring himself he would be on time for his next meeting. Quickly, he ducked inside.

"Bonjour, mademoiselles."

"Bonjour, monsieur, can we help you?" they said in unison, as if struggling with an urge to giggle at one another.

"Why, yes, I'm certain you can." Mirdad, hands in his coat pockets, surveyed the shop. He was in an elegant lingerie boutique, surrounded by soft silky things inviting his touch.

"What would you like?" asked the taller brunette whose skin was pale and creamy.

He strolled over to a table of neatly displayed silk panties, wondering if he should tell her how he would like to see her model the palest pink ones, but in lieu of that, he merely ran a finger lightly over their tiny surface, smiling into her taunting green eyes.

"I'll take a box of these." He reached instead for a small stack of pastel silk handkerchiefs, delicately embroidered. "Gift wrapped, if you please." They would be perfect for Sylvie, Jean Paul's lovely wife, as a thank you for last night's elegant dinner party.

Jean Paul with his carefree, rugged French cowboy manner at times made it difficult to remember that he was also a prominent investment adviser and the man assigned to him by Houdin to train Mirdad in the complex field of finance. A challenge Mirdad greatly enjoyed and unwittingly excelled at. Jean Paul seemed to bring out the best in Mirdad, and Sylvie, the best in Jean Paul.

Merciful Allah had given Mirdad the chance for redemption and a new life he embraced.

Mirdad handed the brunette shop girl his American Express card.

"What color ribbon would you like, monsieur?"

He shrugged. "Whatever you think, mademoiselle. I'm sure your taste is excellent."

"That depends, monsieur, on who they are for," she teased.

"I see." He walked to the counter where she was leaning. "They are for a friend's wife." He watched her eyebrows shoot up, and smiled. "To thank her for a party," he added.

"In that case, monsieur, the silver ribbon will be nice." She smiled approvingly, handed him back his card, and disappeared to the back of the shop.

He must remember this shop for another day, he noted, catching the quiet petite blonde watching him from under her downy lashes. She blinked and turned her glance shyly away.

Life was indeed pleasant on this bright Parisian Thursday. His friend Jean Paul was a real character and a clown socially, but when it came to investments, he was as sharp as a samurai's sword, the kind of associate Mirdad had dreamed of doing business with rather than against. He was also the first male friend Mirdad had known since—

Piercingly, he felt the old knife-like stomach spasm that he had not felt in months. He winced in agony.

His head sagged to his chest.

"Are you all right, monsieur?" inquired the petite blonde who had been busily unwrapping new inventory.

Perspiration began to bead his forehead. He must take hold of himself. *"Pardon, mam'selle,* I must have eaten my lunch too quickly...a little indigestion. I'm fine, really." He walked toward the open door. "Perhaps a little air," he said to reassure her.

Staggering out to the lobby, he took in a slow breath, clouds of doubt floated behind his eyes. Would he ever be free of pain and guilt for his deeds?

He sat on a silk sofa, waiting for the stomach spasms to fade. Clearly last night's message had affected him more than he thought. *Would he ever be rid of his witch of a mother?*

An image of sweet-hearted Madame Tourneau flashed before him, her apple cheeked smile, her undemanding kindness, while his mother's endless demands, her deceptions, lay guilt at everyone's doorstep except her own. Regrettably, he had believed her lies with all his naïve and loyal heart. Anthony's death had opened the door to truth and knocked him on his ass, leaving him cloaked in shame and guilt, an unshakable mantle. And yet he *must* shake it off or *Mother* would own him and his life would be worthless.

He stood, feeling better. But as he looked up at a chic woman in a crimson Dior dress approaching him, his world started to crumble bit by bit.

"My son, I've been searching for you." His mother shoved a magazine into his hands, a copy of *Harpers Queens*, and took hold of his arm. "We must go now."

He shook her off, his pulse racing. "No. I'm not going anywhere with you. I've had enough."

"Don't be ridiculous," Rena said. "I've located our Glories, in London."

She never had listened to him. It was always about her wants and desires. "Not this time, Mother. I've found a home here in Paris."

She stepped forward and he backed away, hating her.

Rena got up in his face. "You see whose picture is on the cover here?" She grabbed the magazine and held it in front of him. "Your blonde bitch, Mirdad."

Mirdad scanned the cover, a photo of Kathryn, as beautiful as ever, wearing the Persian Glories. *Why? How?*

He recalled the last time he'd seen her at the Hilton in Teheran. She'd entered the hotel disheveled, carrying a camera case after a night out at the ball and then with Anthony. He'd given her an engagement ring. *And the sly dog must have given her the Persian Glories, too.* Mirdad wanted to laugh out loud but only snickered. He had driven her to the airport brazening his way past komiteh militia and crooked airport officials all to accompany Kathryn, her crew, and the Persian Glories. She probably had tucked the empress's crown jewels in with the Glories, and he'd sat right next to them.

Rena leaned closer to him. "I eliminated two who wrongfully owned the Glories. With the diamonds almost in my grasp, do you think I'll allow the blonde to stand in my way?"

But the diamonds had belonged to his Aunt Ilyia, Mirdad thought.

She rattled the magazine in his face. "If you want her alive, you'll come with me now. Because if you don't, history will be repeated. After the Evans charity ball the owner of the Persian Glories will be me. As it always should've been."

Memories whirled in his head. *What did she mean by this... history?* He shouldn't put anything past her, but what he was thinking was too horrible to be true. "Mother, my aunt...you. It couldn't have been you."

She smirked at him.

". . . and Uncle Richard? Impossible," he said. "You didn't—did you?"

She laughed and to his horror, he wondered if it were so.

"Let's go, my son."

"Monsieur, a moment!" The petite blonde shop girl ran out holding his package wrapped with silver ribbon.

Mirdad didn't take the silk handkerchiefs. He smiled at the shop girl. *"Pour vous, mam'selle.* So you won't forget me. *Au revoir,"* he said, and towed his mother along briskly, before the girl could thank him.

Another time he might have given them to his mother, but never again.

"Who was that girl, Mirdad?"

"Somebody innocent." *Like Kathryn.* He would make certain Kathryn survived his mother's foul plan before he returned to life in Paris. With thoughts of Kathryn his pulse skipped a beat then raced. There was no denying he would enjoy seeing her again. London might be dangerous, but not all bad.

CHAPTER TWELVE

IRAN

D ark and still, it was the moment that hovered between shadow and light, the precipice before night lifted and became the day. Anthony crouched low next to Ali, Tabriz, and Hans under the bridge leading up to the Iraqi border checkpoint. They would cross into Basra Provence as Islamic pilgrims on the road to Mecca for the Hajj, the Muslim pilgrimage to Mecca, the hoods of their robes pulled low over their faces, hoping to avoid the notice of Iraqi patrols carrying photos of wanted Iranian war criminals. Anthony waited for the right moment to climb the embankment.

His memories of the past churned against Iran's current bloody reality, brothers fighting against brothers. The Islamic Tribunal was now more vicious than the SAVAK. There were mock trials daily with hundreds sentenced to public executions. Fine statesmen such as Prime Minister Amir Hoveyda, a man of infinite charm and warmth, and Mrs. Farrokhrou Parsa, the Minister of Education, a brilliant woman whose work the Ayatollah should've been proud of, were hung instead. She had been a close friend of Anthony's mother. All a colossal miscarriage of justice, a waste.

Anyone could be accused of treason to Islam and was fair game. If Anthony had been caught, he'd have found himself on trial just for his friendship with the Shah. It was all so reminiscent of other revolutions throughout history, bloody and brutal. Only the luckiest would survive. His luck had nearly run out, but now his friends had given him a second chance, another life. He needed to get to a hotel, someplace in Iraq with a phone and arrange for a way home.

Anthony traveled light. Ali had furnished him with small tomes of poetry, Rumi, his favorites, Hafez, Byron. That was all he'd packed from the mountain, that and the name of his family's murderer. He would bide his time, but not for long.

"You must go first, Ali, with Hans. I'll follow," Anthony said.

"No!" Ali insisted. "I will not go if I cannot see you are safe."

"Humor this dead man, Ali, because I'm not moving until you're across. Besides, Hans' Farsi is so bad, he'd give himself away in a moment."

Anthony put his hands on Ali's shoulders. "I'm proud of the man you've become in the last few months, enduring hardships and taking on the responsibility."

Ali nodded, his mouth solemn. He'd gone down the mountain once every week to get supplies and never failed to bring food and clothing to families left stranded and homeless by the revolution. Anthony studied Ali's conflicted expression, loyalty versus safety.

"Your uncles wait for you on the other side, Ali," Tabriz said.

"Caution," Anthony said. "Fake documents could land you in an Iraqi prison."

Ali grimaced. "I'm no longer the impetuous student in Jaleh Square taunting the revolutionary guard . Not after what I've seen." He hugged Anthony and bade goodbye to Tabriz. He took off behind Hans, who'd made himself look more like a Persian than Tabriz, so long as he kept his blue eyes cast downward.

Crouched low and out of sight, Anthony watched their progress until they were through the checkpoint. He exhaled relief and turned to Tabriz, his voice low, "Goodbye, old friend. Promise you'll leave before the end comes. You know how to reach me."

Tabriz said, "I'll leave when I can do no more here. And when you find that swine Houdin, you must contact me. Houdin is mine."

"*Insha Allah*, you'll have a piece of him."

"The head." Tabriz laughed. "On the end of my sword."

Anthony embraced the man from whom he'd been given decades of tutelage and to whom he owed his life. "I am indebted to you, Tabriz, my brother."

Tabriz clasped his arm and nodded his head, looking

Anthony in the eye. "We are brothers."

Anthony left him and turned, climbing up to join the line of travelers passing through the checkpoint. His heart thumped with regret, rage, and despair for Iran. But he didn't look back at his battered country for his mind was already flooded with too many memories both joyous and tragic. He pressed forward, trekking toward the country of his roots and the commotion of a busy border crossing.

Jeeps were parked in a line with armed soldiers leaning against the cool metal frame talking. Two Iraqi soldiers manned the post, smoking filtered American cigarettes, scowling, probably wishing to be somewhere else this night.

"Papers, pilgrim," said the taller soldier.

Anthony handed over his new documents, his prayer beads held in his scarred right hand, his face shadowed by his hood.

"Look at me when I speak to you. Where are you headed?"

Anthony raised his head, senses heightened, his green gaze aimed downward. "I come to worship Allah, sir, for the holy days." He bobbed his head, his colloquial Arabic raspy.

"Go, then." The soldier waved him through.

Almost gagging on his relief, Anthony shuffled away quickly.

A dirty bus idled at the roadside and was being boarded by a line of travelers. Anthony hurried onto it and found a seat, his relief palpable, just as the bus, belching exhaust, took off for Baghdad.

Her private Learjet from Paris having just landed in Casablanca an hour ago, Rena whisked past Demi, who held the door for her, into their Moroccan villa library. She breezed past Omar, blowing him a kiss and snapping her fingers high in the air without looking back as servants followed with luggage and many Parisian shopping bags.

"In there," she said, setting her new Balenciaga handbag on his desk. The servants filed out and she turned to Omar who stood with his arms crossed over his powerful chest.

"Omar," she crooned. "In here." She whirled around at Demi who still held the door for her. "You, little thing. Out!"

She turned to Houdin and saw his pulse jump in his throat, his face flush in a rush of surprise, exhilaration, she guessed, her own excitement surging.

"Ah, my spectacular Rena." He laughed deep in his throat. "God, life is good! It holds such promise," he said, then glared at Demi.

"You heard the lady," Houdin's voice was raspier than usual. "Disappear, little thing."

Demi's eyes were great orbs of anger and humiliation. Cautious, she suspected, because he did not slam the door as she'd heard him do on the phone from Paris.

Rena minced into Omar's private apartment, and he followed. She removed her scarlet silk jacket, threw it across a plush sofa, and sniffed the air: Cuban cigars, scotch, and perhaps Omar's after-shave, Obsession for men. She paced around the room inspecting his domain, her face an impassive mask.

"Your eyes are like glimmers of smoking embers, Rena. Let me look at you," Houdin said, coming to her side. "Your new outfit is magnificent. Dior?"

She nodded. "It cost you."

His smile was predatory. "I've missed you."

She turned slowly to him, her hand moving up to his face, her petulant lips slightly parted.

He reached for her.

Some hours later Rena sat in her new silk robe with Omar on their terrace overlooking the pounding Atlantic Ocean, sipping chilled vintage Veuve Clicquot, loving the dusky breeze stirring damp hair from her warm neck. She refilled Omar's glass saying, "I enjoyed your friends in Paris, Jean Paul and his lovely wife Sylvie."

"Jean Paul is my financial adviser, first and foremost, Rena." He smiled. "Is his wife lovely, *joon-am*? I hadn't noticed."

She chuckled and ran a hand through his dark curls. "You know, Mirdad enjoys Paris, too."

"Mirdad? What does he have to do with this?"

She straightened. "Our son is not a warrior, my love. He is a scholar. Perhaps he should continue to work in Paris after the Glories belong to us."

"I have been deprived of my son for too many years, Rena. I want him by my side."

"You sent me to France."

"Yes, my darling." He reached into her peach silk robe caressing her breast. "So you could buy pretty things to charm me."

"As you wish, my love." *For now*, she thought, as a pounding came at the front door.

She listened, as a servant below admitted none other than "little thing," Colonel Nassiri.

"What is he doing back here?" she asked, standing and tying her robe closer around her body.

Omar patted her hand; a sly smile curved his full mouth. "He comes bearing gifts, *joon-am*. For you." Omar picked up the intercom. "Send the colonel up," he said, and Rena dashed into her dressing room.

She threw on a paisley silk caftan and stood watching as Demi presented Omar with a wooden crate about eighteen inches square.

"It is done, sir," Demi said.

Curious, Rena stepped out beside Omar. "What is that?" she asked.

"It is for you, my love. Open it," Omar said gesturing to a round glass table nearby where Demi placed his mysterious crated gift.

Rena tossed back her hair, lifted the crate's lid, and gasped, willing herself not to step back. She would not let Demi's antics cow her no matter how vile.

She steadied her gaze instead at the human severed head of a man, his eyes rolled back under his eyelids. His dark beard matted with blood, his cheeks sunken. And yet there was something she recognized.

She glared at Demi. "Is this some lunatic joke, Colonel?" She held her horror tightly inside, blood pounding in her head.

Omar came to her, wrapping an arm around her. "Ah, sweetheart, you do not recognize this face?"

She shook her head, breathing heavily.

"Meet Azi, your filthy blackmailer, never to trouble you again, *joon-am*."

"At least it's part of him," Demi smirked.

"And where is the rest?" Rena asked.

"Rotting in the desert sun, my love, like the lizard he was."

"Gone," she said. "Azi, gone forever from my life." *Gone. For twenty years I've had to pay him all the money Anthony sent each month—five thousand dollars every month, leaving me with barely enough to survive all those years in poverty.* She turned into Omar's supportive arms. "Oh, thank you, thank you, love of my life." She held him against her. "Thank you."

"You must thank Demetrius. He searched long and hard to do this deed for you, Rena."

She pulled back and composed herself, facing Demi.

"Colonel, perhaps I've underestimated your abilities." She nodded respectfully. "I thank you for your service to me and my husband. I will repay your resourcefulness," she assured Demi. "Now if you will excuse me." She walked to her dressing room thinking, *Demetrius Nassiri could be useful.*

Sitting at her mirror, Rena pondered her many years of regret over the sloppiness of her crime. She did not regret killing Ilyia or Richard, but the following twenty years of poverty and struggle, of becoming a social pariah, none of that was part of her plan. It had been embittering, horrid.

Her husband Valik, then Iran's prime minister, had been brought so low, was disgraced, had paid the ultimate price for shielding her—death. She hadn't counted on the scandal, nor her own fall from grace, to be no more a member of one of the top Iranian families. She had expected to inherit her sister's Persian Glories and to marry Omar. She was instead handed over to Valik's pious brothers to live with and to raise her son there. If not for Anthony buying her that little house on his twenty-first birthday, she would still have been trapped with Mirdad's unbearable uncles. But she'd had to scrimp to stay in the little house. And with Azi blackmailing her for murdering her sister, she had paid him his blood money. *Galling.*

Azi, the vermin, was now dead. She picked up her hairbrush, brushing out her thick tresses, and with every stroke she whisked away fear of ever being caught, of ever going to prison for her crime. She was free to flaunt her good fortune and rejoin society, even if it was in Paris. She slid her brush through the last stroke. *Free.*

Anthony's hand shook as he waited in the telephone booth at the hotel in Baghdad for the overseas operator to put through his collect call to his grandfather, and heard, "Yes, I'll accept the charges."

Hearing his grandfather's old raspy voice was a most

welcome sound. Anthony yearned for home, his thoughts vibrating with his desire.

"Good afternoon, sir," Anthony said.

There was silence.

"Grandfather, it's me. I am alive."

"My dear God, it *is* you! Anthony!" He heard the old man's voice crack and knew his own would, too.

"Yes, sir. I'm in Baghdad. But I need help getting back to England without calling attention to myself. Can that be arranged? I'm anxious to come home."

"Naturally, I'll take care of it on this end, my boy, but you must give me a few hours then call me back, unless I can reach you somewhere."

"I don't know yet where I'll be. It was Mirdad, sir. He ordered my death and everyone's on our property. He's Black Glove—an officer."

"You can't mean it? No."

"I'm going to make them pay."

"Then let no one know you are coming. Especially not Kathryn."

"Kathryn? You've seen her?"

"She's staying the weekend. She's marvelous. We've planned your photographic exhibition—in memoriam. She mustn't know you live. I mean it. Stay in the city for a few days, get acclimated."

"Thirty seconds," a voice announced.

"Expect my call in three hours, sir."

"I'm so glad, so glad, Anthony." For the first time in his life, Anthony heard his grandfather weep.

He waited for a moment. "Grandfather, there is something I must tell you, something you must know—" and the line went dead.

Hours later, huddled in a deserted Baghdad alleyway, Anthony waited in dusky light alongside a mud-caked concrete building. A dirty Range Rover pulled up next to him and MI-6 agent Jess Hartmann stepped into view, squinting through the dust. "Took you long enough to get out," Jess said. "Thought the Iranians had you."

Relief flooded through Anthony. He embraced his friend and contact for over a year since the first week his Iranian missions began.

"We're for home?" Anthony said.

"On our way. Get in," Jess said.

Anthony leaned back, the efficient Rover eating up tarmac, his eyes at half mast, his excitement boundless at the thought of England growing nearer, peaceful, green, and welcoming. His grandfather, Philippe, and of course, the shining star on his horizon, Kathryn, his beauty.

They'd driven for miles when Jess said, "Wasn't sure you'd made it. No one was."

"Didn't know myself."

"Good to see you, mate." Jess kept his gaze on the road. "You look a bit roughed up though."

For the last twenty-four hours Anthony had ignored the irritating pain riddling his body. The burning, tightening skin and fused bones still healing, but the sand chafing inside his clothes was the worst.

"I'm sure you thought this a disguise, my white, rough hands, scars, the unruly mane. But this is what I look like now—a fucking beast."

"Seen worse," Jess said.

Kathryn was in England! Not in the States as he had pictured her. His memories, a banquet of her image he'd clung to: flying together over the twilight desert, stars strewn across a purple sky, hands full of each other, laughing, touching, lying with her in a grotto, limbs entwined, her silky skin sliding over his, their need building...He longed to go to her and entice her to come back to him. He didn't fear his enemies or the revolution, not the Turks, nor the Iraqis. Only, he admitted, his heart seizing, finding Kathryn could no longer love him. She thought him dead. Everyone did.

Once again, he wondered, had she found someone else with whom she could ease her sorrow? The notion pressed in on his chest, constricting, and jealousy stabbed his heart. But scores had to be settled, because if ignored, his soul would never be free. He must remain under the cloak of his death, an invisible man, and he must act quickly before being recognized somewhere.

This last week, Hans had finally shown Anthony the Iranian and English newspapers he had saved until they were ready to leave.

"The world knew renowned photographer and jet-setting bachelor was still missing, or worse," Hans had said. He'd handed Anthony the latest copy.

News of his presumed death had trickled into L.A. papers and trades. Pictures of the deceased Anthony Evans had been splashed everywhere. Too much publicity for him to feel safe.

They reached London after midnight. Anthony was dropped off as planned, anxious to reconnect with his best friend, to shower and stretch out in a real bed. Jess stopped the car at the top of the mews behind Philippe's posh Mayfair gallery apartment and said, "Hear me out."

Anthony reined in his need to shed itchy clothes and listened.

Jess explained. "Kathryn, Lord Charles, and Philippe paid me a visit at MI-6 home office with a strategy to catch your killers."

"And?" Curiosity and alarm sizzled inside him.

Jess nodded, his smirk crooked. "It's in the works."

"No," Anthony groaned. More than ever he was determined to have a discussion with Philippe.

"Rena and Mirdad were seen in Paris," Jess said.

"Paris. So close."

"And Houdin is staying in a Casablanca villa at the moment."

"What is this plan?" Anthony was sweating.

"An exhibition honoring the Persian Suite, photographs by Anthony Evans—in memoriam, followed by the grand December charity ball. It's all planned for later this month.

The infamous canary diamonds, the Persian Glories, will be worn by your Kathryn as a lure and..."

Anthony listened to a scheme he thought risky, one he bet his daredevil-love Kathryn embraced. Rena would not stop until she gained the jewels and had gotten rid of Kathryn. She had eliminated everyone else blocking her way. He'd come in time, he hoped, to grab Rena and save Kathryn. He gave Jess a scowl. Jess looked amused.

"Don't worry, mate. We'll have our top security guys there," Jess paused. "There's another matter, however. Philippe arrived at MI-6 overwrought, shaking, his eyes bloodshot. He went on about a missing shipment from Iran. Word on the street is Philippe's gambling again. He's in deep. Drinking, too. He said a freighter carrying cargo you two packed on his last night in Iran, Middle Eastern treasures and what not, has mysteriously gone missing. What is it about this cargo that has Philippe dithered?"

Anthony leaned back, feeling bludgeoned by the news. Volatile scenes replayed in his head. "The night Kathryn and I were attacked by Komiteh militia at Tahkt-e Tavoos, I later joined Philippe at the warehouse. The 'what not' we crated included renaissance chests, Ming vases, Regency armoires, a Rolls Royce, you name it. Everything was stuffed with currency. Including pallets of cash layered between Tibetan rugs, enough to finance a London bank."

"Billions?"

"I'd say."

"We've tracked the freighter en route to Casablanca," Jess said. "So that's why Houdin got his hooks into the shipment."

Anthony frowned at the news. "Iranian immigrants are counting on that shipment to survive."

"And so it seems is Philippe?"

Anthony recoiled. "No, he's not a thief. He earns substantial, legitimate fees brokering the shipment when it gets here."

"Yeah, enough to cover his gaming vowels? I wonder. Until he pays off those I.O.U.s, Philippe's fair game for London's worst thugs." Jess cocked his head. "So Philippe's after the shipment and London's seamy underworld is after Philippe. These guys are mean."

Anthony and Jess traded looks. Both were acquainted with the thugs Philippe was up against. No laughing matter. *Damn it, Philippe!* Anthony thought. *You're better than this.*

Anthony started out of the car, but Jess grabbed his arm. "They're watching, Anthony. They won't let Philippe out of their sight. The shylock collecting the VIG has eyes on him, too."

"Better hope they don't get wind of the shipment." Keeping his voice low, Anthony added, "Pitting London's mob against Black Glove terrorists could start an international crisis."

"I'll keep my home office out of it, mate."

"Thanks, Jess, for everything." Anthony steadied himself, getting his bearings, reaching for a sense of the familiar. "And here I thought I'd returned to a modicum of serenity."

Anthony stepped out of the Rover and scanned the darkness, a habit now. He leapt over a fence, climbed the fire escape, easing through a second-floor window. It had been easy, too easy. Philippe needed to be more careful. Thugs holding hefty gaming vowels were apt to slice Philippe good as a warning. Time to confront his friend.

Anthony closed and locked the window and pressed his back to the wall listening. He needed Philippe to hide him for a few days even with the risk of discovery.

Sounds from the first floor rose, and he peered over the gallery balcony. Below in the spacious showroom, splashed with light, was Philippe, his tawny hair shot with gold flopped over his furrowed, concentrating brow. Philippe was working late. His wonderland of fine European Art Nouveau and Art Deco furniture, glass, lighting, and fine art, a collector's paradise, was filled with pieces Philippe had moved heaven and earth to acquire.

Here refinement surrounded Anthony. A sharp divergence from a Kash'kai mountain stronghold, three months of hiding surrounded by a dozen rough tribesmen, their leader, one ex-Marine, and a gangly student of twenty-two just finding his way. His mountain family had forced him to survive and to look forward, never back.

But now below him stood his past, his childhood friend, tall, taller than he was, blond, with a look of civil grace, a casually refined Englishman who held his undying loyalty. But Anthony felt raw, out of place, his primal instincts honed, hardened and dark.

He gripped the knife he carried in his pocket and knew if need be, he'd not hesitate to use it to save Philippe from some thug.

He breathed in, the fresh scent of polish filling his head with a complex citrus verbena blend. He watched Philippe polish a stunning Jules Lela dressing table, bringing up a rich patina from beautifully veined Macassar ebony. The clean aroma brought back memories of growing up with his friend and how rewarding it felt seeing him care for his art instead of slumped over a roulette table, soused to his ears.

Anthony shifted his weight and the wood floor creaked, echoing through the upper gallery. In the silence it could've been a tree falling.

Below, Philippe spun toward the sound. He made a beeline for the alarm system, setting it. He pulled out his handkerchief, dabbing his forehead and grabbed a pointed letter opener from a desk.

Anthony faded away from the balcony into the shadows, hearing Philippe check doors and windows. Philippe was right to be scared.

He headed into Philippe's second floor office to wait, knowing Philippe would follow the sound. He sat at his friend's desk, flipped on a small Daum lamp, and heard footsteps.

Philippe came in a moment later and paused in the dimly lit office doorway. His gaze dropped to the pair of worn leather boots propped on his desk. He grimaced.

"Hello, old man," Anthony said. "Working late, are we?"

"Who's there?" Silence. "That voice...it can't be."

Anthony rose. "That's a poor greeting for someone who's come back from the dead."

He was bathed in shadows, probably fierce looking with his long black hair, full beard and unsightly scars. He heard Philippe's sharp intake of breath.

"How can it be?" Philippe's head craned forward. "My God! It's you!" He rushed to Anthony's side, gripping him in a bear hug. He felt Philippe choke up and suck in air, steadying himself. "You devil! I should have known you were too contentious to die."

Anthony held on to him, an onslaught of emotion swept him to his great surprise, emotion he thought he'd ground to ashes. Welling up, he eased away and pressed the heels of his palms against his eyes. *He may not be safe, but he was in England.*

CHAPTER THIRTEEN

Anthony waited until Philippe had composed himself before he explained. "Jess from MI-6 sped my journey through Iraq and into England, slipping me in through the back door, shall we say? I came to you first."

"Does Charles know?"

"Yes. I called him from Baghdad."

"He didn't say a word."

"He wouldn't. He doesn't want anyone to know. Not you. Not even Kathryn."

"My God! Why not?"

"Look. I'll explain it all after I get cleaned up. I'm longing for a proper shower."

"Of course. Help yourself."

While Anthony showered and changed into Philippe's clean, pressed clothes, the pants too long, the shirt a bit tight, Philippe made tea, much to Anthony's surprise, and served it with sandwiches in his salon by a warm fire.

As he sat there, Anthony watched his friend's face register a thousand feelings telling the events that had happened since their last phone call. It seemed like years ago.

"So the old man put it all together. We've learned that Rena has joined forces with her new husband, my biggest fan, Omar Houdin. And my grandfather figures Rena will make an attempt to take the Persian Glories."

"The most opportune time, the night of the exhibit," said Philippe.

"And she'll have Houdin's manpower to carry it out."

Philippe stroked his unshaved chin. "Our one ace in the hole is they both think you're dead."

Anthony paced, restless, his gaze traveled around the room lighting on a wall of photographs, records of events in Philippe's life and therefore his as well. Raindrops tattooed an uneven rhythm against the windowpane, and with each beat familiarity of his years in England seeped into him, their time at Eton, Cambridge, and Philippe's gallery on opening night. He spotted a photo framed in ivory of his father and Tabriz in Iran. Behind them stood three smiling boys—Philippe, himself, and Mirdad. How life had been reshaped, distorted.

Philippe sipped his tea. "I hadn't realized how cocked up my life was until I forced myself to put down the bottle."

He'd been told all this but let Philippe speak, knowing he needed to come clean on his own. Anthony stood, leaning against the mantel, his leg stiff and aching with the damp weather, a constant reminder of his objective, while he heard Philippe's anxiety over the missing shipment and the frustration with the Iranian families hammering him for answers.

"And you can't collect fees until we secure the shipment." Anthony fingered the knife in his pocket.

"I gave up the dream of a New York showroom. I'm broke."

"Houdin," Anthony said. "He's got our shipment."

"You sure?"

"No. But he's set himself up in Casablanca, so it makes sense. And where there's Houdin, Mirdad will be close by." Anthony focused on the dartboard attached to Philippe's door. He pictured Mirdad's fake smile and threw his knife. It whizzed past Philippe's head.

Philippe glanced behind him. "Good throw. Haven't seen you do that since we were boys."

"I've been practicing." Anthony studied his friend. "Don't worry. We'll deal with the shipment and have Mirdad, Rena, the lot of them arrested and sent back to Iran's tribunal." Anthony sat across from his friend.

Philippe raised his cup. "I will celebrate that day."

"I'm proud of your restraint," Anthony said. "But this time lives depend on your resolve or you could get us all killed. Can you stay the course?"

Philippe steadied his gaze on the glowing embers. "I've mucked it up again, I know. But I'm determined."

Anthony nodded. "I know what demons are like, Philippe." The scum who had pursued him toppled a nation, trampled its beautiful culture and murdered Persia's finest citizens. "But I'll pursue them in the dark, as long as they think I'm dead."

Philippe ran his fingers through his hair, looking Anthony over.

"You're a bit messed up, old man. Skin pale as a blanched chestnut, those scars, pirate-like. Your eyebrow slice—that's a beauty. And your hand. Is this the lot of it?"

"The worst is under my clothes."

"How bad?"

Anthony stood and yanked off his shirt.

A flash of horror filled Philippe's eyes and was gone as quickly.

"They nailed me."

"Hope you had some good drugs."

"For a few weeks until Tabriz weaned me off. I howled but fought harder to get well." An unpleasant sensation took over when cool air touched the bullet wounds in Anthony's shoulder. Burns down his right side puckered angrily. Nonetheless memories made him stay away from the fire. There was no comfort zone.

"That's most of it," he said, pacing again.

"Not as bad as I'd feared." Philippe cleared his throat. "I can't tell you how sorry I am about Raymond and Tali. I loved them, too."

"You know Raymond defended Mirdad to the end. His affection ran deep for that sod."

"You know my feelings about Mirdad." Philippe frowned and grabbed the poker, sorting out the fire's embers, adding another log. An ember popped and Anthony cringed. He put the shirt back on and glanced down.

A copy of *Harpers Queens*, tossed on an end table, caught his eye. The cover shot of Kathryn boldly wearing the jewels he'd given her blinded him. He picked it up and scanned the article inside. A half-page of stills Anthony had taken on the first day of shooting at Persepolis caught him by surprise. He was thrown back in time.

A torrential downpour covered Persepolis and shooting stopped. Canvas tarps were launched, rustling over equipment and 200 extras with their mounts withstanding the deluge. At this rate the ground would turn to sodden mud, and the shoot would be lost. They waited it out, soaked and shaking, prepared for the worst. But in the next moment the sun burst through, scattering storm clouds, spreading its rays like honey over a brioche, bathing the desert floor in gold.

Tarps were yanked off, extras cued, and cameras rolled. And as he heard Kathryn shout, "Action," a massive rainbow arched overhead in vivid hues. The footage rivaled that of Lawrence of Arabia.

He longed to be with her now.

Anthony turned to face Philippe. "His lordship insists Kathryn and I could never carry on a charade once we get near each other. So I haven't spoken with her."

"Charles is right," Philippe said. "Kathryn may hate me for this, but there's no way she could pretend to be grief stricken if she suspects you're alive. And you'd probably endanger her as well."

"Judas!"

"You know I'm right."

"Then you're to be my eyes and ears around her, Philippe."

"That much I can do."

"Philippe, you've changed. What's happened to you? You've lost your poker face." Anthony surprised himself as his voice broke.

He listened as Philippe candidly admitted to his gambling folly, instigated by his drinking. Drinking brought on partly by the thought that Anthony was dead.

Shifting, uncomfortable hearing of the twists and turns of events in Philippe's decline, Anthony realized his friend was afraid. "Who, Philippe, are you afraid of?"

"His name is Thorne. He's a violent prick who has others do his dirty work. I owe him money."

Anthony was on a first name basis with treachery. He recognized it well. 'We'll sort it out. I promise." He poured himself a generous snifter of Remy Martin and said, "Tell me about her, Philippe. I need to know."

"It's been rough going for us all. I had to tell her you were dead, you know. It was ironic. Just moments before, she'd received flowers from you. It left her totally devastated. As could have been predicted knowing Kathryn, she ran away from me out into a ghastly lightning storm. I found her unconscious near a tree in Hyde Park."

Anthony's heart nearly stopped. "Is she all right?"

"Yes, yes, but since then it's been grim for her, for all of us. But for Kathryn, it's been as if life had drained out of her. Her ex fired her off the Boeing shoot, and she's been like a shadow."

Anthony stood. *The prick, he would...He wasn't finished with Brett.*

"But I must say," Philippe went on, "working on her documentary and your exhibit seems to have brought her back to life. The whole exhibit was her idea, you know."

"No, I didn't know."

"Now that I think of it, you really have been a giant pain in the ass for all of us, and I for one am damned upset with you." Philippe poured more tea. "In fact, I don't know why I'm even speaking to you."

"Then maybe I shouldn't ask to stay here till tomorrow night?"

"Tomorrow night?"

Anthony smirked. "You don't expect a ghost to move about in the daytime, do you?"

CHAPTER FOURTEEN

Anthony awoke before dawn, his tortured dreams of revenge fading as he shook his head. An acute need to reveal to his grandfather what he'd learned on the mountain set him into action. He had changed his mind. Plans for retribution couldn't wait.

He swung his legs out of bed, planted his feet on the floor, taking a moment to gain his footing. In one off guard moment desire for his woman tore at him, the need to hold her in his arms, to breath in her scent. He would beg on his knees just to see her face.

No matter. Impossible.

Shoving away the need, he dressed quickly, penned Philippe a note, and set out in darkness.

Heavy fog shifted around him like restless ghosts of those he'd lost. He climbed on a bus to Paddington Station, and took a train bound for Buckinghamshire, the verdant familiar scenery eating at his heart, as he felt loss, regret, and longing for family.

He walked up his grandfather's long drive at Edyton Manor, hands dug in his pockets, his face stinging from the morning chill and rapped on the massive door, tucking away his anxiety over their first meeting since his return. He wasn't expected for two days yet.

Wiggins, the butler, swung the door open, his face almost impassive as he said, "Welcome, your lordship." Wiggins' glance skimmed over Anthony's different appearance. "If you'll wait in the foyer, sir, I'll bring tea."

Anthony breached all etiquette and hugged him.

He waited outside his grandfather's study in the three-story marble and paneled mahogany foyer. He sat on a padded bench by a tiny table polishing off his second cup of tea and his favorite breakfast, a ham and egg sandwich, the first English food he'd eaten in over a year.

Breaking the ghastly facts surrounding his parents' death was all he could think about. Wiggins opened the door to his grandfather's book-lined study. "He'll see you now, sir." Anthony put down his napkin, took a breath, and entered.

Lord Charles Evans paced, his anticipation apparent.

"Sir." Anthony's beard was trimmed but full, his long hair, cleaned of yak butter, was tied back in a queue. His face weathered by scars added to the hardened expression he'd seen for himself, but the happiness at seeing his grandfather was huge. He waited for the surprise to abate.

"My, you are in disguise. Right off a Kash'kai desert."

Lord Charles opened his arms and Anthony closed the distance, hugging this beloved man. "My boy, you're back from the dead." His grandfather wept as he held him.

Anthony felt him shaking and didn't want to let go. He was home. Home.

An hour later, Anthony sat with Lord Evans in his study after relating the tale of how Rena murdered his parents, her method a bomb, and her unrelenting treachery in the years following. He waited for his grandfather to absorb a shocking and painful answer to the mystery that had haunted him over thirty years before going over his plan.

Charles got up and paced the carpet, puffing on a Cuban cigar while digesting the information, his jaw tight. "So Rena was the one. Not her current husband, the general, and not some mysterious saboteur. Rena had my son killed."

"She instigated unspeakable acts for a handful of cold, dead stones thinking they'd be hers." Anthony couldn't shake off the revulsion. The library filled with smoke, burning his eyes. He waved a hand in front of his face, his mind narrowing in on a way to handle Rena.

"I don't see you smoking anymore," Charles said. "I have acquired an aversion to smoke."

Charles' eyes widened. "Of course you have. Thoughtless of me, sorry." He stubbed out his cigar. "Come, let's walk."

Donning heavy jackets and boots, they tramped out across the lawn into the late autumn woodlands behind the manor, piecing their collective information of hideous events into perspective. The ground, blanketed with bronze, orange, and beige oak leaves, crunched and scattered underfoot. Anthony breathed in fresh English air, redolent with sweet clematis, verbena, and new moss. They tromped ahead through a sodden pasture, stepping over a broken fence and continuing down the estate lane skirting the Crown's Head Pub where they might have been seen.

"I hear a bitter need for retribution in your words, lad." Charles shook his head. "I feel it, too. She murdered my son and your beautiful mother. Now she knows where the diamonds are. How she must covet them." Charles stopped, puffing heavily, his breath expelling in steaming gusts.

"You all right, sir?"

Lord Charles put his hand on Anthony's arm, bracing himself, breathing deeply. All at once, he straightened and nodded, appearing renewed. "Don't fret."

"Grandfather, unless Mirdad and his vile mother are stopped, our family will never survive."

"I'm counting on it. I paid five hundred quid apiece for their tickets to the ball." With a smug smile, he pulled the envelope from his jacket and tossed it to Anthony. "Naturally, I insisted Rena and Mirdad come as my guests."

Anthony read the gold embossed invitations and slid them back into his grandfather's pocket.

"They'll be couriered to the Savoy's concierge."

"A gracious gentleman indeed!"

Charles grinned, leaned into Anthony. "Willingly playing into her conniving hands."

Anthony smiled. "Lock them away once and for all."

Charles raised his gloved fists to the sky, as branches swayed on the breeze, leaves shimmered with sunlight, and clouds danced overhead. "Oh, lucky day! You are home."

Anthony threw his head back, laughing for the first time in months at his grandfather's delight.

Charles held firm to his grandson's arm. "You must listen when I tell you. Go back to London today. Kathryn is coming for tea to go over arrangements for the ball. She'll stay the night."

"She'll be here? I might see her?"

"Absolutely not! The only way our plan works is for you to remain a ghost to everyone, if not Philippe then especially Kathryn." Charles lowered his voice. "You cannot be involved with her before the ball, or all will be lost. I know you, and I now know Kathryn."

Anthony agreed they would of course be too consumed with each other to ever pull this off. If she still loved him when she saw the beast he'd become. Injuries to his skin and bones were not all of it. He'd been scorched deep inside, charred. Perhaps too damaged for her to love.

Lord Charles went on, "Kathryn has spent other weekends at Edyton Hall since she forgave my rude behavior towards her with MI6 at Heathrow, and I've enjoyed every visit." He stopped in front of his grandson. "She set up the initial meeting with Jess at MI6 herself. She is clever and determined." He paused. "But your visit today was not my idea. And I'm incredibly uneasy about even the suggestion of you being here when she arrives." He rushed ahead. "The two of you together under one roof. Harrumph."

Anthony caught up. "I promise to behave, sir."

"I doubt you're strong enough to stay away from her, to stay hidden."

"What? Am I an intruder in my own home?"

His grandfather halted. "Really, Anthony."

"Fine. I'll leave after dark then. I can't risk being seen in the village in daylight. Please trust me, Grandfather."

"If you were not such a hot head, showing up two days early unannounced, I could have avoided this situation entirely."

"I've calmed down."

"It's remarkable how fond I've become of Kathryn in so short a time. She's been a comfort to me."

Anthony's pride swelled. "Unavoidable, she's—"

"You know, I'm bursting with pride to think of what a magnificent couple you two will be when the time comes."

Anthony put his arm around his grandfather's shoulders and allowed a portion of the love he felt for him to penetrate his own hardened heart.

A few hours later, Anthony sat at his open bedroom window overlooking the park-like drive up to the manor, his mouth dry. He watched for the moment Kathryn would arrive, remembering his grandfather's strong words. Stay hidden. He'd promised and his goal was to keep that promise. *Soon he would see her.*

He reached for his water glass, sipping slowly, and heard a car approach. His adrenalin surged seeing the midnight blue Daimler pull up below.

He set down the glass and stood, vertigo assailing him, and sought his balance with his cane, watching as she emerged from the car. *Could he really stay away?* He had sworn he could. But as her long shapely legs and beautiful body came into view he was not so sure.

Her hair was pulled sleekly from her face, coiled at the base of her head. He grabbed his binoculars, wanting desperately to see every detail of her face. There she was, lovely, so sad. *My God!* His chest tightened when he saw the anguish in her eyes. He clenched his fists, wanting only to go to her.

Out of the question.

She suddenly looked up at his window, and he jumped away. With his eyes closed, he struggled to remember what must be done. And when it was done, they'd be together. For now, patience. Keep her safe.

He turned back to the window and heard the front door open. His grandfather, followed by Wiggins, came out to greet her, something Lord Charles rarely did. "Lovely to have you here, Kathryn."

Kathryn hugged him and handed over a white-handled bakery bag. "The drive out was breathtaking on this clear day."

He held up her bag. "What have you brought this time?"

"Scones from Hummingbird off Beauchamp Place, and the pear tarts you like."

"My dear, so thoughtful," his grandfather said, hugging Kathryn back. "We'll have a sumptuous tea, and you'll tell me how plans for the ball are proceeding." Charles handed Wiggins the bakery goods and called for tea. He offered her his arm. "Shall we?" he said as they entered the foyer.

Above in stocking feet, Anthony moved quickly to his bedroom door, quietly stepping out onto the shadowed gallery, listening for Kathryn's voice in the foyer below.

What was he thinking? He braced himself against the gallery wall, his heart pounding. After three months in the mountains in the company of men who wore weapons and grunted a lot, the sight of her fragility stunned him. The love he felt triggered an overpowering desire to hold her, have her.

Downstairs, Charles ushered her toward the blue drawing room reserved for honored guests. Anthony started to turn away and heard, "Rena and Mirdad are coming to the ball," Charles told Kathryn, as she glided into the salon. Their voices faded as the door shut behind them, closing off further eavesdropping.

Those words slammed Anthony's goal back to center and dissolved his doubt. He glanced at the closed doors. *He must keep his promise to stay in the shadows.*

Inside the blue salon, Charles offered Kathryn a comfortable Damask chair facing the garden, her knee touching the tea table. News the doctor had just told her bubbled inside. She was almost three months pregnant with Anthony's child—a child doctors had told her she could never have after she lost Brett's baby. *Her miracle baby must remain secret until after the ball.*

Kathryn couldn't help smiling. Although she was bursting to tell, the news must be kept from Lord Charles for now or he'd never agree to her wearing the Persian Glories to lure Anthony's killers. Instead she was here to get the staggering budget for the event approved.

Hands folded in her lap, she enjoyed the soft breeze wafting into the perfect blue drawing room so like one her mother would decorate in varied shades of blue silk velvet, and a Delft pottery, linen print.

Charles sat across from her and looked up saying, "Here's our tea now."

Wiggins glanced at her discreetly from under hooded eyelids, and served tea astutely in a long, steady stream from a stunning old Tiffany service.

She caught the fragrant aroma, Earl Grey, her mother's tea. Homesick? Yes, she was, a bit, but her goal was to rid the world of the monsters who had killed her baby's father. She gazed at Charles, who regarded her kindly, and they both dug their forks into yummy pear tarts, so good, and sipped tea.

"Charles, our December ball is in less than two weeks and I'm reluctant to tell you the budget has reared its greedy head. I need to discuss costs."

"Really? Ummm. These tarts are scrumptious." Wiggins served him another. "And you brought so many."

She chuckled, knowing her appetite had increased. "You don't sound too concerned about the amounts, but with all the tenting and whatnot..."

"My dear, any second thoughts?" he said softly. "With you and Samantha handling the budget, I'm not worried. Make it wonderful. This will be after all, the last tribute to my grandson." He cleared his throat. "In other words, I approve, whatever it costs. Oh, and by the way, Samantha and Emmaline will be by later to fetch you for a little shopping in the village if you approve."

Kathryn buried a reminder of her own grief and said, "I'd love to go."

Charles glance slid to the tea tray. "Shall we try a steaming scone?"

"Yes, let's." If only the ad execs she worked with were this agreeable. The thought of Wally Brandt shouting over the Boeing budget sprang to mind. She wiped away the image with a dollop of clotted cream and a scoop of strawberry preserves over her warm scone, savoring blended flavors.

Teatime was to enjoy, after all. Security worries she'd leave until dinnertime.

CHAPTER FIFTEEN

It had grown late as the hours ticked by and sleep eluded Anthony, his need to see Kathryn churned within him. He rose from his bedroom chair and let himself out into the silent hall. Stealthily, he came to her door and listened. Satisfied, he tried the handle. It was unlocked.

He entered, and gently slid back the drapes; moonlight bathed her sleeping form. He stood protectively above her, drinking in the features of her astonishingly lovely face. He wanted to touch her cheek but wouldn't. She stirred on a sigh and turned, tugging the duvet away from one shapely leg. He felt his own strong intake of breath at the sight. Aching to take her in his arms, he backed away. Time to go. Covering her, he crept silently from the room, closing the door.

He leaned his head against the door jam, frustrated, his emotions building to a fervor. Damn, damn, damn! He wanted to be with her! He closed his eyes, his fists clenched against the heat building inside. Love and lust warred in him, a desire to take her here, now. He shuddered, gripping his will, clutching on to his last shred of decency.

No, he could never have ravaged the one remaining lovely thing in his life, could he? What had he become?

He heard a noise and looked up. His grandfather stood at the end of the hallway outside his suite. Anthony nodded and joined him inside.

"I won't have this, do you hear?" His grandfather seethed.

He had sworn to his grandfather he could stay away, but now he was not so sure.

"You are not to go near her!" His grandfather furiously paced the room. "I agreed to have you here so you could see she's all right," he said and turned abruptly. "That's our bargain. You will stay away!" He ran his hand through his silver hair. "Anthony, neither Kathryn nor you are safe until this is over. Do you really wish to jeopardize her?"

"I'll always protect her." Anthony turned away, wanting desperately to scream into the night. It was too much for him. Why did he think he could do this? "Then I'll leave for Casablanca and the shipment tonight."

"No! You will remain until after the exhibition! Control your blasted temper and come back here at once!"

"I can't." Anthony flew from the room.

He needed to be outside. He grabbed his boots and ran downstairs, his uneven gait barely slowing him, out into the brisk night.

A full moon illuminated his path to the stables, where he heard his Arabian stallion whinnying. He bridled Darius, coaxing him outside with gentle words, and pulled himself onto the horse's strong, bare back.

He rode with a violent energy through heavy woods, branches smacking together above him, the strong scent of English woodlands filling his head. *Kathryn, you are mine! I want you. God! I need you.* He wanted to break down the door and carry her away with him.

He galloped like a wild man up the side of the hill above the manor, frustration damning him. *This is my house, my woman, and I can't take her! Mirdad, you bastard! This is all your doing.* He galloped harder up to the top and reined to a stop, Darius rearing on his hind legs, whinnying wildly, in touch with Anthony's violent emotions. He stroked his horse's neck, a gesture to calm them both.

Feeling a pull from the manor, Anthony looked back. Kathryn stood at her window, silhouetted in moonlight. For a brief moment she looked up, and he knew she was everything to him. His rage subdued, his torment stilled. A smile twitched on his lips, and he took off across the hillside. The night was textured by elements, the air crackled with energy. The moon, so full, was accompanied by a coterie of filmy clouds, which never quite crossed its path.

He was part of this night and the wind, free for this short time from punishing restraints. Far enough away from the manor, he let out a cry of joy. I've seen my love, and she is safe, safe in my house! When this is over, I'll choose my path, with my woman beside me. No longer your prisoner, you bastards. Your time grows shorter, your destiny sealed by your own hand.

"Mirdad, Houdin, I'm coming for you! And you, witch!"

Kathryn had awakened, alert, perceiving something. Was it a dream? Intrigued by radiant moonglow spilling into her room, she was drawn to the window. She fought with the latch until it opened. The air seemed to pulse, vibrate. She stared, transfixed, At the top of the moonlit hill, a lone horseman reigned in his horse. It reared, front legs high, then pawed the ground restlessly. The rider turned her way. And for a moment she thought—Anthony. They stared at each other, unable to move. Then he'd gone. She'd reached out, but there was only air.

Still she remained for several minutes, her heart thumping, regret gnawing at her stomach. So she returned to her bed, curling her body into a tight ball of sadness.

At the manor stables, Anthony cooled down Darius and put him away, grooming him with sweeping strokes, crooning a Persian song and feeding him extra oats before he went inside the manor.

CHAPTER SIXTEEN

Anthony showered, left a note for his grandfather, and made his way to London, climbing over Mayfair rooftop gardens back to Philippe's apartment. This time he entered the terrace door with a key Philippe had given him. In the cozy guest room he slept like the dead for a day and a half and then woke, dressed quickly, and went to his meeting.

Across town in the basement of a pub owned by Hans's uncle off Piccadilly Circus, Anthony met with his team: Jess, Hans, Ali, Philippe, and eight other MI-6 security specialists. On the night of the ball, a larger group of plainclothes officers would surround the Savoy perimeter. The men here, however, were Anthony's inside team.

"You won't see the Black Glove bastards until they strike, Jess." Hans drew his hand across his throat. "Like that, you're dead."

Jess squinted. "Assassins."

They sat around a well-worn planked table voicing their views on this op. Paper cones previously filled with fish and chips and half empty bottles of vinegar and red sauce littered the table.

Philippe had arrived an hour late. He had received more threats over his gambling debts and was a shaky wreck.

Anthony tossed Philippe a pastry box of sugary buns and handed him a mug of steaming coffee. This was not the first time he'd helped his friend get sober.

Two of Jess' men got up and removed the mess to an unused bar against the wall, crumbs wiped away. Glasses of ale remained on the table.

"Scumbag terrorists can't pull this shit in London," said Jess. "Steal the Persian Glories."

"Not with us on the case," said another of Jess' men.

"We've got your back, mate," said another.

"Fuck 'em!" Hans said, and ale glasses clinked in a toast around the table.

Anthony unfolded a schematic and smoothed it out over the table. Together they scanned every floor on the Savoy layout, memorizing each entrance, exit, elevator bank, stairwell, and loading dock, deciding who would be stationed where, going over a timeline, and from street to basement tested their walkie-talkies.

Hans tapped his square-tipped finger on the blueprint. "Ten quid says the getaway will be here." He pointed at the basement loading dock. He stretched his neck, lacing his hands together behind his head.

"Agreed. It's their only safe exit point," Anthony said. "But we'll still have to cover the Savoy's front entrance."

"It won't be safe when we get there," Ali said, no longer appearing like a boyish student in his gray turtleneck sweater. He caught Anthony looking at him and nodded as if to say, *Yes, I grew strong on the mountain, too.*

Anthony smiled. "Only three of the nine elevators go to the basement." He indicated the locations. "The main lobby elevator, manned by a uniformed operator, a back janitorial service elevator and one off the kitchen."

"Two men will cover each," Jess said.

"Philippe," Anthony said, "Kathryn must never be out of your sight. Jess's man Tim will be your counterpart."

"Tim?" Philippe said.

Pounding footsteps on the stairs brought all heads up around the table.

"Here's Tim," Jess said. "What've you got, mate?"

Tim unzipped his weathered bomber jacket and smoothed back his red curly hair. Like all Jess's men he was well built, trained in martial arts.

"Bad news," Tim said. "Chief says we can't arrest General Houdin or his wife."

"What?" Anthony couldn't believe this. "Why not?"

"Diplomatic immunity for both him and the Mrs. He's the governor of Teheran, appointed by the Shah."

"Houdin is the Shah's enemy." Anthony's voice lowered.

"Not officially." Tim scooted in on the bench next to Hans. "Oh, and that goes for his son Mirdad, too."

"Son of a bitch," Hans said and glugged down his lager. "If we can't arrest them, we take 'em out."

That comment from Hans quieted the room.

Anthony shrugged. "Ex-Marine, black ops." But his

look urged Hans' restraint.

"Ajani is a stepson," Ali said. "His father, not Houdin, was one of Iran's finest prime ministers."

Tim shook his head. "Sorry, mate, sources confirmed Mirdad Ajani is General Houdin's natural son."

Anthony scooted back, his chair scraping the rough floor. He listened in shock.

Tim leaned in. "The general has always known it and has recently recognized him as such."

"This can't be true!" Ali blurted out.

"Hold on," Tim said. "Word is Mama thought to marry Houdin after her husband died in Quar prison." Tim smirked. "By that time she was soaked in scandal, and Houdin wouldn't marry her. Afraid she'd ruin his career ambitions. Wanted to keep her around, though. She wasn't keen on that plan." He shrugged. "This year she got what she wanted, new husband, son, all together."

Anthony's ears rang, his vision blurred, images weaving before him, lifelong images of Mirdad as his tag-along little cousin, memories he'd thought had dissolved. He clutched the table edge. *On a dais at Golestan Palace, a small boy stood proudly by his father, a valued scholar and statesman—not a thieving terrorist.* Shreds of sentiment wound through him. How could he feel for this cur? He hated him.

"Anthony, he does not know Houdin is his father," Ali said. "Of this I'm sure. But I would love to be the one to tell him."

"If Mirdad pulls this heist off," Jess said. "I'll haul his arse in. End of story."

Murmurs of agreement came from both sides of the table.

An hour later they'd gone over the plan to everyone's satisfaction and split up.

Emerging from the dark cellar into a clear brisk afternoon, Anthony shook off the disturbing revelation about Mirdad. He'd spent enough time today on thoughts of his cousin. He turned up the collar on his pea coat, pulled his stocking cap low over his forehead, and glanced up, surprised.

It was Christmas season. How had he not noticed before? London's shop windows dripped with tinsel and garland swags along High Street. Shoppers bundled in dark coats and red and plaid scarves, bustled in and out of stores, carrying bright packages and gift bags. How long had it been since he'd enjoyed Christmas with friends and family in England? He brushed the question away with weightier matters to consider.

The night of the exhibit finally arrived. Lord Charles' driver pulled up into a long succession of shiny cars and limousines among the flashing lights of the paparazzi in front of Philippe's almost unrecognizable gallery. Kathryn patted Lord Charles' hand, tamping down her own anxiety at seeing Anthony's work.

As they both peered out of the car window at the splendid sight, Kathryn smiled without comment, allowing

Charles this moment to come to terms with his own feelings of loss, anger, and grief. After hours of sobbing on her uncle Buzz's shoulder, hers were held in check, and she had her goal clearly in mind. Catch the killers.

A great billowing canopy in the style of a grand Persian tent extended from above the Mayfair gallery entrance out to the curb, draped with gossamer magenta and lilac-striped metallic silk curtains, tied to pillars next to the curb. The silver tent itself rose to a pinnacle where tall white plumes and peacock feathers crowned the point. Two Acadian guards, reminiscent of renderings from a Babylonian palace, stood solemnly on either side of the entrance, with pointed beards, brocade tunics, and flat conical hats. They appeared ready at any moment to use the long sabers sashed to their sides. An electrician Kathryn and Emmaline had hired from Samuelsons Film Service had worked long hours to light the dramatic venue as she would on set. The effect achieved was just as she'd planned, spectacular and dramatic.

"Philippe's done it, Kathryn," Charles said, pounding his hand on the soft leather seat beside her. "By God, it's exciting. You've all done it! Marvelous."

"Hey, over here," they heard.

The paparazzi had spotted them.

"They'll want some comment from you, Charles," Kathryn said.

He blustered for a moment and squeezed her hand. "Thank you for this evening, Kathryn."

The driver came around and opened the back limo door.

Lord Charles stepped onto the Kashmir-carpeted entrance, extending his hand to Kathryn. She followed, her black velvet gown flowing behind her. And before she could turn to the entrance, the press descended upon them, all speaking at once.

"Harrumph!" Charles said, assisting Kathryn onto the carpet. They stood for a moment soaking in the entire effect. Lights flashed around them.

"Good God!" said Charles. "Who are they expecting, the queen?"

"Practically." Kathryn said, holding his arm.

"We'll be blinded for sure."

"Over here, Lord Charles. Can you tell us why your grandson was killed?"

"I am here this evening, ladies and gentlemen, to honor Anthony Evans' work. That is what tonight is about."

With lights flashing, someone shouted, "She's wearing them, the Persian Glories!"

"Quickly, my dear, or we'll be trampled."

After a few quick photos that seemed to take hours, Charles and Kathryn entered the gallery showroom.

The radiant faces of Buzz, Samantha, and Emmaline greeted them inside. Buzz happy, it seemed, with Emmaline and her beautiful mother, Lady Samantha, on either arm.

Emmaline gave Lord Charles a peck on his cheek. "Hello, Uncle Charles," as he was affectionately known to her family, and she took Kathryn's hand in hers.

"Doesn't it all look smashing?" Emmaline gushed, her gaze sweeping the expansive art deco wonder.

Emmaline's infectious delight obliterated Kathryn's nerves, and she took a good look around at the venue, awed and excited, preparing her emotions to go upstairs to the gallery.

"It's grand, Emmaline. Amazing."

Emmaline handed Kathryn a glass of champagne, which she declined, asking for a Perrier instead.

Lord Charles whispered, "Ready to go up, my dear?"

Kathryn's heart beat like crazy along with her pulsing nerves. She reached for calm, determined to do this for Anthony, still unwilling to believe he wasn't coming back to her. She took Charles' arm. "I'm ready."

Before reaching the gallery level, they stepped up to the first landing, and there under low-voltage light hung a life-sized black and white photo of Anthony dressed to play polo, vibrant, handsome. She was struck by his direct gaze into the camera, the familiar mischievous half-smile on his lips, his arms folded across his broad chest. His glorious eyes stared at her. Kathryn clutched Lord Charles' arm, faltering.

"Steady, child," he said.

"I miss him so." Kathryn hung on and walked to the image. She touched the face in the photograph and then his hand, her fingers glided over the surface as if she could feel something of him there.

"I can't face those people. It's too much..." Tears streamed down her cheeks.

Lord Charles handed her his handkerchief. "Be firm. Remember what this night is about."

Buzz moved to her other side. "It's gonna be rough, Kat. We discussed this and you said you could do it." He squeezed her hand. "You put this together for good reasons, but if you want to go, I'll take you outta here. Besides, you've got us both to lean on, you know."

"You're right." Kathryn wiped her eyes, took a deep breath and smiled wanly, hiding heartbreak that would never leave her. But as they climbed to the exhibit level, she glanced back over her shoulder for just one more look at the man whose love still consumed her.

She had insisted Philippe and Emmaline curate the exhibit so this would be her first look at Anthony's final body of work. She couldn't view it alone, not if she wanted her nerves intact for the evening. She held Buzz's hand tightly, Charles on her other arm as they entered the stark white gallery.

Startling photographs, so much like paintings in muted colors printed on large canvases, captured the essence of Anthony's Persia.

A landscape with a mosque nestled among trees like a jewel in the desert, and a single worshiper on his sojourn called to her. Aided by the staff he carried, he seemed to have stopped for a moment, entranced by the vivid sunset, the great sweep of purple mountains and verdant pastures surrounding him.

They moved to the next large photo. Tribal horsemen corralled wild horses, their faces glowing through a break in a dust cloud. She recalled the zeal of Tabriz and his men racing toward Tahkt-e Tavooz after the first shoot.

They moved to a photo of her comforting a small child, who looked with great trepidation into the open door of a helicopter. She remembered seeing similar images with Anthony: the helicopter ride over this mosque at night, Tabriz and his men at Tahkt-e Tavoos with their horses.

A photo in Iran's happier times caught her attention. The Shah stood with the empress, in a candid moment by a lake watching their children. Kathryn saw in her mind, not the Shah and his wife, but another family outing by the lake. *I had hoped it would be us, watching our own children.*

A chilling depiction stopped her. Three lovely co-eds dressed in western clothes, laughing on the steps of the University of Shiraz library. Most of all Kathryn remembered Anthony incredibly attractive in his tux at the Marble Palace, with dignitaries in the grand ballroom in a flourish of celebration. The last moments they had shared together. He had whisked her away into a joyous night and proposed.

At the far end of the room was the focal series called "Wings." One photo in particular drew them close, the largest among them, "The Winged Lion of Persepolis," bathed in the richest golden shades of daybreak, where Kathryn saw herself, perched beside the face of the beast, tears on her cheek as if she foresaw Persia's future.

Her gaze lingered on the photograph, but she saw in her mind flickering light from the fireplace in Anthony's Shiraz studio, when she'd seen its duplicate and had been completely shocked by its existence, by the intensity of what had followed. They had made love on a fur rug in front of the fire, gazing at one another, and in that instant had known they were meant to be together. The night had been theirs, the memory still so powerful it shook her.

Buzz squeezed her hand, bringing her back to the present. "This is something, Kathryn, something wonderful."

And the last one he had taken of her after a bath, wrapped in a length of white silk, wearing the Glories. Drops of water sparkled on her skin, as did the diamonds around her throat, on her ears, and in her hair.

"Looks like you had a better time than I thought." Buzz smiled.

"I had a wonderful time," she whispered, for that was all she could do. "Thank you for giving me the opportunity."

"I never realized..." Lord Charles said with a break in his voice. "I didn't know you had become such an integral part of his life, his work."

She squeezed Charles' arm, wanting desperately in that moment to tell him she was carrying Anthony's child. But it was too soon and too public a place to tell him such intimate news. Tomorrow it would all be different. But she needed to tell someone soon or she'd burst.

Anthony couldn't refuse himself one small glance into the exhibit hall. For so long, this exhibition had been the focal point of all his plans and aspirations, and now he could barely steal a look. He glanced through the partially opened door and saw Kathryn.

She stopped him cold; her hair swept up into a swirl of soft curls held by the Persian Glory tiara, sparkling like sunbursts under low voltage lighting. He needed to leave, but couldn't take his eyes off her. And then she moved away, studying some piece near the entrance that seemed to affect her greatly. He watched, wondering what it was, desperately wanting to go to her. People he had worked with and known forever wandered over and she smiled, chatting with them. He heard some remarks.

"Amazing. They look more like paintings, the colors"

"This is by far his best work."

"Fascinating aspects of Persia we might never have seen."

"Pity, pity."

He closed the door to Philippe's office.

"They've come!" Ali said from behind him.

Anthony grabbed Ali's arm. "Shhh. Voices carry across the hall."

"Mirdad and Rena have arrived," Ali reported softly. "They're drinking champagne in the Savoy ballroom lounge."

"How many men are with them?"

"We haven't seen others. It's too early to tell yet. Meanwhile, limos are stacking up in the motor court." Ali cleared his throat. "I have a message from my cousin, Davood. You did not tell me you had gotten him out of Iran."

"Yes. Along with two of his college friends working undercover for me, spying on Houdin's movements."

"But you have MI-6 spies, no?"

"It takes a cagey Iranian to spy on the Black Glove leader.

Your cousin is both smart and motivated." He studied Ali's face. "You okay with this?"

He nodded. "Thank you for saving my cousin." He looked to Anthony. "Anything else?"

"Make sure no one will be waiting for Kathryn in her suite after the ball," Anthony said.

Ali smiled. "Not even you?"

"I wish," Anthony said. "Are the others in place? Hans too?"

"Yes, yes, don't worry."

"I'll stop worrying when we get that bunch where we want them."

"You know where I want them. Dead."

"No, Ali." Anthony took hold of Ali's shoulder. "You can't do that here. You're not in Iran, and the British definitely frown on murder, even justifiable homicide."

Ali nodded and left with Anthony by way of the roof garden, which had seen more visitors than the front entrance.

The conversation Mirdad had with Demetrius earlier in the Savoy lounge slammed into his thoughts.

Mirdad had leaned in close to Demi. "No harm must come to Kathryn tonight."

"I heard you but don't think you can give me orders!"

"I'm depending on you."

Demi brushed past him.

And now as he entered the silk-tented lounge, the response seemed too ambiguous for Mirdad, but he hoped he'd gotten through to Demi.

Sitar music set a mellow atmosphere inside the hotel's vast ballroom lounge. Billowing silk transformed the ante-room, large enough for two hundred guests. Mirdad gathered two glasses of champagne from a passing waiter and awaited Kathryn's entrance, longing to see her after three life-changing months. Somehow he must atone for at least part of the wrong he'd done her.

He handed a brimming champagne flute to Rena, his mother, although he thought of her as something entirely different now. Tonight Rena looked beautiful in a red satin Balenciaga, this treacherous female who had poisoned ninety-nine percent of his soul and ruined his life. The last one percent, Kathryn had saved by opening his heart.

The poisoned part, to his amazement, still held loyalty to his mother. He had sworn a thousand times to do this one thing for her and he would: get her the Persian Glories. Participating in his mother's caper was his only means to insure Kathryn's safety.

Afterward, it was back to life in Paris, done with Rena forever. He glanced around, noting the amazing transformation of this lounge, though he was unable to see into the step-down ballroom shielded by white gossamer curtains.

"Excuse me, Mother." He held up his glass. "A refill."

Her long lashed dark eyes flashed to his. "Not too much, now. We'll celebrate after."

He inclined his head. "Whatever you wish." He turned away from his dark parent, drawn to whatever lay beyond the gossamer curtains, recalling his appraisal last week of this layout.

Pulling back an edge of white chiffon, he peered into the ballroom, surprised. Gone were the massive arched windows, the gilt and pale paneled walls, the fussy antiques he'd seen here just days ago. Before him, fifth century outer stone walls replicating King Xerxes' palace at Persepolis encompassed the ballroom. He deciphered the elements of Kathryn's design, loving that she had created this from places he'd been with her in Iran. Parts of the stone perimeter, cast in bas-relief, depicted winged warriors. Flanking the orchestra's stage, no surprise, were two regal stone winged lions. Corners of the huge expanse held planters filled with white sand and towering palm trees, lit from below.

These seemingly ancient walls surrounded an oasis of colorful, numbered tables for ten. Purple and white orchid centerpieces held three-foot faux canary diamond-studded white plumes, swaying above gold chargers, flatware, and embossed crystal. Lighting myriad candles on each table, waiters arranged ten chairs of gold bamboo design with embroidered seat cushions to encircle each table. Mirdad nervously checked the numbered card in his pocket. *Table one. Kathryn's table.*

Grateful for his luck, he leaned back his head smiling and noticed an astonishing domed indigo velvet sky overhead, pinpricked with light in thousands of astronomical figures. So like her to treat this venue as a production design for a movie set of ancient Persia combined with Shiraz's Paradise nightclub, all of it inside a classic British ballroom.

Mirdad tipped his glass swallowing his laughter with champagne, excited he now might have two hours with Kathryn before all hell broke loose. If things went badly tonight, those could be the last two he'd ever have with her. If all went well he'd entreat her to come to Paris with him and tempt her with a fabulous new life. He closed the white curtain and returned to his assigned duties, switching his champagne for a glass of mineral water. One glass of champagne was enough to calm him. Another might shake his wits. He must be alert to his mother's tricks.

Rena watched her distracted son's internal battle mirrored in his eyes. He was conflicted over this Whitney woman; his hands virtually tied because the bargain he'd struck stated he would do as promised insuring no harm would befall the woman. This amused Rena. What might happen accidentally was not her concern. A smile quivered on her lips. She spread her gown's red satin skirt around her, enjoying a sip of fine Bollinger and her vantage point from the center semi-circle divan facing the entrance. She awaited her prey.

As expectant guests glided in through open double doors over colorful Persian carpets with a hint of curiosity about them, Rena watched. This staid upper crust set displayed a certain group-like grace rather like a flock. No matter how expensive their well-cut tuxedos and expensive gowns, compared to Iranian society, they lacked flare, panache; they were so stuffy and dull, geese instead of peacocks. They seemed enchanted by this outlandish harem-like atmosphere.

Thank Allah she could leave directly after dinner, jetting off to their little hideaway in Morocco. She looked up to see Mirdad returning to her side.

"No need for nerves, my son. Demetrius will be here soon." She returned her gaze to the entrance. "He'll handle everything." She stood. "Ah, he's here now."

Mirdad's head swiveled so fast he almost spilled his drink. *He knew that tone. She was up to something.*

Rena chuckled. "And look who is on his arm. Gorgeous as always."

Demetrius walked over, escorting a brunette beauty, dazzling in a strapless emerald green beaded gown and matching evening bag. The lethal Alexandria Badiyi, so much more than just a Black Glove spy. Mirdad's mind buzzed with dire possibilities but was pulled back to his goal of getting Kathryn alone to talk, to invite her to Paris. There was so much he needed to say in case the heist ruined everything for him. When Kathryn took off the jewels, they would be seized quickly. But she would be safe. His mother had sworn. *But was she lying?*

Alexandria leaned in. "Mirdad, it's been an age." She air kissed his cheeks, smelling as always, of Chanel No. 5, a lovely scent, but not on her. She gave him a seductive look, always on the prowl. He pulled back. Hard to believe she'd been raised at the Shah's court, her mother, Oriana, the empress's trusted assistant.

"No need for nerves, my son. All will go well."

Mirdad listened to remarks buzzing in many languages, Italian, French, Portuguese, and more.

"Quite a crowd," Rena said, gazing at guests mingling. "Why all the foreigners?" she asked in Farsi.

"She chose the World Food Bank to feed the impoverished," Alexandria said. "This is a worthy charity we support tonight. Dignitaries invited from around Europe have come, it seems, for this event."

Eloquent words from one of Houdin's hired assassins. Mirdad knew Demetrius wasn't interested in her. So why was Alexandria here? Who was her target? Voices stilled around him and it was clear why. *Kathryn.*

His pulse sped. "Excuse me." He stepped away from his mother and headed toward her.

Rena's gaze swiveled to the entrance. People cleared a path and stood back as Kathryn Whitney entered. All seemed captured, certainly, by their first sight of Faberge's infamous canary diamonds in all their glory. *My, my, my, aren't you a vision?*

Time seemed to stop for Rena when the Whitney woman appeared. The woman stealing everyone's attention, wearing the Persian Glories as Ilyia had. Few had seen the parure exhibited.

But it was her turn now and nothing and no one would stop her from possessing the diamonds. Everything was in her favor. She had handled them only once, that night while her sister Ilyia had dressed.

It was then she had noticed the intricacy of the design. The necklace, like a mantle, came apart in two sections, short, three inches or long, six inches. The six-inch bracelet could detach and be worn as two three-inch diamond cuffs as the Whitney woman did tonight.

Rena scanned every inch of the harlot, lit by chandeliers intensifying the brilliance of Fabergé's design, as intricate as his famous jewel encrusted enamel eggs and far more valuable. This was better than a dream. This was real.

She stood before her Persian Glories, worn in full force; the entire mantle-like necklace draped over bare shoulders of the American blonde. The tiara with the robin's egg sized center stone sat atop her golden hair. *Wrong.* Fabergé designed the glories for a raven-haired woman like Rena.

Ms. Whitney wore the three-inch perfect diamond cuffs on each wrist. The twenty-carat canary diamond ring was on her right hand and on her left she still wore Anthony's fifteen-carat engagement ring that had been his mother's. As Rena glared at Kathryn, fury flamed, cinders spread like a river of rage through her veins. Two words came to mind. *You're dead.* She would make sure Kathryn suffered before Alexandria took her life. She sucked in a calming breath and another, cooling her temper to chilled calculation.

The legacy of the Persian Glories was known to be one of great love, but after tonight rumors would circulate about a curse. Everyone who possesses them dies. A small smile curved her ruby lips. *Little do they know I'm the curse.*

From her vantage point, twenty feet from the entrance, Rena watched every gesture of Ms. Whitney who extended her hand to Mirdad. Her son bent to kiss the woman's hand. Rena bristled.

Lord Charles, with Kathryn on his arm and Mirdad beside her, moved toward her. Charles, older but so tall and handsome, like the other Evans men.

"Rena, my dear," he said, and kissed her cheek. "How amazing you look."

Squelching memories of painful surgeries, she beamed with the compliment.

"Good of you to invite us, Charles. Spectacular event." Rena's gaze returned to the Whitney woman. Her fingers itched to yank the Glories off her neck.

"Hello, Kathryn. I believe you know Ms. Badiyi? And, of course, Colonel Nassiri," Rena said as Philippe Kahlil, that French Lebanese sponger, drew Lord Charles away to greet other arriving dignitaries.

Rena toned down her intentions and took a deep breath. Her gaze seared Kathryn. "A lavish event," she said. "And I see you wear more of my sister's jewels."

Kathryn hadn't flinched at her nasty remark.

"They are my jewels now, Rena," Kathryn said with a smile. "And how wonderful it feels to wear them. I'm sure you can imagine."

Oh, you've asked for it, slut. I will enjoy kicking you to death with my stilettos. Rena smiled. "I do imagine." She turned to Alexandria. "You remember Ms. Badiyi, of course."

Alexandria stepped forward. "I'm sure she remembers."

Kathryn nodded. "What a lovely, sparkly green dress, Alexandria. But where is your lavish dog collar? It fit you so well."

Alexandria's fingers clenched and unclenched at her side like cat claws in strike mode, her dark smile more like a grimace. "We were sorry to hear about Anthony," she said. "We all miss him, I can tell you that."

She pushed raven locks behind one ear, displaying a gorgeous dangling emerald earring. "A parting gift," she said, pointedly smirking at Kathryn. "Not as lavish as your canary diamonds, but then I didn't have to work as hard as you to get them."

Kathryn returned her smirk. "Oh, but you tried."

"Ah," Lord Charles said, returning to Kathryn's side. "The orchestra has started up, and the curtains are open. Shall we find our tables?" he raised an eyebrow. "Ladies?"

The room buzzed from hundreds of guests reacting to the Persian Night created for this evening. "Simply, astounding," they all heard, and Kathryn looked over at her small committee, Emmaline and Samantha Samuelson, with a thumbs up.

Emmaline giggled and Samantha nodded, surrounded by awed friends.

Rena hadn't seen these two Samuelson women in over twenty years. Emmaline had been but a small redheaded

222 | THE PERSIAN GLORIES

child. Her mother Samantha a naive noblewoman who had no idea her husband cheated on her. She had not seen them since the day of Ilyia and Richard's funeral. *A wonderful day.*

CHAPTER SEVENTEEN

"Come my dear," Charles said to Kathryn. "I suggest we find our table." He looked at his place card. "Rena, you and Mirdad are with us."

Rena put on a congenial smile. "Lovely."

"Sir, may I show you, Ms. Whitney, and your guests to your table?" It was Robert from the lobby, now in a waiter's tails.

Kathryn was thrilled to see her hotel friend had advanced. "Robert, you've come a long way from bell boy."

"Because of your enthusiastic endorsement, Ms. Whitney. I thank you."

"Well then," Charles said. "Table one, I believe."

"This way, sir?" Robert indicated with a sweep of his arm toward the first tier above the dance floor.

"Shall we?" Charles led his group. Buzz escorted Samantha and Emmaline, Philippe trailing with Sir Vincent and Lady Sybil. The perfect ten. Well almost.

Kathryn heard Mirdad whisper to his mother. "Sir Vincent is a leading art historian and Philippe's long time mentor. His wife Sybil is an influential society hostess.

They'll sit at our table."

"What about Alexandria and Demetrius?" Rena whispered back.

Mirdad shrugged.

Kathryn had placed those two at table thirty-three, not far enough away from her, but back closer to the entrance where Jess' men could keep an eye on them. It would do. Kathryn noticed Robert slip a piece of paper into Charles' palm and Charles glance back at Jess by the entrance.

Robert turned to her saying; "I've ordered Schweppes for you and Mr. Kahlil, Ms. Whitney. Anything else I can do for you?"

"Thank you, all is well, Robert," she said.

He held her gaze for an instant and then bowed and was off.

She wondered about the paper exchanged. But then as the group sat in front of their place cards, the wonderful orchestra segued into a soft samba and the thought floated away.

Mirdad said softly, "May I have this dance, Kathryn?"

She turned to him. "I'm glad you asked." She had waited for a moment to speak with him. When she stood she caught Philippe's scowl and dismissed it.

Mirdad led her onto the dance floor and smoothly took her in his arms. "We haven't danced since the Shiraz Paradise Club, do you remember?"

"I remember every moment I spent in Iran." She wondered how much she could now tell him. "You saved all our lives, and I'll never forget that."

He looked serious. "I'm no hero, Kathryn, believe me."

"To me, always," she said.

Mirdad gazed into her intelligent hazel eyes and wanted very much to be her hero. He'd wasted years being his mother's dupe, but that, he'd shown himself in Paris, was his past, not his future.

As they danced, Mirdad let the warmth of Kathryn's arms and body flow into his. She was everything he adored, respected, and longed to be with. She had brought him back to himself, to the son his father had raised: a scholar who appreciated grace, humor, and talent. He whirled her around and gleaned she wanted to say something that seemed difficult to get out. "What is it, Kathryn?"

Her smile was tight.

"I'll always be here for you...and never betray you. I promise."

She sighed and said, "It's something you must swear you won't repeat."

"Of course."

"Especially not to your mother."

"Truly, you are more important to me than anyone." His eyes narrowed. "And Rena is the last person I'd tell anything personal."

"I've thought a long time about this," Kathryn said. "You are the youngest male relative of my child, the only cousin this baby will have." She gave him a trembling smile. "You're an amazing historian, the one to teach this child Persian heritage."

Mirdad's heart slammed in his chest, his eyes widened.

"Yes, I'm pregnant with Anthony's child, and you are the only person I've told."

Emotions roiled—no rocketed—through Mirdad. Flashes of Anthony, as he had once loved him before he betrayed him. Of Kathryn the first day they'd met on set at Persepolis, when she'd dressed like a boy and challenged him, thrown an American football at him, and every detail of what had happened after filled his head and heart. The buoyant love he had for both, and for the treachery he had dealt them. Colossal guilt roared through him. He gulped down his sins and grabbed ahold of himself. Cinching in his past, he looked forward—for her, for her child. For the child whose father he had murdered. And whether Allah forgave him or not, he would put every last second on earth into loving and caring for this child and Kathryn.

"Mirdad?"

"I can't tell you how overjoyed I am by your news, Kathryn. And honored you chose me to tell." He gave her a gentle hug. "I will love and protect you both forever, if I may."

"You had better. Because I want you to be my baby's godfather. Will you?"

Mirdad's head reeled from all she had disclosed to him, certainly not what he'd expected her to say. But she looked relieved and happy with his reply.

"It will be my privilege, Kathryn." And it was a privilege for her to have shared her news with him.

They headed back to the table. Kathryn noticed several of Jess' men dressed as hotel employees stationed around the ballroom, and she relished a sense of safety. Now that she felt safe, she was starving.

Highly focused on everything happening around them, Kathryn knew things could heat up at any moment. Alexandria and Demetrius were on the dance floor, swirling toward her. She wouldn't let that hussy ruin a good meal.

At her lively table wine flowed and dinner was being served. Mirdad held her chair and they sat. Preselected entrees of either beef tenderloin, filet of Dover sole, or a medley of Persian roasted lamb and kabobs were silently placed at each setting.

"Seems they started without us," Mirdad said, his smile teasing.

"Well, I don't know about you, but I'm ready." Kathryn looked down at her Dover sole and frowned.

"Shall we trade?" Mirdad said, offering his plate of perfectly cooked rare roast beef.

"Um, if you don't mind." They traded plates. "I swear, sometimes I eat like an NFL linebacker."

He bent to her ear. "Perhaps you're carrying one!"

They both sniggered like naughty children. Kathryn glimpsed Rena's disapproval and ignored her.

Dinner conversation continued as Rena regaled both Sir Vincent and Lord Charles with news and stories, her surreptitious looks around the room ignored by others at the table. Philippe, as amusing as ever, charmed both Sybil and Emmaline. Buzz and Samantha had their heads together, seemingly engrossed in a personal exchange though she was certain he watched every move around him. Both

Lord Charles and Sir Vincent discussed the silent auction bids individuals at her table had placed, having both bid on the river cruise up the Danube. Buzz and Philippe went for box seats at Brighton racetrack. The ladies bet on rifle lessons, spa days, and a stay at Portofino's Hotel Splendid. All there acted as if deadly enemies weren't seated next to each other with palms itching for a showdown.

Kathryn caught Mirdad looking over at her plate, noticing she had finished most of her beef. He chuckled, having barely swallowed a morsel of his delicate fish.

With her linen napkin she dabbed her mouth and caught Philippe's nod to her. *A signal.*

"I say, Kathryn," Philippe said. "Shall we have a last go at the auction before they close the bidding?"

"Indeed," she said. "Put your charity money where your mouth is, sir." She turned to Mirdad and smiled. "If you'll excuse us for a moment."

They hurried out of the ballroom to the lobby auction tables.

It took a moment for Rena to discover Kathryn and Philippe had left the table. She'd been distracted by the attractive American, Buzz, chatting her up on her right. She strained to see Alexandria's table.

Demi and Alex stood, heading toward the exit. They had moved not ten feet away when a waiter spilled something on Alexandria. Rena heard glass breaking. Alexandria shrieked and slapped the waiter, swearing in Farsi.

Rena would make sure the fool lost his job over this. She leaned back watching Demetrius rush Alexandria out to the lobby and Rena smiled. Omar would be downstairs with his men, guaranteeing plans went well. *It had begun.*

She kicked Mirdad under the table. He shot her a look and got up, excusing himself.

She narrowed her eyes at him. *Go quickly!*

Mirdad rushed from the ballroom to catch up with Demetrius and Alexandria. He knew where they were headed. A locked emergency staircase off the lobby, and Alexandria, the best lock-breaker in Teheran, would take care of it. He raced.

Alexandria had the door opened before he reached them.

"Demi," Mirdad called out. "Demi, wait."

Demetrius looked back over his shoulder. Alexandria gave his arm a tug.

"I'll follow," he told her. As Mirdad caught up to him, Alexandria hurried up the stairs.

Mirdad leaned in close to Demi. "Remember, you cannot harm one hair on Kathryn's head or your death will not be swift," he hissed into Demi's ear. "Not one bruise."

Demi did a slow turn to him, his look inscrutable. "She means something to you."

"More than you can understand," Mirdad said. "Don't test me on this, Demetrius."

Demi hesitated. He clasped Mirdad's arm then said, "I'm clear." He smirked. "But tell that to your mother."

"My mother hears only what she wants. I'm counting on you. No matter what happens to me. Understand?"

For an instant he couldn't tell what lurked behind Demi's expression. Perhaps jealousy. Then it softened to one he knew well. Mirdad held Demi's forearm, the muscles rippled under his tux. He left his hand on Demi's sleeve and saw lights dance in his dark eyes.

"I won't fail," Demi said and walked away.

The response was too vague for Mirdad, but he felt Demi was on his side.

Mirdad followed Demi into the stairwell but he did not ascend. He dashed down to the basement to join his well-trained Black Glove team.

Kathryn and Philippe left the lounge. Jess and two men fell in beside them. Kathryn heard Jess talking quietly into his wrist walkie-talkie.

"Tim, you read me?"

"Copy," came the security man's reply. "Floors one through ten clear. You bringing them up now?"

"On our way. Open up."

She was shaking, her pulse racing. She hadn't liked seeing Rena and Alexandria there, hadn't liked it at all. They were formidable. If Rena were going to attempt anything, now would be the time. Every instinct in her wanted to call this off for her baby's sake, and run across the lobby back to her flat and hide under the covers, but it was too late now. She'd do her part, get it over with once and for all. It had been her idea after all. And now they would move on it.

The elevator doors opened, and Jess hustled them inside. Seven of them entered the elevator, rising toward who-knew-what?

Tim, with his curly red hair, pushed the button for the eighth floor and nodded to her. The other three security men looked straight ahead, one with a shaved head, one with short brown hair and the third, a blond GI-Joe type with a buzz cut. They would accompany her to the suite she had taken for the night.

Philippe leaned toward her. "Hold on. We're almost there."

"I can't," she said, ready to explode with nerves. She fumbled with the tiara, about to yank it off.

Philippe took hold of her wrists, stilling them. "Calm down. We're almost to your room."

Kathryn took in a long breath, the best she could in the close elevator. To be honest, she couldn't wait to hand the jewels over to Philippe to be placed in the Savoy's main vault.

Philippe put an arm around her. "Don't worry. Another few minutes and we'll have the Persian Glories safely stored."

Kathryn squeezed Philippe's hand. She *was* worried but couldn't say it. What would happen to him after he took the jewels from her?

They reached the eighth floor and stopped. The elevator doors opened. Tim edged out, checking the hall. It was empty. With his back to the door he said, "Let's go," and Kathryn almost leapt out into the hall, turning toward her room.

They heard a click—the cocking of a weapon.

"Down!" Jess yelled.

Thwap. Thwap. Thwap.

Three shots had whizzed close to Kathryn's head, and Tim jostled her behind him, shielding her. Kathryn caught a glimpse of a figure in glitzy green, ducking around the corner. *Alexandria Badiyi. The second time Anthony's jealous ex-lover had taken a shot at her. Why now?* She must have been hired to kill her. Kathryn's blood ran cold.

Jess chased Alexandria, gun drawn. He fired a shot.

Philippe rushed to the end of the hall after Jess and stopped.

The other three security guards had fanned out, covering other hallways of the H-shaped floor.

"Tim, Tim," Kathryn said as he slumped against the wall, blood oozing from his blue jacket sleeve.

"You all right?" he squeaked out.

"Me? I'm fine." Two more bullet holes smoked from the back of his jacket, but no blood.

"Vest," he moaned, breathing hard. He held his chest, catching his breath, and managed to stand.

"All clear," Kathryn heard over Tim's walkie-talkie, and the three guards appeared. Two others guarding her door hadn't moved, their expressions fierce and aware.

A commotion rose from around the corner.

Jess called out, "Sonofabitch!"

They heard thuds and shrieking. Philippe stood at the end of the hall, wincing.

"Got her," they heard and Jess hauled the shooter, Alexandria, toward them, her wrists cuffed in front. Jess's lip bled. "Get this wildcat into the elevator," he said, handing her smoking .38 to a shaved-headed guard.

But Alexandria's eyes widened as she got closer to Kathryn. She shrieked, "Whore, bitch!" She lunged, her cuffed arms shot out, her fingers, like claws, raked her nails over Kathryn's shoulder, gouging a deep scratch.

Instinctively Kathryn's baseball throwing arm came back, then shot forward. Slugging her.

Alexandria howled. Blood gushed from her nose.

Kathryn leaned in. "You did everything in your power to get Anthony killed and you succeeded. But you're done, lady." Kathryn didn't turn away though Alexandria cursed like a banshee in Farsi, spitting blood.

"I've had it." Jess peeled off a strip of duct tape from inside his jacket and slapped it across the whole bottom of Alexandria's face, blood and all.

She kicked him hard.

"Bitch!" Jess peeled off more duck tape and wrapped her ankles.

The big GI-Joe guard shoved up an abandoned laundry cart and unceremoniously dumped her into it.

Alexandria writhed and bucked.

"You asked for it," the big guard said. He shoved the cart another ten feet, and two other security men handed her out.

"Tim. Call down, warn Ed. He's in the basement near the chute," Jess said. He held the laundry chute door open.

Tim made the call, and they dumped Alexandria head first down the vent.

"A long way down," Philippe said dryly. "And she'll shoot out the other end, reborn—as a towel."

All of them laughed, shaking their heads at the absurdity, then laughed harder.

Tim pulled out his Glock before they entered Kathryn's suite. The others stood guard. "Clear," he said after he'd checked out every corner and stood back for her to enter.

"Please come in, Tim," she said. "Let me see to your arm." Perspiration matted Tim's red curls against his forehead; his lips were pinched with pain.

Jess nodded okay and helped get his jacket off.

Kathryn got some hydrogen peroxide and cotton squares from her overnight case and ripped open Tim's sleeve. She cleaned the bullet wound on both sides of his arm and tore off a piece of white fabric from his sleeve, making two small pads. "Who's got more duct tape?" Jess handed her a strip, and she covered Tim's wounds. "Good for now," she said.

Tim smiled at her. "I've never had a princess fuss over me before."

"I'm no princess," she smiled back.

He shrugged. "You look like one."

The tiara. "Just for tonight," she said.

Jess motioned to Tim. "We'll give you a minute, Miss Whitney. Be right outside." Jess and the other guards left her with Philippe and closed the door.

Kathryn stood in front the mirror over her dresser somewhat dazed, taking a long look at herself, touching the stones at her throat. She needed to hurry and get them off, but her hand shook.

Philippe stepped forward. "Let me help you."

"Other women tonight wore extraordinary gems," she said, removing the glittering tiara. "Do they always have to put up with such precautions?"

"Well, one takes ambitious precautions when the jewels are worth over two hundred million pounds, and someone wishes to kill you and steal them," he said. "In your case, given all the publicity, Lord Charles's heart, I'm sure, is pounding with apprehension."

"Remember how unprotected the jewels were when I came through customs?"

"Oh, God!" Philippe gasped. "Don't remind me!" They both laughed at the memory.

Together they replaced each piece into its original position in the golden box, and she closed it. A flicker of relief crossed Philippe's face.

"I saw you speaking to Mirdad." Philippe's tone was not as calm as she was sure he wanted it to be. "What did he have to say?"

"He's made big changes in his life. He seems different," she said.

Philippe's eyebrow rose suspiciously. "I doubt that."

"You don't like him, do you?" She sank into a sumptuous, overstuffed chair and kicked off her shoes, rubbing her sore toes.

Philippe stood across from her. "Mirdad is not what he seems, Kathryn. I don't think he knows who he is, and when he wakes up, he's in for a shock."

"What do you mean?"

"Nothing." He smiled. "I must go."

Kathryn handed the box to Philippe. "There you are, safe and sound."

"I'm not leaving you hear alone, a guard will stay here in the suite's front room."

"But Philippe..."

"No discussion on this, Kathryn. We've already had an incident." He called outside the door. "Jess, send in a guard to you stay here and guard the princess tonight, right."

"Right, mate," one of the guards from the elevator entered. "I'm Jeb," he said and sat on the sofa. "Just forget I'm here, ma'am."

"Okay. Goodnight then."

"Goodnight, ma'am."

Philippe placed the box in a black satchel and went out.

Kathryn's room felt so stuffy. How was she expected to sleep after all that? She unlocked the French doors in her bedroom, letting the music drift up to her from the ballroom below. The air was cool; it felt good. She lifted her hair off her neck.

The first part of their plan was complete. The bait was set. Alexandria had jumped at it. She recalled Anthony's comment about Alexandria in Teheran when she shot at his car. *She is more than she seems.* Just what Philippe said about Mirdad.

Right, she was an assassin. Kathryn had been focused on the she-devil Rena, and hadn't anticipated seeing the killer side of Alexandria again. But they were rid of Anthony's ex-lover and Kathryn was too tired to let bittersweet memories upset her, she hoped.

She undressed, wondering if Anthony would have enjoyed this evening's exhibit. How brilliant it would have been sharing it with him, viewing his work, remembering places they had seen together, dancing, laughing, and after. She placed her palm over her tummy. *How I miss your daddy...*

Enough.

She slipped on her nightgown and robe, shoving away useless sorrow, and stretching out on the bed, looked at the next options for her life. Should she go back to L.A., work on another documentary, or try to get another commercial to direct? She could build a life here in England, near Anthony's grandfather. Somewhere, somehow she needed to jump start a career and make a home, because this baby was coming. Tomorrow, she promised herself, she would choose a path.

She placed a glass of water on the bedside table, remembering Philippe's concern. She was so tired, but she got up again reluctantly to close the French doors. Philippe carried the diamonds now, making him vulnerable, open to Rena's next move. He was surrounded by protective MI-6, but she asked anyway. *Please, Lord, keep him safe.*

Trying to push aside her worries for Philippe's safety, she threw off her robe. It was too hot! But she climbed into bed. Curling up beneath the smooth sheet, sliding one hand beneath the pillow next to her. She clutched the little pearl-handled .22 Lord Charles had given her and fell into a fitful sleep.

CHAPTER EIGHTEEN

"Anthony, you ready?"

Anthony leaned into his walkie-talkie. He and Ali were hidden in a dark stairwell. "Jess. Everything okay?"

"Security's clear each floor down. We'll meet at the vault."

"You and your black clad ninja squad," he heard Philippe say.

Anthony looked over at Ali, shaking his head. "My ninjas are posted in the basement, old man. We're about to grab a service elevator."

They would come out discreetly at the back of the lobby, close to the hotel manager's office and the safe. "Where is Kathryn?"

"Kathryn is fine, locked in her room, security guards on the door, Jeb inside the door. Tim's with me"

"Any trouble?"

"An interesting run-in," Philippe said. "I'll explain later."

"Okay. See you at the vault, Philippe. Be on high alert."

Hans' voice broke in. "A BG thug pushed past hotel security down here. He's in the power room. Trouble."

Anthony heard a loud bumping sound from Philippe's lift. The emergency alarm screamed. Then static.

"No power," Jess said.

"Jesus...dark...third floor!" Philippe's voice sounded ragged.

"Keep your head, Philippe," Anthony warned, steadying his own nerves.

"What the bloody 'ell?" Tim yelled.

"Smoke's coming in," Jess shouted.

The plan was falling to shit! He heard pounding.

"We're stuck." Philippe coughed. "It's...tear gas!"

"Get on the floor, Philippe," Anthony said. "Cover your face with your coat." Violent fits of coughing and gasping followed.

"Oh God...eyes...burning..." Static...Philippe sounded panicked.

"Calm down. We'll get you out." He had to.

"Doors...opening," Jess coughed out. "Four men...gas masks...inside—" Jess coughed more.

"Philippe, don't try it!" He heard a muffled shot, a moan, and something thumped against a wall.

"Damn it, Philippe!" Anthony yelled and grabbed Ali's arm beside him. "Switch channels. Get Hans."

"Hans, It's Ali. You read?"

"Yep. Power's back."

Anthony said, "It's started! They're coming down. Someone's been shot. Don't know who. They've got the diamonds."

"Black Glove thugs are roaming around here in the basement. My guys spotted the others out by the loading dock in hotel uniforms, havin' a smoke. So be careful. They can be in and on you real fast."

The Black Glove now had the jewels, but they couldn't leave through the main lobby, not coming from a smoke-filled elevator; MI-6 would cuff them before they made it out. No. The basement had to be the thieves' exit route, Anthony decided. No other choice.

"We're ready." Hans said. "You comin' down?"

"Right now." Without another moment's hesitation, Anthony and Ali slipped from their concealed post in the stairwell and raced down the steps, through the maintenance crawlspace, and out onto the catwalk twenty feet above the cavernous basement.

Below wooden crates were stacked on one side and there was a chain-link locked cage with stored luggage. Dolly-carts, a small forklift and other stuff he couldn't make out under sparse fluorescents. Except for shadowed BG thugs, how many, he couldn't tell.

"In position," Anthony whispered. "Copy?"

"Hell," Hans low voice said. "My guys have been in this catwalk so long we know every ghost in these dim lights," he chuckled. "Oops. Watch it. Those cocksuckers are headed back from their smoke. See 'em?"

Anthony crouched with Ali motionless and silent beside him. He pulled out his infrared scope, pinpointing where his own men were located in the catwalk, then focused on the elevator doors. Two returning BG thugs now stood guard at the doors. Numbered lights over the elevator lit up, triggering Anthony's focus.

Philippe...shot? Power was back on and it was moving. Two, one, LL, B.

The cab whined to a stop.

The doors opened. Anthony counted four men through dissipated smoke, yanking off gas masks, tossing them, and pulling down ski masks, covering their faces. They had two of his security guards, Tim and GI-Joe. Kathryn, thank God, was in her room with Jeb. Jess was slumped to the cab floor in a growing pool of blood.

In a swift move, Philippe lunged for the jewel case, grabbing it, but the cold metal of a thief's revolver crashed onto the back of his skull. Philippe sank, not moving. *Shit!*

The thief twisted the black satchel from Philippe's grip. Anthony heard the bastard thanking him in Farsi for the diamonds as the others laughed.

Anthony immediately knew the voice. *Mirdad Ajani?* Hatred boiled in him.

"Did you hear that?" Hans hissed over the walkie-talkie.

Ali rattled off cuss words in Farsi under his breath.

Their GI-Joe guard was still mobile with a gun. A thug pushed him out of the elevator.

"Behave yourself and you'll stay alive," said the thief holding the diamonds.

As soon as Anthony heard the voice again, he had no doubt whose face was behind the mask. He tensed, logic blinded. His instincts roared. Revenge.

Ali grabbed Anthony's shirt, restraining him. "Not yet, Anthony, not yet."

It took every strand of discipline Anthony could summon not to hurl himself on Mirdad and plunge his knife through the scum's loathsome heart.

The two other thieves dragged Philippe and Jess, the fallen head of security, out of the elevator, and dropped them like grain sacks against a pile of cartons in the corner. Blood soaked Jess's shirt, but he coughed—a good sign. Philippe, however, wasn't moving. Anthony prayed he was alive.

Mirdad, who carried the satchel of diamonds, tucked his gun into the holster under his arm, as did the other two men behind him. Only the fourth man had his gun out. Good, Anthony thought, you've made a mistake, you bastards. Relaxed too soon.

Anthony surveyed the enemy below, identifying many of Houdin's A-list black belt assassins. He'd seen them spar at the fancy SAVAK gym. His fighters had trained in the wilds while hiding from these enemies on the mountain.

As he readied himself for the attack, Anthony wondered if there were other Black Glove agents he hadn't discovered guarding their escape route. He would soon find out. He signaled Hans and nodded, ready. He caught a glimpse of Ali's expanding fury.

"Mirdad is mine," Anthony whispered through clenched teeth.

They pulled their ski masks down over their faces. Anthony not ready for cousin Mirdad to know he was alive—not yet. *Time for a surprise, you bastards.*

With roaring war cries:

"Huzzah!"
"Ourah!"
"Allahua Akbar!"

Anthony's team dropped from the scaffolding like a screaming avalanche onto the enemy below, attacking the enemy thugs like the well-trained agents they were.

Anthony's pent-up rage from the mountain erupted. He kicked out, landing a powerful blow to Mirdad's head, stunning him. He punched Mirdad's face and then his body, again and again. Mirdad crumbled, the satchel of diamonds slipping from his hands, falling near him on the cement floor.

Instantly, the man covering Mirdad looked up, and Anthony recognized Houdin's man, Colonel Demetrius Nassiri. He wheeled his gun around at Anthony, aiming. *Damn!* A flashflood of fury and adrenalin flooded Anthony. He brought his foot up into the man's elbow, the gun went flying. Anthony kicked it away, anger morphing into focused resolve. In the melee, through shouts and fists flying, Anthony searched for Mirdad.

He sensed someone behind him and whipped around, recognizing the Black Glove saboteur from Kathryn's film set. A gun butt struck him, sending excruciating pain through his right shoulder.

"Ahhh!" Anthony howled like a wounded beast. With the force of fury, he sliced down a blow on the saboteur's forearm and felt the bone snap. The gun fired wildly and fell to the floor.

For an instant the man was startled, but in a flash a knife appeared from his sleeve. He charged, cutting through Anthony's jacket. The added pain propelled Anthony away. He deflected the blade with a sidekick to the assailant's ribs. The BG thug doubled over. Anthony shouted, "Motherfucker!" With a front kick, and a snap punch, the knife clattered across the cement floor.

Yowling, the saboteur attacked with a series of ferocious jujitsu kicks. Anthony, stunned by the man's strength, blocked the kicks with a gedan barai, a defensive tactic. Giving no time to recover, he thrust heel first into his target. Unstoppable, the Black Glove fighter plowed forward. *No fucking way!* Anthony put everything behind one final kick, and his opponent at last sprawled unconscious in a corner. Anthony spun around.

Ali was in a struggle for his life. His attacker was small but powerful, adroitly avoiding Ali's punches. Anthony recognized him, the odious Captain Aran. Striking out with his fist, Ali jabbed at the attacker. With astonishing speed Aran grabbed Ali's fist before it reached him, twisting it, grinding Ali down to the floor, kicking him in the chest. Anthony went in for the attack, but Aran leaped out of reach to Mirdad's side, grabbing the satchel of diamonds, pulling Mirdad to his feet, and yelled in Farsi for him to move.

Ali jumped up and tackled the satchel of diamonds, tearing it from Aran's grip before he hit the floor. With cool deliberation Aran kicked Ali in the face and took off with Mirdad.

Anthony looked up, seeing Mirdad and his accomplice disappearing down the darkened corridor. Tearing after them, Anthony and Ali raced down the corridor until they reached the open loading dock. There at the exit, a powerful looking man stood, in shadow, backlit by street lamps.

Anthony squinted, seeing General Omar Houdin. Feet planted, Houdin raised his automatic weapon and fired, blasting everything in front of him, covering Mirdad and his man's exit.

Rounds burst in a fiery barrage. Anthony and Ali, both bleeding heavily, dove for cover between crates of freight cargo, covering their heads. Bullets blasted around them, shredding crates, pinging off metal. Finally it all stopped.

Anthony leapt up, waving away gun smoke, in time to see Mirdad escape into the night. Aran was not with him.

He kicked at debris around him and tore off his ski mask, shaking with fury.

Ali ripped off his mask, hurling it to the ground.

Anthony's fists clenched. Not having Mirdad in his grasp drove him wild. He stomped at the concrete floor, cursing in Farsi, his voice growing hoarse as he struggled to deal with Mirdad's escape, striving for rational composure he just couldn't feel.

If it hadn't been for Philippe lying unconscious and some deep uneasy sense insisting he remain, Anthony would have thrown all reason aside and pursued his cousin into hell.

He hurried through the battle scene; men's bodies sprawled on the basement floor amid moans. He came to one and stopped. It was Tim. Anthony knelt beside the body, drowning in remorse that Tim had been dragged into this assignment. Tim had been Jess's good buddy. He closed Tim's eyes and called Hans over. "Take care of him, brother," Anthony said.

Anthony turned to Ali, who rubbed his injured wrist, then smashed more wooden crates against the wall with his boot, mirroring unvented frustration Anthony felt.

Breathing hard, Anthony said, "Good work, Ali. They didn't get the diamonds."

Anthony wiped at the blood soaking through his sleeve.

"Mirdad, the slimy dog, slipped away," Ali said.

"Another day will come for that dog." Anthony wiped his knife, flipped it into the air, and caught it, a gesture that had often calmed him on the mountain. "We'd better see to Philippe."

They found him coming around.

"Ohhhh...! Where the hell...?" Philippe held his head.

Anthony knelt beside his friend. "Nasty blokes weren't they?" he said, still shaking from the encounter.

GI-Joe knelt beside them, checking on Jess's injuries. "It's a damn good thing you lot were here," Joe tossed over his shoulder.

"Tim's dead," Anthony said.

"'e's all right," GI-Joe said, "Bloody bullet went through 'is shoulder, mate. That damn woman shot him."

"Woman?"

"Yes, Alexandria Badiyi," Philippe said. "I was going to tell you."

"Joe," Anthony said. "Tim didn't make it. I'm so sorry, man." GI-Joe looked to Jess.

Jess didn't speak. He turned his face away.

"And the jewels?" Philippe said.

"We have them."

"Did you get Mirdad?" Philippe sat up, his hand to his head.

"Some of the others, not Mirdad." Anthony couldn't hold down his anger at the missed opportunity. "Damn it, Philippe. Are you allright?"

"Yes. But my head feels crushed. At least they waited until Kathryn was safely in her room."

"Kathryn! Oh, Christ, no!" Anthony yelled, panic flooding through him. He looked over at Jess.

"Go," Jess said. And Anthony took off running.

CHAPTER NINETEEN

Kathryn awoke with a start, feeling so hot she could barely breathe. Her heart raced as she lay in darkness after a bad dream and wondered what time it was. She kicked off the covers, closing her eyes, and lazily reached for her glass of water. Instead, she touched a hand.

Her eyes flew open, and she stared up into the dark face of a man poised over her. She screamed in horror as his eyes raked coldly over her scantily clad body; then she kicked out at him and scrambled for her gun. He slapped her face viciously and held the point of a knife to her chin.

"One more sound and you die," he said, his accent Persian.

She couldn't have made another sound if she tried. The point pressed painfully into her skin as she watched a cloth move down over her face along with a sickening smell. *Where was her Jeb?*

"Your guard is dead." He made a motion across his throat and smirked.

Anthony hopped a service elevator to the seventh floor, found the window to the fire escape, and climbed onto it. A dark figure above climbed through Kathryn's eighth floor balcony. A curtain billowed out of the open French doors.

Anthony crashed through the French doors from the balcony and saw his target leaning over her bed.

Enraged, Anthony yelled, *"Hey, arabe kassif.* Dirty Arab!" The intruder whirled around his blade ready. But Anthony was faster; he kicked him in the stomach and threw him out onto the balcony, lunging after him.

Shit. It was Captain Aran, the sadistic bastard. Aran plunged his blade at his throat. Anthony leapt aside.

Captain Aran grabbed onto the fire escape and climbed up toward the rooftop.

Anthony had witnessed Aran's brutality over the years. "I'm coming for you."

Captain Aran paused mid-step. *"Dool! An ru sar it.* Dick! Shit on your head!" He climbed faster, but Anthony had reached him. He grabbed onto Aran's ankle.

Aran kicked out, throwing him off. "Let go! *Madar jendeh!* Your mother is a whore!"

"Khodeto Bokun. Go fuck yourself," Anthony said, climbing onto the same fire escape platform. They planted their feet, facing off. Aran unholstered his .45 revolver, aiming at Anthony's head.

In a flash, Anthony sent his knife whirring, deadly

accurate, into the captain's heart. Aran took one last breath, looked down at the hilt of the knife impaled in his chest, then slumped to the railing. Anthony stood shaking, gazing down at Captain Aran.

He had watched Aran blow a hole through Raymond's head and then shoot sweet Tali. He pulled his knife out of the butcher's chest and wiped it off on the dead man's sleeve before he kicked Aran's corpse, wishing he could boot him into hell. He shoved the body over the platform's edge. The corpse plummeted down nine floors to the concrete below.

Anthony turned away and quickly climbed down to Kathryn's balcony, stepped into her darkened room, and rushed to her bedside, reaching for her.

She was gone.

His mind whirled with rage and frustration. The moist pad lay on the pillow, giving off a faint smell of ether. *Chloroform.* He picked a strand of her blonde hair from the pillowcase, his chest seizing. The duvet and her robe were tangled on the carpet. She had struggled. He stood over the empty bed, his head spinning with images of the terror she must have felt. They had wrapped her in the missing top sheet. He scanned the suite—the guard was missing. He searched for other clues and found Jeb sprawled lifeless in the front room. He heard a pounding at the door. Shouting.

"Scotland Yard. Open up. Where's your key, mate?"

"You think the courtyard corpse could'a fallen from this room's balcony?"

"We'll find out. Draw your guns and break the damn thing down. Now!"

He didn't have time to deal with these buffoons now. His grandfather would have to do it. He was going to find Kathryn.

Just as the door came crashing in, Anthony left as he had entered, through the French doors, down the fire escape, into the seventh-floor window, and finally into service elevator.

Mirdad, I'm coming for you.

CHAPTER TWENTY

Rena slammed the door to her London hotel suite and leaned back against it, her mind whirling.

"Satan's balls!" *Disastrous! They had failed her again.* Failed! For the love of Allah, what had happened? How could they not kill one sleeping woman in her bed!

She stood for a moment, relieved to be away from the crisis after the ball, and back in her own sedate hotel suite at the Berkeley. Had she mentioned to anyone at the ball where they were staying? Surely not.

She must wait for Omar's call.

Mirdad had botched her plan. And that *little thing*, Demetrius, was an incompetent ass. He hadn't shown up at their rendezvous point on time, and she had known immediately something must have gone wrong. Thank heavens she had thought to have a driver waiting for her. She had been so nervous she could have never told a cab where to take her. Her pulse raced. Her temples throbbed. She would have to calm down. The dim glow of the lamp next to the bar caught her eye. She crossed to the bar and grabbed the chilled bottle of Absolut, broke open the seal, and gulped down a swig, the scorching liquid sending heat throughout her cold, shaking body.

She kicked the refrigerator door closed and took the bottle with her to the sofa, flopped down and flipped off her red satin pumps. Omar could be in Tangiers by now or soon would be. He must be furious with her. Her plans had been botched; the blond bitch lived. She was anxious about speaking to Omar. But the very worst part was she did not have her diamonds.

She tossed back another gulp of vodka and heaved the bottle across the room. Before the vodka reached her stomach the bottle crashed into a lamp, sending shards of glass and liquor splattering onto the carpet. Now she would have to listen to everyone bitch and complain, blaming each other. Failure had never loomed as a possibility to her. And it felt like a brick wall had fallen on her chest.

The door to the suite flew open, and Mirdad stormed into the room, one eye swelling closed, blackening, a flaming welt on his jaw and he clutched at his ribs. She had never seen such fury in him.

"You lied to me. It was a goddamned trap! I'd be at Scotland Yard right now if Demi hadn't pulled me out of there. And then he disappeared. Was that *your* doing, Mother?"

"You fool!" she screamed. "Why couldn't you follow my plan?"

"You planned to kill Kathryn."

"It was all worked out. A robbery, the Whitney woman, killed." She marched toward him.

"There was a codicil to Anthony's will! Leaving the

diamonds to me if his wife, children, or intended should not survive." She scoffed. "Had your brain worked, you would have seen it after his death. But no!" She flashed him an icy glare. "You chose drunken whoring. I had to fish you out of bed, you wearing nothing but stained black sheets."

He whipped away from her and threw open the door to the refrigerated bar. "Where's the fucking vodka?"

Rena glanced toward the broken lamp, and Mirdad saw.

"Couldn't you have thrown some other goddamned bottle? Something that I don't like? You inconsiderate bitch!"

"Insolent bastard!" Rena jumped up and lunged at him, her arm raised to strike, but he grabbed her wrist.

"Don't ever call me that again, Mother! Because that makes you a whore!"

"But you, my dear son, *are* a bastard and I am a whore." She spit in his face. He slapped her hard in return.

"I knew my father and love him still."

Shrieking, she fought to get away from him, but he held on, getting up in her face. "Do you want me to hit you again? Or will you calm down?"

Rena yanked away from him and tromped across the room, forcing herself to hold down her rage. There was much her son didn't know.

Mirdad took out his handkerchief, wiping spittle from his face, looking as if he wanted to hit her again.

"What happened?" she asked, her voice unsteady. "What did you mean, a trap?"

Mirdad didn't answer, because the phone at last rang.

He picked it up, and Rena flew to grab the extension across the room by the bed.

"Hello?"

"Ah, Mirdad, good," Houdin said. "You are there protecting your mother." Mirdad flinched.

Rena listened. Omar's voice on the other end had the distinct reserved enthusiasm of a businessman seasoned for success, sure of the outcome. "Where are my men?"

How could she tell him?

"It was a trap," Mirdad said, his eyes blazing across the room at her. "Tell him. Tell your husband all about it, Mother."

"NO!" Rena screamed into the receiver. "We don't have them. They didn't get out."

"Our strategy was sound. How did this happen?" Houdin yelled.

"I don't know," Rena said, glaring across the room at her son. "Ask Mirdad. He's the one who failed."

There was a silent moment before Houdin spoke. "Mirdad?"

"Two taken. Demi and I got away, with your help, and then he disappeared and didn't show at our rendezvous point."

Silence.

"Captain Aran was killed trying to carry out your little scheme. You lied to me, both of you," Mirdad said, his anger thinly veiled.

"Mirdad, listen to me." Houdin's voice now a cold, measured calm. "The two of you must get out of there now. Do you understand? You must not wait a second longer. Is that clear?"

Mirdad sighed. "Yes, yes, it's clear." He threw the phone at his mother and fled from the room, stripping off his blood stained clothes and muttering, "Sonofabitch!"

"Omar, you took the bitch on board with you to Morocco. I didn't tell Mirdad, do you hear?"

"I have her."

"Good, good. Tell me."

"I'll explain everything when you get to Tangiers. But you must go now, understand. A plane is waiting. The driver knows where to take you. Go, *Joon-am*, go."

"Yes, my love," she purred and hung up the phone.

She had something of her own to explain. Her new plan. She would never give up her diamonds.

"Move!" She shouted after Mirdad as he went to change his clothing. "We have a plane to catch."

But as she turned, he stood in the doorway looking at her with indescribable anger and resolve. He had overheard the conversation.

"You double dealing bitch. You took Kathryn!"

An hour later, Anthony hung up the phone in his grandfather's handsome Savoy hotel suite and turned to Lord Charles, who sat at a Chippendale table pouring hot tea from a delicate porcelain teapot, lacing it with cognac and sugar.

He sat across from Charles. "It's arranged. I can be in Tangier by dawn."

"You can't just go off to Morocco on your own, for God's sake, Anthony!"

"Grandfather..."

Charles handed Anthony a cup and glared at him until he drank. "It's out of the question. You know the risks to both you and Kathryn. This lot has gone after a nation, killed their own people. Obviously, nothing or no one will hold back their mania. I know I'm right." His grandfather sat back and finished his tea. "Of course you must go after her. But Scotland Yard and MI-6 advise against your plan, too. They suggest..."

Anthony stood, bumping the table. "They don't know my plan."

Charles clinked his cup down on the saucer and rose. "And you'll protect her against Houdin's hordes on your own?" He pounded the table, the tea set chattering. "Such arrogance. She barely survived your plan last night."

After walking around the room, Charles finally settled on the divan.

Anthony cringed at the truth that hung heavily in the room, but blew it aside, quashing doubts about his strategy for getting her back.

How often had Tabriz drilled into him on the mountain, *"Warriors must be certain of their path."* He'd learned much from there.

He'd listened and done things their way, but not now.

"Sir. I'll protect her." He softened his tone, knowing the

depth of his grandfather's concerns. "I can't allow Houdin and his people to poison my life further."

Anthony sat, sliding closer to his grandfather. "Please listen," he said. "Ali has already departed for Morocco. Ali's cousin Davood and his fellow student escapees have been scouting out Houdin's movements there for weeks, better than MI-6 can because it takes an Iranian to think and track like another Iranian."

"Harumph. I see. Obviously, I can't deter you, but I still question your judgment. Let them—"

"Sorry, Grandfather. This is my call. I'm flying with Hans." He touched a tiny gold lion, a gift for Kathryn he kept in his pocket, and savored the idea of having Kathryn safe in his arms. "I'll bring her back to us."

"Well then, my boy," his grandfather said with a sad smile. "God speed."

Anthony hugged his grandfather, the old man's affection warming him.

As he left, his thoughts shifted through the perils of his crucial mission.

Kathryn, young and alone, lay on a big bed in a strange, dark room. Somewhere beyond the room, she heard party sounds: glasses clinking, laughter, her mother's boisterous friends and then a piano. Her mother was singing, "Stormy Weather." Can't go onnn, everythinnng I have is gonnne, stormy weatherrr...

Kathryn shivered against the cold, curling her small body into a ball. In the darkness she knew she wasn't supposed to, but she snuck out of bed and reached around the room for something warm. There was a coat, her mommy's sable coat draped over a chair. Kathryn slipped her arms into the too long sleeves and reveled in how it felt, soft, warm and light, like a furry bathrobe. Wearing it, she crawled back on top of the big bed, feeling closer to her mommy, breathing in the faint remainder of perfume from the coat.

But it was getting too warm now inside the coat, hot, too hot. She tried to throw off the coat, but it grew all around her, moving. She couldn't get it off her.

Grownups stood over her—laughing. Why didn't they help her? Couldn't they see she was trapped? She tried to scream. Nothing came out. One woman's face loomed over her, her smoke gray eyes turning a fiery red.

Awake, clutching her stomach, Kathryn heard, *"Don't be afraid, I'll keep you warm."* It was her own voice.

She lifted her heavy eyelids and stared into tiny red eyeballs moving closer to her.

She screamed and scrambled away, across a dank floor.

The rat retreated somewhere into the darkness.

Kathryn stayed crouched in the corner, shivering cold, clutching herself into the smallest form, desperate for warmth. Where was she? How long had she been there? She had no sense of time at all. She shifted, searching for some ease, but every inch of her ached, from her toes to her hair. Every molecule of her body and spirit was in revolt. She had to get out of this place!

Anthony climbed down out of the plane, his dark fury barely contained, and strode across the uneven tarmac of a remote airfield outside the ancient city of Tangier. Ali followed. Hans waited in the cockpit while the engines of his small jet whined down. A chilly wind whipped under Anthony's scarf and into his flight jacket, raising goose bumps, a chill that belied a scorching heat to come when the sun reached its zenith in the North African sky. That sun could flay his pasty English skin. No matter, he'd come to work in secret, hopefully with the element of surprise, to save Kathryn. And to send to hell her captors who took so much from his world.

A short distance away he saw the outline of three specter-like figures emerge from shadows surrounding a rusted shed. Were these the men he was here to meet? One bearded man raised his arm.

Anthony tensed, then eased his duffle bag to the ground, freeing his good hand to reach for his shoulder holstered Glock.

"*Shalam*," he heard from the bearded man and two others moved from the shade toward Anthony. It was Davood, Ali's cousin and the older of the three men at twenty-two. Sorgi, not as pudgy as he'd been three months ago, ran forward. Achmed, tall and more muscular than when wounded at Jaleh Square, was by his friend's side. These youths had been targeted by the revolutionary guard, and his last mission had been to fly them out before leaving Iran. His zealous Iranian spies were tracking Houdin's nefarious activities, the stolen freighter loaded with loot, and now his kidnapped love.

"*Shalam.*" Anthony touched his fist to his chest, a meter of tension lifting with the sight of them. "Brothers, I'm glad Allah has kept you safe."

"*Shalam*, Anthony," they all said at once, energy vibrating from them. "We have seen Kathryn," Davood said.

It was the information he wanted. "Is she safe?"

They looked from one to the other, awkwardly shifting their weight. Tall Ahmed stepped closer. "She is alive, a captive at Houdin's hideout, a castle on the cliffs. When you called, we went to the airfield where Houdin keeps his private jet."

"And from there," Sorgi said, "we waited until he landed and his Black Glove soldiers took her away, wrapped in a blanket."

Davood said, "We followed a long way and hid outside in the dark. A huge man carried Kathryn inside an old castle, Houdin's hideout."

"You are certain it was her?" Anthony said.

"We were certain when she struggled and her blond hair spilled from the blanket," the shorter Sorgi said.

"So we rescue her as you did us," Achmed said. "Come. We will take you there."

Davood gestured to the waiting Fiat. "Houdin's castle is many miles away."

When it was safe, Hans would rent a chopper and meet Anthony at an appointed rendezvous point to grab Kathryn. Anthony put a reassuring hand on Davood's shoulder and looked into the eyes of his three spies.

There he glimpsed dark fires burning, memories, he

guessed, of the revolution's brutality smashing their be-loved country.

"There is a man in Houdin's employ we can trust," said Davood. "He will do anything to stop Houdin. I think he wants to kill him himself."

"Let's go, then," Anthony said.

They jogged to the Fiat, and took off down a long desert road, going over the many precautions needed for Anthony's plan to work.

That same morning, Mirdad sat in the passenger seat of Houdin's silver Jaguar, enduring an outrageous hangover and Colonel Demitrus Nassiri's wild drive along the cliffs outside Tangier toward Houdin's hillside hideout.

"Slow down!" Mirdad clung to the dubious security of the passenger door handle.

Demi looked furious and seemed unforgiving in his anger as he rammed the accelerator to the floor, rocketing ahead of a truck and three cars.

"You drive like a demon from hell, man." From his facial expression Demi's mood was indeed foul. "I can only free Kathryn if I'm in one piece!"

"Two days at the villa with your hellish mother, the venomous bitch. How do you manage her?"

"I don't." Mirdad slumped lower in the seat and tuned him out. He knew well enough about his mother's viperous rants. He didn't care, he just had to get to Kathryn before she was harmed.

Demi was going on about some infraction his wretched mother had committed for which Mirdad lacked both the ability and the interest to follow. He'd had enough of the bitch.

With great honking, the Jag roared past a poultry truck, foul squawking, feathers flying, the driver in his Moroccan fez, cussing.

Mirdad gasped. His pulse pounded against his brain like a kettledrum. "What ails you today?" He shoved on his Givenchy dark glasses.

Demi reined in his speed and snorted. "You aren't listening."

Mirdad unclenched his fist. He supposed he could force himself to be polite. After all, Demi had aided his escape from the Savoy shoot-out in London.

"Sorry, Demi. What did you say?"

"The guest house. I've arranged private quarters for you at Villa del Sol."

"Ah yes, Villa Del Sol." Mirdad leaned back and in a theatrical tone said, "A hundred years ago on the Moroccan coast near Cape Spartel, a Moorish castle named Castillo del Corazon, built in 1864 by a Spanish nobleman, Juan del Cordoba."

Demi shook his head. "Always a historical quote. You read too much."

"History eases my mind."

"Valik Ajani was a historian, no?"

"My father, yes." Mirdad closed his eyes for a moment and was back in his father's library, the two of them together reading. He opened his eyes. "Castillo del Corazon remained in its original state until a Libyan renegade purchased it in 1974. It was renamed Villa del Sol, a name chosen by the owner to sound anonymous, nondescript—a name that would not draw attention to itself." He glanced over at Demi, who seemed calmed by Mirdad's little recitation.

"But in truth," Mirdad went on, "Villa del Sol, with vast sums of money spent on it by the new Libyan owner, had reached high standards of nobility and then was leased to your friend and mine, General Omar Houdin in December, 1978."

"How do you know all this trivia, Mirdad?"

"History, not trivia, Demi. It always pays to know what one faces. Don't you agree?"

With a smile Demi said, "I do. So, there is a small guest villa at Houdin's castle, used for visiting dignitaries who care for more privacy. It has four bedrooms. Madame Houdin would not hear of you staying there. She wants her adored son close to her. However, she loathes me and is happy to have me away from her presence, and I'm happy to escape her." Demi smiled. "Naturally my small villa is at your disposal for whatever."

Intrigued at this kindness, Mirdad looked over at the handsome but lethal Greek, admiring his profile. "Blessings be upon you, Colonel. At least I will be spared having to be inside the villa with my mother." Mirdad re-assessed the colonel. Perhaps the alarmingly attractive Demi wasn't as dedicated to Houdin as he'd previously thought. He had risked his own safety in London to drag Mirdad away from the police and put him in a cab.

Mirdad recalled the unwavering loyalty Demi's own guard had shown to him in the London brawl. Demi had treated his men with respect where Houdin demanded devotion out of fear. He knew Demi was almost as appalled at Kathryn's abduction as he was. But would Demi help him get her out?

They drove in silence along the coast until they reached a turnoff where Mirdad looked away from the ocean to see Castillo del Sol, solid in its Moorish elegance, ruling the mountaintop.

But instead of heading the Jag up the driveway, Demi pulled over to the cliffside instead, skidding to a stop. He got out and for a moment just stared out over the pounding sea.

Mirdad got out, slamming the car door, his jaw tightened and walked over to Demi yelling, "I may not seem to be in a hurry, but I am. I have deep concerns for Houdin's prisoner. I need to see her."

Demi's look was now one of compassion.

Mirdad's heart thumped against his chest.

"Is this about Kathryn?"

He sensed there was no joy in what Demi would say.

"Mirdad." He sucked in a sharp breath. "There is something you must know."

MIrdad followed Demi's story of the man he had finally found in a mountain village who had blackmailed his mother for years because he was the man she had hired to kill his Aunt Ilyia and Uncle Richard. How Demi had brought to Rena the man, Azi's, head in a crate.

Mirdad walked a few paces away and faced the sea, letting the ocean breeze wash over him, quieting his nausea. His beloved Aunt Ilyia and Uncle Richard blown to bits by his own mother's cunning. If only the breeze could blow away his guilt and stupidity for not before believing his ruthless mother capable of such crimes. Years of worry for her, always he was driven to protect her from evil only to become her murdering dupe. His stomach burned, burned with the pain of his wasted life. He had become as despicable as Rena.

The only people who had loved him—Anthony, Raymond, Tali—dead at his hand.

Crouched in a dark corner shivering, Kathryn heard a clicking noise. With it a blinding shaft of light shot into the room. A massive male body stood in the doorway, black against the light.

"Please, who are you?" Her voice made a small sound in the empty room.

"I've come to take you out of here."

That even, strong voice—somewhere she'd heard him speak before.

"I'm Mohammed. Do you remember me?"

Her panic rose with image blips of a mystery flight, being cold, terrified, drugged, flying away from safety.

She recalled the man in the doorway, with skin like shiny obsidian. He had taken her onto an airplane from London.

"I remember you, Mohammed." She swayed, scrambling to sit up against a stone wall. Her throat was dry, her voice, scratchy.

The dizzying flight had been a blur of discomfort and harsh sounds, then a bumpy landing somewhere, but where? From her nightmarish fog, she recalled this massive man lifting her into the back of an idling truck filled with soldiers, sour smells, and her terror. Leering glances had fallen on her body clad only in a rumpled silk nightgown.

This man, Mohammed, had taken off a poncho-like garment in a woven Moroccan fabric, and covered her with it before she faded into unconsciousness.

Kathryn regarded him, so many questions racing in her mind. Could she trust him? Would he help her get away? "Where am I? What is this place, Mohammed?"

"I will take you out of here. Can you stand up?" Not waiting, he pulled her to her feet. "Here, wear it." He handed her a dark robe.

Shivering she put it on, tied the belt, and reveled in the robe's soft warmth. "Are you letting me go?"

"I cannot," he said, his expression unchanged.

"Please," she said. "Help me."

He stood back and waited for her to walk out of her cell in front of him, but she stumbled and before she could recover, he swept her into his strong arms and carried her through the corridors and up two flights of stairs.

She tensed. "Where are you taking me?"

"Somewhere more accommodating."

In a haze of remorse, Mirdad turned toward the Jag.

"Wait," Demi said, flashing Mirdad an inscrutable look. "Don't get in yet."

Mirdad didn't care if he ever got back in the car. He wasn't even sure who he was anymore—*a man or a monster?*

"Fine. I need some air before I face her, my mother." He almost choked on the words. They walked over to a parking area and sat on an iron bench facing a hotel and café. Le Mirage resort spread across a cliff in stark white contrast to the roaring sapphire sea below. Mirdad leaned on the iron armrest.

Next to Mirdad, Demi's low-pitched voice broke into his thoughts.

"There is one more thing you must know, Mirdad."

"What else could you possibly tell me, Demetrius?"

Demi leaned over. "You knew your mother and Omar were lovers years ago, didn't you?"

"What?" Mirdad had heard him clearly, but it took a moment to absorb this disgusting tidbit. He wanted to weep. "Go on."

"They continued as lovers long after Rena married Prime Minister Ajani. Mirdad, Ajani was not your father... You are Omar's son. Houdin is your father."

Chilled, Mirdad skittered back in his seat, bashing his

spine against the bench armrest, the metal digging in. "This is not possible. My father was—"

"No, Mirdad. Your father is Omar Houdin."

Nooooo!

The pain of it struck hard, he sucked in air, recoiling.

"H-how can you know this?" he stammered." I don't believe you. Just more of my mother's lies to make me obey whatever plans she's made."

"I've seen proof."

Mirdad leaned forward and in a harsh whisper said, "What fucking proof, Demi?"

Demi yanked a fat envelope from his inside breast pocket and slapped it on the bench next to Mirdad.

Mirdad stared at the damning envelope between them. Perhaps it would amount to nothing.

He ripped it open and read through documents and letters from the illicit lovers. One was from a month before his mother married but hadn't mailed, informing Houdin she was pregnant with his child. Many more letters after his father, Valik died. Houdin evidently wouldn't marry her then, because she had been married for twelve years to a disgraced prime minister. He had, however, wanted her as his mistress. And so it went over years until just months ago when the star-crossed lovers had married. *All's well that ends well.* He crumpled the papers, about to rip them up.

Demi grabbed them away, smoothing them and stuffed them back in the envelope. "Houdin has plans for your future," he said. "You are his heir."

Mirdad's lifelong beliefs were shattered, cracking away the world he had known. *Heir to a despot.*

Rivulets of icy revulsion slithered through Mirdad, his soul freezing, his facial muscles stiffened. "I'll bet he does," he said weakly, looking away. His mind brought forward memories of the fabulous man he'd always thought to be his father, clinging to them. *Father,* his heart cried.

"I miss you," he whispered on a tense breath, afraid to unclench his fingers, to let the stamp of value Valik had placed on him disappear and leave him with only this foul news. He wanted to run....

Be strong, as I have taught you, he heard inside his head.

In that moment a glimmer of warmth touched him, and Mirdad grabbed on to the many gifts Valik Ajani had given him. The love he'd shown a small boy, his love for books and history, his deep laughter. Mirdad would reclaim the examples of loyalty to the right people. *His secret.*

He calmed and turned to Demi. They got back in the car and turned up the long driveway to Castillo del Sol. The iron gates opened for them, and Demi drove forward to the *porte au cochere* and stopped.

"Well, now I know who I am. A bastard. Omar Houdin's bastard, born of a witch and a soulless demon." Mirdad let it all sink in and the clues he'd missed: his curiosity over the many kindnesses from Houdin, his generosity. He gave the matter some thought and realized what he wanted most. "Where has Kathryn been kept, Demetrius?"

Demi's soft look hardened. "I've had her moved from a dungeon where your sadistic mother had her thrown.

She is now in your villa suite. She is well guarded by my man, Mohammed. Don't worry."

"You must tell my dear papa of the ill treatment his valuable captive has received. That should piss him off." His voice tight, Mirdad added. "I must see Kathryn at once. My mother wants her dead, you know. But I won't have it. I can't let one more horrible thing happen to her. Kathryn is pregnant. She and my unborn cousin mean the world to me. This whole thing is wrong."

Hidden behind a row of desert boxwoods at the back of Houdin's castle, Anthony huddled with Ali, thoughts of rescuing Kathryn foremost in his mind. Ali's cousin Davood, his spy, scouted for Kathryn's whereabouts. They waited for Davood's return.

In this scented enclave date palms, mint, and citrus mingled, reminding Anthony of his mother's garden in Iran. Of the cool iced tea Tali used to serve him outdoors when he had run and played with his treacherous cousin who was yet to be brainwashed, still a comely little pest following him everywhere.

He shook off the tender image.

His mind had drunk deep from the well of darkness inside him and churned with hatred for Rena, Mirdad, and their coven. How untouchable they considered themselves. He had survived their murderous wrath on the mountaintop, cocooned in fiery flesh. His need for revenge was well forged.

Davood crawled back through the hole they'd dug under the ornate wrought iron fence bordering the grounds.

"High noon," Ali said. "Not exactly the best time for an escape. No cloak of darkness, no sleepy guards."

Davood said, "I got in through a window and saw a maid bring a tray of food from the kitchen. I followed her to a room with two guards by the door. Maybe four others guard that wing, too. This could be the place where they keep her."

"Six men? That's all?" Ali said. "Three to one, we can take them easily."

"Six men in one wing," Davood clarified. "Sorgi and Achmed are circling the perimeter. They'll meet us around back outside the general's quarters."

"Sounds good to me," Anthony said, checking his weapon and adding a silencer. "We have one chance. If we do everything in silence, no noise, complete surprise."

"Understood," Ali said, starting to move.

"No," Anthony said. "Somebody has to guard our exit." He handed Davood a knapsack with clothes for Kathryn.

Davood nudged Ali. "Just be careful who you shoot."

Ali looked down at the gun. "I'd like to shoot them all. If we don't get back, go to Hans. He set the chopper down behind a bluff far enough away from the property not to be seen or heard. Wait there for an hour only, then go."

Ali nodded.

"Okay, let's do it." First Davood then Anthony slid under the fence.

Dressed in black clothes meant for night, they moved

behind shrubs and trees, at times staying as still as stone, then moving again without a sound. They circled around the tennis court, and as they got close to the villa, Anthony saw Houdin swimming in the pool. There were more than a dozen men nearby, four more on the tennis court. He spotted his young spies, Sorgi and Achmed, huddled behind a thick hedgerow and moved to them. They looked winded and unnerved.

"All together there are more than fifty armed Black Glove guards," Sorgi gasped. "Other Black Glove leaders arrived earlier, a gardener told me. They're here making deals for the freighter's cargo. Two containers have been off-loaded into the castle by orders of Madame Houdin."

"Rena?" He wondered which containers she coveted enough to forsake profit from a sale.

"Anthony, the castle is an armed fortress," Achmed whispered. "So many Black Glove soldiers."

And who knew how many more were inside? Anthony looked from one to the other, at the fear growing in their young eyes.

Just as he'd dreaded. The place was crawling with the enemy. Time to change tactics. But first he must withdraw these young men before they were caught. "You've done well," he said. "Now you must all get back to the chopper and wait. This is over for you, but not for me."

Anthony had formed another plan, one that gave him pause. If what his grandfather and Philippe had insisted was true, he had an outside chance. The notion Kathryn considered Mirdad a good friend galled him. How deceived she had been. Mirdad was a rat.

But this situation called for a back door approach, and he would act on Philippe's info and pray it was sound.

Anthony's attention was drawn up to a balcony where Rena stood.

How the sight of her, surveying her luxurious grounds, unscathed by all her crimes, summoned his boiling rage. He remained still as it pulsed through him.

Roiling inside, he and his men edged back. He'd have to risk another plan.

CHAPTER TWENTY-ONE

It was nearly noon as Rena watched Omar from her bedroom balcony. Swimming the last of his laps under the noon sun, he reached the edge, and his attention was caught by Demetrius. Omar leapt out of the glistening pool, rimmed in lapis lazuli, and tied on his terry robe; his thick hair shiny with pool water.

Demetrius came over and babbled words at him. Omar listened and looked up sharply. He grabbed a towel and bounded upstairs, calling out, "Rena, you devil, where are you?"

Rena huffed. So, Omar had swallowed some new bit of tattling Demi had done on her. What? she wondered.

Demetrius, she vowed, would have to disappear like a stone in the ocean.

"This time you go too far," she heard just before Omar stormed through her bedroom door.

He tightened his robe and said, "Have you forgotten my orders, Rena? I heard how you treat our guest, and it must stop." He shook his fist at her. "What an abhorrent thing to lock a lovely young woman in a dank storage room."

He dried his hair and tossed the towel down, wiping his feet on it.

So, she had a new tantrum of his to deal with.

"Only you, Rena, would do something like that. It was excessive and stupid."

Unflinching, she faced him, knowing what she must do.

He shook his head slowly.

"Rena, love." He stepped close and stroked her cheek. "Silky," he said. "You are so lovely, your luscious body clad in silver, shimmering over your breasts." He moved even closer, caressing her hair, pushing a lock over her shoulder. "I will have to punish you for this."

She challenged him with her expression.

"What makes you so very cruel?" he said softly, looking deep into her eyes. "Has life been so bleak for you?"

"You have no idea," she answered in a husky whisper. "It is only when I look at you, I see the sunshine."

"I wanted to resist you," he said. "Blame you, be angry with you, but it is difficult."

Defiant, her gaze never left his.

His knuckles grazed over her silk clad nipples.

She squirmed on an intake of breath.

"In truth, I don't care if you are cruel. Take out all your anger on the world because it leaves the best for me, the wild fire and ice I crave and always find there." He reached for her hair, pulling it. "But you have tested my limits. I have no choice. You must suffer." He crushed her lips to his, and held her until she felt him gain control.

She pulled away and turned her back on him, brushing

the straps of her gown from her shoulders and let it slide to the floor, then looked back at him.

"Do it now, Omar. Punish me."

"You are always astonishing." He peeled off his robe.

Within a minute she would gain control of this encounter.

A guard opened a door to a brightly lit, lovely old suite of rooms. Mohammed carried Kathryn in and put her down, her feet touching plush carpet. He turned and left her, shaky and weak with none of her questions answered.

A thin middle-aged maid in a fresh, starched uniform waited beside a table where a tray of Moroccan food released billowing, steamy aromas, enticing Kathryn's nagging hunger.

"I prepare bath," the maid said, gesturing toward the bed. "Clothes. For you."

"First, may I have something to drink?"

The maid handed her a glass of milk and lowered her eyes. "You must eat, lady." She gestured for Kathryn to sit at the cozy dining table.

"Please," Kathryn said. "Tell me where I am?"

In a halting voice, the woman said, "You are at the general's castle, lady."

"General Houdin?"

She gave a quick nod but appeared uneasy. "Please, eat. I must to your bath." She hurried off to another room, her footsteps silent as she passed over an array of Persian carpets.

Kathryn eyed the glass of milk, her stomach gurgling, her mouth dry with a bitter taste. Strength was what she needed. She sat and drank from the chilled glass, trying not to gulp it down, the liquid soothing, triggering her hunger. She tasted a mouthful of warm lamb and couscous then another and wiped her mouth on an ivory linen napkin. Her gaze was drawn to the fabric square smeared with not just milk and lamb, but dirt.

Her face, arms, legs, and bare feet were filthy. She felt the back of her head, and a clump of matted hair and realized the prevailing bad smell in the room came from her body. She stank like an alley garbage bin. Half-naked, she still had on the same nightgown she had worn to bed in London, now soiled and ruined.

Dizziness and panic assaulted her. She gripped the table edge so hard the dishes rattled. Flashes of a man over her bed in London, his ski mask—his eyes, the smelly toxic cloth covering her nose. All the foggy images flooded her mind. She prayed the drug had not harmed her baby.

From another room in the suite, she heard running water. Sucking in deep breaths, hoping to gather her thoughts and steady her nerves, she caught the fragrance of jasmine, perhaps bath salts. The longing to submerge herself in a clean, fragrant, hot bath almost made her forget the danger here. But she had faced tough odds before. Kathryn glanced around the room assessing her situation.

Where was she? Houdin's Moorish-styled castle.

The carpets were not Persian but Moroccan.

The door swung open. She stood surprised Mohammed had returned so quickly.

He walked toward her. "Come."

She needed more time before facing her captors. "Please, Mohamed. Let me bathe."

He shook his head. "We must go."

"Hello Rena," Kathryn said, facing the woman who glared at her. "How lovely to see you again." She almost gagged on her words.

Kathryn had been brought by Mohammed into an opulent salon, lavishly furnished with heavily carved Spanish antiques and Moorish style silk velvet sofas, adorned with gold tassels. The room overlooked the sea. And there reclining on a sweeping chaise, lounged Rena, dressed in a black Chanel dress, a fitting color for the queen of darkness. With a wave of her hand, Rena sent Mohammed away.

This could be her chance to get away.

"Sorry I wasn't able to dress for the occasion," Kathryn said.

"Not at all, my dear, you look charming." A slow, strange smile stretched across Rena's face. "Charming."

Rena's eyes raked over Kathryn's body from head to toe and back again, not missing a thing. Kathryn felt like a specimen under Dr. Hyde's microscope. It was obvious from the look on her face that Rena despised her. The woman seemed to carry some personal vendetta. It was not the time for Kathryn to show fear, though she was terrified.

Smoky eyes perused her and suddenly locked on Kathryn's abdomen, and Rena howled her recognition. "You conniving whore," Rena shrieked.

As she continued to shriek her fury, Kathryn froze. For the first time she was deadly aware of the extent of Rena's hatred.

Standing strong, Kathryn steeled herself against an onslaught, spurred by knowledge she alone must protect her baby, she must go on the offensive. "Why have you brought me here?" Kathryn demanded. "What do you want?"

"Silence!" Rena shrieked. "I will tell you when to speak."

Kathryn stepped closer and made eye contact with Rena, hoping to communicate strength in front of her enemy. "How can I help you so we can get out of here?"

"You? You help me?" Rena said. "Ha! It's you who needs help, you fool! Far more than you imagine. Unless of course," she stepped closer to Kathryn, "unless you become exceedingly cooperative in every way." Rena threw back her head, filling the tense atmosphere with harsh laughter.

"Let's cut this petty intimidation," Kathryn broke in. "We both know what you want. The Persian Glories. My Persian Glories. They're mine now, Rena, not your sister's and not yours!" Kathryn smiled.

"Slut!" Rena screamed.

"You're pathetic," Kathryn went on, consciously increasing the sound of her fury, bracing herself for Rena's inevitable response. "You wanted everything your sister ever had, didn't you? Isn't that why you killed her?"

Rena shot her hand out, slapping Kathryn across the face.

Barely flinching from the blow she'd expected, Kathryn screamed back, "Murderer!" She planted her feet squarely and returned the slap with greater force. "That's for Anthony!" Then not waiting for Rena to recover, Kathryn pulled back her fist and slugged Rena in the jaw, knocking her to the floor. "And that's for what you did to your own son."

Seizing the moment of surprise, Kathryn bolted, but before she made it to the door, she ran into a solid mass of humanity, Colonel Demetrius Nassiri.

From behind him Mirdad barged in the room shouting, "Mother! Where is she?" He stopped and looked from his mother holding her purpling jaw to Kathryn writhing as Demi held onto her.

Rena howled and charged Kathryn.

Mirdad stepped between them. "Mother, calm yourself," he said harshly. He pulled his mother into an embrace, spinning her away from Kathryn, moving toward the open terrace doors overlooking an undulating sapphire sea.

"Shh, shh, dearest Maman. You are so close to having your heart's desire."

"The bitch struck me!"

"She will be gone soon, Maman, shh, shh..." he crooned, soothing his mother, and waved a hand to a cowering servant. "Bring ice and a cloth for my mother at once." He led his mother to her dressing table.

Nassiri backed Kathryn from the room.

Demi hurried Kathryn away, and they climbed another flight of stairs, her nerves still racing. She had enjoyed slugging Rena, knocking her to the floor. A smile curved on Kathryn's parched lips. Even the sting of Rena's slap was worth it. But now more than ever she had to escape before Rena retaliated. That wouldn't be pretty.

Demi said, "I'm moving you back to Mirdad's suite."

"Mirdad's suite?" She had been in Mirdad's room? Oh God, she must persuade him to help her get away and soon.

Demi unlocked the door to the sumptuous suite. "A better place for your safety and privacy."

She almost laughed at herself, a filthy captive in this sparkling room, walking on priceless carpets with filthy bare feet. She was dirty, gritty, bruised, and she stank. She must get clean. They entered the suite and were greeted by the same kind housemaid she had met earlier.

"I will refresh your bath," the maid said to Kathryn, eyeing the welt on her cheek. "Yes? And a poultice perhaps."

Nassiri nodded. "Yes. Go." He turned to Kathryn. "You must eat, bathe, and rest. You will be well guarded."

Kathryn's longing for all those pleasures swept over her like sunlight illuminating memories, always of Anthony, her bath with him in his apartment in Teheran, dressing and undressing for him, sharing a lovers' picnic on his bed next to his warm, male body. Bread, cheese, and oranges consumed, the juice drizzling down his chin, her licking it off. Momentarily Rena was gone from her sphere of thought.

Demi went on, "We brought you clothing and such from Tangier." His voice deepening as he added, "Be assured, neither Mirdad nor I will let anyone do you further harm. Rest well."

"Wait, Colonel, please. Can you tell me what is going on?"

"My name is Demetrius. And yes, I believe you know why you are here, no?"

"For a mad woman's obsession to own the Persian Glories."

"Perhaps."

"And Mirdad? Is he obsessed with the jewels, too?"

"Only with keeping you and your child safe from his mother's unpredictable nature. Mirdad cares deeply for you. He wants to have a relationship with his new cousin when the time comes and will be proud to be your child's godfather and only Persian relative."

"Please," Kathryn said, "find a way out of here for me and my child."

He nodded and left Kathryn with all her longing to be free pent up inside. She shoved her filthy hair off her face and took in a heavy breath. Could she trust Mirdad or Demetrius? She'd find out. The maid led her to a steaming bath.

Mirdad's heavy heart weighed on him from many angles when he met Demi on the path to the guesthouse. He pondered how to save Kathryn from his mother's deadly grip, and go on to live in Paris, away from his parents and still care for his Iranian orphans. And his absolute need to be finished with the Persian Glories, once and for all. They walked around the back of the manicured property in full view of the Mediterranean Sea.

"Mirdad, you need to relax. You're wound too tight," Demi said. "I've arranged a massage for you."

Mirdad glanced over at his companion. "Once again, your kindness is welcome, Demi."

They came around a bend where Mirdad saw a mini-Moorish villa sparkling with more charm than he could have imagined. Carved arches in the sand-colored stone, inlaid tile, and soaring dark, carved doors with massive brass hinges, beckoned. The path was flanked by flowering plants giving off a pure fragrance, ridding his senses of Rena's cloying perfume.

The front doors swung open. Mirdad stepped inside and felt a great weight lift from him.

"You seem to have sprung to life in front of my eyes," Demi said.

"I'm amazed," Mirdad laughed softly. "That's how I suddenly feel—alive again."

A valet awaited him, taking his jacket and his drink request.

"Not bad," Mirdad observed.

"Well, let's see if we can make it even better." Demi clapped his hands.

A long-legged beauty in a short, transparent top and gossamer harem pants with nothing underneath appeared, offering a tray of drinks and snacks. Another sat at Mirdad's feet, removing his shoes.

"I had no idea your tastes ran in this direction, Demi. I'm well pleased."

Demi smiled back, and Mirdad once again noticed the colonel could be charming—and damned attractive—though admittedly arrogant.

"I've seen to further preparations..." Demi ushered him into a massive, elegant bathroom. The walls, floors, and ceilings were tiled in aqua, beige, rose, and gold as intricately interwoven as in any Moroccan palace. A large oval pool was the focal point of the room. Mirdad moved to the side of the pool. Four slender columns surrounded it, spiraling upward into a domed Moorish ceiling of tiny mirrors, reflecting fantasy images from below. He was transfixed by the orchids and palms, and a cage of exotic birds flanked the pool filled with steaming, scented water. A beautiful silver hashish pipe, inlaid with lapis lazuli and pink tourmaline, stood filled on the tile ledge.

"Ha! What are we waiting for? This way, *ma cherie.*" Mirdad stripped himself naked, then peeled the filmy fabric off a blond girl, his hands lingering on her soft body. Laughing, he took her with him and sank into the water. "Delicious. Aren't you coming? There are two girls, you know."

Demi blushed, then smiled and clapped his hands again. "You mean four!"

Another pair of beauties appeared from the bedroom already undressed except for the delicate gold chain belts and ankle bracelets they wore. Mirdad watched Demi's response as he looked from one to the other.

"Lovely," he said. "Come on."

Demi undressed at the side of the pool, staring into the water.

Mirdad appraised the body Demi was so proud of, his smile fading, and his urges growing more intense. Once again, his smile returned, his eyebrows raised slightly in acknowledgement of what he saw.

He looked away when Demi grinned and slid into the water.

The girls were silky soft and slippery under Mirdad's hands. He turned away from them and lit the pipe. Together he and Demi smoked, exhaling into the steamy room. Mirdad stretched in the water next to Demi, the sensual effects of the cannabis taking over. His glance fell away from the women and into his companion's eyes.

Demi returned the look. "I'm captivated by this regal manner of yours. Like a young prince, graceful and haughty, your smile, those eyes." Casually, Demi extended his powerful arms and skillfully stroked Mirdad's shoulders and back with a technique that must have taken years to perfect.

Without seeming aware of it at first, Mirdad relaxed under Demi's touch. Then he turned to him and saw a look of rapt expectancy, and Mirdad was hooked.

The one piercing glance penetrated Mirdad's studied armor, his pretense of seduction. He knew then it was he who was being seduced, and he never wanted anything more.

Mirdad clapped his hands and the girls quietly left the room.

Demi watched him—always his disarming smile—and Mirdad moved toward him.

"I am yours to teach," he murmured, moving into the circle of Demi's arms, running his hands over gorgeous, muscled forearms, biceps, and shoulders. "Isn't this what you were after, Demetrius?"

"I cannot lie, even to myself. Yes, for some time now. You're exactly what I want." All restraint gone, he took hold of Mirdad and brought him into his fantasy. Mirdad let go. He had a few fantasies of his own to share.

Neither of them held back.

Mirdad awoke with a start and focused on his surroundings. They had bathed and napped, Mirdad cloaked in Demi's warmth, his first time ever sleeping next to someone. Quietly he stood, put on his robe, and left the bedroom. Finally, he'd had his first consensual homosexual adventure, and it was exciting. It was great, however...

It wasn't the fact he had been with a man that disturbed him but images of Anthony and himself swirling in his mind. Anthony's eyes the color of the Elburz forest where they'd run, or the Caspian Sea where they'd splashed. So filled with life—a life Mirdad had taken.

The picture slowly unraveled, plummeting him back to the present. Mirdad groaned, clutching his chest as if he could keep his heart from cracking open to his long denied yearning for another.

Anthony. *How I loved you,* Mirdad mouthed, unable to hold back the sea of sorrow he had freed. *Always you. Was it so terrible to love you? So terrible I needed to kill you, to deny it?*

Chest heaving, he brought himself back under control. He stood and looked around, only now noticing the envelope someone had slid underneath the door. He picked it up and glanced at the address. *Cousin Mirdad,* in Anthony's handwriting. Shaking, Mirdad tore open the missive and read the text.

> *Sorry to disappoint you, cousin. I'm alive.*
>
> *Tell me Kathryn is all right, you haven't hurt her.*

Mirdad staggered back, his world tilting on its axis. He read on.

> *I watched Aran put a hole through Raymond's brain. I watched him die. I watched them kill Tali. Your men took my family ring I had placed on Raymond's hand before my world exploded.*
>
> *Come to the seaside café on the bluff—alone—now. Or I'll find you.*
>
> *Time to talk. A.*

How could it be? He shuddered with a combination of fear and hope. Perhaps? He threw the note on the table.

Mirdad dressed and ran from the guest villa into the courtyard and hopped into the idling Jag he had ordered. His mind tormented him, as well as his stomach. Those Parisian doctors. *Merde*! What did they know? He needed to calm down. He could well be trusting the wrong person. He would find out.

Mirdad straightened his ivory linen sport coat and saw Demi running after him. "Go back inside, Demi."

"Don't go, Mirdad." Demi ran after him, grabbing his jacket lapels. "You're taking a huge chance. I read the note."

"I must know if it's him." Mirdad read anguish in Demi's eyes. Now look what he had done. The amazing warrior, Demetrius, was falling in love with him, he was certain. So what, he smirked at his own chastisement.

Demi said, "I'll hide with my M14 rifle. I won't interfere—unless you signal for help."

Mirdad put his hand over Demi's, adoring the warmth there.

Demi relaxed.

"Go back to our guest villa," Mirdad said. "Swear you'll wait there!"

Demi nodded and left.

When he arrived at the café, Mirdad charged through to its entrance, hoping Demi would keep his word.
In the cliffside café, Mirdad took off his dark glasses and fought for composure. This was not one of his favorite places, too many tourists. But now he wanted people

around for some sense of safety. Thankfully, the decor wasn't overpoweringly elaborate; that was a plus. He'd had enough of his mother's gaudy surroundings at the castle.

Musicians in white *djellabas* and silk turbans, sat behind a railed balcony overlooking the sea, and played traditional Moroccan music.

He headed for his table, set for two, inhaling the aroma of lemon chicken with couscous. He was not hungry, but he ordered *pasicillas* and a drink, as if he was calm. He had cash ready to slap down on the table if he needed to make a sudden exit.

As he sat back sipping ouzo, steadying his nerves, he heard laughter around him, and a voice he would know anywhere said, "It's not every day a man gets to face his own murderer."

Mirdad looked up. There stood Anthony, scarred, his skin quite pale as if he'd been in a cave for three months. Quickly, Mirdad set down the glass of ouzo before he dropped it and stumbled to his feet, his facial muscles tensing as Anthony faced him.

"True," Mirdad said. "Nor the murderer to face a corpse resurrected."

"Sit, Mirdad."

Mirdad sat, feeling naked under Anthony's scrutiny. He shifted his seat slightly more into shadow.

"I did come close to death, if that makes you feel any better."

There was a hint of a smile from Anthony, a sinister smile. The changes to his debonair cousin were arresting.

"Where is Kathryn?"

"She is safe and well."

"I want her away from this place."

The waiter placed a glass of ouzo in front of Anthony, and Mirdad waved him away.

Anthony shook back his long hair, tucking it behind his ears and drained his glass. His right ear and right hand were veined with purple scars. Another sliced his right eyebrow, and from below Anthony's dense beard, a similar webbing of scars ran down his neck. His beautiful green eyes burned with a dark fire.

"Actually," Anthony said, "did you know, if exposed to sunlight, second degree burns will turn purple and stay that way?"

"I—I didn't know that." Hence, Anthony's pallor.

"However," Anthony continued, "in order to heal without severe scarring, one must scrub the burns each night with a cloth—until they bleed."

"Painful." Mirdad loathed himself.

"Quite. But effective. I'm told within a year or two, most scarring, the second-degree scars anyway, will fade away." He raised his dissected eyebrow. "The majority, you do not see. But it gives one hope for a brighter, if not more attractive future."

Mirdad's immediate impulse, oddly, had been to hug Anthony. Perhaps not such a good idea after his despicable behavior.

Stupid, stupid, stupid. Anthony would surely prefer shoving a knife through his heart. Mirdad searched around the restaurant for foreseeable threats, but saw none.

"How you must hate me."

Anthony's jaw tightened.

"I won't ask you to forgive me," Mirdad began. "I can't forgive myself. And although I can never undo what is done, please believe me, I have regretted it every day and night since. And I will tell you this, I am not the same person I was before."

"I don't give a fuck who you are." Anthony started to get up, but Mirdad caught his arm.

"Please, I'll do whatever it takes to help you. You see, Anthony, I love her, too." Mirdad watched Anthony fume.

"You have a sick way of showing it."

"I have done an evil thing," Mirdad said.

"Which one? Which evil thing are you referring to, cousin?" Anthony's body stiffened, and it was as if Mirdad could feel his rage surge.

"But I did not do this thing to Kathryn." Mirdad's face heated. "It was Rena's doing."

"Your mother is insane," Anthony said. "Isn't that obvious?"

"I came to make certain Kathryn is not harmed in any way."

"Is that anguish on your face or self-pity?"

Mirdad did not answer him.

"For God's sake, Mirdad, tell me where she is. I have to get her out of here now. If she's hurt, I'll kill you."

Mirdad steadied himself. He must play this right. "No, not hurt," Mirdad said. "She's resting. She's fine." He leaned in across the table. "I have a plan to get her safely out, and to satisfy my mother."

"Rena will never stop, will she, until she has the Glories?"

"You are correct. So, Anthony, do you live in danger from her obsession? Or give up the diamonds?"

"You think for a moment I give a crap about those diamonds when Kathryn is threatened?"

"Then hear the plan I've laid out to save Kathryn."

CHAPTER TWENTY-TWO

Returning to the castle property, Anthony trailed Mirdad, carrying a bulging laundry bag on his shoulder, his face hidden under a burnoose, more than ever anxious to make his call to London then to see Kathryn. And that would happen if Demetrius Nassisri, a wild card, was on board with the plan.

They made their way to the guesthouse, and Mirdad pushed open the door. Nassiri looked up at the ghost and staggered out of his chair gasping transfixed at the sight of him. "No! It can't be!" A flood of emotion washed over his face.

Aware of Demetrius Nassiri closing the door behind him, turning the lock, and reaching for his gun, Anthony held his anger in check. "Let's get on with this, Mirdad, and get Kathryn out of here."

Mirdad walked over, perched himself on the edge of a carved desk, and picked up the phone.

"Sit down, Colonel, we have a plan to discuss." Anthony motioned toward the plush sofa. "You won't be needing the Glock."

"Oh?" he looked to Mirdad.

"We have come in peace to solidify a way out of this mess—forever," Mirdad said.

"I don't have much time, you'll note," Anthony said, nonetheless walking by the marble coffee table and lighting a cigarette before he sat down and looked up at Mirdad. "Funny, how I once wanted to do nothing but protect you," he said. "I should have killed you both at the Savoy when I could. Then we'd all have been spared this."

"That was you?" Mirdad let out a sarcastic laugh. He, too, lit a cigarette. His hand still trembled but he seemed calmer to Anthony. He went to the bar and poured himself a soda water.

This was not the picture Anthony had expected. He remembered Kathryn saying Mirdad had changed. He was starting to see what she had meant. Still, it was hard to believe.

"So convince me," he said. "Tell me why Houdin is doing this. I know what Rena wants, but what's in it for Houdin?"

Mirdad sat down in the chair across from him. "It's the crown jewels. Houdin knows your grandfather has them. And he wants them."

"In fact," Nassiri added, "he's already made a deal to sell them."

Anthony stared. Only the empress knew he had taken the crown jewels. "How? How did he find out?"

"Alexandria Badiyi," Mirdad said.

"Don't looked so shocked." Nassiri laughed. "She was able to get a lot of useful information out of her mother, the empress's assistant."

Right. It all made sense. "The self-serving little bitch," Anthony said.

"A ransom request for Kathryn has already gone to your grandfather," Nassiri said.

Anthony closed his eyes, knowing full well his grandfather could never let the crown jewels of a foreign country be used in a terrorist act. No matter who they could save, even someone he loved, even for me. He looked up.

Nassiri watched him. "It won't be easy to get Kathryn out. And if you're thinking you can take her by force, it only takes one bullet to kill her. I know how Houdin thinks. Believe me, this place is heavily guarded."

He glared at him. "Don't give me that crap, Nassiri, you're his fucking adjutant! You can arrange anything."

"Madame Houdin doesn't trust either of us. She'll have us watched. We're off her favored list," said Nassiri. "So call your grandfather, Evans. Negotiate, that's what you know, so do it well."

Anthony sat looking at the glowing ash on the cigarette in his hand, knowing what he had to do. He got to his feet and smashed the cigarette in an ashtray. "I have a plan of my own, so listen up. Once I secure the exchange details with my grandfather, I leave here—with Kathryn. We fly to Marrakech. I'll give you our destination, where we'll stay. When I know the diamonds are in Moroccan airspace, Mirdad and only Mirdad will come to pick her up with just enough time for the meet-up. At no time will Rena have access to Kathryn."

"And why the hell should we believe you, Evans?" Demi said.

Mirdad stood. "Because we want the same thing. To live our lives free from Houdin and Rena. Let them have all the jewels, just not the people we love."

Nassiri and Mirdad exchanged telling looks. They were a team, Anthony guessed. "So be it."

"Make your call, Evans, then I'll guide you to Kathryn's apartment," Nassiri said. "You will have time together before the guards change and then you go." He paused. "She is brave for a woman. She slugged Rena."

Mirdad and Anthony grinned.

"Yes, she is," Anthony said. "All right, we'd better act fast because my grandfather won't do anything unless he hears from me."

Nassiri stood and gestured to the phone.

"And you'll have to shower before I allow you to see her." Mirdad said. "You smell like a desert rat."

In less than three minutes, Anthony's call was through to London, and he heard the familiar gruff voice. "Grandfather, they have her at the general's castle."

"Morocco?"

"Yes. We were delayed by the storm. I'm here now with Mirdad. He will help."

"You can't be serious!" Charles said.

"He wants her safe, as we do. You received the request?"

"You know as well as I do the crown jewels are the

property of a sovereign nation and can't be touched. I won't do it even for you."

"We both know what you must do, who you must call. The crown jewels are a deal breaker."

Silence. "Hmmm...I haven't spoken to my old Parisian friend Monsieur Arpel for a while. I'm sure he could part with his best replica of the crown jewels for a price anyway. Afterall he did make twenty-five copies. One must be worthy of Kathryn's life. I'll do it at once...but, Anthony, you must realize by now that woman wants Kathryn dead."

Anthony continued his phone arrangements for the jewel exchange, waiting as Charles made calls on another line to coordinate.

With Anthony busy, Mirdad pulled Demi into an alcove.

"Do you have any regrets, Demetrius? Are you sure you don't wish to change your mind?"

Demi turned to Mirdad sharply. "Should I?"

Mirdad put his arm around Demi's shoulder. "I want you with me, but you must know for certain if you'll regret turning against Houdin."

Demi's dark eyes glowed when he said, "Never, never. I have no regrets. I'm going with you."

"Good. We'll be together soon enough. After the exchange I'll meet you in Paris. We'll drive to the Cote d'Azur from there. It's just that I want you safe, out of here in case things go wrong." Before Demi could protest again, Mirdad went on. "Don't worry, I have no intention of going down with Houdin on this. You and I, we will have one last task to insure all goes well at the hand-off outside Marrakesh and then..."

Mirdad could say no more or his emotions would weaken his resolve.

Deep compassion shone in Demi's eyes. "It will be done and then Paris. The two of us."

Mirdad cleared his throat. "Here's your letter of credit and the other papers you'll need when you arrive. And the key to my safety deposit box and to my flat." He smiled.

Demi's hand grazed his. "I'll be waiting."

"Till then," Mirdad said. "I must go to Rena now. Later, Houdin." He touched Demi's shoulder. "My cousins must be kept safe from now until after the exchange. Their safety is our main objective throughout this operation. No telling what my mother will try."

Anthony hung up the phone and waited for Mirdad, pretending he hadn't overheard Mirdad and Demi converse.

"Are we set?" Mirdad asked.

"The Persian Glories and Iran's crown jewels will be at the airfield outside Marrakech in two days. My grandfather and Philippe will see to it."

"Good. Then I'm on my way to meet with Mother and Houdin to get our plan underway." He motioned for Nassiri to wait outside and turned back. "Please, Anthony, hear me just for one minute."

Anthony did not want to hear what Mirdad had to say, but since he had agreed to make this plan possible, he paused. "I'm listening."

"This is not an excuse," Mirdad said, "but all those years back, I never knew anyone cared for me or knew you had helped us. All I heard was you left us in the dirt. There were no calls, no letters, no communication, no money, nothing from the day you left Iran. I wrote to you, I even tried to call."

"Not true," Anthony said. "I wrote dozens of times."

"Well, I never got your letters or knew you sent money. My mother, no doubt, made certain of that after my father was imprisoned."

Anthony, of course, had known this from MI-6.

"And now I know he wasn't even my father. I don't even know who I am." He laughed, a hollow sound. "You see, I'm a bastard. Omar Houdin's bastard. Isn't it funny? Everything was taken from me—even my identity. I saw nothing but the veil of hate my mother put before me each day. I'm sorry, sorrier than I can possibly tell you, Anthony."

Anthony sighed and leaned heavily against the doorway. Fathomless pain in Mirdad's eyes revealed that he spoke the truth. His energy was so different, one Anthony recognized from long, long ago. Maybe Mirdad had been resurrected from the dead, just as he had.

At one time Anthony would have embraced him, but that was beyond consideration now. Understanding what had happened to Mirdad was one thing; but forgetting or forgiving the horror his cousin had created for everyone, Kathryn, sweet Tali, Raymond and Ali was challenging. He tried to lay these thoughts to rest. Anthony still needed

Mirdad's help and diplomacy was his ally. "Peace, brother," Anthony said.

Mirdad shined with a look of courage. "Peace to you, brother."

Bright sunlight from a clear afternoon sky reached into Rena's salon. Mirdad reentered her room armed for battle, feeling like he'd been gone a thousand years, but in fact it only had been a few hours. She hadn't noticed him yet.

He stared at his mother, still reeling from the truth he had finally seen clearly, the knowledge she had always been the chess master and he, her pawn. The realization gnawed his gut. He was being eaten away from within. His own mother—the royal bitch of all times.

Rena lounged on her sofa, beside a vanity table, sipping espresso with one hand, and holding ice to her bruised face with the other. She still hadn't seen him.

He took out his handkerchief and wiped all emotions from his face. It was his own demons he needed to crush. He was no longer a brainwashed child, but a man about to go his own way—and he wanted to make her squirm.

Rena swiveled to him and then back to her mirror, repairing her make-up. "Mirdad, you've returned to me," she said, her voice purred like a malevolent cat, drawing him to her.

"Why are you here, my son? Did you miss me so much you managed to tear yourself away from the casinos and your whores at La Mamounia?"

"The ransom note has been sent. We've had an immediate response," Mirdad said.

"My! News travels fast." Her eyes sparkled up at him.

As the light crept closer, its rays reaching her, Rena grabbed her sunglasses, put them on, and turned her head away irritably. She snapped her fingers and a servant poured espresso then left the room.

Rena glanced over her son. "Mirdad, how wonderful you came back! You, dressed in your fine linen suit, have become even more handsome, my son." She gestured to a delicate porcelain cup of steaming espresso set out for him. "Drink your coffee while its hot, darling."

He took a sip, still standing. "I have something to tell you, Mother, and I believe you have something to tell me, too." He finished his coffee, set down his cup and and moved closer to her. "My cousin, Anthony, left a will." He pulled a sheaf of papers from his inside coat pocket.

He watched her pulse speed up at the base of her throat, her hands clenching and unclenching as if clammy.

"Is this fabulous news or dire? Obviously, you've read it?"

He kept his reaction in check.

"Really, Mirdad, I'm not a mind reader!" She glared. "You look red-faced but seem quite calm."

"Here, Mother, wouldn't you like to see for yourself?" he held the document out to her.

"Well, of course, darling, but it's so bright out. Can't you read it to me?"

"Certainly," he said taking his time unfolding the papers.

"'In the event of my death, I, Anthony Evans'—no, I'll skip the preliminaries. Let's see, 'my estate in Shiraz and all the property in it goes to my cousin, Mirdad Ajani...Why that's me, isn't it, Mother? Oh, but the house burnt to the ground, didn't it?"

Rena suddenly sat up straight and stared at him, looking appalled by the fabulous wealth that had been destroyed. "What?" She slammed her cup down on a side table and yanked the paper from his hand. Her gaze followed her finger, skimming down the page.

Mirdad said, "Doesn't it say something about the house we have lived in for the last fourteen years?" He forced a smile. "Your house, costing you so much?"

"That insignificant place!" She waved her hand at him. "Quiet!" Her eyes burned up the page, and she was unable to believe the rest of it. "There's resort property on the Caspian Sea, a lodge in the mountains, and a ranch in the north of Iran! How fabulous!"

She looked up at Mirdad. "Where is this ranch? And the Caspian property? Is there a villa on it?"

"Oh, yes, with ten bedrooms. Lovely place. But as you have done occasionally, I've forgotten to mention one catch." He stepped closer.

"What, sweetheart? What did you forget to tell me?"

He heard a slight edge of nerves in her voice.

"It's Anthony, Mother." Mirdad leaned closer. "He didn't die."

"What do you mean, he didn't...?"

"He's alive. In fact, he paid me a visit today."

"WHAT ARE YOU TALKING ABOUT?" Rena leaped from her seat, but Mirdad grabbed her and pushed her roughly back down onto the sofa.

"Yes. He agreed to our ransom request for the diamonds." He stood looming over her and continued to speak in the same irritating tone.

So the half-breed was alive. She was no longer to deal with Anthony's ancient grandfather to gain back her Glories, but Anthony himself. Well, she would use him and then would settle his destiny with a final tragic death. She would enjoy the spectacle.

"He said he would be happy to see you again, Mother, and would set a time to meet us at a private Marrakesh airport in a few days, giving him time to secure all the diamonds at the appointed hour. Tsk, tsk. Can you imagine, Mother, loving someone so much as to give up the Persian Glories for their safety?"

Rena turned away, rubbing her brow, vexed by this notion Anthony lived. "How could this be? Are you certain, Mirdad? Anthony was burned in a fire. It must be an imposter, you fool."

Mirdad came close up in her face.

She cowered. "Who is this monster child of mine?" She gave him a shove, but he was unmovable, an iron man.

He stood and moved the hair off his forehead, looking down at her. "And he did ask me to mention one more thing to you. He expects you to be gracious to Kathryn, because he doesn't want to have to slit Auntie Rena's throat like the two guards we found downstairs."

She jerked back. He wouldn't be alive long enough to get to her. "Whoever it is I don't care. The man must be disposed of."

Mirdad sat calmly in a chair across from her and crossed his long legs. "Now. Isn't there something you have to tell me?"

Rena caught her breath. "What else is there to say? The plan is working. My Persian Glories are coming to me." Rena eyed him suspiciously. "What the hell are you getting at?"

"Didn't you want to tell me who my father really is? Or maybe you've forgotten." His eyes narrowed. "Or maybe you don't know. You slut."

Rena's mouth gaped. But this time she held her tongue.

Once Demetrius Nassiri led Anthony to Kathryn's guarded door, he knocked lightly, and a housemaid answered.

"Sir?"

Anthony stepped up. "I'm here to see my wife," he said and walked in. "Where is she?" A moment of surprise flew across the maid's face before she looked to Colonel Nassiri for confirmation.

"Yes," Nassiri said. "Fetch her." He bent to Anthony. "You have three hours until the guards change shift and then you go. Houdin will be busy negotiating with his partners longer than that. My guards will insure your privacy." With this last reassurance, he left.

"The lady, she is in the bedroom," the maid extended her hand. "This way, sir."

"And what is your name?" Anthony said.

She looked stunned someone would ask this. "My name is Mina, sir. I will wait outside, until you call." With that, she left.

Anthony walked to a doorway and entered a bedroom large enough for a palace. He looked around stunned, seeing recognizable objects, many he knew quite well. Resentment hammered at him.

And then he saw her. *Kathryn...*

She stood on top of the bed, her back to him, examining an enormous carved wood headboard. Her damp hair was longer, it hung in waves over her shoulders. Her curves even through a Moroccan, cerulean blue cotton skirt and blouse, were luscious. Her trim ankles and long slender feet made him smile. The smile felt foreign, good.

Riveted to the floor, he absorbed the tableau, knowing he would never forget the sight of her at this moment, wearing garments embroidered with butterflies and daffodils the same gold as her hair. And though every part of him longed for her, he would move slowly as he was still a ghost.

Across the room Kathryn's engaged energy vibrated around the room. She ran her hands over smooth, deeply carved wood, clouds, and the heads of winged cherubs, polished to a glistening umber.

He heard, "This is beautiful, Mina, where is it from?"

"A church in Holland," a male voice said. "It was part of an altar piece. It belonged to my grandmother."

Kathryn's mind whirled at the sound of the voice. Her body froze. The accent British, rich, husky, and familiar caught her breath.

"What...what did you say?" She turned and faced a tall, bearded man removing his burnoose. A trimmed beard, overly long hair, dressed in faded jeans, and a loose white collarless shirt.

"The carved angels...they're part of an altar piece. It's signed on the back by the artist and dated." He moved closer. "The signature is burned into the wood. It belonged to my grandmother."

She stared, in shock. "Anthony." Their eyes met. From a distance she heard her own voice calling him. "Anthony?" She gaped at him, unsure.

"I didn't mean to frighten you, Kathryn."

She heard every word, or some part of her did, as if from a great distance. Hearing him speak her name she felt the room begin to spin. Was this still another apparition? On a rainy street in London, on a stallion under moonlight. Was she imagining him now? His face, oh God, the eyes. She relived her horror and loss in that London park, learning he'd been killed, the pain of it strangling her again. And now? "Anthony?"

The walls, the words, the smells from the furniture polish, and the general strangeness of the day were suddenly overwhelming. The voice of the man who moved so slowly toward her. She felt hot, no cold. She leaned away, not believing what she saw, tears spilled down her face and she stumbled falling forward.

"Kathryn..."

Anthony lunged awkwardly and caught her to him, then set her free. He gazed down at her, breathing heavily. "Kathryn, my love."

Wobbly, she stood before him, her eyes widened, her mind striving to adjust. She gained her focus and fixed warily on his face, absorbing his reappearance. Her senses came alive, senses she thought she'd buried with his memory. She was hungry to drink him in, to fill her eyes, her yearning heart and her arms with him.

"I missed you more than words can say," he whispered.

Tentatively she touched his face, her fingers connected with his flesh, warm and real. She gasped softly. His quiet smile formed under her fingers.

Her gaze traveled over his face as her fingers had done, from the beard he'd grown to emerald eyes brimming with emotion. He could be an actor or the brilliant photographer he was.

His wonderful scent enveloped her, and his lopsided grin took hold of her heart.

She smiled. "You smell so good."

His smile stretched across his face. "Let's get you some air," he said, lifting her.

With Kathryn cradled in his arms, Anthony carried her out onto the covered terrace garden.

She was barely aware of sounds from birds, the gurgling fountain or the scent of jasmine filling the sun-bright day, for all she could see or feel, was this man, real and alive.

"A fine thing," he murmured. "I've not seen you in three months and first thing you almost pass out on me."

"You make me weak in the knees."

He pressed her hand to his lips. "I'm sorry it took me so long to come back to you, Kathryn."

Her eyes filled, and for a moment his features blurred. "I thought I'd never see you again." Kathryn's mind strived to adjust. "Where were you?" She must know what happened to him. "Do you want to put me down?"

"No, not ever," he said. "I revel in this treasure in my arms." He kissed her brow. "And the feel of your velvety skin next to mine." His eyes closed briefly. "No, I never want to let you go."

Tears stung her face. "Those are love words."

"For the woman I love."

"I thought I'd lost you forever."

She slid down his body, and he pressed her close, pushing the hair from her forehead.

She touched him again, first his shoulders, his biceps. "You're not a ghost."

He brushed her hand with his lips. "I'm getting us out of here."

"How?"

"I've negotiated. We have a few hours together."

"Really?"

"I promise." He grabbed her to him.

"They told me you were dead...gone...a terrible accident..."

"I know."

"When I heard, I couldn't listen. I wouldn't believe it. I thought I would go mad. It was the worst moment of my life." Agony locked in her heart broke through, and she sobbed until she could regain composure, still hiccupping.

He brushed her hair from her face.

"You are real and alive, aren't you?"

His low voice filled with emotion, he said, "Very much alive."

She leaned closer. "Then prove it," she whispered back.

He held her face in his hand and bent to her. "My supreme pleasure." His lips met her yielding mouth with soft kisses. His tongue traced her upper lip. "God, how I've missed you."

His mouth tasted of such sweet passion, exploring, taking, yielding, wiping out lost days, weeks, months of separation and longing. She pushed closer, lost in love. Her need unleashed her fathomless desire for this man, no longer a ghost. He brushed her cheek with his lips. "I've longed for you." He gathered her to him.

Anthony was here, and their baby thrived between them. Should she tell him? Perhaps it was too soon. She studied him.

"Anthony, was that you I saw in London, in the rain?"

"I couldn't resist following you." His grin became mischievous.

"And I see..." She ran her fingers lightly over faint webbing down the right side of his neck. Her heart lurched. There must be more. Her incredible, beautiful man had gone through hell.

His lips brushed her cheek. "I'm here." It was almost a whisper. "Remember our last night in Teheran, when I proposed. The happiness we felt."

"I remember it all." The thought of making love with him made her glow.

"I said then I'd never leave you. How can I? You're my life, my home, my heart."

A breeze floated into the room, and she remembered other moments.

He kissed her neck, lingering there.

"Please don't let me go. This could be my mind playing tricks."

He pulled back his expression full of mirth. "From now on," he lifted her, "I'm going to love you each day as if there is no tomorrow, and you'll know it's real. I can't let you go. I need you, Kathryn!"

He bent and swept her inside, lay her on the bed, and nudged the door closed. "I've waited so long," he said. "But I should take it slow."

She knew his need was great, but no more than her own. This was not a time for restraint; she craved the physical assurance he lived. She looked back at him and pulled her blouse over her head, tossed it and her bra aside, reaching for him with open arms.

Slowly, his mouth came down to meet hers, hot, expectant. They stripped off their other garments until their bare skin touched, his pale, hers flushed.

She opened herself to him and they came together like missing links, joined again, no past, no tomorrow—now, part of an eternal chain of love. Her exhilaration, her joy was real.

After making a lovely mess of the bedroom, sheets rumpled, pillows scattered about the room, they showered together quickly and donned cotton robes.

"I'm so hungry," Kathryn said. "Aren't you?"

"When have I known you not to be hungry?" he teased and went out into the salon.

As Kathryn shook out the top sheet and retrieved pillows, arranging them again, Anthony brought a covered tray of refreshments through the bedroom and out onto the enclosed terrace. "Mina left this for us," he said.

She followed, and they ate with gusto, lamb and vegetable stew in a saffron paprika broth garnished with lemon and mint and Moroccan flat bread topped with Feta cheese. Anthony glanced at his watch. "We're okay."

They went back to bed, and for a while barely moved, each gazing at the other.

Kathryn's gaze followed her hands' movements as she quietly assessed the changes in Anthony's body. His wounds had been severe; it was unbearably evident. It made her crazy when she thought of what he had endured to be left with such angry scars. Except for this, he was lean and tight, his muscles defined under firm skin glistening with perspiration. It was so like him to fight back with the only thing he had, his own body, to make it better, stronger than ever.

"Tell me about these, Anthony," she said, touching his scarred right hip.

"Really?"

"If you could overcome them, I can listen."

He raised himself on one elbow and gazed down at her. "I realized they'd hit the gas tank and leapt from the Jeep. The effort saved my life, and I'm told, my limbs. But the fire all around me was excruciating. Scorching metal flew from everywhere. I smelled my own flesh burning."

Kathryn forced herself not to react, to subdue the shuddering she felt inside and let him get it out.

"I was in a living hell, but luckily, both Hans and Tabriz were looking for me. They pulled me clear of the wreckage and put me on a stretcher. They flew me to a small hospital near the Iraqi border, used to dealing with soldiers who had burns and shrapnel wounds from military skirmishes with Iraq." He bit his lip, silent for a moment. "Are you sure you want to hear this? It's not pretty."

"Yes, go on." She needed to hear it all.

"I hallucinated for days at first," he continued unsteadily. "I saw you—as you were at Persepolis—on the winged lion. I was certain for some strange reason that I was being flown on wings of the lion to safety, but it was Hans' helicopter. In and out of consciousness, somehow I clung to the notion I would survive. When I didn't think I could anymore, I still held onto that belief and fought for the will to recover.

"We stayed safe in Tabriz's mountain lodge, high in the Elburz. Every day I fought a little more to move. As soon as I could, I waged war with the mountain and learned again to climb. It was challenging—often brutal—scrambling across rocky ledges, almost being blown from its cliffs."

"Somehow...I knew," she said. "Really. I felt like part of me was there, too. I'd wake up and be on a ledge overlooking a thousand-foot drop or in a desert. I thought I was going mad. One night I woke and went to the window, threw it open to the pouring rain, and thought no one on earth could be this lonely. But I felt you, didn't I? The emotion was overwhelming."

"I think we felt each other."

She smiled timidly. "Anthony, do you think when we were both lonely children away at boarding school that I perceived you then?"

He looked at her a long time, then reached for her. "I'm sure of it. It was just a matter of time before we met."

She turned in his arms, and he clung to her.

He followed her fingers as she ran her hand along the uneven surface of his right shoulder.

"I was never so glad I was left-handed." Changes of emotion flashed across his face, a darkness. "The scars will heal more, Kathryn. They won't always be this ugly."

"I don't care about your scars. They're badges of a battle won."

"Almost won. Almost."

She closed her eyes and felt afloat on a sea of love, but in an instant she was afraid he wasn't really there and quickly opened them. He was. She nestled close to him.

He caressed her belly. "You've changed," he whispered. "So womanly, round." He caressed her fuller breasts, his finger circling the areola, now a deep rose color, then her hips and stomach. She had a wonderful feeling right then that he would love her however she was shaped.

"You're like an Odalisque painted by Goya. Stunning. You'll definitely fit in my harem."

"What harem?" She pushed him onto his back, straddling him, brushing his chest with her bare breasts, her sensitive nipples.

"You could get into trouble up there, little girl."

"I'm a big girl now."

"Big enough for this?" He rubbed his erect cock across her shapely bottom.

"I've been looking for that," she said. "I thought I'd lost it." She raised herself up on her knees. "It does seem bigger than I remembered. Much bigger." Deliberately, she lowered herself onto him. Slowly, she rode him, the tempo building until Anthony groaned and swept her under him.

"Now, I've got you." He smiled wickedly, his hands reaching under her buttocks, and he plunged deeper inside of her.

Her gaze fixed on him; her own heat flared. "I want all of you!" she cried.

Later, when the afternoon sun slanted into the bedroom, Anthony was jolted awake by a knock at the salon door. He looked around for Kathryn and heard the shower turning off in the bathroom. He wrapped his shower towel around his hips and walked out of the bedroom to the salon door.

"Who is it?"

"Time to go." It was Mohammed's voice.

He opened the door just a crack.

"The Black Glove guards are changing shifts. You have ten minutes. Jeep is waiting out back. Hurry."

He closed the door and glanced at his watch. Time to risk this hasty exit. He'd better move fast.

Kathryn had put on her bra and panties and was towel drying her hair. She watched Anthony return to the bedroom.

"We're leaving," he said, and slipped on his faded jeans then tossed a gray knapsack on the bed. "Mina packed this for you. More clothes Mirdad purchased for you in Tangier," he said, his lips tight.

He dropped his own dark knapsack on the bed and pulled out a pair of her khakis, a white blouse, and a tribal scarf. He tossed them to her. "I brought you these." He tossed her a pair of dark glasses.

She grabbed them and put them on, and throwing her hands in the air said, "You believe they're just going to let us walk out of here? Rena and Houdin?"

"Kathryn. I'm giving them your Persian Glories for your life. That is, if you approve, since the jewels are yours." He raised a quizzical eyebrow.

She finished dressing and walked away to the window, gazing out. Sounds from the call to prayers wafted into their room on a soft breeze from across the bay of Tangier, breaking the still heat of afternoon. The sheer curtain billowed inward, lightly touching her skin. She pushed it aside, gazing out across the bay to the city bathed in a burnished apricot glow, reciting her own silent prayer, awed in gratitude that Anthony lived, and they were together. She thought about their safety. She thought about Anthony, still wounded, she thought about their baby he didn't know about yet was safe. But she couldn't think about the joy of being far away, having tea in an English garden with Anthony, and Lord Charles, or she'd lose it. All she knew was they had to get the hell out of here. She would tell him when they were away from this place. If it meant trusting his arrangement, then she would. "Approval granted."

Anthony came up behind her and caressed her shoulders. "We've got to go."

She turned to him. "I can't see trusting liars like Rena and Houdin."

"Mirdad is covering for us. His mother and Houdin will think you're leaving with him, for your safety from Rena's high-handed treatment."

"Then we are done here." She grabbed him to her and kissed him. "On to our next adventure."

He held her. "Life is always an adventure with you, Kathryn."

There was knock at the door.

Mirdad stood back in the villa's main salon and watched Houdin pour chilled bubbles of Dom Perignon into Rena's glass, then Mirdad's, then his own. He couldn't wait to get away.

"To us! To our success," Houdin said.

"And to forgiveness," Rena added. "You have forgiven me my wickedness, haven't you, Mirdad, my love?"

Mirdad stepped in for the toast. He needed to play this well. "Of course, Mother. I was beside myself at first, but I'm over it now." He raised his glass. "And to love," he added and tossed back his head, swallowing the welcome chill of the beverage.

Rena grabbed Houdin's arm. "I'm so glad all our secrets are out in the open. It's wonderful, our family being together." She reached up and kissed Houdin's cheek.

"I'm so proud of you, Mirdad," Houdin said, clinging to Rena's waist and smiling at Mirdad. "This is the happiest day of my life."

"We all only want to be good to each other," Rena said, "so very good." She whirled to grab the champagne bottle, refilling everyone's glass. "And Mirdad, you will see how much I've changed." She nodded to Houdin as if for assurance.

Mirdad watched his mother carefully, a part of him still hoping to see a glimmer of truth emanating from her, some feeling, warmth, a sign she had indeed changed. He truly didn't want to hate her as he did. But searching deep in her eyes, down to her core, he sensed only hollowness within her. He smiled inwardly. This empty space was a good sign, for when she was filled, it was always with malevolence, making her dangerous.

"I must go, Mother."

"Don't you want to see the woman first? To see that she is unharmed?"

"I trust your word, Mother," he said almost choking on his words.

With a flick of her hand, Rena ordered a guard, "Put her in the car."

Mirdad stepped forward. "Actually, Mother, Colonel Nassiri and I will take Kathryn to Marrakech, for her safety." Mirdad looked to Houdin.

"But..."

"This is my idea, Rena," Houdin said, and winked at Mirdad. "A better plan, no?"

Relief washed over Mirdad.

Rena's smile looked forced. "Whatever you say, my love."

She handed Mirdad a briefcase from the table.

"Why the briefcase?" Houdin asked.

"For Anthony's stupid papers," Rena said. "We're making a switch, you see, the woman and the papers for the jewels, no? A trade. Mirdad has learned from you, Omar."

"Indeed." Houdin beamed. "Very wise. That's my son, our son, Rena."

Mirdad held down his revulsion because now he could get Demi and leave this place forever.

Kathryn's need to get far away from Houdin's villa pounded in her veins. Mohammed drove the 4X4 Land Cruiser. He pressed ahead, over roads she had not seen before, the sky swept with the powerful afternoon sun illuminated the cobalt Mediterranean. She leaned closer to Anthony, and he hugged her against him.

They drove further away from the fertile coastal plain into a denuded desert, all so different in the daytime from her nighttime arrival. Kathryn fought to keep her mind relaxed, calm, focused on the changing scenery and not on the terror of getting caught locked in her mind. She pushed it away.

The day was warm, but her hands lay clasped in her lap like clumps of ice. Anthony put his hand over hers. "Relax, darling. For the next two days we're on holiday."

"With killers after us? Are you mad?"

"Perhaps, however this is the very best day I've had in a long while," he said, and drew the back of her hand to his lips. "I'm where I want to be—with you. And until we have to meet up with these jackals again, I intend to enjoy every second we're together. Okay?"

She shook her head but said, "Yes, I want that, too."

Dust spitting up around them, they reached a desert plain hidden behind boulders where an enormous gunship of a chopper waited.

The door flew open, and Ali and his cousin Davood jumped down.

She was overjoyed to see them.

"Lady Kathryn!" Ali and Davood yelled, running over. They stopped in front of her, appearing unsure.

"No mullahs are watching, my Muslim brothers," she said, and hugged them both. Leaning from the cockpit,

Hans saluted her and started the engine. Two other younger guys waved from the open door.

"My fellow student exiles," Ali said, pointing. "Come, we go now." He and Davood grabbed their gear, tossing it to their friends on board. Kathryn, Anthony and Mohammed got in.

Kathryn sat in front with Hans, Anthony in back with the guys. They lifted off to the sound of whomping rotors and radio static, and of young men laughing, retelling their truly scary stories of Iran, making light as they flew into clear skies and headed southwest toward Mohammed's remote village just twenty miles from the Marrakech airfield. The village would be the drop off point for Kathryn and Anthony. The guys were headed to the airfield to beef up security before the meeting with Rena and Houdin. Dirty tricks were expected with those two.

The chopper flew over Cape Spartel and Castillo del Sol. Kathryn didn't look down. She was overjoyed seeing her Iranian cohorts together again. Hans was her greatest surprise. She hadn't known he had made it out of Iran. She put her head on his shoulder, hoping she wouldn't blow her tough-guy cover and cry.

Hans apparently sensed her emotion; he gave her a one-armed hug. "There, there, lovey," he said. "We got you now." Her smile was wobbly until he said, "Don't be thinking you're gonna fly this bird, 'cuz it ain't happenin'!" Bubbles of laughter erupted from her and floated through the cabin carrying away a bushel of apprehension.

Anthony sat behind her in the borrowed eight passenger Hind, a Russian-made gunship used in Iran. That was when she noticed the stored weapons, mostly M14 sniper rifles, with many rounds of ammunition, some Ak47s, and a few 9mm Glocks. They must be Houdin's.

They left behind a smaller Alouette aircraft rented in Tangier. "We'll straighten it out later," Hans told her.

She glanced again at Anthony, sitting smugly with his arms crossed over his body and a slight grin on his face, the younger men chattering around him. She reached back and squeezed his hand, his grin widening.

He'd made her happy, and he knew it.

It was almost dark when the chopper landed outside Mohammed's village just twenty minutes from Marrakech and lifted off again quickly, leaving her with Anthony and Mohammed, who directed them on foot to his dilapidated garage workshop. Inside, Mohammed closed the rickety doors and turned on work lights. "You'll like this one," he said to Anthony and pointed out a matte black, tricked out Jeep. "Off road V6 extreme Rubicon," Mohammed said. "I modified it myself. Heavy grill, lights, tires—everything you'll need in the dunes. The gas tank is full."

"Looks like it just came off an aftermarket showroom." Anthony circled the car. "Fine looking machine, Mohammed. I won't ask how you managed this."

Anthony handed him a bulging money pouch, and the men shook hands. "Find a safe home for your family soon, man," Anthony said.

"This I will do." Mohammed turned to Kathryn. "I am sorry I could not do more for you, madame."

"Thank you for guarding me," she said. "Be safe."

He led them farther into the wooden building then out through a covered back entrance, down a few steps, and across a small courtyard.

He handed Anthony two sets of keys. "For the car," he said, "and for a place—" he opened a door and flipped on a light "—where you will be safe." Mohammed smiled and his somber face lit up. He stepped through the door saying, "My wife has been here. All is ready."

They entered a studio apartment with a view of the small town and a souk winding down a narrow street.

"The shops are still open if you wish to walk in the twilight hour."

While Anthony and Mohammed stood across the simple room at a writing table going over maps, Kathryn gazed around. Rough white stucco walls, a covered settee with bright cushions of turquoise, lime green, orange, and yellow with more placed around a circular low well-used brass table. A bowl of fruit, figs, pomegranates, tangerines, and dates rested there with a note of welcome.

From across the room she heard, "La Mamounia, less than an hour...private airstrip." She didn't really want to know more details right now. For these few days she was simply a woman enraptured by her lover.

She walked into a small bathroom with an open shower, a sink, and a fairly modern toilet with a pull chain flush. Ivory Moroccan towels with fringe tassels hung on an iron towel bar. She let her fingers slide over the fringe and picked up a fresh bar of soap on the sink stand. It smelled of star jasmine, reminding her of Tehran. Her memory pushed back further to her little Hollywood house on Mulholland and the scent of jasmine wafting onto her patio garden. Would she ever get back there?

A door closed behind her. She turned and Anthony was there. "Ready for a walk?"

The sights, sounds, and pungent smells in the small Kasbah were overwhelming to Kathryn, especially walking with Anthony through a busy fish market. What assaulted her senses the most were the legions of flat boxes lined up, filled with different sizes and shapes of scaly, slithery things—snakes, eels, and God knew what else.

Kathryn began to feel quirks of pregnancy and grabbed a low wooden railing, bracing herself against the queasiness overtaking her. Instinctively, her glance dropped to her hand, and she saw a squirming thing inching up through a box nearby toward her fingers. She recoiled so quickly she nearly fell over.

Anthony, wide-eyed, caught her. "What is it?"

"I don't know, I..." She didn't know what to say. Of all things, she didn't want to be a spoilsport on their first evening together.

"When did you eat last?" he said.

She shrugged.

"Well, I'm going to pass out if we don't eat soon!" He looked around and found a little café.

Kathryn no more wanted to look at food right now than

at the eels, but she did like looking at Anthony and was not ready to leave the marketplace. They ordered Fesanjan, an aromatic chicken stew with pomegranate and walnut sauce. Naturally, she ate more than he did.

Later, when they got into bed Anthony held her, whispering soothing, romantic notions, "Be happy, my love."

She mumbled back, "We are," and he became still.

She looked up at him. He gave her an almost smile, and he stroked her hair, apparently preoccupied with the exchange day after tomorrow and everything that could go wrong. Then his face cleared, and he kissed her forehead. She went right to sleep.

They awoke early after their first night together in so long. He still held her, and with the gods on their side, there would be many nights like this. They were happy.

Quickly, they ate, packed a bag of fruit and dates, and backed the stellar V6 extreme Rubicon out of the garage.

For hours they drove on their own sight-seeing excursion across a strange, changing terrain, the noise of the Jeep drowning out much of their conversation, so they spoke mostly in shorthand, vigorously pointing out any new thing of interest: a cluster of local henna plants, a small camel caravan, or part of an ancient building in ruin.

He leaned in and said, "I have something extraordinary to show you."

She couldn't wait, but in truth, for her it was all amazing, a time Kathryn wished could go on without end. Two travelers excited, discovering parts of life together, sharing both awe and laughter. Mostly, Kathryn had to admit, she was in awe, while Anthony laughed.

They passed through a town where a moussem, a religious festival, was in progress and stopped for a time to watch. Men and women dressed in candy-colored silk garments of orange, lemon yellow, raspberry, and mint proudly carried tall banners overhead like billowing rainbows as their procession wound along the dusty streets toward a soaring minaret, watching over their medina as it had for centuries. Varicolored turbans and flowers bobbed on their heads. Sounds of their music and arm and ankle bands jangled rhythmically with their movements.

Anthony drove her away from the village to the edge of the world—the Erg Chebbi sand dunes near Erford. "Moroccan splendor," he said. "Come see."

Looking up spellbound, she got out of the Jeep. He pressed close to her back his arms wrapped around her. They faced the dunes. "Watch," he murmured.

Dunes rose in slow motion as if on cue like mighty tidal waves to golden heights of unimaginable magnitude from a primordial sea of sand like something from an awesome movie. A whooshing sound came with the movement. The overwhelming majesty was pulse-stopping when the waves in countless numbers reddened like great flames ignited by the setting sun, illuminated some with a deep crimson glow, the others were washed in rich amber.

It was a staggering sight, so unexpected Kathryn couldn't speak. The great sand mass seemed to flow as a subtle ocean in a shifting movement. Almost imperceptible, it was nonetheless steady, strong, and unmistakably meaningful, for as one peak rose to an incalculable height, the adjacent dune seemed to be sucked from beneath by a great mouth, all in Technicolor.

And so the constant shifting, sinking, and swelling of a great desert affected Kathryn's reflection on her life and Anthony's, always scrambling for the next move. Dragged and pulled by incalculable forces taking hold, they were constantly resetting the stage to resist being dragged under, barely able to claw themselves back up to the cliff's edge.

She shivered, humbled to her trembling knees. "I'm blown away," she said.

"As am I." He tucked a strand of hair behind her ear, nuzzling her closer. The darkness she had sensed in him seemed lighter somehow. Perhaps being together helped.

In the last bronze rays of desert sun, they were about to get back in the Jeep when the intense heat having burned well into the day grew strong again.

"Wait," she said, sensing something great yet to come.

Anthony dug in his knapsack and pulled out his camera, removed the lens cap and went to work. In that moment the sky exploded in a symphony of intense color, the vivid tints varying from shades of magenta, blood orange, and indigo to a deep purple engulfing the vast horizon.

Anthony shifted his moves like the sand, taking shot after shot.

His first in a while, she bet.

"Anthony?"

"Hmm?" He'd put his camera away and scooted behind her, leaning on the Jeep, his arms encompassing her, she leaning into him. "Is this all part of a dream?"

"No," he responded softly. "This is real. The rest of life is the dream." He buried his lips in her windswept hair. "You know, I would go through it all again if it was the only way I could be with you."

"But it shouldn't have to be this way. Everything a trial by fire."

"True, but one day...one day, you'll be ensconced in your own English garden."

She shook her head and he chuckled.

"Or walking in your Malibu sunshine with small feet padding beside you, and you'll long for this excitement."

"That may be sooner than you think."

He pulled away. "You mean you're leaving me? You're going back to California, after all this?"

"No." She turned into him, cradling his face. "I mean the small feet." She placed his hand over her stomach. "I'm... we're going to have a baby. I'm pregnant."

His look of surprise was priceless.

She gazed up at him.

"A baby!" He threw his head back and laughed. "Mine?"

"Ours."

"You're brilliant!" He leaned over and kissed her, full on her lips, his eyes ablaze with fiery green sparks.

"And when were you going to tell me?"

"Now, since we're away from killers and that place."

"Perfect timing, you marvelous creature. I adore you."

He leaned away and said, "No wonder you fainted when you saw me. Oh, my darling!" he bellowed, laughing. "I'm sorry, it just seems so funny now, my coming at you like a shrouded ghost. Oh, I love you."

"Then stop laughing at me, you beast, and tell me!" The wind whistled across the dunes.

He took her shoulders firmly, their eyes locking. "I'm elated. Thank you."

"For what?"

"For wanting our child. I'm sure under the circumstances it must have been...difficult."

She stepped back. "You mean it would have been easy to get rid of? I would have sooner ended my own life. I didn't know at first," she said. "It was too soon. And when I did, I had part of you. And for that I felt blessed."

He pulled her to him, and she felt protected in a way she never had before. It was just what she had always longed for, even while pushing people away.

"Anthony, tell me, were you on a hill riding a black horse at your grandfather's house?"

"I didn't know you saw me."

So it was he. "I wasn't sure myself." She nudged closer. "Soon we'll be safe," Kathryn said just before the sunlight finally faded, bringing a faint chill. She leaned into him, her arms around his waist.

Anthony seemed to recognize how vulnerable she felt here on the rim of a foreign world, the toll taken from the harrowing journey of the past months.

"You're tired. Let's go. Tomorrow will come soon

enough."

"Okay, but Anthony, no more secrets—no more secrets."

"Look who's talking."

They drove back through all the same sights, now more subdued with the dwindling day. In a village they had passed earlier, they stopped for a meal of kabob with hummus and flatbread. And when they finished, and headed back to the Jeep, Kathryn sensed something more than fatigue bothered Anthony.

She took hold of his arm. "What are you keeping from me?"

"It's time to go," he said, clearly impatient. Shaking loose of her hold, he walked to the Jeep and leaned against it, his arms folded across his chest.

"All this intrigue. I'm sick of it. Do you hear me? Sick of it!" She was shaking.

She had mourned his death and rejoiced at his life; his child grew inside her body. But something was tearing them apart, a force as clear as if it stood in front of her and with it came a threat of which she was certain. Why was he unwilling to speak of it? She walked up to where he stood.

"There's some problem, isn't there?"

He stepped toward her. "Kathryn!"

She backed away. "Don't try to manipulate me, Anthony. This time I want to know everything."

"Get in the car!"

"Can't you feel this shift between us? We're tilting in

opposite directions. More than ever, I need you to be straight with me." She grabbed his arm. "I need strength."

He reached for her.

"Inner strength," she said, and held her arm out between them.

"You aren't going to like it."

"I don't like it now."

"Does Rena know you're pregnant?"

She nodded.

"Then it's not over, Kathryn."

He guided her to a large boulder and sat her down. "You see, love, while I was concealed in the mountains fighting to regain my strength, an informer, an old man, was brought to our camp."

Anthony's eyes narrowed slightly, and she could tell he was reluctant to go on. She stood and walked away, making it easier for him to tell her. She waited for him to continue.

"The man told of his brother who had been hired to plant explosives on a diplomatic flight from Teheran to London years ago. The two primary passengers on the plane were my parents. This bomb expert was hired by a woman called Rena Ajani."

"No! Mirdad's mother killed your parents? Her own sister?"

"Yes."

"It's too horrible!"

"And saw her husband hang for it."

"Mirdad was only a boy."

"She poisoned his mind against me years ago. I knew

his feelings had somehow been twisted but refused to admit it. I thought in time I'd repair the damage she had done between us because as we had once been so close. But Rena's efforts were far too successful."

He turned his face to the indigo sky. "Kathryn, I heard Mirdad order Raymond's death myself." He faced her. "Then he gave the order for my death."

She stepped away. "I don't understand. Why?" Her heart hurt with this information about her friend.

"Two of the oldest reasons in time: jealousy and greed. You see, Rena can't rest until she gets not only the Persian Glories but sees to it that everyone else who has owned them is dead."

She blinked, trying to absorb what he said.

"Does it make you afraid you're next? It should," he said, kicking his boot into the lumpy sand. "It makes me very afraid."

He shook his head as if dispelling something dreadful and looked at Kathryn strangely. "Why did I not figure out the depths of her obsession while in London? I could have saved you this mess."

It was then Kathryn ran through her mind everything she'd seen, heard, and ignored about Rena. "I see it now. The Glories won't be enough because what's driving this woman runs deeper than diamonds. Something rotten has festered inside Rena for a long time." Kathryn walked up the ridge to him.

"Neither of us will stay alive as long as Rena is free."

"That's why your grandfather didn't tell me you were

alive, isn't it? Because of the danger."

"Could you have pretended grief when you experienced the joy we've had today? I couldn't, I know. No, my grandfather knew what Rena was after, and knew she would let nothing stand in her way. As much as I hated it, I had to agree. And the robbery? Mirdad was one of the thieves I fought, one of the faces behind the masks, but he got away. I let him get away."

Kathryn shuddered.

"Now I wish I'd done more, crushed every bone in his body—smashed him—as he has smashed everything in my life."

"No. You don't know all of it with Mirdad. He's changed, you have my word." Kathryn stood firm, watching Anthony struggle with her declaration.

"Reluctantly, I'll take your word."

"There's been too much pain for all of us, Anthony."

He moved to her. "I want to bring you only pleasure for the rest of our lives," he said. "I wish I could send you back to London while I deal with them."

"I wouldn't go. I won't leave you."

He laughed, running his hands over her shoulders and back. "If you only knew how far the fist of Omar Houdin's Black Glove can reach."

He whispered so low she could barely hear. "I'm so desperately in love. You're my life. I can't let anything harm you or our child." He pulled back with a hint of mirth. "But getting your cooperation is never that simple, is it?"

When they reached the cozy apartment, they came in and locked the door.

"A shower?" he asked, and she nodded. They shed their clothes, leaving the sandy pile right there. Anthony turned on the shower.

Kathryn unwrapped the new bar of fragrant soap and stepped in behind him. Under steamy water, she pressed herself to Anthony's back, her arms around him, soaping his chest. Between kisses, they washed each other and dried off with soft-fringed towels. He lifted her and carried her to bed.

CHAPTER TWENTY-THREE

At first light the next morning, Kathryn watched Anthony dress quickly and leave for Marrakech to meet Philippe at his hotel. Groggy, Kathryn rolled over and went back to sleep. She awoke two hours later and reached for him. Her hand touched the empty sheets, and she realized the day of reckoning had arrived. She showered and dressed, wanting more than anything to survive this day with Anthony.

When Mirdad came for her, she was ready.

Mirdad had covered every aspect of the plan to ensure Kathryn's safety. He would make certain, no matter how.

In the backseat of his limo, anonymous behind tinted windows, he turned to Kathryn, and whispered, "There's nothing to worry about. Our driver is Mohammed, and we'll soon see Anthony at the airfield. Rena will never bother you again, I promise you. All that is behind you now."

Kathryn clutched the supple leather armrest and looked at him sharply. "Mirdad, you have not seen the looks of naked hatred on your mother's face, the evil living in her eyes." She swallowed. "She hasn't turned on you yet."

"Oh, but you are wrong there," he said, chills washing through him in a river of shame. "She turned on me when I was twelve and has managed to destroy my life since."

"So you woke up to her games? Before or after you ordered people to die?" Her mouth twisted.

"After." He jerked toward her. "Not until Captain Aran brought me Anthony's papers from his safe, letters addressed to me that had been sent back to him. And I read his will. He left me most of his Iranian wealth, a great deal except for the house I had already burned to the ground. But it was the deep caring in those letters, like I was the little brother he would never forget. Reading that cracked my mother's hold on my mind."

"Mirdad, I don't know if Anthony can forgive you."

"Perhaps not. I doubt I can ever forgive myself."

The car raced on with an eerie chill inside. With one look at Kathryn, he knew they both felt it.

Mirdad turned away from her, as if searching for warmth outside. "I must have stayed drunk or stoned for three weeks, until I was dragged back to Houdin and involuntarily sobered up. From there I went to Paris determined to change everything about myself, until the inside of me matched the outside."

Seeing a glimmer of compassion in her eyes, he shook off dark memories.

"Yes, Rena came between me and Anthony, but I'm finished with her."

When he spoke her name, he tried to cover his bitterness by clearing his voice. "My mother is damaged beyond hope. I'm getting away from her after this exchange."

"Then you must go far away," she said.

"And when I find someplace I can feel warm, I'll write and you'll send back pictures of my new godson, I hope."

"So you think Papa will be busy with his cameras?" Kathryn teased, and he saw their mutual hope to relieve the desperate apprehension choking the atmosphere. He managed to quash another flood of emotions rippling through him. Only a small bit of the soul-searching turmoil he still went through surfaced, and he turned to her and said, "Take this."

He handed Kathryn a passport.

She rubbed her fingers over a worn leather case and looked inside and frowned.

He chuckled. "Not a great picture, I agree."

"It's due to expire in August of 1980." She looked up. "How did you...?"

"Anthony brought it to me at the villa. I apologized to him, a small thing in the face of it, but I want peace. For all of us."

Kathryn touched his cheek. "I remember a time not long ago when your face barely registered anything at all."

The limo had pulled to a stop on an expansive tarmac in between two jets parked a good distance apart.

"You have changed, Mirdad, I'm sure."

His smile held great tenderness. "In many ways. But I still love you, Kathryn. And Anthony. Anthony, too. I only wish I had known sooner."

They gazed quietly at one another until Mirdad turned away, looking out the window. "We've arrived."

The moment to say goodbye had come.

"I will always carry you in my heart," he said softly.

"And I you, my friend. I'll never forget your kindness to me." She took his hand.

"Goodbye, Kathryn." Mirdad hugged her. "I wish you great happiness."

"Stay well, Mirdad," she said.

"Don't be nervous. It's simple," he said. "You and I stay together until I'm given the jewels. Armed men surround the area protecting us. But remain calm."

The day was cloudless but gray with gloom. Outside the flight office, Anthony tried to restrain himself from pacing the tarmac. It was useless. Kathryn was with Mirdad, which made him uneasy. He wanted her safe next to him. They were due to arrive any minute.

He straightened his tie, buttoned the jacket of his light linen suit coat, and touched his clean-shaven chin, courtesy of Philippe's expert barber at La Mamounia early this morning.

Anthony's hair was cut and groomed; his shoes polished—a well-dressed business executive waiting for a colleague. He turned to Philippe who leaned against the wall scanning a copy of *The London Times*, pretending to be calm. Philippe had flown in with his valuable cargo of precious gems an hour ago, and he and Anthony had discussed at length what had happened and the pitfalls of what could go wrong. Had they taken every precaution? He knew until he handed over the jewels, he controlled the situation. After? They would have to move quickly. Anthony paced again.

Anthony's own Iranian team was armed with M14s. Philippe carried his own 9mm Glock. Other riflemen with M16 sniper rifles were hidden on rooftops covering the plane. More were stationed unobtrusively around the airstrip to cover Kathryn and him if the situation got heated.

But Houdin's men were all over the place with enough weapons concealed to start a Moroccan uprising.

Anthony leaned next to Philippe, looking at the two planes, a Learjet, and a Gulfstream on the tarmac closest to them. After they traded the jewels for Kathryn, the Gulfstream would take him and Kathryn and Philippe away to England. The Persian Glories were true, but Iran's crown jewels were fine replicas made by the great Pierre Arpel for the Shah's coronation.

The smaller Learjet, General Houdin's plane, surrounded by his guards, had their hidden weapons waiting to go into action. Their flight plan destination read Casablanca, but who knew for certain?

"Lord, let it all go well." Anthony closed his eyes. He'd found himself praying constantly.

"If you keep this up, old man," Philippe said, "you'll wind

up in church on Sundays instead of out riding your horse."

After a moment, Philippe nudged Anthony's shoulder. "Look alive, my friend. They're here. I'll see you on board." He handed Anthony the briefcase loaded with the infamous Persian Glories worth an impressive fortune.

Two limousines pulled in front of the small building. Anthony moved to the doorway.

The doors to the first limo swung open and Rena stepped out, followed by Houdin. Rena flashed Anthony a withering look then turned her back. Houdin led her quickly to his waiting jet.

"Shall we?" Mirdad said, getting out and holding the door for Kathryn himself.

When Kathryn emerged from the second limo, Anthony was brought back to the first time he had seen her at Persepolis. She wore a simple white dress; her hair, the color of the sun, moon, and stars all at once, floated loosely over her shoulders. Sunglasses covered her eyes. She was the vision in his dreams on the wings of a lion. Had it been less than a year?

When she saw him, she removed her sunglasses and bit the lower lip of her generous mouth. No make-up, her large wide-set eyes raised to him were clear and hopeful. She was beautiful. Her movements were easy but cautious, nervous but poised and vulnerable. He wanted her with him, but he remained focused.

As they had arranged, Mirdad moved her onto the tarmac, closer to Houdin's jet. Anthony followed and met them there.

"Just as I promised," Mirdad said. "Here she is."

Anthony ignored Mirdad. He could wait no longer and gathered Kathryn next to him, holding her close. She felt wonderful in his arms.

"Are you all right?" he asked, feeling her tremble. "What's wrong?"

"Nothing. Nothing. I'm so glad to be with you."

"Hold on, my love. We're almost through this."

"Get on with it, Anthony," Mirdad said. "My mother is not a patient woman."

Anthony opened the case for Mirdad to inspect the jewels.

"I have no doubt all the jewels are there."

"Well, take them." Anthony extended his hand holding the case. "Go on. I want to get her out of here."

"Anthony..."

"Take them, Mirdad."

Kathryn stepped forward, taking the case from Anthony. "The legacy is yours, Mirdad. And I give the diamonds to you with love and gratitude for doing everything you could to save me, and the baby."

"And for bringing Kathryn back to me," Anthony said.

"No," Mirdad said. "Just listen to me. Your case looks like mine as I requested. I'm going to reach for it. But I won't take it."

Anthony squinted. "I don't understand."

"What is the legacy? The diamonds are to be given in one's lifetime to someone you love, right? Well, I give them to you, Anthony and Kathryn."

"Mirdad, Rena won't let you do this," Anthony said.

"We'll do this carefully and she won't know until it's too late."

"She'll kill you!" Kathryn said, handing the case back to Anthony.

"Don't worry about me. I'll handle her," he said firmly. "Just do it, Anthony. Now. And you'll be wanting your papers from your safe in Shiraz. They'll be sent on to you."

"Mirdad," Anthony said, "give Rena her jewels and come with us."

"I'm afraid the jewels won't be enough for Rena." With his back to Houdin's jet, Mirdad extended the case when Anthony did, but did not take it. "There. It's done. You go. Goodbye, Kathryn. Anthony. Good luck."

Anthony grabbed Mirdad to him and hugged him, relieved he didn't have to kill him. "Thank you, Mirdad. Till we see you again," he said.

"Yes." Mirdad smiled. "Now go. Goodbye, my friends, and take care of my baby cousin."

Not thirty feet away, the engines of Omar's Learjet roared to life around Rena. She stood in the plane's open doorway; her binoculars focused on the briefcase filled with her diamonds. Her chest was heavy with anticipation. A marksman, concealed on a nearby rooftop, had his rifle trained on his target, the blond and Anthony. He waited for her signal.

As Mirdad turned and came toward her Learjet, Rena signaled the marksmen.

The man leaned into his M-16 sight and two shots were fired.

She smiled.

But Anthony didn't fall, he only jumped away. The tarmac at his feet sprayed chunks of asphalt around him. He threw his arm around the blonde and they ran toward their Gulfstream under a barrage of inept gunfire.

Rena jerked back, in shock. *Merde. Merde. Merde*! She swung her focus over to her marksman. The shooter slumped on the rooftop unmoving. She searched the other rooftops. On one, a man crouched low dressed in black and ran out of view. There was something familiar about him.

Rena rushed inside her Learjet and flopped into her seat beside Omar. She buckled herself in.

A moment later Mirdad came on board and the copilot shut the door behind him and entered the cockpit. Mirdad nodded, his eyes lighting up with a smile. He took his seat across the aisle and to Rena's annoyance, stowed his briefcase under his seat and buckled the seatbelt.

Rena started to undo her belt, but Omar restrained her. "No, Rena. We're ready to take off." He kissed her neck.

"Father's right," Mirdad said. "Don't be foolish. There's plenty of time to enjoy your treasures. Be patient, Mother."

"Patient! Why should I have to wait now?"

With his infuriating calmness, her rebellious son reached across the aisle and patted her hand. "Because it's not safe, Mother."

She averted her eyes and didn't argue further. Her pulse raced with wild desire, but she waited and pulled her compact out from the small Chanel bag her on the seat. She gazed at the truly beautiful face of success. She now had everything.

Mirdad closed his eyes hearing the plane engines rev up. Thank God, thank God. Kathryn and Anthony were safe. It was not often a man got another chance to rewrite his destiny. He had redeemed himself as much as he could. For the first time in so long, he felt great. No shooting pains in his stomach, no emotional terror. He had made peace with the world and perhaps with Raymond who had always gently told him the truth. God, he felt good.

He leaned back, exhaling a deep relief, his chest filled with pride. Demi had taken out Rena's sharpshooter a moment before the bastard tried to shoot Kathryn and Anthony.

Demi was by now on his way to Paris, his last task complete. A pang of longing pressed in on Mirdad. It was all so bittersweet. He had found Demi, his love partner, who would be waiting for him in Paris. And Ali, Mirdad knew, would sneak back into Iran, avoiding Islamic revolutionaries to rescue the girl he had fallen in love with, lovely Nina, Anthony's secretary—a Jew. Mirdad loved how Ali fought for the oppressed.

"Excuse me, darling," she purred across from him. "Haven't I waited long enough?"

He looked at his watch. "Ten minutes." The Gulfstream started taxiing into position. "Yes, you have been very good."

The planed rolled out to the end of the runway.

Methodically, Mirdad unbuckled his seatbelt and casually reached for the case at his feet. He handed it over to her with great flourish. "Finally, Mother," he said with a big smile, "you get what you deserve."

"Let me have them!" The engines revved.

He gave her the case and walked to the front of the plane. The plane was ready to take off. It sped up.

Omar leaned back comfortably in his seat. Rena's fingers fumble on the clasps until they sprang open. She gasped.

The Learjet lifted off.

Omar screamed at her. "Where are they?"

"NO! You fool, Mirdad! He tricked you!" Rena screamed.

The case exploded in her hands, blowing her world apart.

Anthony jumped. Everyone still preparing the Gulfstream for takeoff, everyone inside the flight office heard the explosion and felt the ground shake. "It's a bomb."

Kathryn whirled to the plane's open door.

Anthony held her, watching shooting flames, burning remains and debris hurled through great dark clouds of churning smoke, covering the sky. He shook with utter disbelief then denial of what was before him—and pain.

The blast had blown every part of the Learjet into bits, killing everyone on board. It was like his parents' murder all over again only this time, it was his cousin, his little brother. He thought his heart would burst with pain. His little brother, forsaken by everyone who mattered to him as a boy, as a man, disintegrating into pieces.

Baradar koochooloo.

His mind raced back through the years, years when Mirdad had no one there for him, no one he was allowed to love. Always made to feel he must protect his diabolical mother.

Tears ran sad rivers down Anthony's cheeks and jaw. He wanted to howl for the boy with a deep yearning soul, for the man who favored history and truth but succumbed to evil. So few had gleaned the best of him.

And then it hit him.

This was Mirdad's last act of contrition—of love.

"He knew," Anthony whispered, turning to Kathryn. "He recognized Rena would make an attempt, and knowing what she had done, he made certain he would beat her to it. Mirdad accepted Rena would never rest while we were alive." Debris continued to fall until there was only scorched, charred metal succumbing to the earth's pull.

Kathryn's face was white with shock, questions written all over it.

"You see, he wouldn't trade cases. Mirdad perceived Rena's malice and used it against her. Her plan to destroy us, you, me, the baby, he denied her—so we would live. *Baradar koochooloo.*"

She put her arms around his shuddering body. "The brother of your heart, my love. We will never forget him."

CHAPTER TWENTY-FOUR

AMBASSADOR HOTEL
HOLLYWOOD, CALIFORNIA,
January 1980

Commotion engulfed Kathryn when she took Anthony's hand and stepped from the limo onto the red carpet for the thirty-sixth Golden Globes award ceremony outside the towering backdrop of the L.A. Coconut Grove. Giant klieg lights illuminated the glittering sea of fashion, ambition, fame, beauty, jewels—Hollywood celebrity. She had healed from the past and with her husband and her film team, they walked a new, brighter road. Cameras flashed around them, paparazzi and TV newsmen vied for her attention. Kathryn floated beside Anthony in a white chiffon Dior gown, her hair swept up in an elaborate chignon, topped with a glittering canary diamond tiara from her Persian Glories, the center stone the size of her baby's fist.

Anthony, tall, effortlessly elegant, wore his glossy dark hair fashionably long, tipping the collar of his crisp white shirt, in contrast to a black Armani tux, his three-day stubble covered fading scars.

Kathryn clung to Anthony's arm, concentrating on an outward show of serenity, while bubbling excitement and joy filled her. The wonder of stepping up to the goal line of a shared dream was near. Whether a trophy waited at the goal post or not, it was miraculous they were alive, together for this moment, and their baby was safe at home with his nanny.

Buzz, Wally Brandt, Peter, and Teddy in tuxedos, sauntered beside them through throngs of celebs, enjoying their nominee status for best full-length documentary film, *Faces of Iran.*

Cameras flashed, paparazzi called out, "Over here, Ms. Whitney, Mr. Evans."

"You're not even movie stars," Wally said.

"It's the bling," Teddy said, pulling his Hemmingway hat lower on his brow.

"So you're a Pulitzer Prize winner, Evans. Big deal." Buzz smoothed back his thick salt and pepper movie star hair; his blue eyes alight, merry.

Wally Brandt mimicked him, running a hand over his Air Force flat-top. "Yeah, we're producers, man."

Fans behind corded barriers shouted, "Look, director Kathryn Whitney, the Persian Glories."

She looked over smiling, only slightly nervous.

"She's countess now, dude," a reporter yelled back.

A flurry of photos, near blinding, ensued.

"Steady," Anthony murmured.

A serene smile on her lips, Kathryn held her head high, until Anthony leaned in and brushed her bare shoulder with a kiss. She blushed with desire and the crowd went wild, roaring applause.

On to her confidence building masquerade, he leaned closer, and whispered, "Just who am I accompanying tonight, my love?"

"Grace Kelly," she glanced up at his mischievous grin and her smile widened. *"To Catch a Thief."*

"Perfect, only you are lovelier."

Coaxed aside for a few TV interviews that went by in a blur, Kathryn gave them her best, nodding while Anthony answered the questions about their almost star-crossed romance and their brushes with death.

Kathryn commented on their blond baby boy, eight months old, and of course, the Persian Glories. Anthony was congratulated on his Pulitzer for photos of the Radical Khomeini uprising, now a full-blown Iranian revolution. Was there another film in the offing for the two of them?

"Perhaps," Anthony said as they stepped away.

She and Anthony looked at one another silently affirming; the scope of what they had been through was theirs alone to know.

"Good luck," he heard. They were ushered inside the Grove's lavishly decorated ballroom.

Kathryn paused to soak in the sight.

Cascades of white flowers spilled over dramatically lit, dark velvet draping along the walls leading to a circular stage, the backdrop, a shimmering curtain with a sparkling chandelier. A delicate table sat center stage covered with trophies, marble pedestals topped with a world globe, encircled by a film strip.

Fanning out from the stage, tiers of round tables covered in white linen and adorned with gleaming silver, crystal, and low centerpieces of more white flowers: peonies, roses, orchids, and lacy greens beckoned. Elite filmmaking guests, some still being seated, displayed their own finery.

Kathryn paused to peruse the amazing array of talent in this glamorous crowd. She glanced down close toward the stage, the big-name section. There was Meryl Streep, nominated for *Deer Hunter*, her favorite film this year, at a front row table with her husband, alongside Robert De Niro, Christopher Walken, and director Michael Cimino. At another front-row table sat Jane Fonda and John Voight, up for *Coming Home* with their director, Hal Ashby.

Teddy, standing behind her, said, "Man, it's Brad Davis." Teddy's favorite film was *Midnight Express*, directed by Oliver Stone, seated at another star-studded table accompanied by their dates.

It seemed tonight Kathryn's group were all star-struck. She had been to film award ceremonies, Clio, Sundance, Venice, AFI—all more low-key. This, however, was film royalty in all its splendor, and she was awed to be included.

Before she took her first step forward, she was aware of heads turning to her entrance, the hum of background noise and she felt a flutter of self-consciousness. *Grace Kelly,* she inhaled, allowing Anthony to guide her. "You do make a grand entrance, my love."

"I'm wearing the Persian Glories."

"Without the diamonds you would still be the most beautiful woman here."

"Oh, do go on," she murmured.

He chuckled. "Enjoy tonight. You've earned every delicious moment. No matter the outcome, you've won." He pressed her fingers to his lips.

Cameras flashed.

She felt an odd prickling sensation on her neck. Just jitters, she suspected.

Kathryn's table, set on a high tier, designated by film category, was lively with enthusiastic banter. Wally Brandt's wife, Teddy's date, a cute script girl, and Kathryn's mother, Patricia, who Peter had graciously invited, had all arrived in a second limo. Patricia, overjoyed, now looked at Kathryn's best friend anew, appreciating his well-groomed attire and his quick wit. Peter had, after all these years, won her mother's approval

Her animated table quieted, listening, watching when film clips from each category of nominees were played on a big screen above the stage. They toasted award winners who hurried to the stage to accept.

Jane Fonda and John Voight won for *Coming Home,* Warren Beatty and Dyan Cannon for *Heaven Can Wait,* John Hurt for *Midnight Express,* but sadly, Robert de Niro, Meryl Streep, and Christopher Walken had not won for

Deer Hunter. And even more irritating, Kathryn had felt again as though someone watched her every gesture and not in a kindly way. She dismissed it until Peter leaned toward her.

"Brett is here. He's watching you."

At that moment, a waiter delivered a note to Kathryn. With the only unpleasant feeling she'd had all evening, she stared at the card. Perhaps he wished her well? She opened it and read:

You don't stand a chance.
Tough Luck

Wally looked up at her slight gasp. He eyed the note. "May I?" he said.

She handed the card to him.

He barely looked at it before he walked down a tier to Brett's table and said something to Brett she couldn't hear. Wally tore up the note and dropped the pieces on Brett's lap.

"Oh, Brett always was such a bore," her mother said, negating the bad vibe. She raised her crystal flute and spoke. "To us, 'A' listers."

Wally returned and joined in. "Winners all!"

"Damn straight," Teddy said.

And when the tense moment came to announce the winner of a full-length documentary, her table hushed.

Presenter Warren Beatty announced, "And the award goes to..." he opened the envelope, "To, *Faces of Iran,* producers Kathryn Whitney, Buzz Anderson, Wally Brandt, Peter Shuman, and Teddy Wright. Then, Best director award, Kathryn Whitney."

Her team almost leapt out of their seats. They filed up to the stage, *Faces'* musical sitar theme played in the background.

The moment was surreal; her heart danced, her breath fluttered like butterfly wings, her spirit soared with gratitude. She had come far from her dark days in California and Iran.

As she climbed to the stage, images of her harrowing journey to tonight raced through her mind. But she looked out and caught sight of Teddy passing Brett's table and flipping him off and she laughed, refocusing in this superb moment.

Kathryn accepted her two awards and a hug from Warren Beatty, ever the flirt, her whole being soaked with humility and appreciation. She stepped closer to the mic and said for her team, "We thank the Hollywood foreign press for this great honor." She held up the award. "And in London we thank Samuelson's Film Services for the generous loan of their editing bay, and to the endangered families flown to safety, we thank them for their trust, and we offer a prayer for those still brutally oppressed by the Revolutionary Guard.

"Above all," she said. "I thank my amazing husband, Anthony Evans, for his photographic contribution to this film. His talent is obvious, and I thank him mostly for his courage in saving so many lives, including my own."

Buzz, Peter, Wally, and Teddy stepped forward; their clasped hands held high. They spoke together, "Thank you all," and with Kathryn leading the way, they fled off stage. Applause erupted filling the room, people stood and applauded louder, TV cameras panned the audience's response.

Buzz, just behind Kathryn said in her ear, "This group is tuned into the world stage, Kat. They've read the articles in *Time, The London Times, Rolling Stone, Variety*. Hell, some of these dudes here wrote half the stories about this film. They get what happened in Iran."

She squeezed Buzz's hand.

The stories behind *Faces* that Kathryn and Anthony had reported on the QT, were published by leading journalists worldwide. Cueing the world into information, while skirting openly politically offensive data against the Khomeini regime was too risky for Iranian citizens who remained on the revolutionary guard's radar. Anthony was there to greet her. "Happy now?"

"I've been happy since you found me," she drew him close.

The minute the awards concluded, Teddy called out, "Let's party!"

And beginning with Sir Elton John's charity bash, they did.

Under purple and pink lighting and a glittering, mirrored disco ball at Morton's West Hollywood glamour spot, Kathryn's unbelievably attractive husband took off his tie, stuck it in his pocket, and unbuttoned his collar. He looked at her with the sensuous look that had entranced her in Shiraz dancing an incognito samba, when they hadn't even known each other's names. She wanted that feeling back. He took her hand and moved her onto the dance floor.

"Hello," she said, her voice breathy, passion zinging between them.

Anthony gripped her waist, his words husky. "Let's dance." He spun her into the pulsing rhythm of Donna Summers' disco song, "Last Dance." The music came on slow and built to a compelling rhythm that said, *I want you.* And she was lost again in fantasy, the added attraction now of being wildly in love.

The song hadn't ended when he held her to him and said, "Ms. Kelly, may I take you home now?"

She took a shuddering breath. "Yes," she said, so ready to be alone with him.

By the time they were in front of Morton's, the car she knew Anthony would have waiting to return home idled there.

The driver opened the Rolls Royce door. Once inside, the opaque window separating the passenger cabin was drawn up. A Chet Bake ballad played, a bucket holding chilled champagne waited, wrapped in a towel beside two glasses.

A shiny walnut box sat on the carpeted floor. Kathryn took off her tiara, and he helped her remove the rest of the infamous canary diamonds. Anthony lifted open the satin-lined case and locked away the Persian Glories.

He turned up the music, popped the champagne cork

and poured Kathryn a bubbly glass. They sipped from the same flute.

"I've waited all night for this." He caressed her cheek and extracted her hairpins, loosening her chignon.

She leaned into his hand, warm and strong, a hand offering undying devotion to her, to their baby. Each day he offered anew his protection and a love she had never dreamed possible. She shook out her long hair. Her mouth curved in a half smile, desire in full flame.

"You excite me." He kissed her neck, her jaw. "Everything about you turns me on."

"You're a mad man," she said, breathless.

"Mad about you." He brought his lips to hers.

She tasted Bollinger champagne and sweet love.

He reached down and caressed her ankle. His hand slowly moved Kathryn's gown up her calf then further along her thigh. He knelt before her and pulled her body to his mouth, taking control, expressing his passion. And over the next hour, they both did.

Once again dressed and almost home, Kathryn nuzzled into Anthony, well pleasured, relaxed, her heart buoyant with gratitude. She had the love she hadn't dreamed possible.

The taped music changed to John William's haunting theme "Cavatina," from *Deer Hunter*. Her thoughts played back to Iran and her first meeting with Mirdad, the time when she had asked him if he'd seen the film. A brief look of longing had flashed in Mirdad's eyes before he had said, "Not yet."

Her thoughts rambled through more images of him, recalling his obvious amusement at her berating comment, "Lord Anthony Evans, prince of tardy," Mirdad's melodic laughter, his willingness to learn to throw an American football, his openness discussing his love for film, especially film noir, the small book he'd given her that she kept on her bedside table. Her sadness that Mirdad would never see *Deer Hunter*.

But more profoundly she recalled dancing with him on the ballroom floor in London, the night that had changed their lives. Myriad expressions had passed over his face then when she'd told him she was pregnant with Anthony's baby, expressions she only now understood. The love, the guilt, a plea for redemption, his curious reverence for her, for Anthony, and for the baby had played over and over in her mind. Months ago she had received a package, a gift from Cartier in France, a sterling silver baby cup inscribed in Persian, and below the baby's birth date. She had looked up the words in her *Farsi* dictionary. "For my golden nephew with love."

"We're home, darling."

She was quiet.

"Are you asleep?"

"No, just reminiscing." She looked about. They had stopped in front of her little rental on Mulholland Drive where they stayed for now.

When she had mentioned they might look for a bigger house, he'd said, "I like it here."

How she adored this man.

She took his hand and held it to her lips, the fine trace of scars barely there, fading more with time as he had said they would.

"Does one ever stop recalling so many memories?" she asked. "Some wrenching, some awful, some...tragic?"

"Perhaps not, but it's time to make new, happier ones, together," he said, lifting the box with the diamonds and her Golden Globe trophies. "And I believe we're well into happy."

"Oh, yes," she giggled because brighter images filled her thoughts, those of her own small cherub, so like the ones carved into his great-grandmother's headboard they slept against. "Let's go look at him!"

Anthony's eyes beamed at her through thick lashes. "And then?"

She tingled. "Absolutely."

CHAPTER TWENTY-FIVE

Walking along the beach in Malibu the next day, young Richard Taylor Evans, perched atop his father's T-shirted shoulders, chortling, smacking Dad's head as they walked along the Sand. Today Anthony's cup overflowed, yet he was bothered, out of balance.

Their black lab, Max, trotted ahead, investigating every sand crab on the Malibu shoreline. It would be dusk soon.

At low tide, waves lapped around Anthony's ankles with the Malibu pier at his back and ten-feet out, Kathryn, in running shorts and a crop top, roamed a tide-pool investigating. Un-squeamishly she held up a baby octopus and bent to the water, lifting a second moving prize from shallow water, a golden starfish. She beamed, her smile lighting her sun-kissed face. With careful steps she rejoined her husband and eight-month-old son, waving squiggly creatures in front of baby Richard. The boy studied the creatures and held out a chubby fist, poking each sea soul. He looked at his mom and grinned and bounced his delight. She turned and released the animals into the water.

Today, Anthony and Kathryn were dedicated to having

this time solely for relaxation, basking in familial intimacy, and friendship, a great treat for insanely busy people. Film awards, the Iranian revolution, and whatever else would take a backseat, he'd insisted.

The Cartier baby cup Kathryn had received was an enigma. He'd told himself it must have been ordered by Mirdad in London before the kidnapping with a request to fill in the date later when the birth announcement appeared in the papers, as all noble births did, and then to send the gift on to the child's mother. That theory would have to satisfy him because that was all there was to it.

But something else niggled at him. He'd not been able to get hold of Philippe in over a week. Perplexing. Philippe had mentioned he might go off for an ancient art auction, but that wasn't for months.

He glanced away from Cross Creek Bay tide pools, along the coastline to the row of colony "bungalows." Five houses up, from a wide terraced deck, he heard a loud whistle.

Buzz, with his athletic physique, leaned over the balcony rail of Kathryn's mom's house, waving a statuette, the Golden Globe trophy he'd won last night for producing *Faces* along with Teddy, Peter, Wally Brandt, and of course his remarkable Kathryn. After partying late into the night, the guys would arrive at some point soon for hangover remedies and a barbeque.

It was time to rejoin the family.

Kathryn took Anthony's arm. The baby lunged toward her. "I'll take our little lordling," she crooned, and wiggled him loose from his dad's grip.

The scent of barbeque wafted down the beach. "I'll bet you're hungry," he said to his wife.

She hurried ahead with her little bundle. "You know me well."

Anthony's grandfather had arrived this past week and was amusing his new friend, Patricia. The two had become fast friends in England at Anthony and Kathryn's wedding, a garden wedding, naturally, on the family estate per Kathryn's choice. She seemed delighted her new husband had become her glamorous mother's chum, an equestrian buddy. Anthony enjoyed going to the Polo Club with Patricia.

He had overheard his mother-in-law say to Kathryn at their wedding, "Well, Kathryn, finally you stepped into the garden of love and didn't pick a lemon!"

He'd had to turn away because he'd been laughing so hard.

That was her feisty mother. Not difficult to see where Kathryn got her spirited nature.

A commotion grabbed his attention, and he came up onto the deck to greet arriving guests.

"Such a great party house," Wally said. "Enormous deck, the pool, all of it overlooking the Santa Monica Bay. Nice." Just then lights flickered on around the wide bay. "The Queen's Necklace."

"Come, let's get some food," Anthony said, then glanced down at Wally's full plate of starters, crab cakes, rémoulade sauce, and chunks of lobster.

"Makin' you hungry, Anthony?"

"Yes," he said grabbing a juicy chunk of lobster off Wally's plate and popping it into his mouth, smiling and enjoying the morsel. Wally shook his head and grinned. Anthony heard the phone keep ringing inside the house but ignored it.

"Oh, Patricia, I'll get it for you," he heard his grandfather say.

Anthony headed for where Kathryn stood, sipping a margarita; she grabbed another off a tray and held it out to him. He took a swig and saw his grandfather rush toward him, his face a ghostly pallor. He held the phone out to Anthony. "It's Philippe."

"Not a great time to chat, Grandfather. Tell him I'll call him back tonight."

"I'm afraid that won't do, Anthony. You see, Philippe is in a Turkish prison." Charles shuddered. "He won't be allowed another call."

Kathryn, Peter, and Teddy looked at each other's panicked expressions. Teddy shook his head. "*Midnight Express*, man."

Anthony set the glass down, took the phone and headed inside. "Philippe, what can I do?"

Over the crappy reception he heard, "Lou, twenty-four... key in...drawer...come!"

CLICK.

What the hell? Was that a code? He'd figure it out in flight, if he could get one.

Kathryn had sent Peter upstairs to put together some things for Anthony before coming into the study. She

364 | THE PERSIAN GLORIES

stood close, expressionless, waiting. Wally and Buzz followed her in. Her mother was there too, holding the baby.

"I need a flight to Istanbul, now," Anthony said.

Wally stepped up. "Got it. Give me five minutes to see what I can do."

He took the phone. "As head of Boeing, I'd damn well better be able to get you a flight."

Meanwhile, Buzz called overseas on Patricia's private line. "Anthony, its Jess at MI6. He'll meet you at the private airstrip by Heathrow with details."

Wally said, "I've got you a flight if you can make it. Half an hour." He handed Anthony the info.

Anthony looked to Kathryn. "You drive."

She grabbed the Porsche key off the desk.

Peter ran in and tossed Anthony his duffle bag.

They were gone in seconds.

Kathryn's Porsche screamed down PCH, breezing through barely missed red lights. She roared past Topanga Canyon, making good time, her attention riveted to the road. She had a close timeframe and an adored passenger to keep safe.

Anthony yelled over the whine of the turbo engine, "I had your mom hide your passport. So no big ideas to join me."

"I know. She told me."

He shook his head.

Kathryn tried not to show how she cried inside.

"Please kiss my son for me."

"And you make sure to bring his daddy back home to him—to me."

"Always, my love. Always."

She accelerated into a turn at the California incline. They would make it.

THE END

BENEATH
THE
CRESCENT
MOON

CHAPTER ONE

ISTANBUL, TURKEY,
April 1954

Under a blistering noon-day sun, Philippe lowered his head and charged like a young bull through the old-town spice market. He raced below awnings, shadow into sunlight, dodging quibbling shoppers, his skinny seven-year-old limbs pumping, his breath heavy. His nostrils were laden with scents of cardamom, chilies, garlic, nutmeg and humanity. The school knapsack, slung across his chest, beat against his side. His nerves burned with his need to escape.

Shouts disrupted the bartering. "Stop thief! Catch him!"

Sweat dripped from Philippe's forehead into his eyes, his path blurring. He swiped his face on the sleeve of his only dress-shirt and ran on. One quick look back and he knew he must hide.

Blocked from view by a crowd of tourists, Philippe slid under a draped spice counter and scooted back, clutching his scraped knees to his chest, his arms wrapped tightly around his shins. He fought to slow his breathing while searching for an escape path. Peeping out from under the drape, he spied an entrance to the Grand Bazaar. Adrenalin pumping through him he chose his moment and darted out into the busy bazaar archway. He cut through the vaulted labyrinth, searching for a way to get back to the Blue Mosque before the call to prayer. He must be there to meet his father's envoy, or he would be forever lost—a waif roaming foreign streets. For his father would not return for him. His hand shook as he took out his wrinkled city map and regarded it closely. He shuddered knowing a greater fear than he'd ever known in his seven years. He'd be okay. He was almost eight.

Feelings were no good. He must stay with facts, observations, numbers. His father had told him. "Maps, books, words and their meanings, science, art and music, these are things you can rely upon, my boy. Trust your instincts. Sentiment will foul up your goal. Avoid it. Life is a game of logic."

He must trust his father's words.

His pursuers out of sight for a second in the crowded bazaar, Philippe ducked into an arched alcove and pressed his body against the ancient stone wall, leaning his head back. He heaved great breaths, this resting place cool. Dizzy for a moment, he stayed quiet. An uneasy feeling crept along his neck. He was tired, hungry and thirsty. He shook it off as he'd been trained to do. Perhaps he'd lost them.

He heard more shouting outside. "He's in here, I can feel it."

"Find him!"

He gulped knowing he must go or be caught for stealing bread left uneaten on a café table. Bread he'd only smelled but not tasted because he'd dropped it in his haste to leave when the waiter shouted, "Stop thief!"

For this small theft, they could cut off his right hand. Who knew what would become of him? His father had warned him of what might befall a blond child. He could be taken as a slave, sold or sent to a work camp, or thrown into the Bosporus. He blinked away these images, his eyes becoming accustomed to the dim space. There deep in the alcove, he glimpsed a narrow stone stairway leading up into darkness. He didn't care what it led to. He'd take it.

He ratcheted down panic and clamored up the narrow steps, his hand skimming along the bumpy wall until he reached a landing and a doorway. Hearing a commotion below, he quickly stepped into a dim hall. This escape route was his choice, and he must meet any challenge it presented.

He proceeded down the narrow passage until he reached an ornately carved wooden door. He looked carefully at the etched carvings. "Mohammed is the light," it said. He wanted light. He gripped the heavy iron doorhandle and pushed down. The big door creaked open.

Philippe entered a large, richly appointed salon leading out to an equally large terrace where, under dark blue awnings, eight men sat on benches along two sides of a long table where four chessboards rested. Fate was with him! He knew this game. Two turbaned servants stood on either side of the wide terrace opening. A matronly woman rushed forward and grabbed his shoulder.

"What are you doing here, boy?" she scolded.

Philippe wanted to yell, Sanctuary. Please, I need sanctuary. Instead he reigned in all emotional impulses and put his hands together nodding, *"Selamunaleykun, Hanfendi,"*—May God's peace be with you, Madame." He continued in Turkish. "I am here for the chess game."

Two men seated at the head of the terrace table turned, their penetrating gazes inspected him. One wore traditional Turkish clothing made of fine cotton in shades of blue and white, simple loose pants, an elaborately embroidered vest over a dark blue tunic, his head wrapped in a slanted turban. Then Philippe noticed each man at the table wore clothing from other countries. He ventured a guess: Persia, Egypt, Saudi Arabia, Tunisia, Somalia, Jordan and Syria. This looked to be more than a casual chess game he had stumbled into.

Philippe cleared his throat and said, "A million pardons *Beyefendi,* I meant no disruption." His voice cracked, but he kept his face still as a pool of water.

The Turk at the table stood, looking him over as if deciding. He stated calmly, "This is a game of wager boy."

Philippe noticed the cash on the table and dug into his pants pocket grasping an object. "I brought my wager, sir."

The Turk who seemed to be the host, said. "Come here chess player,"

His guests sent sly glances over Philippe.

Philippe swallowed, which was difficult because he was parched and insanely nervous and walked out to his host and stepped up. He pulled from his pocket a round brass compass that resembled a pocket watch and clicked it open for his Turkish host to see.

"Wait your turn." The Turk glanced at the inscription, and showed it to his opponents, looks passing between them. They grunted their acceptance of the wager.

"Will you not greet your fellow players?"

He was in! Philippe cleared all emotion from his face and said, "*Selamunakeykum, Befendi,*" then added. "*Gunaydin,*"— the day shines. He turned to the man across the table and said in Farsi, "Greetings to you, sir." In Arabic he greeted the Saudi player. He had just run out of languages for this group. He added in Arabic, "Greetings to all, sirs." His heart thumped in his chest, his upper lip was moist with sweat, but his face remained serene. "Adim Philippe," *my name is Philippe.* "I am British."

The men nodded, grunted "Selam," and his tension ebbed slightly. He glanced around the table, not so much at the men but their chessboards. They were locked into well-played games except for the Saudi player who had two pieces in jeopardy. Philippe quickly looked away.

"Take my seat," the Persian player said, "and finish my play. "My name is Tabriz and I wish to see what the *English* have brought to our table."

Philippe did not hesitate. He took off his knapsack and quickly sat across from the Turk, tucking the bag in next to him. For luck Philippe casually felt the medallion lying below his collar.

"Ahmet," the Turk said. "I am called Ahmet." He glared at Philippe. "Your move, English."

To hesitate would be a mistake. With one cool scan of the board, Philippe saw his move. He moved his rook three spaces. "Check."

Three moves more and he said, "Checkmate," knocking over Ahmet's queen. The other players were silent until Ahmet burst into laughter, the others joining in at Ahmet's expense.

The matron hurried up to him with a bowl of water and a cloth and Philippe thought he would be given a drink, but she dipped the cloth in the water and washed his face then his hands. "Undo your collar, boy. You are too dirty to sit with these fine men."

Philippe wanted to object, but obeyed, unbuttoning his shirt collar.

The matron lifted his medallion out of the way and washed his neck.

Tabriz stood next to him, staring at the gold medallion; a diamond glinted over a horned ram. "I am also Aries," said Tabriz.

"I am the lion," Philippe said, holding up his medal turning it over. There a ruby gleamed above a lion. "Leo."

"Button your shirt, English," Tabriz said softly. "There is nothing Turks love more than gold." He turned to his host. "Ahmet," Tabriz said, "Young English deserves a prize for his win, yes?"

"But of course," Ahmet said. "He has offered entertainment for our group if not begrudging respect from me." Ahmet looked stern before he smiled at Philippe.

"I am thirsty," Philippe muttered.

Ahmet gestured to the woman.

The matron seated him at a small table in the salon. She served him cool tea and chicken kabob wrapped in flatbread.

He smiled, relishing every bite, the fine tastes sliding into his churning stomach. He wiped his mouth on a soft linen napkin and stood. "Most humble thanks for this good meal, Hanfendi." He bowed and went to the terrace where the eight men sat in muted discussion. "Pardon the intrusion, sirs, but you see, *shoan in tooni ke. Komakam konid?*—I am lost. Can you help me

Before leaving the chess-player's apartment, Philippe, with some new won cash in his pocket and his knapsack slung across his chest, said goodbye, and again thanked his hosts, Ahmet, Tabriz and Matron. In her plump hands Matron held a small bag of delicious smelling sweets.

Turkish delights, he murmured and popped one into his mouth. *Pistachio, his favorite.*

Matron put her warm, motherly hand on his shoulder. This sensation conjured up feelings, an onslaught flooding his heart; home, family, mother, father, longing, loss. Too many feelings he'd held at bay. He stiffened.

Stay the course, Philippe, he heard his father's voice inside him. *Be brave. Use your massive mind, my son. Stay with facts, observations, numbers. Lock your feelings away until you are truly safe.* Philippe looked up. "Many, many thanks, for your kindness, madame. *Selamkunalekkum*—Goodbye."

While escorted down a hallway, the last words Philippe overheard were, "Guard him with your life," Tabriz growled at Philippe's escort.

Gosh, he would never have thought winning a small chess game would garner him such concern. Nonetheless, he was glad of it. Philippe already felt safer from his nasty pursuers. He believed he would be back at the blue mosque in time for the call to prayer.

They descended a different stairway to an exit that spilled out into the fish market. Seafood smells had never bothered him as they had his mother and apparently so the man escorting him who pinched his nostrils with one hand and tugged at Philippe with the other. This giant man was tan with hairy arms.

Giant wore dark pants and a tunic cinched by a belt with an empty scabbard. Philippe wondered where his weapon was.

"Move," the raspy growl threatened.

"But Ahmet said we had plenty of time."

"You have time. I don't. Move!"

"I could move faster," Philippe said in Farsi, "if I had your gigantic feet!"

The man had strange pale eyes, but he smiled, and his skin crinkled kindly.

Philippe noticed Giant also had a missing tooth on the upper right side of his mouth, and as they rushed on, Philippe wondered if he had ever seen a dentist. Philippe remembered his father warning him, "If you eat too many sweets your teeth will fall out." Philippe patted his knapsack filled with Turkish delights and gulped. Worrying now would be pointless. It would take years to become a man.

He and Giant moved quickly toward the Bosporus wharf where he had slept on a fishing boat hidden beneath a tarp for the last two nights.

He squirmed. The prickling sensation was back. He wondered if they were being followed.

Photo by Chloe Buccetri

ABOUT THE AUTHOR

Susan Wakeford Angard graduated high school on the lot of Twentieth Century Fox Studio. During this time she had leading roles in major television shows at Fox Studios, Warner Bros, Paramount, Universal and MGM. Her fascination for Ancient art then led her to study for an art history MFA at UCLA.

After leaving UCLA, Susan joined a family-owned TV Commercial Production Company, shooting consumer product commercials from McDonald's to Budweiser, Purina and Boeing. She traveled much of the world filming on location, including in the Middle East during the last months of the Shah of Iran's regime. Susan became an eye-witness to the Islamic Revolution.

Her attraction to visual arts persisted leading to a career as an architectural interior designer and owner of an award winning Los Angeles design firm and has won competitions on several episodes of *Designer's Challenge*, an HGTV design show.

Susan wrote briefly for CBS episodic television but with a need to tell her own stories, she changed genres to write fiction. She attended the UCLA Writers Program and the advanced writers program at The University of California at Irvine, and is currently involved in a follow up writer's critique group. During this time she raced vintage autos, was director of a prominent Arts Décoratif Collectors Gallery as well as raising four children. Susan lives with her present husband, her love, and is currently finishing her next novel.

susan.angard@me.com

Made in the USA
Middletown, DE
12 October 2022

12520210R00229